There are no safe words. There is only surrender.

When Alice leapt into sexual games with her neighbors Henry and Jay, she didn't plan to fall in love. She sure didn't expect she'd be the switch between Henry's commanding mastery and Jay's submissive playfulness. But now she's moving in with them, and she'd better figure it all out—fast.

Trouble is, she's never been a live-in girlfriend. The day after a traumatic first night at a BDSM club might not be the best time to start.

Struggling to find her place within the lifestyle, Alice seeks equality in a relationship built on surrender. Learning to lean on Henry challenges the foundation of her self-worth. He'll have to lean on her in return for their triad to find stability. But can her stoic dominant lover accept her as a confidante as well as a submissive? And will their love be enough to silence Jay's emotional ghosts?

Books by M.Q. Barber

Neighborly Affection Series

Playing the Game
Crossing the Lines
Healing the Wounds

Published by Kensington Publishing Corp.

Healing the Wounds
Neighborly Affection Book Three

M.Q. Barber

LYRICAL PRESS
Kensington Publishing Corp.
www.kensingtonbooks.com

For those who know what it is to feel less than whole.
You are worthy of love.

CHAPTER 1

Alice sectioned her pancakes into a neat grid. Focusing on the spongy bounce in the stack kept her hands from trembling. Breakfast was the most important meal of the day. Especially when Henry served the living-together discussion as the main course.

A flip and sizzle sounded from Henry's spot at the stove. "I believe my studio might be repurposed."

"Your studio's already in the smallest room. Alice and I can share closet space. It's not like we'd sleep there anyway." Syrup dripped as Jay stopped his pancake-loaded fork halfway to his mouth and twisted around in his seat. "We won't, will we? You're not, I mean, your bedroom is—"

"Jay. Don't borrow trouble, please." Henry loaded fresh pancakes on the serving plate and turned off the burner. "I would not move Alice into my room and leave you alone."

"And I wouldn't let him if he tried." She shook her head at Jay as he swung around to face the table.

"But as Alice has a much more organized aesthetic, Jay, it might be best—"

"I can be neat and clean." Jay powered through without a hint of offense at being called a slob. Interrupting Henry right and left. Christ, he wanted this bad.

Not that she didn't, but displacing Jay from his room fell short of ideal. She refused to make moving in a panicked reaction to last night's disaster at the club.

"Jay."

Ouch. Henry's gentleness cut sharper than his command voice. Jay's suggestion would go down in flames.

"I can." Jay vibrated in his seat. "Put it in my contract. 'Keep bedroom to Alice's standards of cleanliness.'" His usually rich tenor bristled and cracked. "Add it. I'll initial the change."

He seemed manic this morning, and for once bereft of sexual innuendo. God knew he had plenty of material. Her sharing his bedroom, and he hadn't thrown a single suggestive remark.

Henry's expectant stare weighed on her. He didn't need her permission to alter Jay's contract, so why—she'd be acting in a dominant role. The woman who couldn't even figure out how Jay felt today.

Shoving aside her apprehension, she nodded. Serious responsibility came part and parcel with moving her relationship forward. She'd need to be consistent and set rules she could praise Jay for obeying. Make a ritual of checking the room so he knew she was paying attention to his efforts. Caring. One thing amid a sea of hundreds Henry handled. He thought that way all the time, for both of them.

Henry carried the serving plate to the table and set it between them. Taking his seat, he glanced at their plates before filling his own.

Jay stared, intent but restrained enough to refrain from asking again. She hadn't believed him capable of such impressive self-control. Although, when he wanted something enough, he always managed to surprise her.

Finally, Henry quirked one corner of his mouth in a smile. "That's a fine idea, Jay. We'll add it to your contract today."

Jay gave an exuberant shout. His fork clattered against his plate. He hopped up from his seat, rounded the table, and dragged her chair back.

Annnd there's the lack of self-control.

"You're done eating, right, Alice? We can go to our room and you can tell me what you want fixed and I'll—"

Henry's silent laughter greeted her pleading glance. She'd have to get him for that later.

"—and we can pack your stuff and I can move the boxes and—"

"I'm not done eating yet," she said, breaking into Jay's chatter.

Henry had warned her, while they lay talking late into the night and Jay slept beside them, that the new living arrangement would cause excitement.

"But I'm excited about moving in, too." And carried the teensiest terror of making a wrong decision. For Jay. For Henry. For herself. "How about if you start by, umm, dividing your clothes into piles for laundry and putting away."

He fidgeted with her chair. Henry would understand his anxiety without a prompt. *Okay. Unravel Jay-threads.* He needed to know she didn't blame him for his panic at the club or her public discipline. That she loved him. That she wasn't sending him off alone to punish him.

"I'll join you when I'm done with breakfast. We can work on it together all day, and by tonight—" She lacked the authority to promise her hope.

Henry tipped his head and nudged the tips of his fingers in a go-on motion.

"By tonight we can all tumble into Henry's bed together."

"For good," Jay said. "No more nights apart."

"No more nights apart, Jay." Henry's decisive tone formed the firm bedrock of their relationship. "Now, I believe Alice has set you a task regarding your shared room. Perhaps you'd best get started."

"Yes, Henry." Jay pushed her chair in and swaggered into the second bedroom.

"You did very well, Alice."

"I was terrified."

"Nevertheless. You found your courage, and you gave Jay the reassurance he needed. Thank you."

Cutlery clinked in their silence. Without Jay's chatter, the hallway and its open door—the bedroom soon to be half hers—spawned a whirling tornado of questions.

She wasn't a spontaneous person. She planned. Researched. Tested. Yet she hadn't run design models before agreeing to move in. Why the fuck not?

Henry, that's why. He whispered to her as he cradled her at night, and her questions and fears crumbled like improperly cured concrete. Love, that's why. As long as she loved them and they loved her, everything else was fixable. Open to negotiation.

"You know I'll never be as obedient as he is." Loving Henry and

Jay didn't blind her to reality. Henry already knew. He had to. But saying the words mattered.

Henry laid his fork and knife across his plate.

Maybe he'd give her an answer key to this new world. The first time she'd been in love.

Henry's persistent stare and slow-spreading smile gleamed with a touch of I-know-something-you-don't-know smugness.

"What? You think living with you all the time will change me?" The first time she'd lived with a lover. Two of them. One who'd dominate her at least part of the time. Fuck, she didn't do things by halves. "Make me more submissive?"

"No, Alice." Chuckling, he clasped her hand in a comforting squeeze. "It might, as change changes us all, but no. What amuses me is merely that even *Jay* is not so obedient as Jay."

"He's been on his best behavior? For our nights together?" If he'd been trying to impress her, she didn't know the real Jay. She didn't know weekday morning Jay. Cranky, bad-day-at-work Jay. Or what Henry was like when a burst of creativity struck. If he disappeared into his studio for days.

"You believe Jay has never defied me in front of you?" Henry raised an eyebrow.

"No, I guess he has." Hell, Jay'd defied him at their anniversary dinner, moving things forward faster than Henry had intended. The very first night. In January, too, taking advantage of the relaxed rules granted for his injury. And the night she'd safeworded. He'd begged her and Henry both to listen to him. "A lot more than I realized. But he's so easygoing. Jay-like."

"He's happiest when he has a clear task to complete and unconditional affection. He can be quite stubborn when he's unhappy, for which I give thanks." Closing his eyes, he bowed his head. "Convincing him that saying 'no' or disagreeing with me in some way would not result in the loss of my love and approval took a long while."

"While I bulldoze ahead with my own two cents." She turned her hand in his, running her fingers over his palm. His hand delivered pain and pleasure both. She hadn't feared losing Henry's love and approval before. She hadn't known they were hers to lose. But she'd worried about losing her place in his life with Jay.

Now she'd traded the periphery for the center. No, not the center.

An equally blended mix, one she wouldn't know how to create and could never replicate. Corinthian bronze. Gold, silver, and copper alloyed into a form beautiful and precious. Yes, now she had something valuable to lose.

"You know your own mind very well, dearest." He closed his hand, capturing her fingers and stilling their motion. "I don't expect that will change. You'll challenge me more often than he will. That, too, is a joy. You each complement the other in my heart, Alice."

"You're not expecting complete obedience from me? Even though we'll be living together?" A recipe for resentment and hurt feelings if Jay had to answer to Henry and she didn't. "Is that fair to him?"

"The question here is what's fair to you. Submission gives Jay a sense of security. It is not a burden to him. Its weight on him does not grow heavier if your share is lighter." Henry shook his head. "We'll find a proper balance, whether that requires continued restriction of the hours in which you answer to me or some other method. So long as I have you both with me and happy, the rest is a matter of fine-tuning details. We'll adjust as needed."

"We're going to memorize a table of on-and-off hours like a bus schedule?" A color-coded timetable on the fridge. Right beside the star sticker chart she'd never made for all the sex acts she successfully tried with Henry and Jay. A snicker slipped out.

Henry's lips twitched. "If you'd prefer to expand your submission into something more akin to Jay's, though perhaps with less oversight outside the home, I've no objection. It's certainly something we may try. In that case, your safeword would take on a greater role. If you became uncomfortable with something—at any time, not only during a stated game—your safeword would instantly indicate such to me."

"Even when we aren't playing?"

"Even then. We would, in essence, always be playing. The games simply wouldn't always have the sexual emphasis to which you're accustomed." He released her hand and gestured at the table. "If, for instance, I asked you to gather the dishes now, you might playfully protest. If you persisted, I might suspect you wanted to be commanded to do so or wished for more of my attention. But if you meant your protests in earnest and it seemed I had not recognized it, using your safeword would reset the conversation and our roles within it."

"But I don't have a problem clearing the table." Henry cooked nearly every meal they ate. If she and Jay helped under his guidance, they fulfilled a necessary function. Contributing as equals according to their skill sets was sense, not submission.

"My hope is that I will not ask something of you that you cannot give, dearest. But you may at some point have a conflict of which I'm unaware. Be unable to take care of the breakfast dishes because you must rush to work for an early meeting, perhaps. Or you may have bruised your arm on the subway ride home and prefer not to carry the supper dishes." He raised a finger. "In which case, I'll examine the injury before we play games of any sort. But the point remains. Your safeword will indicate to me the serious and sincere nature of your objection."

A safety valve. If the pressure of submission overloaded her tolerances, he'd adjust the flow rate to compensate and leave her the option to yank the emergency brake. "I'll keep alert for those T riders throwing elbows. I'd hate to miss out on a game with fun rewards because some jerk muscled past me during rush hour."

The hint of a smile accompanied his elegant shrug. "The real world must take precedence over my own control, Alice. Even when I have you firmly in my dastardly clutches every day."

She imagined him twirling a cartoon mustache, ridiculously oversize and sinister, as he tied her to a set of railroad tracks. Well. Maybe not railroad tracks. Maybe his nice big bed. "Got it. Good thing I don't like to eat pistachios. I'd hate for there to be any confusion."

"Shall we try it, then, my sweet girl? When you're in the apartment, you'll answer to me as Jay does, with the exception of the second bedroom, which will have its own rules."

A trial run. Fuck if she'd turn down a new adventure. "I'd like that. You want me to clear the dishes?"

"No, I'll clear today. If you've finished eating, I'd like you to come here and give me a kiss before you go and reassure Jay of the value of his labor."

She was up in an instant. "That I can do."

Henry kissed her, tender but brief. "Go on and make him work for it, then. The more instructions you give him—"

"The more I can praise him for following them to the letter."

"You see? No need for terror. You've thoroughly grasped the concept."

"Time to implement it." She preferred implementation over theory anyway. Moving in with her lovers. Practicing a larger submissive role with one and learning to take a dominant role with the other. What grander experiment could there be?

Alice's studio apartment almost matched the pristine whiteness of the day she'd moved in. Not much left. Not much to start with.

Fresh from hauling the vanity across the hall, Jay zipped through the door and thrust his arms out in front of her. "Load me up."

She hefted one of the waiting drawers. "You want 'em all now?"

"Do I ever." He rocked and sprang like a sweet, demented jack-in-the-box. "Gimme everything you got."

She laid the first drawer across his arms. Every one of Henry's handwritten notes to her snuggled beneath her PJs. "No peeking, stud."

Bras in the second drawer. "A girl's gotta keep some secrets."

Panties in the third, stacked beneath his chin. God, he'd get great mileage out of that.

"I'm trusting your discretion, here." As if he hadn't seen her in—and out of—more than half the dainty delicates safe in his arms. She flashed him her best winning smile and waited for the joke.

Blank-faced and blinking, he stumbled half a step back, caught himself, and zoomed toward the door. He nearly took out Henry coming the other way before he danced sideways and disappeared.

"Hey." She waved at Henry.

At least he smiled back. No unexpected dodging there.

"Almost done."

A scant two boxes of dishes and cookware had gone downstairs with one of towels and bed linens and another of assorted odds and ends. Clutter. The sort of thing Henry wouldn't appreciate in his apartment. Their apartment.

Her new home.

She'd spent almost two years in this apartment. Despite the thrill of having her own place, she'd never made the space hers the way Henry's apartment breathed beauty and elegance. Offered warmth and comfort.

Mmm. She'd awakened this morning wrapped in the circle of his arm, opened one eye, and gazed across his chest at the mop of shaggy black hair burrowed against his other side. Comfort for sure.

"Second thoughts, my dear?" Henry stepped beside her and rested a hand on her back. "This is not an insignificant thing you're doing."

Not insignificant, no, but not unwelcome. If moving in turned out to be a mistake, she'd learn from it and plan accordingly next time. Except there wouldn't be a next time, because she'd make this work. "Not second thoughts."

She sagged into his side, and he shifted to cradle her. He understood how big a step she was taking today. A leap. A huge fucking leap. But she'd taken one last night telling him she loved him. And he'd caught her with a declaration of love in return.

"Excitement. Trepidation, a little." She nudged his shoulder. "And a big pinch of 'Wow, Jay works fast.'"

Henry chuckled and bestowed a light kiss on her hair. "He does at that. My eager boy."

"Somebody call for me? Are we giving out hugs?" Jay swarmed them, darting in front and throwing his arms wide. "The more the merrier, right?"

"Absolutely." She planted a loud kiss on his cheek. "We're admiring your work ethic while we stand around and slack."

Jay squeezed them hard and stepped back. "Gives me more chances to flex my muscles." He posed weightlifter-style, which emphasized his lean cyclist's body.

She tickled his ribs.

He yelped. "Flag on the play."

"Do they have flags in weightlifting?" She pulled her hands back. "I think the rib tickle is a legal move." They swung their heads toward Henry. "Ruling from the ref?"

Henry dragged his fingers up her ribs.

Senses alerted, muscles tensed, she slid a hand across his chest, fully prepared for a counter-tickling campaign.

But he flattened his hand and delivered a firm stroke. "Tickling, my dears, is enjoyable in small doses. Beneficial in some cases."

The feathers. Somewhere in Henry's special dresser lived the feathers he'd teased her with on the night she'd discovered the joys of flogging. An arousing night made more so by the faint tickle of the feathers between each new sensation.

Smack.

The sound crashed in her head, and it wasn't the paddle or the crop or the flogger. It was Henry's hand landing on her ass last night. Whispers and laughter and that fucking bastard Cal shoving his dick in her face. She sidestepped. A tiny shift. Nothing suspicious. Nothing calling attention to the narrow sliver of space she'd put between herself and Henry.

"But perhaps now is not the best time for play. If you wish to shower before supper, you'll need to finish up soon." Henry inhaled with ostentatious exaggeration. "And I do suggest a shower when you've finished moving furniture and carrying boxes, delightful as your musk may be."

"I always knew I was delightful." Jay sniffed under his arms. "You think we can bottle me and make a fortune?" He crowded forward, arms up, ducking his head and catching her eyes. "What do you think, Alice? Am I delightful?"

She fended him off, laughter sluicing fear from her mind and tension from her muscles. "Right now? You reek like a sweaty forest. Henry's right." Not much left to go downstairs but the futon. The lumpy, banged-up bed belonged to another lifetime. "We can leave this stuff for another day and you can hop in the shower."

Jay followed her gaze. "No, I can get it done. Today. Now." He hustled over and hefted the floppy mattress.

Bare, the frame revealed the long scrape where she'd lost her grip and dragged the damn thing on the pavement hauling it into her first apartment with no Jay to lend a hand. Exposing the bones of the bed the way Henry exposed hers, only he'd used gentle care and she never managed more than rough bluntness.

"Won't need this tonight." Jay balanced the weight on his shoulder. "I'll square it away downstairs. Come back for the frame." He rushed past them out the door. "I'll be done in time for dinner, Henry. Promise."

Footsteps echoed from the stairwell.

His bouncing between moping and mania nagged at her. "Does he seem off to you?"

"It's an exciting day." Henry lifted her hand and kissed the back. "And some small cause for nerves." He tilted his head toward the futon frame.

A lonely bed for a lonely woman who hadn't recognized her loneliness until Henry and Jay poured love into the layers they'd scraped through to reach her. She tried to see the bed as Jay might. More than a job to finish to please Henry. "An escape clause," she whispered. "He's afraid I'll back out."

"He'll settle down, sweet girl." Henry rubbed his thumb over her knuckles. "His behavior is neither a reflection upon the reality of your emotions nor a lack of trust in your love for him."

No fucking way would she let their love go. She'd rope herself to them and growl a warning at anything trying to send her back to that place without them. "I'm not backing out."

Henry pulled her to face him. "This is not a race, Alice. It isn't a test. It isn't a competition of any sort. Do you remember what I told you the night of your anniversary dinner? If events move too quickly, we will stop and reassess." He stood broad-shouldered and sturdy, his green-eyed gaze steady on her. "The words are as true now as they were then. You will never disappoint me by being honest with me."

"It's not too fast for me. The timing was a surprise, yeah, but I want this." She'd hit the right note. He didn't worry she'd back out. He'd have contingency plans for that. And everything else on the planet. Giddiness tickled her throat. "I want you. I want Jay." She stepped into his embrace.

He hugged her close. "Shall we give our boy a hand? The sooner your belongings are settled, the sooner he will be as well."

Alice wiped down the table while Jay carried the last of the supper dishes to the dishwasher with the flair of a court jester. Clearing her apartment hadn't slowed down her energetic lover. He'd start juggling plates in a minute if Henry didn't stop him. No sign of Henry down the hall yet, but he'd been gone mere minutes.

"Jay. Think fast." She tossed the dishcloth.

He snatched it out of the air left-handed.

"Hang that on the faucet for me, will you?"

He saluted and flashed a cheeky grin. "Day one and I'm already taking orders from my new roomie."

Shit. She'd meant it in fun, a little bit of practice, but she'd been ordering him around all day. "Jay, you know you don't have—"

"I'm not complaining. I swear I'm not." He draped the washrag in the sink and hurried around the island. "I love having you here." Close but not touching, he hovered beside her. "I'm happy to do whatever you want me to."

"Excellent." Brown accordion folders tucked under his arm, Henry strode into the room. "Then you'll be quite pleased with what I have here. If you've both finished your tasks, would you join me in the living room, please?"

"*Yes.*" Jay sprinted past her. "Contract time?"

"Contract time." Henry sat on the couch and laid the folders on the coffee table. "Alice, come sit, please."

She settled in next to him.

Grinning like a fool, Jay bunched up on the floor in a loose waiting pose and crossed his arms over Henry's knees.

"Our contracts are in those?" They hadn't made an appearance last month when they'd added exclusivity and nightly dinners to her contract. Even with the additions, hers couldn't total more than a dozen pages. The thinner folder was half an inch thick.

"Among other things, yes."

"Other things?" Notes? Sketches? His insights on their likes and dislikes? He'd stacked his attention so neatly. The full extent of the seriousness with which he treated their needs.

Henry kissed her temple. "Other things. Now, I've drafted an addendum concerning the second bedroom and the responsibilities the two of you will share in regards to it."

And she'd thought Jay worked fast. Henry must've been busy while she and Jay had organized the bedroom.

Henry leaned forward, tousling Jay's hair along the way, and retrieved two sheets of paper. "I'd like for you each to read it over, and then we will discuss what changes, if any, you'd care to propose."

She accepted her copy of the proposal, and Jay took his. Silence descended as they read.

The morning's nerves melted away, absorbed by a growing sense of security and confidence with each line. Henry hadn't left her to muddle through on her own, to make a misstep and hurt Jay. Of course he hadn't.

Her responsibilities included conducting weekly spot checks at a time of her choosing. Surprise inspections. Jay would immediately correct any minor imperfections she noted. If she observed none or he corrected them to her satisfaction, she was free to praise him with whatever combination of verbal and physical affirmation she found appropriate. Excepting, of course, she wasn't to employ toys without consulting Henry.

Verbal and physical. A whistle echoed in her head. She and Jay had always been free to fool around, even without Henry, though they'd only done so once. Nothing comparable to her, in charge. A heady sort of power, but not unlimited.

Should Jay fail to meet expectations and require corrective action—discipline—she was to bring her concerns to Henry. The decision to determine and impose a suitable punishment would remain his alone. Likewise, he'd arbitrate any disputes. Otherwise, he'd allow their little game to proceed without interference.

Rights. Responsibilities. A clear chain of command.

"I don't have any objections, Henry." This challenge she could accept. Something Jay craved from her. Something Henry trusted her to accomplish. "The language is fine as-is for me."

Jay heaved a vast sigh and sagged against Henry's legs. "Me either. I was just waiting on Alice to say okay. She's the one who has to make time to supervise me."

How like Jay to think of the deal backward. He was the one promising to complete chores. To follow her directions. He'd keep their room clean, and all she had to do was praise him for it. Although the thicker folder had to be Jay's, and it neared three inches high.

"Jay, if you'll fetch a pen, please."

Jay dashed off to root in the kitchen junk drawer.

"Nothing so exacting is required, my dear," Henry said in an undertone. "It's best to start simply. You won't be required to make formal reports to me." He stroked her back. "Merely enjoy yourselves."

This experiment wasn't a project for work. Detailed notes might be overkill. Still. Picking up a notebook wouldn't hurt. She'd track what she'd asked Jay to do. How well he'd accomplished it. The rewards she'd bestowed and his general satisfaction level with them. "It'll be fun."

Henry chuckled. "An elaborate system is already taking shape in your mind, no doubt."

She tipped her head onto his shoulder. "You know me too well."

"Blasphemy." He nuzzled her hair. "I could never know you too well. Though you may be assured I'm making the attempt."

He thanked Jay for the pen, and the three of them signed. She resisted the urge to peek as Henry slipped the sheets into their folders.

Jay replaced the pen.

Henry left the room to put away the folders wherever folders went. The special dresser's drawers did have locks.

She sat alone on the couch. Saturday night. Not even nine thirty. Henry might expect playtime when he returned. She lifted her feet and curled her legs to her chest.

Last night had been fun until it turned into a clusterfuck. Could've been worse, though. The spanking he'd given her had probably been the bare minimum. It had been bare, all right. The entire room had witnessed her bawling like a baby. For ten swats.

As if she hadn't gotten three times that on her birthday. Although those had been for fun, with rubbing and touching between spanks and with her own arousal as the goal.

Henry emerged from the hall. He might ask now. Or demand. She'd given him that right. Her first real night with them as a full-time, live-in lover should be something to celebrate. She'd never told him no.

A drawn-out hum, descending, proved to be Jay yawning. Ever-fidgety, full-of-energy Jay leaned against the dining room table with drooping eyelids and a sleepwalker's posture. "Henry?"

"Yes, my boy?" He changed course without pause to stop beside Jay. "Is there something you need?"

"Just sleepy. I figured I'd go to bed early. If that's okay."

Henry laid a pale hand against Jay's tanned cheek. "Of course. You've worked hard today, my dear boy. Go on and get ready for bed, and Alice and I will join you shortly."

Jay squirmed, half nodding.

Henry studied him in silence for a long moment. "Perhaps it's a good night for story time. 'To me, you will be unique in all the world,' hmm?"

Jay's eyes widened. He grinned, head bobbing. "Yes, please, Henry." He shot a glance her way, and his smile dimmed. "I mean, if Alice doesn't mind having story time."

Pfft. As if she'd deny Jay something he so obviously adored. Besides, story time meant she wouldn't need to find a polite way to turn down sex. "I liked our last story time. It'll be tough to beat *Winnie-the-Pooh*, though."

Jay opened his mouth.

Henry tugged on his hair. "She'll find out soon enough. *The grain, which is also golden, will bring me back the thought of you. And I shall love to listen to the wind in the wheat."*

The words weren't familiar. They both stared at her.

Jay kissed Henry's cheek. "Thank you for the wasted time, Henry."

"My responsibility, brave boy. Forever." Henry gave him a gentle push. "Off to bed."

Jay hustled down the hall, and Henry came to collect her from the couch. "Thank you, Alice, for indulging us tonight." He enfolded her in his arms as she stood. "My lovely roses."

He'd completely lost her.

Henry led her by the hand to the bedroom before going to collect the book. When they'd all brushed their teeth, used the bathroom, and shucked their clothes, she and Jay cuddled close on either side of Henry. *The Little Prince.* Not a story she'd read before, but Henry's voice was sure to make it a favorite.

"... All grown-ups were once children ..."

CHAPTER 2

Alice stared blankly at the television.

She didn't think Jay was watching, either, and Henry sure as hell wasn't. He held a magazine, an art journal of some kind, and he occasionally turned a page. Sometimes she watched his hands just to watch them. He sat in the chair angled toward the couch, at the far end from where her head and Jay's lay.

It wasn't an unfamiliar after-dinner scene for them in the last week. But it was strange. The wrongness persisted despite Henry's sensitivity to their emotional upheaval. The extremes as Jay cycled between cheerful excitement at having her sharing the apartment with them and uncomfortable distance in bed, even with Henry. He professed to being uninterested, shrugging away anything beyond light kissing, yet he acted desperate for closeness, never more than three feet from her or Henry, both if possible.

Though she and Jay shared the couch, they hardly touched. He hadn't tried to kiss her. Hadn't tried to grope her. Hadn't even wrapped an arm around her, for all that he lay on his side behind her. No, his right hand propped up his head and his left formed an unmoving, featherlight weight on her waist. He acted like a sixth grader at his first slow dance.

Her, too.

Equally skittish, she hadn't scooted back against his groin or tangled their legs or even rested her head on his chest. The distance grew every time they shifted and accidentally touched. He hadn't gotten hard all night so far as she could tell, unnatural for him in general but perfectly in line with his behavior this week. She couldn't understand it, that he hadn't wanted her sexually all week but could be so desperate for her attention and Henry's every evening, and yet she felt it, too.

She was starting to wonder if his discomfort was more than encountering his tormenter last Friday. If it was her, somehow. Her thoughts churned in an endless loop of dropping confidence, rising shame, and paralyzing confusion.

She wanted Henry and Jay to desire her. But she didn't want them to touch her. Not as men, not when that sonuvabitch Cal's voice rang in her head. No—no, she did want them to touch her. She ached to erase that voice and make them feel good, too, to know she *could*. Only she needed a way that didn't bring confusion and shame and whatever she was so damn afraid of. Arousing them. Not arousing them.

The problem wouldn't fix itself. She lacked the courage to address it. God knew Jay wouldn't. He kept jumping away as if he didn't want his cock touching her, hard or not. The overwhelming emotional dance made an escape across the hall tempting.

She hadn't informed the super of her move yet. Even with her stuff here now, her apartment—

"Alice. Jay." Henry had been tender all week, comforting them with snuggling and story time. Now his voice snapped with command.

"Both of you, into my bedroom." He laid his magazine on the side table and checked his watch without even a glance in their direction. "You have three minutes to be naked and kneeling on the bed in your waiting pose. Side by side, not touching."

Terror and exhilaration warred in her, kept her frozen in place until Jay's breath gusted against her hair. He needed this, too. He wouldn't find his courage if she couldn't find hers first.

She swung her legs off the couch and stood.

"Good girl, Alice, thank you."

Henry's praise was warm. Maybe he'd seen the nervous tic in her legs. She forced herself to walk to his bedroom, aware of his quiet praise to Jay before footsteps followed her.

She stopped at the edge of the bed and pulled her shirt over her head with trembling fingers. Ridiculous. She'd slept naked in this bed all week without sexual contact. Three months ago she'd believed herself incapable of spending a night in their bed without having sex with them. Now she'd done it seven nights running.

Congratulations. She'd killed the passion in the relationship. What would she do for an encore?

She turned her back to Jay and undressed. He was faster, positioning himself on the bed as she unhooked her bra and pushed her underwear to the floor. She felt exposed. Uncomfortably so. But when she turned to sit, he averted his gaze. He couldn't look at her. Or didn't want to. And she didn't know if she wanted him to.

They knelt in silence. Her heart thumped. Waiting for Henry was torture. Longer than three minutes. Had to be.

Henry stalked them, circling the foot of the bed with slow, careful steps. "I've been lax with you both this week. Hoping you would come to me with these troubling feelings you mistakenly believe you've been hiding so well. But neither of you has done so, have you? No."

His judgment stung with pinpoint accuracy.

"You've chosen avoidance." Henry nodded toward Jay and turned narrowed eyes at her. "And paralyzing numbness."

She hung her head to avoid the disappointment sure to be in his face. But his silence drew her in, and his undressing held her there. Henry often emphasized that distance, directing them while he remained fully clothed. Now he folded his clothes neatly on the chair and came to stand at the end of the bed. Nude.

He wasn't aroused, not yet. Soft, wrinkled skin dangling amid brown hair offered no menace. She rubbed the sheets, the smooth silk a damn dissatisfying stand-in for the vulnerable man who deserved her embrace.

Until his cock rippled and grew and resettled, beginning to stiffen. She clutched at the sheets, folds of cobalt blue bunching between her fingers. Her knees trembled. Her pounding heart urged her to run for no reason at all.

"Alice." Henry spoke in the coaxing tone he used when he wanted her to try something new. "Up on your knees, Alice." The gentle one with the firm undertone accepting her fear but telling her she'd take his suggestion anyway, because he had faith in her even when she didn't. "Come here to the edge of the bed."

Too high for intercourse. Far out of position for a blowjob. The added height of Henry's bed, perfect for bending her over, now placed her face nearly level with his.

He cupped her cheek.

"Nice and slow, Alice." His murmur wrapped her in comfort, cozy and sensual and safe. The low, intimate voice of love she craved. "Jay. Watch, please."

He kissed her. Searching, molding his lips to hers, mouths opening, his tongue stroking. His kiss wasn't pushy or demanding, the way she'd seen some submissives treated at the club. But it was intense. Passionate.

Arousal sparked through her nerves like circuits reconnecting after a thrown breaker in a power outage.

Not frightening. And the singular voice in her head was Henry's.

"Touch, Alice." He clasped her hands and raised them to his chest, pressing her fingers flat. "Touch me. Here only, dearest."

She smoothed her hands across his chest. Broad and solid, he grounded her with his steady breaths. His flesh yielded to hers, pressure curving muscle and fat in little furrows. Displacement. He'd granted her the freedom to sink into him, to take up space not just in his bed but in his life. Her slow, teasing scratch raised his chest hair. The dark strands tickled as they curled around her fingers.

Warmth surrounded her breasts, firing a startled shiver down her back. Henry caressed her nipples with his thumbs. Mmm. Pressure somehow soft and firm and fantastically comfortable. He deserved his share, too. She mirrored the motion on him.

"This is nice, isn't it, Alice? Hmm?" He leaned in close, nuzzling her cheek, breathing across her ear. "You want me to touch you. You want Jay to touch you. You haven't been certain these last few days, but you are now."

She was. The need to escape and her nerve-racking thoughts of Henry's touch had been nothing but the fear of fear. The fear that he didn't want her or she wouldn't respond to his touch in the same way after her punishment at the club. But her body recognized his voice, his touch, as its cue for arousal.

He kissed her with more force, and she matched him eagerly. The first real stirring of desire made itself known as her body tightened around emptiness and her stomach jumped.

Henry knew where her passion lived. He wouldn't let her fears kill it.

Ending their kiss, he turned her face with his until their gazes fell on Jay, still in his waiting pose, his head bowed.

"Is watching too much, my boy? Alice does have innumerable charms. But even when you aren't gazing at her, you can't escape the way your body reacts to her, hmm? Hearing her moans, inhaling her deepening arousal . . . Will you touch her next, Jay? Give your fingers the pleasure of her soft skin?"

Jay shuddered. His harsh breathing almost drowned out Henry's voice.

"You've waited very patiently. It isn't easy, not when you're stiff and aching to be inside her."

Jay hunched forward, hiding his erection.

"No, no, fingers won't be enough, I think." Henry gripped her right bicep.

A reassuring squeeze, but why he thought she needed reassurance—

"We'll put Alice on her hands and knees, Jay, and you'll mount her and take what you need."

A convulsion rippled through Jay's abdomen. He scrunched his face up tight and shook his head.

Oh, Jesus. She groped for the trust woven through their lives. Henry wouldn't cause unnecessary harm.

"Yes, that's what we'll do." Henry squeezed her arm again.

His blood-pressure-cuff routine slowed her racing heart and shoved truth in front of her face, quieting the voice chanting *what the fuck* in time with her pulse. Jay couldn't see Henry's motion. Doggy-style fucking wasn't really on the agenda.

"Get a condom from the nightstand, Jay, and you'll give Alice the beautiful hard-on you have there."

"N-no." Shaking, Jay wrapped his arms around his chest. "I can't." He whipped his head back and forth, his flying hair hiding his eyes. "I can't."

"Tell me why you can't."

"I just, just can't." He rocked in slow, broad sweeps, as if he'd topple on his side with the slightest push.

Her happy-go-lucky lover seemed off-balance inside and out. Needing them.

"You're hard. Alice is wet."

Henry's grip kept her from scooping Jay into her arms.

"You're both quite capable of figuring out the mechanics of insertion."

Jay bent over his knees, pressing his face to the bed. "I can't. I can't, please." He dissolved into sobs.

Henry pushed with unrelenting calm. "Do you remember your safeword, Jay?"

He nodded, his hair rustling the sheets.

"Do you wish to use it now, my boy?"

"No. No." Jay treated the suggestion like a threat. He'd tucked in so small. Her strong athlete, her charming sweetheart, cowered alone in their bed.

"Then tell me why you haven't touched yourself all week. Why you've turned away in bed at night and in the morning, hiding your erections from your lovers."

"I . . . I haven't wanted . . ."

"Have you touched yourself in the shower this week, Jay?"

Naked and sniffling, Jay lay almost prone, a slave prostrate before his master. "No, Henry."

"No, I didn't think so. Twice this week you've slipped out of bed past midnight to clean up after yourself. Your dreams have been giving you what you claim not to want."

And she'd been fucking oblivious.

Jay clawed at the bed. No amount of effort would create a hole big enough to crawl into and pull the sheets over him, but his tender heart seemed hell-bent on trying.

"Tell me why you're punishing yourself, my boy."

"I was bad," Jay whispered in a broken voice thick with tears. "I was bad."

"What does your contract say about punishment, Jay? Who decides if you've been bad?"

"You do."

"And who decides what your punishment will be?"

"You do."

"Are you me, Jay?"

"No." He fell limp, terrifyingly still. "No, Henry."

"Then why have you usurped my role here?"

"I'm sorry, Henry." All the Jay-ness drained from his voice, and he sounded eerie and hollow like he had on the way home from the club.

"Tell me why. Tell me why, or use your safeword. You still remember it?"

His dull, hopeless loll might've been a nod.

"Tell me your safeword, Jay. I want to hear that you know it."

Jay choked out a garbled sob and then, "Popcorn."

Henry sucked in a breath. Popcorn wasn't Jay's safeword. Tilt-A-Whirl was.

Pain radiated from his grip on her arm. She winced but didn't pull away.

"Oh, my darling boy, no." Henry released her arm, pulled her head to his, and whispered urgently in her ear. "Relaxed rules, my dear girl. Intuition and compassion."

Leaving her behind, he climbed onto the bed and cradled Jay. "Tell me what you did that was bad, Jay. It's all right. Tell me."

"I was, I was . . ." Even engulfed in Henry's sturdy strength, Jay shook like a sapling in a windstorm. "I was hard. I *wanted* it."

She'd missed the damn warning sirens. A tornado filled the horizon, and she'd done nothing but stand powerless on the porch while the force uprooted Jay. God help them if Henry couldn't hold him tight enough.

"They aren't the same thing at all, my boy." Henry stroked Jay's back. "Your dreams made you hard this week, didn't they? You weren't even awake to want that. You wanted the opposite, but your body didn't listen. Your dreams managed to make it happen despite your wishes, even with no further stimulation."

Huddling closer, Jay took a long, shaky breath.

Henry kissed the top of Jay's head. "How much more difficult, then, to fight your body's natural reaction when a skilled manipulator is in control? He was already an expert sadist."

Jay lurched.

Henry wrapped him tighter. "You were so new."

A skilled manipulator. Hell of a partner she was. She'd babied her own insecurities and ignored Jay drowning beside her all week.

"The blame is his, Jay."

A sadist.

"It always has been."

Cal. Nearly five years of Henry's love swept out, and the jagged rocks of Jay's pain resurfaced. He'd reverted to a man she'd never met, a shame-filled submissive shell.

"I would've—I was gonna—if you hadn't stopped him . . ." Jay shook his head, the back of his neck slender and bare, his face hidden against Henry's chest. "He saw—he said I wanted it and he was, was gonna let me come and punish me for it."

Eyes welded shut, Henry laid his head atop Jay's.

"He was laughing be-because he knew I was a bad boy who wanted it and if I, if I came, that proved it and he'd, he'd f-fuck me bloody until he made it happen again."

Gentle, smiling Jay. Teasing, playful, eager-to-please, beaten and shamed and— Her stomach wrenched.

She inched closer and knelt beside Henry's leg. "Jay, sweetheart, I want to touch your hand. Is that all right?"

Nodding and sniffling, Jay shuffled trembling limbs. One hand emerged from Henry's embrace.

"Thank you, Jay." She closed her palms around his offering and traced his knuckles. She spoke through tears herself. Repeated his name to be sure he understood and registered what she said. She needed to fucking hold it together. "You're amazingly brave, Jay, do you know that?"

"M'not . . . you . . . brave," he mumbled. "Saved me. Like Henry." The tears came faster.

Oh Christ. "Not nearly so brave as you, Jay. You've come so far with Henry's help, haven't you?" Henry had saved him. She'd let that man get back inside his head and hurt him again. "I know you don't want to let what happened have so much control over your life. You're a good boy, Jay. An amazing man. I'm so proud to be in a relationship with you, sweetheart. To love you."

He shook his head, stubborn in denial. "I'm bad. I don't deserve you and Henry. You shouldn't love me."

"Jay, even women—" She squeezed his hand, grounding herself. "Even women sometimes orgasm during rape."

He flinched as if she'd flayed him open. One word. Four letters rippling through the tense muscles down his back and arms, crushing her fingers in a panicked grapple.

"It doesn't mean they want it, Jay, not any more than you did."

She pushed on. Like Henry would do. Honest, firm, and kind. "It's biology. The body compensating and responding the way it's wired to. You didn't do anything wrong. I want you to know that, really know it, and believe me when I say it. You didn't do anything wrong. Not then, and not last week."

Jay sang a chorus of pain in hitching breaths and silence. Clutching her hand and huddling in Henry's lap, he'd listened. If she said the words often enough, maybe the letters under his skin would spell out love and safety.

"Alice is right, my boy. Cal is a sadist with a great deal of training. He knows how to obtain the responses he wants. And what he most desires is to humiliate and harm his partners."

Henry opened his eyes, and she gazed back at him with every shred of trust and confidence she could muster. Nothing would erase the tears, but his consoling smile presented a glimpse of shared understanding.

"Jay, my dear boy, do you believe it would have been any different for me? If Cal had treated me in the same fashion, I likely would have climaxed no matter how much I fought against it."

"Not you." Jay shook his head.

"Yes, me." His voice gentle but allowing no argument, Henry pressed his cheek to Jay's head. Lines pulled at his mouth, strain running in grooves toward his clenched jaw.

"Henry wouldn't lie to you, Jay." She squeezed his hand again, refusing to force any further interaction on him. "He'll give us the truth, every time. And he has, what, four times the years of experience you have with this scene? Twenty times the experience I have? He understands physiological responses better than we ever will. Trust him to tell you the truth."

Jay's sharp angles softened, his shoulders reclaiming their natural curve and his neck losing the thick bands of over tightened muscle.

"I know it's difficult, my boy. That's why you refused to give a detailed account to the board, isn't it?" Henry's soft tone enveloped Jay in protection. His intense stare pinned her in place. "Why you agreed to sign the papers calling the incident an 'unintentional miscommunication between two consenting adults'?"

She slammed her mouth closed on a gasp. Intentional malice and cruelty masquerading as mistake. No one but Jay and Henry and Cal knew the truth?

"It's why you've never stayed with the counselors and psychologists for more than three sessions."

Jay sniffled. "Didn't want them to know. I couldn't talk to them."

Oh God. No wonder he'd fucking lost it Friday. Christ, they were lucky he was coherent now. Jay had lingering trauma, and Henry had coped alone for years. The only one Jay would open up to and depend on. Jay's anchor.

Jay tugged on her hands.

She freed him with one hand.

He clamped down on the other and tugged again.

Reluctant to disrupt his comfort in Henry's arms, uncertain whether he truly wanted her touching him, she scooted forward with caution.

Jay stopped hiding his face in Henry's embrace and lunged. Both arms out, he slammed into her chest with a hug.

She followed Henry's lead, holding Jay and crooning to him, telling him over and over of her pride in him for talking about what happened, and his bravery, and her thankfulness to have him in her life. He settled while she spoke, his head slipping from her neck to her shoulder to her chest as he relaxed. Beside her, Henry rubbed Jay's back in light circles.

Henry must've intended to break through their avoidance tonight, to bring healthy and fulfilling sex back into their lives. They'd cleared an emotional hurdle. The physical might have to wait. Things would move at Jay's pace.

She loved them, no matter the challenges. She never could've predicted this would be her life. She had no idea how she'd ever explain their love to her family. But she'd found the keeper relationship.

Jay's sobs subsided and his breathing slowed. Maybe he'd fall asleep, exhausted from the emotional release. She'd talk to Henry later, alone, when she wouldn't make Jay relive those weeks and months to improve her understanding of what loomed after such a fresh reminder.

Jay closed his mouth over her breast.

Her surprise squeaked through closed lips. *Not a squeak. I do not squeak.*

Head pillowed in the center of her chest, he cupped the outside of her breast as his lips fumbled and finally sucked at the nipple.

Her arousal spiked with alarming speed. Unintentional. He sought comfort, an instinctive need, innocent and childlike. But aside from Henry's caresses tonight, her breasts had gone all week without stimulation. Jay's contented murmurs escaped with each tug. Biting her lip, she tried to ignore the rush between her thighs.

She struggled not to jump when Henry tucked her hair behind her ear.

"All right, Alice?" He tipped his head toward Jay. Voice a bare whisper, as if he hesitated to interrupt their communion, Henry kept rubbing soothing circles on Jay's back. He had to consider what was best for both of them, not just Jay, even on a night like tonight.

Arousal claimed a small part of an inseparable mix of feelings. Jay drawing comfort from her without fearing rejection brought forth pride and tenderness. But keen awareness of Henry's separation dogged her. He couldn't provide this comfort, and if he felt left out he'd never mention it to allow what Jay needed. He wouldn't take what he needed.

Unless she asked. "Kiss me?"

The tender concern in Henry's eyes gave way to a smile. She'd found the right way to offer what he needed. Months of misunderstanding she couldn't change, but they'd led her here. She ought to be happy for this moment.

"A request I'll happily fulfill for you at any time, dearest." Henry bent toward her, Jay's curled-up form between them, and kissed her sweetly. His lingering kiss did nothing to alleviate her arousal and instead encouraged it. Not because it was passionate or full of thrusting tongues, as it was neither, but because he so clearly communicated his love.

She uncurled her legs as he drew back, and he shifted his hips. The erection that had flagged while he addressed Jay's pain likely had returned in force. After a week with neither of them touching him, he'd be as sensitive to contact and emotion as she was, if not more so. She'd damn well find a way to satisfy him tonight.

Jay snuggled more tightly against her, his mouth slowing.

She braced herself on outstretched arms to keep his weight from pushing her to the mattress.

Henry frowned. "Perhaps it would be best to lie down under the covers and allow sleep to arrive as it will. You've had a long evening, my dears."

Dammit.

Jay's hand fell away from her breast, and he slipped his mouth free.

She smothered the whimper in her throat at the loss.

"But, but we need this." He sat up between her legs and faced Henry. "All of us. You brought us to the bedroom 'cause we've been avoiding it all week, right? So we need to stop avoiding."

Selfish joy tangled urgency and guilt into a knot in her stomach. He'd said in one determined rush what she yearned to but wouldn't. He trusted Henry to find a way to help him push past the rough patches.

"Otherwise we'll let things fall apart. And I can't let that happen. Please, Henry?"

"It's no longer avoidance, my dear boy. Merely a concession to the late hour—"

Jesus, the bedside clock swore three hours had passed since he'd ordered them to undress.

"—and the difficult emotions you both are dealing with tonight."

All three of them. Hearing their pain and supporting them challenged him as much as expressing the emotion did them, no question.

"But I still want—" Jay stopped and hung his head.

"It's all right to share what you want, my boy." Henry brushed Jay's knee. "Or what you would prefer not happen, if that's easier."

Bravery seemed to have taken Jay as far as he'd go. He shrugged, punching softly at the sheets.

Henry opened his mouth, and certainty flooded her. He'd tell Jay no, that he wasn't ready, and Jay would feel rejected. As she would if Henry turned her away later tonight.

"I could, umm . . ."

Two male gazes locked on her face.

Her stomach flipped.

Jay's raised brows bespoke cautious hope.

Henry's narrowed eyes and tilted head displayed studious interest. Figuring her out.

"I could go first."

"You've something you wish to share, my dear?"

"Something I—" Admitting the fear she'd battled this week was embarrassing. "Something I don't want to happen." But Jay had admitted so much more, and he'd been so brave. Henry probably already knew. Saying the words might coax Jay to share his needs, too. She breathed deep to settle her stomach. "Blowjobs."

Jay's eyes widened, but Henry nodded encouragingly.

"I, umm, I've been so—you both know I love you. I know you wouldn't hurt me. And I don't normally, I mean, it's not like it's a chore. I like having my mouth on you and hearing how excited it makes you and feeling soft skin around hard need and knowing I'm in control of making you feel so good. But this week—this week it's been so—" She shook her head, wishing she wasn't about to cry and knowing she couldn't prevent it, because the sting in her eyes was sharp.

"I've been afraid. Because you're men. You have cocks. And I didn't want to see them or feel them or think about them. I keep, I keep hearing his voice and seeing—" She choked back a sob. She needed to admit this. For Jay. For Henry. For herself. "He was rubbing himself through his pants and saying he was going to—he was going to fuck my mouth—and I couldn't move and I was so, so angry and scared and hurt and I wanted out."

Struggling for breath, she waved off Henry reaching to comfort her. She needed to finish this, to say the most important part. "And then Henry said we were leaving. And Jay picked me up. You think I'm the one who saved you, Jay, but that's not—you both saved me, too. I needed to get out, and I don't think I could've even stood up on my own, and you carried me home. To safety."

Henry clasped her hand. "I'm sorry, Alice. I very much wish I could have prevented you from seeing that image, from hearing those words."

She squeezed his fingers. "I know, Henry. It wasn't your fault."

"I wanted to hurt him." Jay spoke quietly. "For acting as if he had a right to think about you that way."

A start. But for him the pain centered on her. As if he didn't register that Cal had done worse to him.

"I was—" Jay scraped at the sheets. "I think I was gonna try. I dunno exactly, but I wanted to put my hands around his throat and—" He closed his fist.

"And I wanted to kill him for the things he said and did to you," she said. "And if you ask Henry, he'll say the same."

Jay looked young and vulnerable, his slender shoulders bowed, his eyes rounded, and his brow lined.

"Alice is right, my boy. The world would be better for his loss, and what he's done to you and to her upsets me terribly." Nostrils flaring, Henry executed a slow blink and exhaled. "But I'm very pleased she was able to share her fear with us. It was a difficult thing to say, wasn't it, my dear?"

God yes. Compressing everything into a tight ball and stuffing those stomach-knotting feelings into a dark corner would've been easier. Except her denial would've given Jay one more reason to pretend his pain didn't exist. To man up. She dredged honesty out of the muck for him.

"Not just because it still bothers me." Made her doubt herself. "More because I'm ashamed to say I've been afraid of you." Amazing men who didn't deserve her fear. "I don't want to feel afraid. I didn't know how not to until you made it so nonthreatening tonight. And then I remembered how much stronger the other things I feel are, the love and desire and safety."

Nodding, Jay let go of the sheets. Tension drained from him.

"Would you like to share something, Jay?" Henry coaxed with steady patience. "Something you want or don't want tonight?"

"I—yes." Jay sat up straighter, and his intent stare pulled her in. "I want to apologize to Alice."

She fought the urge to cringe. He still didn't understand. "Sweetheart, it wasn't your fault. I don't—"

"No, wait, that's not—" He shook his head and turned to Henry. "I want like the first night, when you let me touch her for the first time."

"You want your mouth on her skin. To taste her, sweet and flowing with desire."

She flushed, her skin growing hot and needy.

"You won't be able to avoid becoming aroused, my boy. Can you accept that?"

"I . . . I don't want—" Ducking his head, he cast a quick glance at her.

The words he'd shied from scrolled through her head. "It's okay, Jay. I know you don't want to fuck me tonight. You won't hurt me by saying it."

He relaxed. "Thank you, Alice."

Henry smoothed Jay's hair. "You've made a lovely suggestion, Jay. And you needn't penetrate Alice. But you can help her with her fear. In fact, we might find something from that very night that will help, hmm? Alice greatly enjoyed watching you touch yourself for her. I felt the difference inside her as she tightened around me. There's nothing shameful in that, my boy. You'll make your apology to Alice, and then we'll remind her of how beautiful you are when you come."

"Henry's right." She let Jay see her desire for him, recalling with pleasure how mesmerized she'd been to watch him work himself to climax with thoughts of her. "I'd love that. Please?"

She associated words like reverent and slow with Henry. Not Jay. Tonight, she had to revise her mental map, to recategorize "eager to please" as "devoted to pleasure."

Slow kisses on her inner thighs became warm breaths across her sex. He didn't probe for entrance but teased her lips with long licks until her body opened for him.

She ached for him to move faster, to push her over the edge with typical swiftness. She'd waited all week, and only her imagined fears had held her back. Her body wanted to make up for lost time as much as she wanted to share this time with Henry and Jay.

This wasn't for her, this apology. It was about her, maybe, but it was *for* Jay. The comfort he needed. The welcoming embrace of her thighs. The love and gentleness he wanted to show her.

She hardly suffered, lying beside Henry's warmth, he teasing her nipples and kissing her neck while Jay took the time he needed to feel safe expressing his desire. She wasn't so fragile, not even after last week at the club. But he was.

Still, Henry capturing her mouth made for a pleasant addition. He brushed her hip with his cock but didn't press or demand a response.

Raising her knee, she draped her leg against him.

Jay stroked the back of her thigh. He flicked her clit with his tongue.

She tensed, hips pushing up, seeking more.

He retreated.

Shoving down a frustrated growl, she forced herself to calm. He might succeed in teasing her into annoyance if he couldn't accept, what, her arousal? His?

Henry touched his lips to her shoulder. "Beautiful, isn't she, my boy? So wonderfully responsive."

Jay's breath washed over her sex.

"It's tempting, isn't it? To lie with your nose buried in her scent and taste her sweet welcome and do nothing more than that, hmm?"

Dark hair tickled her thighs. Brushing his mouth across her lips, Jay sent a shiver through her. His gentle, closemouthed kisses fluttered around her clit.

"You don't wish to hurt her or to push her. To make her feel as though she must come for you. As if it were a demand you made of her, of her body, without her consent."

Shit. She should've seen that. Of course Jay would be nervous about making her climax, no matter how much apologizing he intended to do between her thighs.

"She doesn't have to," Jay whispered. "If she doesn't want to. It's okay not to. It's okay."

He tongued her despite his words.

Deeper, please.

Henry sealed her mouth with a heavy finger. "But if it were her choice, my boy?"

Spilling a quiet moan, Jay leaned in and pressed his forehead to her sloping belly. His plea and nudging promise vibrated through her with muted intensity.

"Surely if Alice asked, you'd help her climax."

Help. Not make. Jay's way forward. She nodded to Henry.

With a tap at her lips, he freed her to speak.

"Please, Jay?" She cradled all she could reach of him, pushing back his soft, shaggy hair. "Will you help me feel amazing?" Requests and permission, Jay's most fluent language. "I feel how much you love me, sweetheart. You show me with every look and every touch."

Henry had placed her hand on the switch.

She had to throw it for Jay herself. "Will you taste how much I love you?"

Her tentative, sweet boy gave way to the urgent lover she knew so well. Bracing her thighs, he rolled his thumbs across her clit in a rapid, alternating rhythm sending her spiraling up to his mouth.

Thrust. Suck. Repeat.

Jesus, she needed this. Needed him, needed his stiff tongue inside her and his mouth wrapped around her and the *whoosh* of hot, heavy air striking her clit as he beggared himself of breath to satisfy her.

Buried between her thighs, he uttered a muffled whimper teasingly familiar. A shadowed Saturday morning, both her men breathtakingly beautiful, Jay on his knees worshipping Henry's cock.

Her hand throbbed. Fuck. She'd mimicked Henry's hold on Jay's hair. Tight and clenching, and she wasn't Henry, she shouldn't be treating—

Henry covered her hand and squeezed. "Do that again, dear boy. You feel how you've pleased Alice, don't you? The way she pulls you closer? How she demonstrates her desire for your touch." Henry kissed her cheek. "Give her the sweet rush she seeks."

Jay thrust forward with redoubled effort.

She rocked into the pressure, greedy and drunk on Henry's approval and Jay's inexhaustible devotion.

He breathed faster, harder, the higher pitch near whistling as she danced to his tune. He pulled back—God no, he couldn't stop, not when she'd gotten so close—swiped his tongue between her lips, and sucked at her clit like she held the last sip in the bottle.

She tumbled.

Shivering against Henry, clamping her legs around Jay's neck and shoulders, she babbled her thanks in incoherent syllables.

"Another," Henry murmured. "Give our girl another. She's been too long without."

Her body clenched in agreement.

Spreading her lips, Jay sank his tongue between and lapped with eager attention. He abandoned finesse for speed, rocking the bed, maybe grinding his cock into the sheets. Pleasing her, pleasing Henry, made him so fucking happy.

He fluttered teasing taps across her clit.

She pulled off Henry's move with greater confidence, tugging Jay's hair to signal her readiness for more.

Jay leapt into action, his hard swipes driving her to the edge.

Henry traced a path along her arm and across her stomach, stopping at her breasts. He nuzzled her neck with nibbles and kisses and circled her nipple, a faint tickle. "My strong, beautiful girl."

He pinched.

Fuck. Sharp, sweet pain, her body lifting, need pulling at her. Jay held her in place, his tongue deep and moving and God—

Mind scattering, she shook.

She fell limp to the bed, her legs dropping, knees wide, arms sliding to her sides. Tiny blips of excitement kept coming, spikes in the lazy satisfaction settling in her muscles.

Henry cradled her. Jay dotted her thighs with kisses.

She thanked them, once she'd found her voice. "I'm so glad you suggested it, sweetheart. Your love was exactly what I needed."

Jay left a loud, smacking kiss below her belly button.

Henry nipped her earlobe, rumbled, "Beautifully done," and planted a firm kiss on her lips.

She'd pleased him. Fulfilled a vital role in this relationship. Helped Jay shed some fear and guilt, hopefully. Warmth rolled through her.

"Up on your knees, my boy." Henry sat up, too. "Waiting pose, precisely where you are."

Jay knelt between her legs, his knees sliding under hers in a vee. He settled his ass on his feet and waited. Hands at his sides. Cock hard, the tip gleaming.

"Back straight, please." Henry ran a finger along Jay's erection.

Jay's chest rose. His shoulders broadened. No more hunch in his posture.

"We want Alice to see this beautiful gift you have to show her." Half-hard himself, Henry settled behind Jay in the same pose. He pressed in close, legs sliding forward alongside Jay's. "How the thought of her fills you with desire."

Jay's cock, a gorgeous sight, tall and satisfying, same as its owner. Threatening would never describe him. Not by a country mile. Playful. Boyish. Charming. But her eyes tried to skitter away from his decidedly male presence.

Henry held Jay's knees. "All right, my boy?"

Jay nodded, his gaze pinned to her face. "If Alice is," he whispered.

With a kiss to Jay's cheek, Henry squeezed her thigh. "Share with me, sweet girl. How are you feeling?"

She wanted to answer *relaxed*. To say the orgasms Jay had given her had been enough, because they had, except—*I'll fuck her mouth while she quivers in your lap*—stray flashes bounced at unexpected angles, disorienting and quick and irrational. Embarrassing. No wonder Jay'd needed a spur from Henry to push past the chaos.

"A little, a little nervous." Confession was good for the soul, right? Henry demanded honesty from her, and Jay needed to see it, and they both deserved it. "And irritated with myself. For being nervous."

Jay's wide, sad eyes fueled second thoughts.

"Good girl," Henry murmured. "There's nothing wrong with a bit of nerves." His gentle touch on her thigh soothed in its repetition. "We'll see if we can't increase your comfort level, dearest. You need only watch." He leveled his gaze at her over Jay's shoulder. "And if that demands too much of you, what will you say?"

"Pistachio."

His smile calmed her. "Exactly right."

He rubbed Jay's cock with his knuckles.

The way Jay'd been denying himself, she half expected him to pop off the second Henry touched him.

Whimpering, Jay trembled. His cock softened and flopped over Henry's hand. Jay bowed his head, chin to his chest, eyes scrunched closed.

Lose an erection, Jay? Fuck, he walked around with a perpetual hard-on.

Henry curled his left arm around Jay's chest. His right hand guarded Jay's cock, protectively cupped over his groin. "Tell me, Jay." In contrast to his tender hold, Henry's voice commanded obedience. "The truth, now."

"I'm sorry. I do want to. I do." Pleading with her, Jay opened eyes brimming with tears. "You know I want to. You know I love you."

"I know, sweetheart. It's okay." Whatever the problem, it sure as hell wasn't that he didn't find her arousing. She'd never doubted that Jay did.

"The thought, Jay. The one that distracted you. Share it with us."

He clenched his fists atop his knees. "I don't want Alice to be afraid of me."

Henry held him tighter. "Of course not, my dear boy. Nor do I desire for you to inspire Alice's fear."

She tugged Jay's hands alongside her hips, coaxed them open, and slipped her fingers between his. He wouldn't need them, not with Henry taking care of him.

"It's not you that frightens her, no more than it was I who frightened you at first." Henry nudged Jay, bending their heads together. "Do you remember, brave boy? Better associations. Pleasant memories. We'll help our sweet girl together."

She couldn't imagine the work they'd done to make Jay as comfortable and playful as he usually behaved in bed. As secure in Henry's love. She'd had a slim fraction of the exposure to Cal's viciousness. "I'm not afraid of you, Jay. But I do need your help."

Saying words she'd expected would make her feel weak made her oddly stronger. She didn't have to defeat Cal's echoes alone. She had Henry and Jay to help banish them. "I'm ready to watch. To remember how beautiful you are."

Jay nodded, a low moan escaping.

Henry's doing. Not caused by the hand secure over Jay's heart, but by the one squeezing and tugging his balls with gentle strength. Henry rubbed with an almost flat palm, avoiding more than incidental brushes against Jay's cock.

"An excellent example, my boy. Exactly what Alice needs to see from you."

Palms pressed to her hips, Jay leaned into Henry's hold. His cock gained thickness and length and the deepening colors of arousal. Her own private showing, Henry creating art before her eyes.

"Not a demand." Henry ran his fingers up Jay's cock. "A gift. An offer." He traced the thick ridge along the underside and circled the plump head. "One she may accept or decline."

A gift she wouldn't refuse, just as she never refused Henry's demands. He could've demonstrated using his own cock. A deliberate choice, a rejection of intimidation.

Not that he always intimidated her, but she encouraged that forceful demand from him. The one that told her he would, and could, take care of her needs without making her ashamed of craving his dominance.

She didn't seek that treatment from every man. The jackass trying it at the club had turned her off lickety-split. She loved Henry's singular brand of control.

"He's a beautiful gift, Henry." She stroked upward, over the curves of Jay's knuckles and past the narrowing of his wrists to the lean strength in his muscled forearms. Her gentle partner and playmate. Her sometimes-submissive boy who yearned for forceful control from her, too. "Thank you."

Henry half shielded his smile beside Jay, white teeth and black hair and a quiet kiss. "You see? Alice calls you beautiful." Sparks danced in his green eyes, his energy lighting her up. "She loves the sight of you hard and ready for her. Obedient to her desires."

Pink-cheeked and flush with praise, Jay accented his panting breaths with a moan in their depths.

"Tonight, she wishes to see you climax with thoughts of her. You see her own beauty spread out before you, don't you?"

Jay thrust into Henry's hand, pre-come beading at the tip of his cock. Sleek and straining, he made little bouncing hops, his ass wiggling along Henry's thighs. Her speedy hare zipped toward the finish line with adorable, contagious delight.

"Her stomach, pale and smooth. Her breasts, round and soft, always eager to welcome her lovely playmate." Controlled and coaxing, Henry lowered his voice. "Shall we decorate them for her?"

Jay uttered a thick, *"Yes, please,"* amid heavy breaths. His focus flashed between her face and her nudity sprawled out before him.

Henry added a twisting slide to his strokes.

Stiffening, Jay laid his head back on Henry's shoulder and arched forward. He thrust hard and groaned. He came in a rush, spurting in long streaks, splashing her skin with heat.

Henry murmured to him, guiding Jay through his orgasm with practiced ease. Pure perfection, the both of them, no wasted motions, form and function in harmony.

Jay gasped for air, and Henry patted his chest.

Love.

Evidence all around her.

And on her.

Her giggle slipped out. "I love you."

Tears spilled down Jay's cheeks and collected in the corners of his smile.

Henry released his cock and crushed his chest in a bear hug.

Sympathetic tears gathered in her own eyes, and she blinked them free.

"So much emotion," Henry soothed. "My brave boy and girl. How deep your bond runs. How sweet to see you acknowledge it. You make me proud when you play so well together. Happy tears, isn't that so, my boy?"

Sniffling, Jay nodded. "Happy tears, 'cause Alice isn't scared. I did good."

She gripped his hands and crowded her men with her legs, a near hug. "You did fantastic, loverboy."

He giggled along with her, Henry's dry voice topping their amusement. "You both performed quite well. Now we only need work on expanding your use of proper grammar. 'Did good' indeed."

His snort ruined the oh-so-proper sniff of disdain, sending her and Jay into uncontrolled laughter. They fed into each other, the laughs lasting longer than they would've without the echo chamber, but eventually they subsided into an air-sucking competition to refill starved lungs.

Henry hummed. "Catch your breath, my dears, and we'll have a bit of cleanup. It seems we've made something of a delightful mess."

Jay tipped his head and raised a single eyebrow. Twice.

Yes, she knew. He probably had firsthand knowledge—well, first-back knowledge, given his position—but fuck if she'd leave Henry out either. Not tonight.

"Henry?"

"Yes, my girl?" Kneeling behind Jay, Henry rubbed his thigh in a soothing rhythm.

"You gave Jay what he needed. And you gave me what I needed."

"And I'm very pleased to have done so, Alice."

She met Jay's eyes above his tear-stained cheeks, knowing hers likely matched, and sensed complete agreement. "But there's something else we need."

"Oh?"

Right track. His calculated, neutral tone clued her in. Henry's equivalent of concern when he needed to be strong for them.

"We need to give you what *you* need. Please, Henry."

"Please," Jay repeated, his voice quiet but equally determined.

"You've already pleased me tonight, both of you, with your openness and trust." Henry squeezed Jay's thigh with one hand and Alice's calf with the other. "There's nothing else you need to do for me, my dears."

"Maybe we need"—she took a deep breath and waded in—"to feel like you need more from us. That we're still desirable. We're yours, Henry, but we aren't children. We want to satisfy you. We need to." She cast around for another way to make him understand how badly they needed this. "When we—those first few months—when you wouldn't—I was so confused. I thought, for the longest time, that you didn't want me at all. That I didn't really arouse you."

"Oh, Alice." Henry closed his eyes. "I'm so sorry, dearest. That was miles from my intent."

"I'm not saying this to hurt you. I don't ever want to hurt you. I just need you to understand. I don't want to feel like you don't want me. Or that I let you down or—" This would be the hardest one to admit. But Jay had been so brave tonight. Could she be any less brave? "Or that you don't want to touch me because . . . because of Cal and the things he said."

Jay gasped and nodded, vehemently, fresh tears spilling from his eyes.

"You both feel this way?"

They answered with an echoing, "Yes."

Henry's calm facade cracked.

After a lengthy silence, Henry wrapped his arms around Jay in a tight embrace. He kissed Jay's cheek and patted Jay's side. "To the left for a moment, Jay, please. Alice, if you'll give me your hand and sit up a bit, my dear."

She straddled his thighs.

He pressed her against him until her breasts flattened against his chest and Jay's ejaculate transferred from her skin to his.

"Jay, pile the pillows against the headboard."

Face tucked against Henry's neck, she rocked as the bed shifted with Jay's movement.

"You recall the first night you took Alice?"

"Red flowers and music."

Henry caressed her back. "Yes, precisely. So lovely. So nervous. You recall how I held her for you? Yes? Good. I want you to hold Alice for me, Jay, just like that. I want to look at both of your beautiful faces while I make love to you tonight. That's what I need from you. To see that love and trust and lack of fear in your eyes. Can you do that for me? Yes?"

Alice nodded against his neck.

Jay added a soft, calmer, "Yes, Henry. Thank you, Henry."

Henry lowered her onto Jay's lap. He coaxed Jay's knees up, spreading her legs with them, and wrapped Jay's arms around her. She rested her head beside Jay's, their faces nearly level.

"Beautiful," Henry murmured. "So lovely together."

He knelt between their legs and kissed them, deep and slow, first Jay and then Alice. Limp in the aftermath of her earlier orgasms and the emotional release, she stirred with new warmth from his delicate attention.

"You see how Alice trusts you, Jay? How she allows you to hold her like this, open and vulnerable?" He nuzzled their throats with soft kisses and softer words. "You feel the relaxation in her muscles, don't you? She's not afraid. She's not thinking that you have harmed her or disappointed her. She's thinking that you are her trusted partner, her lover, and she is entirely safe in your arms. Isn't that right, Alice?"

"Yes, that's—"

Henry brought his mouth to her nipple.

"S'true. So safe here."

Jay stroked her sides and rubbed his cheek against hers.

Henry's fingers replaced his mouth on her breasts.

"And my sweet girl, my Alice, you know how desirable you are, don't you?" He brought her hand to his cock, hard and ready. "How eager you make me to feel your body around mine? I'll tell you a secret, dearest." He slipped a hand across Jay's arms and down her stomach, ending at her clitoris.

"When Jay and I reconsidered his contract in August, his opening bid—"

Jay buried his face in her neck.

Henry chuckled. "His opening bid was a request for three climaxes with you per day. Only three, he tells me. That's all. I, of course, explained the unreasonable nature of his request while we were trying to lure you deeper into our den of iniquity. But what I didn't tell him . . ." Henry parted her lips.

She rocked against Jay, the long-legged barrier holding her back.

Henry dropped his voice to a whisper. "What I didn't tell him was that I, too, wanted to write you a contract that had you in my bed three times a day."

He thrust fingers inside her and swept his thumb across her clit. "No alternate Fridays. No waiting. No guiding you slowly into this relationship, this lifestyle. Just sweet Alice, mine to take whenever I pleased. And I please *now*, Alice."

His fingers left her, and he rolled a condom over his cock. He thrust slow and steady, intent on their faces. His rhythm rocked her and Jay. Their moans mingled above Henry's breathing and the slick suction as he stroked deeper into her.

He clasped the headboard and delivered kisses on their upturned faces. The tension behind his thrusts strained her body, tightening her against Jay, squeezing his erection between her back and his stomach.

Henry thrust almost downward, pushing forward, colliding with her clitoris.

Desperate to match him, to keep him, to please him, she braced her shoulders against Jay's solid chest and arched into Henry. Her toes curled.

"Love you both . . . so much . . . my dear ones." Henry thrust hard, giving her the fullness she craved.

Her body responded to him as it always had, obeying his unspoken need for her to come with him. Because she wanted it to. Because she loved him. She leapt over the edge, a willing victim to the free fall that shook her and both of them with her.

When her shaking slowed, he thrust quickly, repeatedly.

She cried out again, chasing the pleasure he gave and demanded she accept.

He growled and dropped his head to theirs, foreheads touching, and drove them back on the mattress as he came.

CHAPTER 3

Alice hummed and danced her way around the kitchen on Saturday morning, getting out supplies to make French toast. Eggs, check. Milk, check. Bread, check. Vanilla extract and cinnamon for flavor, check. Butter and syrup, check.

Finding a wide, shallow bowl for dredging the bread took a couple tries. She wasn't entirely familiar with Henry's kitchen—their kitchen—yet, not as a chef instead of a guest, but she wouldn't hesitate to make herself at home.

Besides, Henry was occupied.

She smirked as she cracked the eggs one-handed and tossed the shells. She'd gotten her morning treat in bed, sweet kisses from Jay and his fingers on her clit as Henry took her from behind while she lay on her side. Their climax had been quiet, gentle, but no less fulfilling for that. She'd bowed out of the postcoital shower quickly to give her boys time to themselves, promising to put breakfast on the table if they promised to work up an appetite.

She whipped the eggs and added the milk, vanilla, and cinnamon while the griddle warmed. The motion of her wrist stirred fantasies of Jay's morning treat. Henry's hand tight around their lover's cock, stroking him off in the shower. She'd have to stay next time. The show had been fantastic last night.

Jay could be so vocal in his pleasure. Not like Henry, not verbal, but vocal. Grunts and groans. Moans and whimpers. Strained breaths and a raspy edge in his voice when Henry did make him talk. Wind him up, and his teasing charm transformed into an uninhibited, driving need coursing desire through all of them.

French toast mix sloshed onto the counter. Whoops. Distracted by the sexy Jay-soundtrack in her head, she'd gotten a little overexcited with the stirring. She wiped up the mess and wet her fingers under the faucet.

The sprinkle of water sizzled on the griddle. She dipped the first slice of bread.

An unfamiliar ringtone trilled from the entryway. Bread dropped and fingers wiped clean, she popped out to the side table. Henry's phone. He didn't get many calls. If it was his agent, a sale might be on the line.

She picked up the phone. The display read *Em*.

Not his agent, but the name teased her memory. Em. Emma. The woman from the club. *She kissed Henry.* The submissive who sat on the board. The call could be about Cal and whether her punishment had affected Henry's status at the club.

Her thumb swiped the screen without permission. "Hello?"

"I think I must have dialed the wrong number. Pardon—"

"No, you're Emma. You're labeled on the phone. From—" She strove for nonchalance. "From the club, right?" Like she talked about sex clubs all the time to women who had seen her half-naked and kissed her lover.

"And you're Alice." Surprise colored the lilting, feminine voice. "You answer his calls?"

"Sometimes." Times like now. And possibly times in the future. So sometimes was an accurate answer. Not one she'd try on Henry, though.

"I see." Emma's tone implied she did see. "Is Henry available to talk?"

"Not right now." If Jay was enjoying being aroused, comfortable being naked and even arousing Henry, she refused to interrupt their shower for anything short of Armageddon.

"Is he—" A long silence followed. "Is he refusing to speak to me?"

Was he *what*? Did this woman think Henry would sever all ties with the club? Had he? He could've met with the board while she and Jay were at work. Fuck. She never should've picked up his phone.

"Should he be?" She tried to keep her voice cool.

"Please tell him—no, I'm sorry, Alice. I've called to apologize, not only to him, but to you and Jay as well."

"You're worried about him." And felt guilty, somehow.

"About the three of you, yes."

Emma had approached them as a friend in the hall. Warm. Laying her hand on Henry's shoulder and kissing his cheek. Complimenting him. About *her*.

"But you'd rather see him in person." Meeting her, Emma hadn't seemed jealous or threatened. She'd seemed happy for Henry. Like a good friend. "To make sure he's okay."

"You're a perceptive and forthright young woman, Alice. I expect it's part of why Henry . . . enjoys you so."

Loves, she mentally corrected. Henry loved her so. And this woman knew it. If she was his confidante, he'd appreciate her support and advice.

"Yes, I'd rather see all three of you in person, but I suppose that would be out of the question."

"We aren't going back there." She rushed out the answer. "Not anytime soon."

Henry had promised. Though the promise seemed as much for him as for them. He'd punish himself for his perceived betrayal of their trust in little ways until he felt he'd atoned. He wouldn't let Jay get away with it, but himself he'd punish for no reason at all.

". . . didn't think you would."

"But you could come here." It was a fabulous idea. Henry needed to talk to someone who'd help him stop punishing himself, and he considered this Emma woman a peer.

"I couldn't possibly."

"You should come for dinner." For Henry, she could keep her jealousy under control. He wasn't in love with this woman. He loved her and Jay. "We eat at seven."

Emma laughed, her voice thin and fading. "Do you? Victor's influence, I suppose. Henry often joined us at suppertime when he—" She clucked. "And now I'm talking out of turn."

"Come to dinner," Alice urged. "I won't ask about your history with him."

"Which I won't be divulging to you in any case, you realize."

"You wouldn't be a very good friend to Henry if you did."

"You're not going to try to push me for information? You were blazing with curiosity when I saw you last."

"Henry gave me the answers I needed. And if I needed more reassurance, I'd ask, and he'd give it." The truth radiated warmth in her chest. She didn't have to feel guilty about asking for what she needed. Henry wanted her to need him.

"Hmm. He would, wouldn't he?" Emma sighed. "But I cannot accept your dinner invitation, Alice, not without his approval. I understand you aren't in the same—that you don't answer to him in every area of your lives, but I won't drop in and surprise him in his home."

The shower had stopped. Jay stood in the bathroom doorway naked and smiling as he rubbed a towel over his hair.

"Just a minute, please." She muted the phone, waved to get Jay's attention, and called down the hall. "Get Henry."

"Demanding little thing, aren't you?" Jay smirked at her. "Where's my breakfast?"

Oh, shit. Breakfast.

"Jay, catch."

He dropped the towel and grabbed the phone in midair.

"Tell Henry Emma's coming to dinner and he needs to tell her it's okay with him."

Thank God the smoke rising from the pan on the stove hadn't set off an alarm. At least she hadn't dropped bread on the griddle. As it was, she only had to turn down the heat and fish soggy bread pieces from the egg mixture to trash them.

Potentially burning the place down probably wasn't a reasonable way to demonstrate her prowess at breakfast duties. *Make a note, Allie-girl.*

A stack of French toast waited, warming beneath a foil tent, when Jay sauntered into the kitchen. Fully dressed, sadly. She was rather fond of the look he'd sported right out of the shower. He sidled up to her as she turned off the stove.

Aluminum foil rustled.

"Hey." She blocked him with the spatula. "Breakfast at the table, goof, and not until Henry's ready, too."

Jay walked his fingers up the spatula. "But if I don't taste them first, how do you know they'll be good enough for Henry?" Wide, innocent eyes gazed at her with puppy pleading. "I'm doing this for you, Alice. From the bottom of my heart."

She snorted. "From the bottom of your stomach, more like. Can you carry the plate to the table without sampling?"

He heaved an exaggerated sigh. "If I must, my cruel-but-beloved chef." He kissed her cheek and danced away with the plate.

Following with the syrup and cut fruit, she surveyed the table, mentally checking things off.

Henry caught her as she turned, trapping her against his chest. Freshly showered and scented, his chest warm and broad. Mmm. Good morning.

"I forgot the juice."

"Jay will fetch it."

She tipped her head back. "So serious. I can—"

"Jay, will you fetch the juice and glasses, please?"

"On it." He raised his eyebrows when he passed her.

Henry prowled her back with his fingertips. He still hadn't smiled.

A prickle of not-lust crawled up her spine. Concern.

"Now, my dear girl, shall we discuss what orders *I* am to carry out?"

"Orders?"

"Mmm. I believe Jay informed me I was to tell Emma to join us for dinner because it was *okay* with me."

Oh. Fuck. Yeah, she'd pretty much said it like an order. Jay would never have done what she'd done. He might've brought Henry the phone, but arbitrarily invited someone to dinner? When hell froze over.

"Imagine my surprise to be handed my phone as I stepped from the shower, a caller already waiting on the other end."

Shifting from foot to foot, she squirmed in his embrace. "I shouldn't have answered your phone, Henry." She'd known she was in the wrong as soon as she'd picked up the phone. "It was rude." No point trying to hide. "I know that, and I'm sorry."

He studied her with narrowed eyes. "I note your contrition only extends so far. What of your spur-of-the-moment invitation?"

A trickier question. If this was going to be her home, too, she had to be able to invite people to meals without being intimidated. With more courtesy next time. Especially when she was rarely the one responsible for providing those meals. "I should've told her one of us would call her back instead of assuming." Even if her intent had been to help repair Henry and Emma's friendship, she'd acted like a kid walking in the door with a friend after school and expecting Mom to stretch dinner without notice. "But I'm not sorry I invited her."

One corner of Henry's mouth twitched.

Her suspicion rested on that microscopic evidence. "And you're not mad at me, either."

"Oh? Aren't I?" Deceptively neutral, but he was neither an angry man nor a violent one.

"No." She had nothing to fear, though his low tone raised the hair at the nape of her neck. "You like it. You like that I invited her, and you like that I'm not backing down now."

"Wrong, Alice." Eyes dark, voice harsh, he gripped her tighter. His cock ground against her stomach. "*Like* is not at all the proper word."

Shivering heat swept through her. Another pair of panties for the laundry pile. Was it wrong to dream of him taking her to bed morning, noon, and night? Last night, he'd said three climaxes a day. Could she get that in writing?

"Love, on the other hand—" He growled in her ear. "Yes, that I feel in abundance, even when you so aptly display your distaste for being ruled by others."

"Not all of the time," she murmured, despite the expanded contract terms with which she'd granted him such power. "Just—"

"Some of the time, yes," he finished with her. He nipped at her neck. "Such a delightful challenge and a constant temptation. But one I'll wait to indulge."

Her whimper, so much like Jay's frequent refrain, surprised her. No wonder the poor boy made it so often. No other sound so thoroughly encapsulated the frustration of desire denied.

"Only for you," she mumbled. She took a deep breath to clear her head.

He let her go, mostly, clasping her hands as he stepped back.

"But I still think dinner is a good idea."

"And why is that, my dear?"

"She sounded like she needed it. And she wanted to apologize in person."

"Well." Henry frowned. "One thing at a time. I suppose you know you'll be giving up your free time this afternoon to go grocery shopping with me."

"So you told her it's okay? She's coming to dinner?"

"She is." He pumped her hands in a shared heartbeat, one-two, one-two. "I expect it won't be what she's expecting. Nor, perhaps, what you are."

Her Sunday best behavior might not get tons of use, but she'd mastered politeness, for God's sake. "I wasn't going to interrogate her."

"No, my dear, I know." He sighed, a fleeting breath. "I believe we've a lovely breakfast growing cold at the moment."

She allowed him the abrupt change of subject. "Yeah, I made—"

The foil covered a much shorter stack of French toast. A mass of bread and syrup rested in front of Jay, a heaping forkful headed toward his mouth.

"Well, I did have a big breakfast of French toast ready."

Henry ushered her to her regular seat, kissed the top of her head, and seated himself.

"You guys seemed like you'd be a while." Jay speared another piece on his plate. "But I'm happy to report the food's super-good and totally safe to eat. Job security, you know."

Henry snorted over her laughter. "Thank you for your extremely useful assessment, my boy. Now I needn't worry that Alice is attempting a poisoning. I do hope you left some for the rest of us."

Jay grinned. "There's lots of fruit left."

CHAPTER 4

Henry sent Jay to the door. The soup didn't need tending, the salads had been plated, and the main course wouldn't go into the oven until the salads had been served. He'd opened the wine bottle a few minutes ago. He could've gone to greet Emma himself.

But he stood in the kitchen with his arm around Alice and his hand splayed on her back. Resting his forehead against her temple, he breathed warmth in her ear.

She closed her eyes and took a deep breath. Let it out slow.

Jay's voice anchored a distant murmur of polite hello and may-I-take-your-coat chatter. On his best behavior for their guest. Having another woman in the house wasn't a threat to him. Ugh. It shouldn't be a threat to her, either, not with Henry's reassuring attention. Though Emma's presence served as a reminder to them both of last week's disaster. The memory might be all that had her on edge.

"No, thank you, Jay." A light, feminine voice. "That's a gift for the chef."

Henry kissed her, leaving behind a whisper. "I love you, sweet girl." He straightened, though his hand stayed on her back.

Opening her eyes, she nodded once. No problem. She could handle this. She'd been the one to make the invitation. Impulsively. Out of equal parts compassion and curiosity. Which everyone knew only killed cats.

Emma turned the corner with her escort, her hand resting on Jay's forearm.

Yeah, no. Definitely more than nerves over seeing a woman who'd been at the club. Irrational fear seized her chest.

Emma was the sort of woman who screamed perfection. Well, not screamed, because ladies didn't do that. She dressed impeccably without Henry's guidance. Alice nurtured a polite smile as she studied their guest. Outside the club, she wasn't distracted by other concerns.

Mahogany hair, a deep brown glinting red in the light, twisted up in some elegantly simple design. Not a strand out of place. A knee-length sheath dress not unlike the one Henry had chosen for Alice to wear tonight. Emma's was a smoky blue-gray. Not flashy and designed to draw eyes from across a room, but tasteful. Understated.

Bet she didn't own a pair of jeans. A woman who'd never run to pick up takeout in a T-shirt, pajama pants, and sandals. With this expert woman right in front of him, Henry had to be wondering what the hell he'd seen in the beginner model.

"Emma." Henry extended his hand. "It's lovely to see you. I trust Jay was the consummate butler."

Emma patted Jay's arm as she let go. "He was indeed. He's grown into quite the proper valet." She stepped forward and laid her fingertips over Henry's cupped hand as if it were a dance they performed. One ending with a half embrace and a kiss on Henry's cheek before Henry released her hand and Emma stepped away.

Her smile at Alice raised tiny lines around her eyes. The eyes matched the dress, a shadowed, winter blue. A choker of platinum and pearls circled her neck above the slight vee of her dress. She clasped a book to her chest with her left hand, upon which rested two rings. Antique sapphire engagement ring. Platinum wedding band with intricate scrollwork.

Relief fizzed like a fresh can of soda. Emma might be widowed, but she wasn't in the market for new love.

Henry petted her back in slow circles. "As we have the opportunity for a proper introduction this evening, Alice, this is Emma, a dear friend."

"It's a pleasure to meet you, Emma." Alice added a wry twist to her smile as they shook hands. "I hope you'll excuse me for not saying hello at our first meeting."

Emma laughed quietly. "Entirely understandable. I've been in the same situation many times myself."

Manners. Kindness. Two more to add to the List of Things Emma Excels At. Alice growled at her jealousy in silence until it settled down.

"My boy, would you pour the wine, please?" He'd set out a dry white for the evening, a Verdelho that paired well with every course. She'd gotten the full rundown while they'd prepared the veggies and Jay set the table.

Jay went to work, and Emma held out her slender book to Henry. "I know, I know, wine or dessert for the host is traditional, but I wouldn't dream of usurping your prerogative in your own kitchen. I hope this will suffice in their place."

Henry accepted the book with both hands, leaving her back cold and empty. He opened the cover. Flowing script inside ended in the words *With love, Em*. Alice forced herself not to read the lines above.

Henry turned the page with a soft hum. The elegant script continued, page after page, but those pages, at least, held titles with words like *chicken* and *beef* and *pastry*.

"Victor's mother gave me a copy of the family recipes when I married him. The collected wisdom of her kitchen and her mother's kitchen and so on back down the line." Emma took the wineglass Jay held out to her and inhaled the bouquet. "I don't suppose I'll have a daughter to pass the wisdom to, but you've a family to feed these days, Henry. Surely you can find some use in it."

"You wrote out a fresh copy for my own kitchen, Em?" He caressed the edge of the pages. "A thoughtful and tremendous gift."

Her gut twisted. Henry's gentle tone belonged to her and Jay, for their gifts. Disliking someone who made Henry happy was irrational at best and shameful at worst.

"They're all in there, Henry. Including that spicy beef dish you loved for Saturday supper and the sweet *pirozhki* for Sunday breakfast."

Irrationality ripped through the room and took the floor under her feet with it. Emma's wedding ring might not mean she still mourned her husband or even that their marriage had been monogamous. Santa had a wife, yet he'd been playing at the club. And Henry had Jay, but now he had her, too. But he'd said he and Emma weren't lovers.

"Thank you, Emma." Henry closed the book with care. He dropped his arm into its former place, curling Alice into his side.

She rested her hand below his breastbone. *Mine.*

"I do enjoy the opportunity to instruct my dear ones in the kitchen, though some of them have terrible thieving manners."

Distributing the remaining wineglasses, Jay boasted an unrepentant smirk. "I'm chief taster. It's an important job."

Emma laughed. "William used to insist he fulfilled the same function in my kitchen until I shooed him out."

Henry raised his glass in a toast. "To hearth and home, and all those who gather therein. Where'er they roam, may they find their way back again."

Glasses touched. Smiles passed around. The wine was cool and dry going down, with a sharp citrus aftertaste.

Emma surveyed the room, making a show of peeking at everything in sight. "In all the years we've known each other, and all the time you've spent in my kitchen, do you realize this is the first time I've gotten a look at yours?"

Her brain was developing whiplash. Categorizing Henry and Emma's history necessitated revision with every conversational turn.

"It's that secretive quality of yours that kept all the girls and boys so intrigued before you settled down."

His kitchen wasn't a secret. He'd invited her into it from day one.

Her. Not Emma.

"And here I'd labored under the mistaken impression that my skills held their interest." Henry hung his head in mocking mourning. "All they sought was a glimpse of my kitchen."

"I want a glimpse of more than a kitchen," Jay faux-whispered.

Alice giggled. "Because you know Henry's skills are excellent in every room."

"Ah, my lovely chorus of defenders to the rescue." Henry's eyes gleamed dark and intense. "I'm pleased to be more to you both than a full stomach. Though that, too, is important." He gestured toward the dining room. "Jay, if you'll seat our guest, please, and then come assist me at the stove."

Jay offered his arm to Emma and waggled his eyebrows. "Soup's on. I haven't tasted it yet today, but the chef is excellent. May I show you to your seat?"

She laughed, polite but genuine. "By all means. I can't recall the last time I had such a handsome escort."

Henry led Alice to the table and lowered her into her regular seat. Adjusting the back of her chair, he brushed his mouth against her ear. "I do so love to see you sitting here, dearest. Such a pleasant temptation."

Heat rushed to her cheeks and less visible places. She'd been sitting right here in August when he'd spoken his first command to her. An order to stand. If she hadn't listened then, no way would she be here now. Did he think of that life-changing moment as often as she did?

Emma smiled as she unfolded her napkin. "I finally had the opportunity to drop by the gallery this week and see the fruit of Henry's skills in the studio. One of those rooms in which he excels, wouldn't you say, Alice?"

She accepted the conversational diversion, holding up her end while Henry ladled soup and Jay carried bowls. Maybe the ability to pick a route through a potential verbal minefield wasn't strictly a dominant skill. Henry masterfully directed conversation without seeming to, but Emma wasn't bad herself.

Years of dinner parties or small talk at the club would teach subtlety. Henry and Emma shared a knack for it. Not a skill she possessed. Directness, that was more her style. Jay's too.

They kept to safe topics, agreeing that Henry's agent, though a cheerful fellow, drooped with a cadaver's gauntness.

"The nerves, I expect," Emma said. "I've never met that man when he was standing still."

"He did seem high-strung when I met him. Jay fidgets a lot—I mean, a lot."

Bringing the last of the soup bowls, Jay stuck his tongue out.

"But Henry keeps him well-fed." She resisted the urge to return Jay's gesture. Better not to open the floodgates and spill the less-cute juvenile shit clogging her head in front of the intimidating woman across the table. "Enough to put meat and muscle on his bones. Otherwise he'd be a dancing skeleton."

"Dibs! I'm calling it now, so nobody else can be a dancing skeleton for Halloween." Jay's enthusiasm caused laughs all around. "Henry, you heard me call it, right?"

"I did. We'll investigate the possibilities of body paint at a later date." Henry set his hand on the back of his chair.

Jay slid into his seat at the foot of the table.

Emma swiveled, one perfectly manicured eyebrow rising. "You don't have a server? I would have thought—" She glanced at the floor beside Henry's chair. At Alice. Settled on Jay and shook her head in a single slow motion.

Jay had already brought the soup to the table. Full-service wait-staff.

"No, no pillows this evening, Em."

Her glance again went to the floor beside Henry's chair as he sat.

Holy shit. Emma expected someone to kneel at Henry's side instead of participating at dinner. A cold night in January. Henry's voice snapping commands. The hollow feeling in her stomach, the chill in her chest. The unpleasant distance between herself and Henry. To be loved and rewarded for her submission was one thing. To sit ignored like a slave unless the master needed something was another thing entirely. Not a game she wanted to play.

Henry picked up his soupspoon.

With the quiet *clink* of the metal against the ceramic bowl, Emma drew her chin up and focused an unwavering stare at Henry.

Her intensity matched Jay in his best waiting pose.

"Grateful though I am for Victor's training in the formalities, I don't run my household in the same fashion." Henry steered the spoon in a slow curve through his soup. "As he balanced his needs with yours, so I balance mine with Jay's and Alice's."

"No, of course." Emma nodded, more to herself than to Henry. "Of course you would."

The talk turned to inconsequential chatter, Henry smoothly encouraging Jay to share stories of the week's most amusing deliveries. He settled down as Henry guided him, Emma asked polite questions, and Alice chimed in on occasion. The charming comedian. Untroubled by the deeper currents. Definitely not thinking about Emma's marriage or what her submission had involved. Things Alice couldn't stop thinking about.

Jay even remembered to tip his bowl properly away to spoon up the last of his cream soup. Henry laid his own spoon down as he surveyed the table. "Salads are in order, it seems."

Jay stood, picking up his soup bowl. Emma half stood.

Shit. No point in standing when she'd already been out-subbed by both of them. Whatever the mindset needed for a submissive, she didn't have it. The instinctive desire to serve. Fuck. Henry would've done better to pick this other woman, the one who spoke art fluently and offered her service with smooth elegance.

"Just Jay to clear, thank you." Henry gestured to his left. "Emma, please, sit. You're our guest tonight."

"Of course." Emma retook her seat. Her hand went to the choker at her throat. "My apologies, Henry."

Silence fell over the noise of Jay bustling about with the dishes, swapping soup bowls for salad plates. Henry excused himself to put the main dish, a baked seafood ravioli tossed with fresh vegetables, served in separate ramekins, in the oven to heat while they enjoyed their salads.

Alice chased down a stubborn piece of lettuce with her fork and stabbed. "Your necklace is beautiful." Three rows of pearls circled Emma's neck, little silk knots between them. "Was it a gift?"

"Oh, yes." The depth of Emma's smile dazzled, a brilliance more than simple politeness, and her eyes shone. "Victor gave it to me many, many years ago."

"A wedding present?" Expensive, for sure, with vertical bars of platinum evenly spaced after every five pearls.

"Our first anniversary." Cheeks pinking, Emma lowered her eyelids in a slow blink. "I knew of his pursuits when I married him, but he refused to begin training me until after we were wed. He surprised me on our anniversary with a collaring ceremony." She shook her head, her voice little more than a whisper. "Told me I was exquisite. That he was well pleased, beyond even his hopes for our joining. I feel his hand on me even now when I wear it."

She'd felt an inkling of that herself. When she wore clothing Henry had chosen for her. Emma had spent decades with a reminder of her husband's claim around her throat. No wonder if the sense memory of him lived in her skin.

Jay ate his salad, seemingly unaffected, but surely he had moments, too, when it took nothing at all to recall the warmth of Henry's hand. The pressure of his lips. The sweet stroke of his tongue.

With the main course snug in the oven, Henry stood in utter stillness, watching them from the kitchen. No. Watching Emma, though he couldn't have seen more than the back of her bowed head.

Lust for his knowledge, his insight, his history, bit Alice with fierce teeth. He saw more than the woman before him. An echo of who she'd been or the memory of his friend and mentor or something Alice couldn't name and might never know.

His parting lips and shifting shoulders bespoke a sigh, though no sound emerged. He came to the table and took his seat. "Moonlight," he murmured. "Victor once told me that was why he'd chosen the pearls."

Emma looked up, one elegant eyebrow arched. "Moonlight?"

"I'd asked him about collaring. The personal significance and how he knew. He said his grandmother told him a story when he was very young. Poetic, though hardly scientific. I'm paraphrasing, of course, but . . ." Henry paused, head tilted. "When the full moon holds sway over the tides, its brilliance keeps the oysters from their beds. They open, and the pearls inside bathe in the luminescence. Forever on they glow with an inner light, a shard of the moon hidden within."

He grimaced. "I was young and clumsy and entirely too ignorant of the nuances of love at the time. I asked if you were his moon, if he meant the pearls as a reminder that he had trapped bits and pieces of you and knotted them into a net to hold you fast."

Fine, if Emma liked that sort of thing. *Not me.* Dishonest. She clamored for Henry's ownership. Greedy desire and pride had shot through her at the club when Santa William said Henry considered them collared. But if Henry had that claim, she demanded an equal claim in return. Another failure to be submissive. She was racking them up tonight.

"Never before nor since did I ever see him so offended, so personally affronted." Henry shook his head, his eyes distant and clouded. "And rightly so. He told me I'd gotten everything backward, and he would have to begin again with me, because for all my skills I lacked wisdom."

Ridiculous. She'd never met a more insightful man. Who was this Victor guy to say otherwise?

"The moonlight, he informed me, could never represent you." Henry leaned forward in his chair, elbows resting almost on the table, hands clasped in front of him. "You were his sun, Em. He filled himself with the light you shared with him. He gave you the pearls not as a show of his ownership and mastery over you, but as a reminder to himself of how thoroughly *he* was tangled in you. That each pearl carried a shard of his love for you, the reflected light he thanked God for each day. The gift you gave him.

"You *should* feel his hand on you when you wear it, Em. You're carrying his love with you."

Shuddering breaths drifted across the table.

Alice averted her gaze. Intruders, she and Jay. Eavesdropping on an intensely private moment. Henry wouldn't have told the story if he didn't believe Emma needed to hear it. And maybe because she needed to hear it, too.

Whatever the rules of their marriage, Emma had loved her husband deeply. She did still. The undercurrents between her and Henry belonged to something else. Nothing Alice could rigidly define, but if Henry had a sun, it wasn't Emma.

"He—he never told me that. Not like that." Emma cleared her throat. "Thank you, Henry." Voice growing stronger, she became the poised perfectionist once more. "That was very kind of you."

She transitioned to a question about the salad with little more than a breath between, as if she hadn't learned something surprising about her husband's view of their relationship. An understanding between them that allowed others, even ones so insightful as Henry, to view Victor as the one who shone brighter. But Emma's husband, her dominant, knew better. Where the rest of the world, even his loving, submissive wife, saw him at the center of things, he saw only her.

As it should be, Henry whispered in her mind. Alice shivered, drawing his eyes, and she shook her head. No, it was nothing. She was fine. Just analyzing. Evaluating.

Wondering how Emma could shrug off the emotion and so easily accept Henry's decision to even talk about it now, in front of her, in front of Jay.

The conversation meandered down lighter paths, the main course served and lauded.

Irritation itched at her shoulder blades. Henry wasn't Emma's dominant. Whatever her training, her years of experience, she didn't have the right to act as if he was.

A sliver of doubt wedged itself deep. Every last bit of Emma's perfect, poised, submissive charm and grace revealed Alice's shortcomings. She'd never be this woman. A woman Henry admired and cared for. A woman brimming with praise for his culinary skills as forks slowed and plates emptied.

"Thank you, Em. It's always lovely to have one's efforts appreciated and acknowledged. But you haven't come to dinner merely to compliment me on the output of my kitchen."

"I owe you an apology, Henry." Emma laid her fork down with precision and gazed at each of them in turn. "All three of you, truly."

"If you feel you must, Em." Kindness emanated from Henry's voice, his eyes, even the tilt of his head. "Was there an egregious breach of which I am unaware?"

"You asked me for one thing, Henry, and I failed to manage it. In the past—" Lips pinched in a thin line, she glanced at Alice and Jay. "You've never failed me when I needed you. You asked for such a simple thing. I should have been more vigilant. My failure led directly to traumatizing young Jay and leaving poor Alice to cope with a situation far outside her experience. Victor would have been disappointed in me." She rubbed her necklace like a talisman. "I'm disappointed in myself. I concede your right for recompense in this, Henry, and submit myself to your judgment."

Alice struggled not to gape, her fork held in nerveless fingers.

Jay, too, had stopped eating.

Judgment. Not forgiveness.

"You believe you deserve punishment for your actions, Em?" Henry slipped into unreadable neutrality, the tone of game nights and safeword demands.

"I believe your Alice suffered a punishment as a direct result of my failure to alert you to Cal's presence in the club. If you judge I ought to share in that punishment, so be it."

"Jay." Henry's voice was quiet.

Fuck. He wouldn't play with Emma the way he played with them.

"Yes, Henry." Jay's whisper drifted from a trembling lip.

Never send Jay to fetch a flogger or a paddle or whatever implement suited the grievance.

"Do you feel Emma is responsible for the injury you suffered last week?"

"No, Henry." A sworn vow, Jay fervent and overflowing with feeling. No way was he ready to watch that. No way would Henry make him.

"Do you feel she deserves to be punished for her oversight?"

Jay studied each of them in silence, but his gaze rested on her last and longest. "I think whatever Alice feels is fair is right." He tapped his fork on the edge of his plate, a chiming metronome in disarray, gaining speed. "Emma thinks she failed us all, and I know I failed you and Alice, and you probably think you failed us, too. But Alice is the only one who got punished."

"Alice?"

Jesus. Did she want him to punish Emma? Was that seriously the question? Ask an eye for an eye when the person truly at fault suffered no punishment. Cal. That fucking jackass and his bully tactics, trying to intimidate Jay, trying to intimidate her, threatening to harm them and—

Henry held out his hand, and she put hers in it, letting his touch calm her.

"I don't blame Emma." Trust. Understanding. The sexual exclusivity their contract demanded wouldn't prevent Henry from disciplining another player in some other fashion.

"She doesn't owe me a share of the punishment." He loved her. He understood the precarious nature of her footing in this new environment. He wouldn't intentionally slight her.

"What she feels she deserves and what you feel owed are"—she forced the rest of the words out—"are your decisions. I won't interfere or usurp your right to determine what's best. But for me, no. The one responsible is Cal. If he were punished, I'd be satisfied."

The smallest tic jumped in Henry's cheek as he squeezed her fingers. The flash in his eyes cleared with his blink. "Tell me, Em, where did the failure originate? You took steps, I'm certain, to prevent the outcome that arose."

"Yes, Henry. Of course. I flagged him in the database. Had he reserved a room or requested special equipment, I'd have been informed well in advance. I investigated his visit log. Saturday nights only. He hadn't attended on a Friday in more than a year. The door and desk staff knew to inform me if he arrived, a small lie about a matter regarding his membership. I intended to know in an instant and send a runner to warn you." She shook her head. "But I wasn't there. I wasn't there, and by the time I'd heard, you'd already gone."

"What drew you away, Emma? Some trivial matter, easily handled by another?"

"No, no, not then. Ultimately, yes. One of the patrons had chest pains and slurred speech. His partners caterwauled like children and refused medical assistance. They wouldn't trust the discretion of the private ambulance service on call. I had to calm the fools before they'd allow him to be moved. Useless. Utterly useless. All the while a true emergency was happening, and I did nothing to stop it. Of no more use to you than those idiots were to their dominant."

"You took extensive precautions on our behalf, and fate intervened. I might as easily say I should have taken Alice and Jay home sooner. Let their first night on display together be a short one. My own desire to see them enjoy themselves blinded me to the potential difficulty."

He couldn't possibly believe those things.

"Or I might have refused them permission to leave my side. Taken them myself. Spent more time training them beforehand."

What was she thinking? Of course he blamed himself.

"Perhaps my desire to surprise Alice with a night out overrode my sense of caution." His dispassionate delivery concealed the guilty currents. No telling how deep they ran.

"Shall I go on, Em? We might play this game all night." Henry tapped the table twice in quick succession. "Or we might accept that what's done is done, and for all the possible missteps each of us made, the one person whose actions caused this is Cal."

But Henry would shoulder the responsibility to fix it.

"All other things being equal, his choice to pursue my dear ones, to corner them and verbally assault them, was the choice of a man who cannot control himself. And a man who cannot control his own actions has no business attempting to control others'."

She'd slept in safety and comfort. He'd spent hours chewing over concerns she'd given no thought to. Repaid his selflessness with selfishness.

"You won't accept my apology, then?" Emma bowed her head. "Nor punish me for my failure?"

"The latter is unnecessary, Em. Any failure on your part was a single snowflake in an avalanche. His voice, not yours, shouted it down. No, I will not punish you, as I perceive neither negligence nor malice in your actions." Henry pushed his chair back and stood. "I will, however, accept your apology on behalf of my family."

He stepped around the corner of the table and touched the pearls at Emma's throat with two fingers.

Alice bit her tongue and swallowed a pained gasp. If Henry had put collars around her and Jay and another dominant tried to handle them, surely he would've taken personal offense. The closeness and trust in Emma's acceptance of Henry's touch struck her like a blow.

He used the same fingers to lift Emma's chin, and she gazed at him with eerie calm. Jay's acceptance without the joy. A neutral mask. If Henry weren't the man he was, he could slap Emma across the face right now and she'd thank him. Not the sort of pain Alice enjoyed. Emma seemed more of a masochist, and even she wanted to ban Cal's brand of sadism. How much of an ass did he have to be for a masochist to find him unappealing?

Henry bent at the waist, the bulk of his body a fair distance from Emma's, and pressed a closed-mouth kiss to her forehead. "I accept the apology of Victor's gentle flower, knowing she intended no offense, and grant her forgiveness. The debt is paid."

Emma sighed, soft and low. "Thank you, sir."

A ritual. Some kind of ritualized apology, and no she wouldn't leap across the table and demand Emma not call him *sir* like she had a right to. Because she was the hostess here, and it would be poor manners, and she wasn't a child, and Jesus Christ it still hurt.

Pink-lipped and pouty, Jay blew her a kiss across his fingertips.

She soaked up the welcome in his deep brown eyes and caught his kiss against her cheek and held it there. Thanked him silently. Her sweet boy. Hers and Henry's.

Henry straightened and turned from Emma.

Alice hastily lowered her hand.

A flicker of something crossed his face.

"Coffee and dessert, please, Jay. In the living room." Henry rounded the table with controlled swiftness to reach her side. He held his hand out. "Ladies, if you'll join me?"

She laid her fingers in his and let him help her to her feet. A formality he didn't insist upon when they dined alone. Trying to meet Emma's expectations. Or set Emma at ease with behavior she'd find familiar. The woman crackled with upper crustitude.

But Henry had reached for *her* hand, though he'd had to leave Emma's side to come to hers. He gestured Emma in front of him to the living room, where she took the plump formal armchair angled toward the couch.

Henry seated Alice at the end of the couch nearest their guest. He settled beside her, leaving no gap. The warm weight of his hand against her spine pressed her closer.

"Comfortable, sweet girl?" he rumbled in her ear.

Never more so than in his arms. "Very."

Realization dawned. Henry intended his possessive behavior as a lesson for *her.* Emma already knew who held Henry's heart. Across the coffee table, she tucked unknowable thoughts behind a wistful smile.

"Perhaps you'd care to choose a topic for conversation, Emma?" Henry leaned against the cushion and wrapped his arm around Alice's back, squeezing her hip.

"You've already accepted my apology, Henry. I may have exhausted my conversation starters for the evening." Emma sat as straight as she had at the table, her legs neatly together.

"Em." Henry chided with familiar firmness. "We both know you've more than an apology on your mind."

Jay knelt beside the coffee table and set the tray down. Henry hadn't made a complex dessert but a variety of bite-size pieces. Fancy little cakes, she and Jay had dubbed them. *Petits fours*, he'd insisted.

"You've always been good at that, Henry." Emma accepted the coffee Jay offered with quiet thanks. "What gave me away this time?"

"You haven't relaxed, Em. If the apology were all that weighed on you, forgiveness would have been enough. And you would have set the stage for it with flowers or a fruit basket earlier in the week." Turning, Henry addressed Jay. "No, thank you, my boy. You've provided lovely service this evening. Come join us on the sofa, hmm?"

Jay popped one of the little cakes in his mouth and sat beside Henry. He squirmed, his body straight and tense, as unsure of his place as she'd been of hers all night. He'd probably rather be snug in his waiting pose at Henry's feet.

Henry studied Emma. "You learned something more recently— last night, perhaps?—that affects us."

If he'd tensed, Alice would've followed suit. But he rolled his shoulders, settling comfortably against the back of the couch and rubbing his hand over her hip. *Relax. Henry's not worried.*

"So, Emma, tell me," he continued, his voice casual. "How did the board meeting turn out? Was there a challenge?"

Jay stiffened, a rabbit in a hawk's shadow.

Henry touched his shoulder. "Lie down, my dear boy." He patted his thigh. "Head here, please."

The younger man settled on his side in a loose fetal position, his head in Henry's lap. He draped a hand over Henry's knee, fingers moving in a steady pattern of gentle squeezes.

Alice ruffled his hair, and he let out a quiet hum.

"You're good, Henry." Emma sipped her coffee. "But this time you're not quite on target."

"Cal didn't object? I admit, I'm surprised. I expected he would attempt to bring a complaint over what he perceives as an inadequate level of punishment."

If he'd expected a problem, why the hell hadn't he mentioned it to her and Jay? *Because he's the dominant and you're the submissives, Allie-girl.* This was part of it, and she'd have to get used to it. Sometimes she'd be insulated. Sometimes he'd worry and wouldn't say a word until and unless the trouble directly affected her.

I don't like that. As his partner, she had to be allowed to support him and share his burdens.

Emma clinked the saucer as she set her cup down. "He didn't have the standing, not after last week."

The startled reflex in Henry's muscles didn't sound in his tone. "I know the board wouldn't have revoked his privileges for being an ass, Emma. You haven't the votes, and his behavior has been overlooked before."

"Not revoked, no. But suspended." The glee on Emma's face matched Alice's at the idea of cutting off Cal's balls and feeding them to him. "For fighting."

"Fighting?" Henry frowned. "It's unlike him to be baited into blatantly violating the rules." He stroked Jay with a light touch along a smooth cheekbone. "He's more likely to take out his frustrations on the defenseless in private."

In the chaos of the night at the club, the image she'd seen over Jay's shoulder as Henry shepherded them out had stuck with her. The one question she needed answered tumbled free. "Is Santa okay?"

Henry whipped his head around and studied her with a look not unlike the shrewd one on Emma's face. Approval and a whiff of admiration, if she hadn't imagined it.

"William really does earn the nickname, doesn't he?" Emma's smile might have reflected her affection for William or her enjoyment of teasing Henry by withholding the answer. "I keep telling him he ought to shave, but—"

"Em, delightful as it is to see you bonding with Alice, I would greatly appreciate an answer to her question *before* you enumerate Will's various charms."

"He's fine, Henry. A bruised jaw and a highly satisfied ego." She waved it off as nothing. "Probably listening to his harpy's complaints over how it looks to their friends."

Henry loosed a single chuckle. "I suppose he let Cal get in a free punch to make a clear case? In front of witnesses, no doubt."

"You'd have done the same thing yourself for him." Emma chose one of the little cakes, orange with white icing, and ate it in two dainty bites.

"Sanctions?" Watching Emma, Henry squeezed Jay's shoulder. Reassurance. No matter how the subject disturbed Jay, he'd refuse to leave.

"He accepted disciplinary action equal to Cal's, a two-week suspension, for provoking the altercation."

God, to have heard William take down that prick. He'd proved to have a quick tongue when it came to goading Cal.

Henry snorted. "Would they have suspended Cal otherwise? Or do we no longer even have the votes for enforcing basic civility?"

"We could." Emma squared her shoulders and lifted her chin. "If you stand for Jacob's seat."

Henry and Emma studied each other in silence. Tension hung between them.

"So we've come around to the real purpose of your visit, have we?" Unflappable, Henry settled back as if he'd expected Emma's gambit.

Were subtlety and sly moves a submissive approach? It wasn't *her* approach. Except when she and Jay had worked together in January to forestall disaster. Henry had seen through them in an instant.

Yeah, he had. But he'd still given them what they needed.

"You have the support among the voting members, Henry." Emma picked up speed. "Victor was grooming you for the job."

She'd have killed for her laptop to take notes.

"Your behavior is above reproach." Emma ticked off points on her fingers. "The novices respect you."

This conversation had taught her more about Henry's standing at the club in three minutes than she'd discovered in the month and a half since she'd learned the place existed.

"Andrew would back you. His niece and her husband thanked you at their wedding, for God's sake."

"And six years ago, I wouldn't have hesitated." Draping his arm over Jay, Henry patted his chest. "Even two years ago I might have considered it." He rubbed his other hand along her ribs and squeezed her close. "But I have other priorities now."

"You don't think they'd benefit from it, Henry?" Emma narrowed her eyes and shook her head. "I know you've ideas for updating the code of conduct. For providing better protections for submissives and specific safety and training requirements for dominants. They're good ideas."

"I'm not saying the job isn't worthwhile. I'm saying it would take too much of my attention from the people I love." He raised his hand from Jay's chest in a dismissive wave before settling again. "Find someone else to implement the ideas. Will would relish the greater involvement. More time away from his . . . lovely wife."

"If he hadn't just baited another long-standing member into a fight, I might agree with you." Emma sighed. "But the older members see him as a hothead. One who needs more seasoning. Whereas you followed protocol. Your subs conducted themselves well and so did you."

Emma set her coffee cup on its saucer and laid them on the table.

"I nosed around afterward, Henry." She leaned in, her elbows resting on her knees, her hands clasped. "A good portion of the people watching Alice's punishment considered it a well-choreographed show."

Alice nudged forward, certain she'd misheard. "They what?"

Emma nodded. "Many of them have seen Henry direct scenes. Some have had instruction from him."

She shoved aside the voice in her head asking what the hell that meant.

"He showed up with subs when he normally attends alone and has for years. It created a buzz." Emma spread her hands, palms up. "They saw what they expected to see, a lesson in trust, affection, and gentle discipline, with you, Alice, cast as the unwitting novice, and Cal as the villainous poacher, and Henry teaching the appropriate course of action. A dominant must always put the health of his sub first and adhere to proper behavior, even when provoked. He must remain in control." Emma shrugged lightly and leaned back in the chair.

All the confusing emotions swirling in her head, the sobs she'd been embarrassed by, the fear that she'd disappointed Henry, her anger at that man—was it better or worse if no one had known how real the punishment had felt to her?

"Alice gave them the emotional center." Crossing her ankles, Emma shifted her attention to Henry. "You gave them the calm control. Jay highlighted the sweeping romance. Several players interpreted him as your loyal watchdog eager to attack the enemy but instead playing the defender, cradling Alice to his chest. A bit of Lancelot. Honestly, Henry, if I didn't know you so well, I might've thought it scripted myself. But you would never put an untried sub through that deliberately."

"No." Henry growled, thick and heavy. "A scene fraught with emotion, soaked in bitterness and violence—I would not have chosen *that* as an introduction."

She'd forgiven him. The outcome hadn't been his choice. She squeezed Henry's thigh, hoping to offer comfort without breaking any unwritten dom rules, and combed her fingers through Jay's hair. No rules against offering him comfort, and he'd retreated. Her carefree playmate found refuge in submission and silence. "Wait. If William only let Cal take a swing at his jaw, why was he suspended?"

"He let Cal take the first swing." Ducking her head, Emma only partly concealed her broad smile. "And then he took the bastard to the floor, not gently, and held an arm across his throat until a bouncer got to them. I received a thorough report."

"I wish I'd seen that." She scratched Jay's scalp in slow circles. Her tender stud deserved fierce defenders, friends who shared Henry's decisiveness, compassion, and protective nature. Tonight's dinner had acknowledged Emma's effort, but William had done his share, too. "I want to thank Santa."

Henry kissed her forehead. "We'll discuss something appropriate, sweet girl."

"You're certain I can't persuade you to take Jacob's seat?" Emma rubbed her hands together. "He intends to step down before Christmas and spend half the year in Arizona with his grandchildren."

"I'm sorry, Em, but I don't think so. My strength belongs to my family." Henry deepened his hold on them. "It's been a difficult week, and we've more work to do."

"Teach a class, then." Nodding, Emma almost stepped on the end of Henry's answer. "You're still training Alice. It's an excellent opportunity."

"Take her back, you mean. No." Henry shook his head, and Jay echoed the movement beneath her hand.

She couldn't, at this moment, unreservedly say going back rated high on her to-do list, either.

"I have no intention of returning, Em."

Emma rippled in a single shudder. Concussive blast, a woman standing too close to a building demolition shoved back by the force.

Alice studied Emma differently from the way she had all night. Not considering what Henry might see in Emma or want from her. Not considering how Alice herself might measure up beside her. What did Emma see when she looked at Henry?

"You have—" Emma cleared her throat. "Henry, may we speak in private?"

Jay curled tighter, rustling Henry's pants and clutching his knee.

"I'm afraid not, Em." Henry rested his hand on Jay's neck, rubbing his thumb back and forth. "Not tonight."

Alice stared, beyond caring about the rudeness. She needed data. If she hadn't been staring, she'd have missed the tightening around Emma's mouth. The tension in her calf as she flexed her leg. Emma had acted pleased for them earlier, for their little family or Henry's happiness. Her friendship with Henry had begun when Alice and Jay were in elementary school. And now Henry had placed himself in their corner.

"No intention at all?"

Emma's requests wouldn't budge him.

Voicing her sympathy wouldn't help. Apologizing for having Henry's support when Emma feared losing it smacked of gloating.

"Not even if they asked? If they needed it?" Emma gestured toward Alice and Jay, but her eyes stayed with Henry. "Do you recall what we discussed last summer, the irreparable harm—"

"Emma." His voice a low command, Henry tightened his arm around Alice's shoulder.

She barely dared breathe. This near stranger might know things about her. Private things.

"We spoke in confidence."

"But your concerns were unfounded, weren't they?" Emma's voice rose in volume and speed. Their eyes met, Emma's tight and pinched and ringed by deep lines beneath drawn brows. Emma flipped her gaze to Henry, her fingers tapping the chair arm. "Here she sits, accepting your discipline and your love—"

"Emma."

Emma's gaze dropped to her feet.

Alice almost expected her to fall into a waiting pose. She felt the impulse herself. Hell, Jay had startled as if that tone had carried instructions for him.

"Your behavior tonight—" Henry shook his head. "Victor would have taken—"

A high, thin note pierced Emma's clamped lips and cut off in an instant.

Henry's struggle, his leashed anger, spilled into Alice's skin. He turned his face into her hair and breathed out, hard.

Across from them, Emma curled bloodless hands in her lap.

Henry left a ghost of a kiss against Alice's head.

"Emma." Henry softened his voice. *"Sverchok.* Even were I to renounce my membership at the club, our friendship would not end." He took another deep breath.

Alice attempted to identify what he'd said. A command? An apology? A nickname? Her lack of knowledge itched at her.

"But we've finished with the subject for tonight. I won't hear more about it. Not one word."

Without looking up, Emma nodded once. "Not a word, Henry. Of course."

"Good. We've kept you overlong in any case. Jay." Henry patted his back, encouraging him to rise. "Retrieve Emma's coat, please. It's late, and she ought to be getting home soon."

Jay rolled off the couch and onto his feet, trotting to the armoire that served as a coat closet. If he moved fast, well, Jay did everything fast unless Henry specified slow. But his hope for some alone time manifested in every bouncing step.

Emma, in her stillness, rode the inverse line. Head bowed, she wore the blank face she'd had accepting Henry's judgment at the table. If not for her slow blink, she'd have been a store-window mannequin.

Alice scrutinized Emma for a shift from potential energy to kinetic. A sign of irritation. Of frustration or resentment at being silenced. But it didn't come. Maybe Emma didn't feel she'd been treated like a child. Or was accustomed to it. Or had the good sense to recall she was a guest in Henry's home. Or maybe Alice didn't know her well enough to know what the hell went on in her head. Dammit. She'd tie herself in knots trying to figure it out.

"Yes, thank you, Henry." Emma straightened. "I'm . . . tired. A bit of sleep will set me to rights again."

Refinement. Poise. Emma had it in spades. She accepted Henry's reproach without complaint. Took the excuse he offered her with grace. *She's a better submissive than I am.* Alice resettled her shoulders, channeling Jay's clinginess, wishing she had Henry to herself right now.

Henry cupped Alice's head and kissed her cheek, his forehead warm against hers. "A moment, sweet girl," he murmured. He stood, leaving her on the couch alone. "Of course, Em. I'll walk you out."

Jay brought the light dress coat over while Henry helped Emma to her feet. Henry accepted the coat, thanking Jay, and held it open. Polite words rolled off Emma's tongue, thank-yous for the lovely dinner and the gracious host and the opportunity to spend time getting to know Jay and Alice better. She turned her back and allowed Henry to slide the coat up her arms and onto her shoulders. He didn't button it for her. Emma didn't reach for the buttons herself, either.

He might do it for her downstairs. Where their interaction wouldn't be seen.

Ugh. Her jealousy was unworthy of her and them. He wasn't having an affair with this woman. The hour was late, and although the guest parking area was well-lit, he wouldn't send his guest out alone. Couldn't, not and still consider himself a gentleman. She didn't understand what they were to each other, but he wouldn't hide an affair.

Ex-lover, though, that was possible.

Fuck.

Jay closed the door behind Henry and Emma. Turning, he cocked his head like a puppy trying to understand a new command. "You're thinking."

"Huh?" The dishes hadn't been taken care of yet. Jay had cleared, but he hadn't rinsed them or loaded the dishwasher. She could do that now.

"You're thinking something."

"Not really." Yes really. All sorts of things. None remotely worth mentioning to Jay.

He followed her into the kitchen. "Yes, you are." He nudged her with his hip as she opened the dishwasher. "What'd you think?"

"Think?" Why had he chosen now to be perceptive? If he could tell, Henry would know in an instant. "I think—" She'd better not be thinking when he returned. "She's very—" *Get it out and let it go.* "Mature."

Jay slouched against the counter, facing her as she rinsed salad plates. "Funny, you don't sound catty when you say that, so I know you don't mean old."

"She's elegant." She kept moving under his stare. Loading dishes. "Poised. Refined." They could have the place cleaned by the time Henry came back. "Very, umm . . ."

"Art crowd. Upper crust."

"Yeah." And now Ms. Upper Crust had Henry downstairs spending time with her. Talking about things Henry liked. Things they both liked. Things she didn't even know Henry liked.

Jay slid closer, boxing her in with his body, the sink, and the dishwasher rack. Leaning his head against hers, he kissed her cheek. "I used to think it, too, you know."

She set the glass down. Jay couldn't really read her mind. She traced the edge of the hammered copper sink apron. "You did?"

"I was a massive bundle of insecurities, and for months I couldn't have sex without panicking, and my hobbies were nothing like Henry's. Of course I did." Wrapping his arm around her back, he pressed her toward him. "You're thinking, 'What does he see in me? What if I'm not good enough for him? He could have all that class and sophistication if he snapped his fingers, and I'm just *me*.'"

She closed her eyes and sighed. Jay did know. He did understand.

"I know he loves me," she whispered. "But she's so . . . perfect."

Jay slipped his head against her own, a slow *no*. "Not for me and not for Henry. For us, you're perfect."

"Absolute perfection." Henry startled her, but Jay didn't budge.

How much had Henry heard? Had he hurried back to them? She twisted around, desperate to read his face.

Henry locked eyes with her. He stalked them, crossing the kitchen with deliberate steps.

"Jay." His voice was soft. Controlled. "Fetch me a condom. Quickly, now."

Jay darted from the room, leaving her to Henry's mercy. He didn't look merciful.

"My sweet girl. Do you know"—with his body he herded her to the kitchen wall—"how many hours"—hiked her dress to her waist—"I've been waiting"—hoisted her with hands beneath her thighs and leaned into her—"to do this?" Fully hard, he pushed into her panties.

He raked her neck with kisses and ground his hips, his cock the strike of a match across her clit. Trapped against the wall, she whimpered and stroked him in return.

"Thank you, Jay. Lend me your hands, hmm?" Henry squeezed her thighs, lifting her up and sliding her back down. "Mine are occupied."

He returned to kissing her—her throat, her collarbone, her earlobes, her jaw, finally her mouth. All the while, Jay worked between them, unbuckling Henry's belt and opening his pants. Knuckles bumping her through her panties with accidental strokes, he lowered the condom over Henry's cock. When the kisses paused, Alice held her breath.

"Is she wet for me, Jay? Best to check. Be a good boy and give Alice two fingers."

Her panties slipped to the side. A finger stroked between her lips with an audibly wet slide. Drenched. No hiding the truth of her eager response. Jay thrust inside. Her bucking hips locked him between her and Henry, shoving the heel of Jay's hand against her clit. Fuck yes.

"More than wet enough, Henry." Jay spread his fingers, readying her for a larger invasion.

Henry forced her hips to the wall. "Show me."

Jay pulled free and raised his fingers.

Henry sucked them into his mouth, his cheeks hollowing.

Jay moaned.

Henry let go and licked his lips.

"Thank you, my boy." He kissed Jay softly. "Hold our girl open a moment. I've a gift to give her."

The best gift. Her breathing quickened as Jay pushed her panties aside and the tip of Henry's cock rested just inside her. Jay stepped back. But Henry made no move to enter farther, and his hands kept her still.

"You want to watch, don't you, my boy?"

"Yes, Henry." His trembling tenor flirted with the edge of a whimper.

"No touching. Neither us nor yourself. You'll wait your turn like a good boy, hmm?"

Jay rasped *yes* between heavy exhalations. He'd wait. Wait like she was waiting now. Wait for Henry's pleasure. His choice of when and how to take them.

The tingling need firing along every nerve shivered through to her skin. "Please . . ."

"You want your gift, Alice?"

"Yes. Please."

Henry thrust with a single, smooth stroke. Her thighs spread as he reached his depth. She clutched his shoulders. He drew back and thrust again, starting a deep, rocking rhythm that carried her along until she was whimpering with need and unashamed of it.

"Who makes you feel good, Alice? Who gives you this pleasure?"

"You do."

"Who am I, Alice?"

"Henry. Henry-Henry-Henry." She called his name with each thrust, a rolling chant.

"And why do I do it, Alice? Why do I allow you so much pleasure?"

She almost fumbled the rhythm, but then certainty filled her as surely as his carefully measured thrusts. "Because you love me."

"Say it again, Alice."

"Because you love me."

She repeated the words until she couldn't, until her throat grew tight and her head pressed against the wall and she met Henry's every thrust with violent force of her own. The drape of her dress and the slide of the fabric teased her as they had on their first night. The tension in her body teetered on the cusp of uncoiling.

He tightened his hold on the backs of her thighs as he drove into her.

Even Henry lacked the breath to speak now, she thought, until he growled against her throat. "Come now, Alice. Come *now* or not at all."

The pure command in his voice and the realization she'd somehow driven him to the very edge of his control gave her the final push. Enough to leave her shaking uncontrollably as pleasure unwound beneath her skin.

He came, pressed deep inside her and groaning as she rippled around him, pinning her to the wall, a thin membrane of latex keeping his heat from spilling into her. Curiosity laced her satisfaction. She'd never allowed the elimination of that barrier with previous lovers. But with Henry? With Jay?

She curled her fingers in the short hairs at the nape of Henry's neck. Might be time to start.

Henry raised his head and pressed his lips to her forehead. "All right, Alice? No fears, hmm?"

Maybe he meant the emotional insecurity she'd been sharing with Jay, but his predatory behavior registered with a tumbling *click*. He'd used his body, his size, his voice, to crowd her against the wall. She'd sat across from a reminder of the club all night, but Henry's stalking hadn't once awakened her fear and anger over Cal's jackass intimidation tactics.

Her euphoria set off a string of giggles. "No fears." She wrapped her arms around his back, burying her face in his neck and rocking. "Just love."

"Good girl." He pushed off the wall. "Shall we take Jay to bed? Show him how loved he is as well?"

She tightened her legs around his hips. "Definitely."

Past Henry's shoulder, Jay stood at the kitchen table with his pants tented.

"We haven't shown him for hours."

Leaning toward them, obedient to Henry's command not to touch, he threatened to crack the chair behind him with his grip.

"We should fix that."

"Wonderful. Come along, Jay. But don't *come*. Not quite yet."

She grinned like a fiend at Jay, who followed behind while Henry carried her to the bedroom. The clutch of her legs around Henry's waist seemed all that kept his pants from tripping him. He set her gently on her feet—well, the heels she'd worn at his request—near the foot of the bed.

Her dress cascaded into place around her knees. His pants dropped to the floor. Henry casually stepped out of them, as if he weren't flustered to stand in front of her with his shirttails draped over his softening cock and his boxers hitched under his balls. Poised and elegant. She resisted the urge to giggle again.

"Jay. Come here, please." Henry positioned Jay in front of Alice and raised her hands to his chest.

Jay's heart thumped hard under her palm. Eager desire beamed from his smile and his eyes.

"Undress our boy for me, Alice. Slowly."

Henry's movements around the room divided her focus as she worked open Jay's buttons. Images flickered like a gif set.

Henry, disposing of the condom.

Jay, nuzzling her hair and inhaling.

Henry, removing his own clothes.

Jay, his skin paler below his neckline.

Henry, watching her push Jay's shirt down his arms.

She knelt to take off Jay's shoes and socks, helping him balance as she made him stand on one foot and then the other. Lifting her head and moving her hands to unbuckle his belt, she slammed up against a twinge of nerves. His cock stood *right there*. In front of her mouth. Bulging behind a pair of dress slacks.

If someone's a good boy, he can watch me fuck her after his whipping.

She gripped belt leather in tight, immovable fingers. Cal droned on.

I have a lovely coachwhip.

"Alice." Henry coaxed her in quiet, understanding tones. "It's all right, my dear. Finish the task I set you. You haven't been asked for anything more than that, dearest."

Her fingers fumbled through unfastening Jay's pants and lowering them as he stood unnaturally still. She was careful with his boxers, pulling them out and around to avoid teasing him, and then she was left with nothing more to remove. Jay's erect cock waited inches from her face. He jumped, and her gust of breath resounded in her ears. She'd been blowing air across sensitive skin. Aside from one uncontrolled jump, he hadn't moved a muscle. Hadn't made a sound. Hadn't cracked a joke.

"Alice. Stand up, please."

She forced herself not to rush. She wasn't afraid of Jay. She wouldn't let him think she was. His erection stirred arousal and affection. But kneeling, and while his pants were still on, that was . . . difficult.

"Raise your arms, please, Alice." Henry stood behind her, his nearness swirling in her awareness before he stripped her sheath dress off over her head and laid it aside.

She curbed the impulse to check for unwanted eyes watching her. Henry nuzzled her face. "Up unto the bed, my girl."

Jay gifted her with a compassionate gaze. He knew fear and vulnerability beyond any she'd encountered. Seeing her shaky responses, helping her, gave him purpose and permission. If she hid, he would too.

Henry stepped aside, gripped her hips, and lifted her.

She sat on the edge while he and Jay removed her shoes with synchronized motions, right down to the playful kisses they planted on the balls of her feet. She flexed toes happy to be free of their long confinement in fashionable footwear.

Henry removed her panties and gave her a gentle push. "Go and sit at the head of the bed, Alice. Make yourself comfortable with the pillows."

Reclining against a pile of pillows and the headboard, she mimicked Jay's position from the night before. If Henry meant to let her cradle Jay while he made love to him, he'd need lubrication. The nightstand displayed no condoms, lube, or toys.

Henry ordered Jay onto the bed. "On your back, my boy. Lay your head on Alice's thigh."

Not in her arms, not like she'd been with Jay behind her.

Jay followed directions quickly. Of course he had. Jay, duh. With a raging hard-on. He settled his head, nestling up against her with his face tipped toward the slight roundness of her belly. A pleasant weight but an unpleasant reminder. If they'd given up condoms, he might've enjoyed licking her clean. As it was, she wouldn't get oral stimulation until she'd bathed, and things were a little busy to request a washcloth. She ran her fingers through his hair. He clasped her ankle, fingers circling in ceaseless motion.

Henry paced around the foot of the bed and stopped at the far corner with his head tilted just so and a soft smile on his face. He breathed deep and let the air trickle out.

She'd see this scene again. Not soon, and not until he'd finished, but he'd disappear into his studio tomorrow to sketch. Possibly even tonight while she and Jay slept.

"My patient, patient boy." Henry lowered himself to the bed beside Jay. Now she had two heads in her lap, and neither would be giving her any attention. Last straw. They were done with condoms. She was a responsible adult about birth control, and the three of them were a monogamous—*God, that's hot.*

Kissing Jay with fierce intensity, Henry pushed him harder against her thigh, one hand in a firm grip on Jay's shoulder. He left Jay's lips wet and swollen and his expression dazed.

"Tell me your safeword, Jay."

"Tilt-A-Whirl." No hesitation. No confusion.

"And when should you use it?"

"Anytime I feel uncomfortable or unsafe."

"And if you're uncertain how you're feeling?"

"I should use it anyway, and you'll help me figure it out."

"Good boy." Henry leaned his torso over Jay's when he kissed him again. The muscles in his back worked to keep him balanced on his arms, the right tucked along the inside of her left leg and the left outside her right leg. He stayed in close contact with both of them, no one alone or unwanted.

Jay squirmed. God, could that boy squirm. He wasn't a quiet kisser, either, emitting whimpers and half-vocalized moans Henry swallowed. A private lap dance from her two favorite men, entirely focused on each other. The intense, personalized eroticism made their show so much stronger than the distant arousal she'd experienced at the club. Watching strangers lacked the intimacy of Jay's head tipping back across her thigh as he bared his throat.

"You want to submit to me, don't you, my boy?"

Jay moaned his agreement, and Henry covered his throat with harsh, biting kisses.

He'd done the same to her in the kitchen. Had it looked this way to Jay? Primal, and violent, and fucking rip-off-my-panties-and-bend-me-over hot?

The mattress rolled as Jay bucked his hips. Lean muscle thrust him high, his erection bobbing past the flexing in Henry's back. He put on an entrancing peep show, there and gone with a wet, shining tip. Excitement brought on by Henry's punishing kisses.

Sitting up, Henry added to the show. He wasn't hard, but he'd come with her less than thirty minutes ago.

He stroked Jay from neck to navel, and Jay wiggled and whined. Henry closed his hand around the base of Jay's cock and squeezed.

Jay groaned. His hips jerked.

Henry held him too tightly to let him come so quickly. A handjob, like he'd given Jay last night. Jay working himself made for a fun show, but the excitement of Henry working Jay even beat the thrill of solving a complex design puzzle on the first try.

Henry leaned across Jay's thighs, pinning him to the bed, and surrounded Jay's cock with his mouth.

Jesus.

Jay gave a strangled gasp and dug his fingers into her calf.

Surprised you too, huh, stud?

Clamping his mouth tight, Henry built up pressure like a hydraulic cylinder and Jay the piston rod driving home. Henry's jaw stood out in a stark line, the tendons in his neck a relief map of tension quaking with every hard suck. He raised his head, licking his lips, leaving a wet and shining cock beneath his chin, and his gaze fastened on Jay's.

"It's all right to enjoy this. I want to hear your pleasure." Soft at first, Henry dropped into his low command voice by the end. "Let me hear you, Jay."

He closed his mouth over the head of Jay's cock again. Sliding lips took him to the root. Henry gave blowjobs. Paradigm shift. Better than she could. Better than Jay, and he got bucket loads of practice. Sucking cock seemed so un-Henry-like.

Yet Henry retained control. Dominant, even with Jay's cock in his throat. Whimpering and writhing, Jay was helpless to do anything but accept his gift. Bold and confident, Henry commanded Jay's submission to having his cock sucked.

Jay arched his back and dragged his feet up the bed, swaying the mattress. His shoulder blades jutted into her stomach and thighs as he rose to meet Henry's pull. The strain outlined every gorgeous muscle beneath his toned stomach. His teeth flashed, his mouth wide and pouring forth sweet, wordless whines.

The power dynamic was the opposite of what Cal would've done—had threatened to do—to her. But a blowjob didn't have to be a demeaning, frightening act. She'd enjoyed giving to Henry and Jay before. She would again. The people, not the act, made it what it was. She brushed back shaggy black strands of Jay's hair falling in his eyes.

Henry's right arm, bent at the elbow, rested on Jay's stomach, his hand mostly out of sight. Hidden between Jay's legs, shadowed by the movement of Henry's mouth as he sucked. Massaging Jay's balls. Or lower. Teasing and circling Jay like he'd done to her months ago.

Her body clenched, and it wasn't in fear. It was curiosity. A stirring of desire.

Jay's groans grew louder, their familiar eager note signaling his imminent orgasm.

Henry gained velocity, his lips sliding with a twisting motion from root to tip and back again, his cheeks hollowing out. His breath was harsh and loud and all but drowned out by Jay's noises.

Jay shouted Henry's name, hips jerking beneath Henry's weight.

Henry's Adam's apple bobbed as he swallowed.

Holy fuck.

Henry let Jay's cock slip from his mouth and covered Jay's chest with his own. "To whom do you belong, Jay?" His voice was hard and commanding and punctuated by his breaths.

"You, Henry." Limp and smiling, Jay stared up at Henry with wide, adoring eyes. Bliss. Maybe the same sort of muddled bliss she floated in when Henry mixed pain and pleasure into a devastating cocktail for her.

"You enjoy belonging to me, don't you, Jay?"

"Love you, Henry. Want to be yours always."

Henry's breaths quieted, and he stilled. "You know I'll never hurt you."

Jay's head shook vaguely. "Never ever."

"Good boy."

Henry kissed him, a kiss that started fierce, like the ones he'd given Jay earlier, but this one softened, and gentled, and slowed into the lingering affection of longtime lovers. And when Henry pulled back, he brushed his hand through Jay's hair, running across Alice's fingers, lifting them to his mouth and kissing her knuckles.

"Never ever," she echoed.

Henry raised startled eyes—grateful eyes—to hers.

"I know it." She sank into the love in his steady stare, the weight as real as his embrace.

"My sweet girl," he murmured. "I'm going to kiss you now."

He delivered the barest brush of his lips on one corner of her mouth, a chaste and reverent touch, before he claimed her lips fully and gave her the lingering attention he'd given Jay.

Afterward, they lay together in silence, Henry's head at her neck and Jay's atop her thigh, her hand and Henry's meeting in Jay's hair.

A long while passed before they rose from the bed, all three of them together, unwilling to part even to send one for a washcloth. Henry washed his hands and face in the sink while Alice and Jay nuzzled and kissed. Affectionate but not passionate, at least for her. With libidos satisfied, the emotional closeness mattered now.

Henry patted the countertop and urged Jay to lift her onto it as he wet a washcloth. Wary of the edge beside her hip, she spread her thighs at Henry's command.

Henry frowned. "We must give thought to enlarging this countertop. It's entirely too small."

Jay smiled at her over Henry's shoulder.

She clapped a hand to her mouth as a giggle escaped. And another. She and Jay cracked up, unable to stop themselves.

Henry watched with a half smile and his I'll-have-you-figured-out-momentarily squint.

Jay got himself almost under control first. "I had"—snort—"the same thought"—gasp—"myself"—chuckle—"last week."

"He did." She sucked in a breath and held it until she could talk without giggling. "He was going to ask you about redecorating."

"Ah—I said two words. Alice. Mirrors." Jay gave her a smug smirk.

Henry waggled his eyebrows.

Alice's giggles erupted again.

"Such a brilliant boy. We'll put it on the to-do list. But right now—" Henry pressed the washcloth between her legs, and her giggle deepened into a moan. "I believe the to-do list is full."

CHAPTER 5

The rich aroma of beef in the oven enticed her the instant she opened the door Monday night. Greeting her with a kiss, Henry sent her to change out of her work clothes.

She wandered back to the kitchen. Six o'clock. "No Jay?"

"One of his couriers neglected to come to work today, it seems, so he'll be late to dinner this evening." Henry manned the stove, browning what smelled like bacon, but in chunks rather than strips. The meat crackled and popped over the classical music on the radio.

"Smells good. He's gonna be sorry if he misses it." Not just him. She'd miss Jay's running commentary about his day at the table.

"Mmm. I've lowered the temperature on the roast. We may wait on him. He'll call when he's on his way." Henry fiddled with a pot on the stove. "Drain this, please, and I'll show you how to prepare them once they've cooled a bit."

She dumped the hot water and refilled the pot with cold water to keep the baby onions wet and her eyes tear-free. A quick demonstration from Henry had her cutting off the ends, removing the skins, and slicing a cross pattern into the little onions.

He hummed along to the music as he worked. The melody floated and bounced, light and springy, a confidence booster. His contentment steadied her.

"Favorite song?" Not the question she meant to ask. A warm-up.

"Haydn. One of the *London* symphonies." His sidelong glance and slight smile prompted hers. He always said he couldn't help if she wouldn't ask.

"Henry?" She cursed her tentative tone. Jay's reassurances and Henry's forceful desire Saturday night should've been enough for her.

He finished moving the bacon pieces to a plate to drain. "Yes?" The weight of his stare dropped across her shoulders.

She cut the final cross and set the knife down. "What's 'fair chalk'?"

"What's fair—ah. I see." He gathered the onions and slid them into the pan with the bacon grease and butter, settling them and adjusting the heat. "*Sverchok*, you mean. Has this question weighed on your mind all this time?"

Two days was practically light speed for her. She'd waited so she'd only embarrass herself in front of Henry and not Jay. Waited until her quietly obsessive two-day search online for a word she couldn't pronounce, let alone spell, in a language she didn't know, turned up nothing.

"Share with me, sweet girl." He reached out and tipped her chin up. "You've taken the first step by asking the question—for which I'm so very proud of you. Will you take another step for me? Tell me what you fear?"

She couldn't say no, not when he coaxed her with his tender rumble. Not when he looked at her with patience and confidence, as if he knew she'd come to the correct decision.

"It sounded affectionate." She winced, ashamed to sound like a jealous child. "Loving."

"It is." He faced her and stroked her upper arms. He wouldn't hide the truth. He might welcome the chance to shepherd her through this.

"I was afraid." To still be worried about how she measured up alongside Emma, about what Emma meant to Henry, was silly. Childish. "That you might"—his calm gave her courage—"love her. That you loved her first." She squirmed, uneasiness seeping through in a whisper. "More than me."

"My brave Alice." He stepped forward, slid his arms around her back, and kissed her forehead. "Thank you for telling me what's worrying you. You know how important your feelings are to me, don't you?"

"I know, Henry." She didn't know why exactly, and her anxiety hung in hope of a fuller answer.

"Alice." He splayed one hand flat against her back and brushed her hair off her neck with the other. "I am thirty-nine years old. My adult life began many years before I met you. I cannot change that at this late date—nor would I choose to."

She flinched, stung.

He raised the hand at her neck and cupped her cheek. "Those years, those events, those *people* shaped me into the man I am. The man who loves you."

Tears pricked her eyes. He loved her. She knew.

"When I look into my future and imagine the shape of my life five, ten, even twenty years from now, it is a life with you and with Jay. It is many happy years together. It is—" He shook his head and hugged her. "I'm getting ahead of myself. Forgive me."

Twenty years? She had trouble imagining her life in five years, let alone twenty. But the comforting press of his hands overrode the panic in her chest, the thumping of her heart. *I don't—I could—I'll still want this.*

"You have nothing to fear from Emma. The affection I have for her does not compare to the love between us." He held her head in his hands and stared into her eyes. "Emma has never shared my bed, dearest. She is a good friend, almost a sister, but she has never been a lover, nor have I truly desired her to be."

He kissed her, the kind of kiss that made her eager to forget dinner and beg him to take her to bed. But he stepped back to stir the onions and add beef stock and move them to the plate with the bacon chunks. Mushrooms and more butter took their place in the pan. He stirred the melting butter, covered the pan, and lowered the heat. "Come here, please."

He tucked her into him, her back to his chest as they stood together in front of the stove. He sighed, a soft sound in her ear. "It's a complex relationship to describe only because it comes with customs unfamiliar to you."

"I'm sorry, Henry." She sank into his strength. "I don't mean to be difficult."

"You're not being difficult. You're being honest." He nuzzled her ear. "It's quite attractive."

Mmm. Even the suggestion of his arousal ignited hers.

"Perhaps an illustration would suffice, so long as you understand it is merely that—hypothetical—as our family has enough to address without adding to it, hmm?"

"Hypothesis only. I can follow that." She hoped. She wanted Henry and Jay. Staying with them meant understanding this.

"Good girl." He kissed her temple and released her. "I've work to finish at the stove. Set the table, please, while I think on this, and then we'll talk."

She nodded her acceptance and set the places. Henry at the head of the table, always. Jay at the foot. Her own seat at Henry's right hand. She'd said yes to him at this table. Been taken across it with slow, powerful thrusts. Sat in Henry's lap in that chair and received oral sex for the first time from Jay's well-trained tongue. She couldn't walk anywhere in the apartment without arousing the memory of Henry's skilled attention. His love.

He moved like a dancer, handling multiple tasks at the stove with ease. His phone buzzed on the counter. Checking the display, he smiled. Finally he turned down the heat, leaving the pan's lid crooked at an angle, and came around the kitchen island to sit in his chair at the table.

"Lovely work, Alice. Sit with me. We've time. The bourguignon will be fine to simmer until Jay arrives in half an hour." He pulled her into his lap, sideways, a position guaranteed to tease her memory and make her melt. "I'm certain he'll be quite hungry."

She shuddered at his low tone. A blush warmed her cheeks. "Not fair, Henry."

"Entirely fair, Alice," he countered. "But it's story time, now."

"I'm ready to listen." With an open mind.

"Excellent. Then let's begin." He cradled her back, squeezing once. "Suppose our first visit to the club had gone well, and we began attending regularly. Suppose we meet a young dominant whose scenes we find appealing. A bit younger than you, but showing promise. We begin seeking him out on our visits. Complimenting his skills and offering advice, as appropriate."

She tried to picture it, to understand the story he was telling her and why. "We see potential. It's attractive."

"Precisely. He's a college student with a strong sense for crafting a scene, but he could be more refined. His submissives could be better satisfied—and I tell him so."

"That seems like it would be a blow to his ego." An aspiring dominant wouldn't appreciate that, would he? She had no idea. Dominants were individuals. No two alike.

Henry chuckled. "He takes it well, perhaps because I offer to demonstrate with my lovely Alice, the light in my eyes, how safe and relaxed and euphoric an experience it can be."

"Me? He'd be—"

"Observing only." He draped his arm across her lap and stroked along the outside of her thigh. "Hypothetically speaking. But he would, naturally, be taken with you at first. A bit of a crush."

Was that how Henry had met Emma and her husband? The question stuck in her throat. "Just a crush, though?"

"Misplaced affection. Because of how beautifully you respond to me, hmm? Because of the harmony that flows between us in a scene. He desires that for himself. Not with you, my lovely Alice, but with his own perfect match." He kissed her cheek. "And we offer to train him to that end."

"A new puppy. Like Jay." She clapped a hand over her mouth. *Shit. Please don't let him think—*

"Oh, my dear sweet girl." Henry's shoulders shook, and he laughed harder. "First Jay is your hare, and now he's your puppy, is he?" He squeezed her tight. "You ought to tell him so. He'd greatly enjoy knowing you feel such ownership and affection. But to return to our scenario, our young dominant isn't so exuberant as a puppy, but he has a friend who is. Thick as thieves, the pair of them."

Henry and William. How they'd come to know Victor and Emma. A practiced couple taking the young men under their wing.

"We spend several months working closely with them to perfect their skills. Overseeing their scenes. Providing feedback, both mine as a dominant and yours as a submissive. Demonstrating technique and the more"—he dropped his voice to a low drawl—"elusive, ephemeral pieces of the puzzle."

Wrapped in the seductive cocoon of his body heat, his scent, and his deep whispers, she floated in a hazy fog of agreement. Every step more reasonable than it should be, letting him lead, eager to see the final picture as he fed her each irregular idea and guided her fingers around curving, slick edges. He'd undoubtedly rubbed away the rough spots for her, presented her with the tantalizing image of completion, but—

"Showing them an idealized example of love in our own affection for each other."

These pieces he gave her to explore, they were pieces of *him*.

Curled in his lap, seduced as she was, she held him captive, the shape of his soul coming together in her hands. She clung tight to the pieces, the abstraction manifesting in dawning understanding.

"The boys—they aren't *in* love with us. But we're the strongest example in their lives of what it can look like." The way she'd taken cues from Jay and Henry's relationship. But for her, it truly had been love. Still was.

"An example, yes. Both inside and outside the club."

"Outside how?" Her heart and her head begged for hard data, specs to define his closeness to Victor and Emma.

"Dinners in our home, perhaps. An example of a more domestic, long-term relationship. The sort to which these young men might aspire." He slipped the hand on her thigh under her shirt and stroked her skin.

Muscles she hadn't realized she'd tensed relaxed.

"When we host, their position is in flux. Dominant, yes, but in our home, you have power of your own. The freedom to talk back, to tease them, to chide them, to mother them. Your role in their lives is a large one. In some ways, your behavior will guide the way they approach submissives for the rest of their lives."

"I didn't know. That's so—" Her lungs seized, throat throttling shut. So much influence. Emma had filled that role for him. She'd hold that piece of him until the day he died. "How could anyone compete with that? Ever?"

Henry cuddled her closer, his nose rubbing her cheek as he cradled her to his chest. "Because there's a distance as well. These young dominants are not your sexual partners—I'd never allow it, and you wouldn't desire it—but they worship you nonetheless. They are in awe of the ideal you represent, a key element in the whole we make up together. What they want is not you, dear girl, but their own perfect match as you are *mine*."

Twice now he'd said so, and the message began sinking in. He didn't want Emma. *He wants me.*

"Now, if these boys came to you over the years for advice, sat at your table, built their own little kingdoms and proudly showed you their toys—if I were dead and buried twenty years from now, and you alone—tell me, would you be surprised if those boys still showed some measure of devotion? If they honored our longstanding friendship by watching over you?"

No. They'd be family. She'd have a responsibility to them, as well. Something almost parental, but not. Sisterly. The way she checked up on Olivia.

"Those boys might, when they find their perfect matches, have trouble explaining what you are to them, my dear." His voice softened into . . . not a plea, because surely Henry would never plead, but something asking for her understanding. Needing her understanding. "Translating their own roles as son and brother and friend and protector into some easy shorthand, some simple way to define their continuing affection for you. Even though what they feel for you is not *romantic* love, it is love, nonetheless."

He loved Emma. That truth wouldn't change. But it wasn't the same way he loved her and Jay. Their connection didn't threaten her.

"Without Emma's example nearly twenty years ago, without Victor's tutelage, I would not have become the man worthy of your trust and devotion, Alice."

She turned in his lap, pressing her chest to his and worming her arms around his back, clinging to him in a tight hug.

He squeezed her in return. "And I'm so very glad, sweet girl, that I am that man for you."

"I love you, Henry." She whispered the truth in his ear. "And I know how much you love me. It's just so new. Feeling it. Admitting it. Accepting it."

He massaged her back with gentle hands. "You've jumped in with such courage. When you come to me with your fears, I will do my utmost to help you address them."

They sat cradled together, Alice reluctant to move, Henry humming along with the radio. "Now, as to your question—no, I haven't forgotten—*sverchok* means 'cricket,' nothing more."

She had to laugh. He might not have forgotten, but she had. She'd let him distract her. But an important distraction.

Henry told her another story, one that had her laughing harder as he explained how he and William had transformed a Russian proverb Victor had often used to gently chastise Emma for speaking out of turn into the opposite—a pet name praising her for being a model of submission and the voice of conscience in their ears.

Jay's bike *tick-tick-ticked* on the hardwood. Their teasing laughter and kisses must've drowned out the door opening.

"Welcome home, my boy." Henry spoke over her head.

No sooner had the bike gone up on its hooks than Jay, sweaty biking gear and all, rounded the table and dropped to his knees at Henry's feet.

"Did I miss dinner?" He pressed a kiss to the inside of her thigh below the edge of her shorts. "Because I'm starving, and I see something I want to eat."

She pulled her legs closed, giggling at the wide-eyed pout Jay sent her way. "And I think my sweaty puppy needs a bath first."

His pout dissolved into a beaming smile. "Your puppy?" He flopped backward, belly up, at their feet. "Do I get a tummy rub?"

Chalk another one up for Henry's win column. Far from offended, Jay loved the idea of playing her puppy.

"After dinner," Henry answered him. "Go and take your shower and change. We'll have food on the table in fifteen minutes, and you and Alice may play afterward."

Jay's animated discussion carried them through dinner, a welcome break from the intensity that dominated her talks with Henry. She loved the intensity and the lightness both, the way the scales tipped and righted themselves.

A balance her life had been missing before Henry and Jay.

They cleared the table together. When she reached for the last of the dishes, Jay reached for her, insisting he needed something to carry, too. He hoisted her at the waist. She giggled the whole way across the kitchen to the sink and flicked water at him while she rinsed dishes and he loaded the dishwasher.

Henry watched them with a speculative eye. Impossible to guess his thoughts, but he was definitely thinking. The dishwasher clicked shut. "All finished?" Henry beckoned them over and bestowed kisses on their cheeks. "I've another task for you, then."

Under his direction, she and Jay pushed back the living room furniture and moved various knickknacks. Well. Fine art pieces, aka *fancy* knickknacks.

Jay hadn't lost his overabundance of energy. He rocked heel-toe beside her as they stood and waited for Henry's judgment.

"Nicely done, thank you." Henry tipped his head. "I promised you a bit of playtime after dinner, didn't I?"

"Yes, Henry." Jay tapped his fingers against his thighs.

She nodded.

"Your play boundary is the living room rug. Stepping outside it will pause the game."

Her heart pounded. A pause option dangled the probability of intense play.

"Clothes will stay on."

How was that playtime? Jay's ants-in-the-pants routine begged for clothes-off action.

"The six pillows in the living room are the only acceptable weapons." Henry gestured toward the space. "The game begins in five seconds. Perhaps you'd best arm yourselves, hmm?"

"Pillow fight," Jay shouted, glee exploding as he bounded to the couch and snatched up a throw pillow.

Shit. No way she'd let him win without even competing. She raced to catch up, grabbing a pillow from the chair and stepping onto the rug as Henry called, "One."

"Begin."

They circled each other, pillows up. She lobbed hers at Jay's midsection to distract him and picked up a second.

He walloped her across the back. Almost. The gentlest pillow fight "attack" she'd experienced in her life.

She spared a glance for Henry, watching from the sideline. Her inattention earned her another attack, as gentle as the one before while Jay bounced around her, and told her nothing. Focused and intent, Henry displayed the slightest hint of a smile.

Catching the side of Jay's head, she pulled a laugh from him. He returned fire with a pillow swat at her ass. She battered his legs, a buffet of blows to his knees, and he responded with a flurry across her arms and shoulders.

Henry had said six legal pillows. Throw pillows accounted for four. She dove for the floor pillow. Larger. Greater heft. She swung as she spun, giggling all the while, and slammed the pillow into Jay's side.

He oomphed. Tugging her wrist, he tangled her up as he rolled and tumbled.

Henry lurched, but stopped at the edge of the rug.

She and Jay rolled again.

The pillows fell from their hands.

She squirmed.

He grunted.

They landed Jay on his back with her straddling his hips. God, he was hot and hard between her thighs. Grinning at her with that sweet Jay-smirk and gleaming eyes. Impossible to resist.

She ground her hips against him for the spark of heat the contact woke in her. Leaned forward. Lowered her face to his. They brushed noses.

Grazing his lips, she drew a low, needy whimper from him. She gave in to temptation and kissed him. Hard and commanding. The way Henry kissed him.

Jay moaned. His hips jerked beneath her.

She gentled the kiss despite the craving running through her body and pulsing between her legs. Pulled her head up enough to meet his eyes.

"Fuck, Alice, I'm sorry." His giddy energy drooped into a grimace. "I'm so sorry."

Sorry. Not happy. Not ecstatic that he'd gotten off. Not relaxed, not enjoying it. God, was she that fucking stupid?

"Sweetheart, there's nothing to be sorry for." If she didn't make it right, right now, Henry would have to step in and do it for her.

"But I just—" He waved toward his shorts.

"I know." She beamed at him. Encouraging. "It was incredibly hot."

He blinked. "It was?"

"I don't know if you noticed, sweetheart, but playing with me got you worked up enough to come in your shorts. Which makes me feel pretty damn desirable and good about myself." She stroked his forehead and pushed back his hair. Would that she could smooth his wrinkled brow as easily. "I wish it made you feel good about yourself, too, stud."

The tightness in his face, all scrunched eyes and turned-down lips, pierced her heart. Please, let her not have hurt him. First she'd let that jackass belittle him at the club, and now she'd made him feel inadequate. Fuck. She twisted to search for strength over her shoulder. "Am I wrong, Henry?"

"No, sweet girl, you're exactly right. You're doing quite well on your own." But he stepped closer and crouched beside them anyway.

Would Jay feel rejected if she rolled off him? Maybe he'd be more comfortable without her weight on him. She sat, frozen, terrified of making the wrong move. Of somehow shaming him further.

Henry covered her hand on Jay's hair. "My brave boy, what were the restrictions I placed on your playtime with Alice?"

"Living-room-rug boundaries. Only hit with pillows. Clothes stay on." Kneading the rug, he rattled off answers at full speed.

Henry hummed softly. "Well done. Where in those restrictions does it say you cannot climax?"

Jay tipped his head back, pushing into their hands. He frowned. "It doesn't."

"No, it doesn't. You came home full of energy, and roughhousing with Alice was exciting, wasn't it?"

"Yes, Henry." He cast a bashful, darting glance at her chest.

"And when she rolled on top of you, that was more exciting."

An emphatic *yes* rolled off Jay's tongue.

"You weren't under any obligation to hold back, my boy." Henry kissed her temple and then Jay's mouth. "You played a fine game."

"But I—" Eyelids sinking, Jay turned his face aside. "Like a teenager."

Henry nudged her, the barest brush of his weight.

She shifted off Jay to sit on the floor.

"We'll be a moment or two, Alice." Henry urged Jay to his feet. "Come along, dear boy. It's nothing that hasn't happened before, hmm?"

He rubbed Jay's back as he pushed him down the hall. Bathroom, probably.

"But not in front of Alice." Jay's whispered reply surely wasn't meant to reach her ears. "I didn't even give her . . ."

She pulled her knees up and buried her face. She'd made him ashamed of himself and his stamina. A simple game, a fun night, and she'd turned it into a nightmare for Jay. Not intentionally, but still. Her fault.

Something she'd found adorable. Charming. So sweetly uncontrolled. No matter what Jay thought, he hadn't left her hanging. She hadn't expected an orgasm. Disappointment was impossible without expectation.

Christ, please let Henry talk sense into him. She climbed to her feet and put the living room back in order. Another bout of pillow fighting wasn't likely tonight. Things had been so nonsexual last week, and the weekend had been a sexual explosion. No wonder if Jay'd been hornier than usual.

Henry came back alone.

An invisible vise gripped her rib cage, compressed her chest. "Is he okay?"

"He's fine. A tad embarrassed, but your handling of the situation helped immensely." Lips curved in a slight smile, he studied her with eyes soft as a mossy-green bed. "Shh, dearest, it's fine." He swept her into his arms. "Just as Jay has done nothing wrong, so it is with you. He merely needed reassurance that everyone's needs would be met."

His touch soothed her, and she buried her face against his chest, inhaling the warmth and sharpness of his scent.

"Thank you for cleaning up, Alice. Shall we move the couch back together?"

They each pushed an end and settled the gray behemoth into place with ease.

"Henry?"

"Yes, my dear?"

"Why a pillow fight?" She wouldn't press if he wanted to keep his reasons to himself, but her conclusion nagged at her. "Was it a test?"

"Did you enjoy playing?"

Until she'd made Jay upset, absolutely. She nodded.

"You weren't nervous or concerned?"

"Should I have been? Did we fail?"

He clasped her shoulders. "It's not that sort of test, Alice. More an assessment of your comfort."

Her sexy artist had *engineered* an experiment to refine his approach based on their needs. God, if his head were a machine, she'd climb inside and study the operations for months. "With roughhousing?"

"One might also name it light impact play. The current state of my dear ones' behavioral responses in a nonthreatening situation, without restriction or expectation, is of some interest to me."

Impact play. A whisper of heat flickered across her back. "Like my suede."

He hummed. "Yes, like your flogger. Tell me, when did you begin to take ownership of it?"

"I guess"—the second she'd imagined the handle in his grip—"after the first time?" Possessiveness had stolen over her. "The others were just toys, but the suede was mine." She hadn't thought to ask if personal attachment was allowed. "That's okay, isn't it?"

"Much more than 'okay,' my dear." He kissed her forehead. "It pleases me."

She searched herself for the eagerness that usually accompanied talk of her flogger. Emptiness echoed. Huddling close, she traced the buttons on his shirt. "I don't think I'm ready to play with it right now."

"No, not yet. Neither you nor Jay." He wrapped his arms around her back. "We'll find our way there again. Not to worry. For now, it's time for bed."

The clock mocked her with a broad smile proclaiming the time quarter past nine.

"It's too early, Henry. Schoolchildren have later bedtimes."

He caressed her ear with a heated breath. "Schoolchildren go to bed to sleep, Alice. And unless I'm doing something very wrong, you won't be sleeping for quite a while yet."

Jay waited atop the covers on the far side of the bed, gaze trained on the doorway.

Naked, of course. Sporting a sheepish grin.

Henry closed his arms around her waist and rubbed his face against her neck. His breathing, deep and slow, as if he might inhale her soul through the pores of her skin, sent a frisson of desire coursing along her nerve endings.

"You've had an emotional day, dearest. Surely you've a glut of thoughts swirling beneath your lovely locks." He kissed her neck with soft lips, gentle and fluttering.

She swayed in his embrace.

"Jay and I agree you deserve our exclusive attention. For medicinal purposes, you understand."

His teasing tone warmed her insides. "You're prescribing a cure for thoughts?"

He hummed, a quiet negative. "There's no cure, I'm afraid." He nudged her forward with his hips, cock prodding at her back, and edged his fingers under her shirt. "Merely a continuing treatment regimen."

She raised her arms.

He tossed her shirt aside and trailed kisses across her shoulder blades. Kneaded her neck with heavy, steady hands.

"Continuing?" She dropped her head.

He pushed her bra straps from her shoulders with his thumbs.

"Is this a weekly regimen? Monthly? Annually? Is it applied topically? Orally? Injected?"

Jay snickered from the bed, and she flashed him a smirk.

Henry growled as he unhooked her bra. "I'm often tempted to make it an hourly injection, my impertinent little minx."

Empty contractions focused her thoughts low between her hips, a heated rush. Hourly. A slave to his pleasure and her own. Surprisingly appealing. Tied to Henry's bed day and night. Hands and mouths and Henry's thick cock to keep her satisfied. Fuck yes. She moaned.

Henry tugged at her pants, lowering them with her underwear, a teasing slide down her ass. "It seems someone approves of such treatment."

Jay watched like a cat eager to pounce on a rolling ball of yarn, his hypnotized eyes following the skin bared by her falling pants. Mmm. He had the right idea. She found Henry's slow-moving hands equally fascinating.

"What's not to like?" She squirmed as Henry tickled her calves.

He lifted her feet clear with delicate precision. What he might see as fragile statuary, limbs extended, at greater risk for breakage. What she might call parts machined within strict tolerances.

"Lounging in your bed all day so I won't miss a treatment? Sounds like a regimen I could get behind."

Henry's delighted chuckle set electrons spinning in her body, creating magnetic fields eager to pull him in.

"It's certainly one *I'm* inclined to get behind." He rose to his feet and pressed himself to her. Clothed. Smooth shirt, rougher slacks, all rubbing and rustling against her bare skin.

God, she loved him like that.

Jay rolled his face into a pillow and laughed.

Henry turned her in his arms and kissed her. Her giggles morphed into a sighing moan as he cradled the back of her head with one hand and cupped her ass with the other. She pressed forward, nipples rising against his shirt from the friction.

He grasped her hands and lifted them to his throat. "Will you undo these pesky buttons? I find my hands have more important places to be."

Those more important places proved highly distracting as she unbuttoned his shirt. He traced the slope of her ribs, fingers splayed. Held the weight of her breasts in the curves of his thumbs and index fingers. Cupped her iliac crest in a squeeze that rocked her groin against his.

She kneaded his chest. Firm flesh, but not hard. Not entirely unyielding. Surrendering just enough to make a place for her.

"Still thinking, dearest?" He spoke in a low undertone, intimate and warm.

"Silly thoughts." She pushed his shirt over his shoulders and down his arms. "Happy thoughts. Belonging thoughts."

"My favorite kind." He draped a soft kiss across her lips.

He took a step forward, and another, and she stepped backward in kind. A dance, ending with bedsheets brushing the back of her legs.

"We'll deliver your treatment on the bed tonight." A smile tugged at the corners of his mouth. "A horizontal delivery method is preferred, as aftereffects may include trembling legs and difficulty standing. Safety first, my dear."

She lowered her chin and looked up, as demure a posture as she could manage, trapped between his body and the bed. "Yes, Doctor. Whatever you think best."

Eyes gleaming, he sucked in a breath and nodded once. "Very well. My physician's assistant will participate in your care today." He lifted her onto the bed with ease. "Please make yourself comfortable while I finish disrobing."

"Nudity's an important part of my treatment, Doctor?" She pushed herself back onto the bed and came up short against Jay.

"Absolutely crucial. Almost impossible to complete without it. You aren't shy, are you? Not such a lovely girl as you."

She shook her head, rolling across Jay's shoulder. "Not even close to shy, Doctor." Tipping back, she gave Jay a teasing smile. "So you're a doctor, too?"

"If he says so, then I guess I'm Dr. Jay." His eyes widened. He laughed. "Don't worry, miss. This treatment will be a slam dunk for sure. But I'm not really known for my assists."

Jay-babble. Incomprehensible Jay-babble. She pecked his cheek and faced front. Henry had his hands on his belt. No way would she miss the show.

Jay wrapped his arms around her waist and kissed her cheek,

snuggling his face beside hers, the two of them intent on Henry's every motion.

"I'm sorry our pillow fight ended so early, Alice," Jay whispered. His lips tickled her ear.

Henry's belt slid free of its loops. He hung it over the chair, turning his back to them, slacks tightening across his ass. Her eyes tracked him, her body focused on the pleasure his approaching nudity promised and her mind diverted by the tremor in Jay's voice.

"It's all right, sweetheart." Her lips barely moved as she matched his low, earnest tone. Covering his arms with her own, she rubbed her palms over his knuckles. "I had fun while it lasted. Totally kicking your ass, by the way."

"I was gonna make a comeback." He laced their fingers together and drew rolling waves across her stomach.

She refrained from making a joke about coming, though it was a near thing. Her athletic comedian sheltered a deep, sensitive center. "Next time, if I don't kick your ass again."

Zipper dropping. A captivating tease. Henry's pants fell, and he stepped elegantly to the side. He bent and picked them up.

She leaned forward and Jay followed, their sighs mingling. Just boxers left.

"You think there'll be a next time?"

"Yup." Boxers hitting the floor distracted her. Or, rather, the firm ass revealed above them. Not that Jay's ass was any less firm. But what her brain called adorable on him became powerful on Henry. Powerful muscles. Powerful thrusts. A powerful attraction that pressed her thighs together and let wetness seep between them.

"I bet if we ask nicely, Henry will let us play with pillows again some other night." They wouldn't even have to ask nicely, if he was rebuilding their comfort through this light impact play. He'd have more roughhousing planned. But not tonight.

Henry faced them, fully nude and partially erect.

Desirable. Mesmerizing. *Yummy.* "We could have a postgame injury clinic. Like the, uh, pros do."

"The pro pillow fighters?" Jay teased with no trace of anxiety, but his breathing quickened.

"Uh-huh." Had she been saying something? Had Jay? Her heart thumped triple time. Eager. Wanting. "A nice soak. Postgame rubdown."

Henry knelt on the foot of the bed. He planted his hands. Stalked them, crowding their legs, kneeling over them on all fours, working his way up the bed as they fell back beneath his advance.

"You neglected to mention the thorough physical exam, sweet girl." He delivered a kiss for her hip and one for Jay's.

She shivered. He whimpered.

Henry smiled at them both. "We'll begin with the neck. We can't be too careful."

He lay on her left side, his cock a pleasant pressure at her hip, his leg a weight atop hers. He nuzzled her neck. "All right, dearest?"

"Heavenly."

Jay shifted beside her, rolling up on his side to mimic Henry. They feasted together, an unending succession of licking and kissing and sucking as they traced the lines of her throat. The curve of her jaw. The edge of her ears.

Her sighs and moans produced a chorus of echoing whines from Jay. Encouraging rumbles, almost a purring hum, from Henry. Soothing. Arousing.

An odd sensation, to be so relaxed and so excited in the same moment. Aware of more, wanting more, but comfortable precisely where she was. In Henry's bed. With Henry and Jay lavishing attention on her. Content to let events unfold at Henry's pace.

"Oh, dear." Henry exuded teasing faux concern. "Your pulse is simply racing. It might denote a medical difficulty. Is this a frequent occurrence?"

She inhaled the mingled scents of leather and citrus and forest. Her boys. "It happens whenever I see you, Doctor."

He kissed her temple. "Jay, this bears further investigation. My medical expertise tells me our patient's heart is located in her chest. Search around and see if you might find it, please. Be thorough."

Jay lifted her right arm, draping it around his back, and nestled closer. She gripped his shoulder as he followed Henry's instructions to the letter. Searching. Hand roaming over her chest. Skimming the tops of her breasts. Breath ghosting over her nipples.

Henry touched his lips to hers. She tilted her face, and he captured her mouth with a deeper kiss. Delivered a series of them. Long, and languid, and arousing something in her beyond desire. A need centered not only between her legs but also between her ears. Between her ribs. Between her everything.

"Henry," she whispered into the gap he gave her to catch her breath. "I don't want to play right now. I just want you. I want—I need—to feel you inside me. Please."

He called softly to Jay, urging him to bring him a condom from the nightstand, but he kept his body pressed along hers. Used one hand to roll the latex over his cock, raising his hips only enough to make it possible. The head rubbed across her clit as he positioned himself, and she cried out, a low, needy whine.

Too much and not enough, all at once, the stimulation a jolt along sensitive nerves. His cock parted her lips, wet and welcoming his arrival. He thrust slow. Settled fully on top of her, his weight pressing her down, and she clutched at his neck and shoulders, her body shuddering beneath him with the first tendrils of relief.

She raised her legs and clung to his hips. Wouldn't allow him to pull back, to leave her body. He rocked them, slow and steady, his scent in her nose and his breath at her ear.

"It's all right, sweet girl." He kissed her cheeks.

She closed her eyes.

He kissed the lids. "Hold on to me. I won't let you go, dearest."

She combed her fingers through the hair at the nape of his neck. Pleasure washed through her. Not an orgasm, but not the unceasing need for it, either. She drifted. Let sensation bathe her.

"You've been eager to rush before, Alice." His low whisper rolled like thunder promising to deliver cleansing rain. "But on those nights, you sought to avoid something, hmm? To escape before it could overwhelm you."

She moaned, a sustained sigh of agreement. She'd spent too long trying to escape this perfection. Not only the fullness of him inside her, but the fullness in her heart.

"And now, my dear? Are you running from your feelings now?"

"No," she murmured. "No, Henry. Rushing toward, not away."

"No, not away, not tonight." His words coaxed. "Tonight you want to feel it, isn't that right?"

Yes. God, yes. "I do."

His body swept over hers, an undulation through his stomach, his hips, his thighs. A wave of clouds scudding before the storm, racing the edge. Power waiting to be unleashed.

She pressed her head back, stretching her neck, striving for breath. "I want to, Henry."

"Good girl." He kissed her forehead and nuzzled her hairline down to the curve of her ear. "Do you feel it now? Understand it with every atom of your being? Tell me how it feels, dearest."

"It feels . . . it feels like—" Like every time he'd told her she'd feel it. That she'd get there. That night in January when he'd been so intense, and she'd thought he meant orgasm. God, how blind and timid and fumbling she'd been. And now she was giddy with it. Dancing in the rain as the storm broke over them both. "It's love. That's what you wanted me to feel."

He groaned. His pace quickened, and she gripped him harder. Pulled him closer. Dared to ride out the storm together.

"I feel it, Henry. I feel it in your hands and your mouth and your words—"

He thrust deep. "And in other places, too, I hope, my sweet Alice."

"Everywhere." Her elation poured out in a laugh. "That's where I feel it when I'm with you and Jay. Everywhere."

"For us, too, dearest. Everywhere. Always." He punctuated his words with kisses to her throat and jawline, until she strained to reach him, seeking his mouth for a true kiss.

No more words. Only the thunderous rumbling in his chest as he pressed her hard to the mattress, the rolling growl that escaped him when lightning sizzled along her nerve endings and she shrieked her joy.

CHAPTER 6

When six fifty-nine became seven o'clock Friday night, Alice was not at all where she expected to be. In Henry's bedroom, almost certainly. Naked, most likely.

Instead, she sat in the back of Henry's car, nearly an hour west of Boston, with little idea of their destination. Her bits of knowledge numbered two. First, she'd spent less than fifteen minutes at home after work, arriving to Jay carrying a cooler down to the car and Henry waiting with her most comfortable pair of jeans and a soft cotton button-down shirt. Second, Jay reported to Henry with pride he'd mounted his mountain bike on the car's foldout bumper rack and stowed everything else in the trunk.

"But I haven't packed anything," she'd protested.

"I took the liberty, my dear." Henry had directed her to change clothes and use the bathroom. "We'll be on the road in five minutes."

No discussion. She confronted the choice to accept or reject Henry's leadership on a regular basis now. She retained the option to use her safeword, even in nonsexual contexts, to halt his plans and initiate a discussion on equal footing. No situation had yet warranted such rebellion.

He preferred to orchestrate events. Faith, rooted in evidence, confirmed his choices ended in pleasurable outcomes for her, with very few exceptions. Her choices had caused those exceptions. Her choice to skip one of their contract nights at Christmas. Her choice to use her safeword, to hide from the love she felt for her boys. Her choice to break the rules at the club.

Brooding, she slid down in the seat. Henry had insisted she have the backseat to herself. *"Lie down and stretch your legs if you like, Alice. I do apologize for rushing you into car travel after you've sat at your desk all day."*

Her decisions didn't always end badly. She was more than competent at her job. She handled her tight finances with no trouble. She gave her sister the support their parents couldn't.

Knowledge and experience made the difference. Where she had the proper depth of field, the deep focus, she did well. She'd never had the right focus for navigating relationships. Where she'd once minimized risk and exposure, now she tried to be open and accepting. Every decision a blurry one. Out of focus. Hard, except Henry made them easy.

So. Memorial Day weekend, and Henry had spirited them away. Somewhere they'd need their own food and Jay could bike off-road. Twisting to lie on her back across the entire seat, she raised her knees and made herself comfortable. Guess Jay'd been right in January about the camping thing.

The passenger seat dropped back, lowering Jay's smiling face toward her knees. He'd been granted permission to control the music, and he'd sung along with every song. In tune, thankfully.

"Whatcha laughing at? Is it my singing? I'm a fabulous singer. Not good enough to sing tenor in the a cappella group at my high school, but absolutely car-trip worthy."

"Not the singing. I'm sure your studly tenor made all the girls swoon." She threw an arm across her forehead drama-queen style. "Camping."

"Exciting, right?" The thrill of anticipation lived in Jay's smile, and his tone, and the way he fidgeted nonstop. "I can't wait to see where we're going."

"I thought you and Henry went camping all the time."

The music abruptly switched from thumping bass to quiet violins, Henry retaking control during Jay's distraction.

"Sure. North." Jay waved, blocking the sun coming through the windshield and sending shadows bouncing around the backseat. "We're going west." Imitation pity saturated his headshake. "For an engineer, you can't orient yourself in space very well." He stuck his tongue out.

She lifted a sock-clad foot and covered his eyes with a gentle push. "You never said you went camping up north, goof. I can only work with the information I have."

"Is there more information you'd like to have?" Henry reached across the seat and touched Jay's arm. "Sit up, please. I know you enjoy playing with Alice, but the passenger seat is not the place for distracting antics while we're in motion. It's unsafe."

"Sorry, Henry." She and Jay spoke together. She lowered her foot, and he adjusted the seat upright.

Henry patted Jay's thigh. "Thank you. Now, shall we play twenty questions, Alice?"

His tone hinted at laughter. Sly man. Probably expected her curiosity since he'd started the car. No. Since she'd arrived home after work.

"Am I limited to yes-or-no questions?"

"Of course. Nineteen left, sweet girl."

She groaned. She'd walked right into that one. "Okay. Okay. Umm, will we be sleeping outside?"

"No."

A cabin, then. "Does this place have running water?" Jay wouldn't care, but Henry would demand it for practical reasons. Hygiene. Safety. Comfort.

"Yes."

Jay swiveled between her and Henry. "Wait, I have an important question, too."

"Alice, this is your game. It's your choice whether to allow Jay some of the questions."

Jay leaned between the seats, puppy-dog eyes at full plea. "It's really important."

"Sure, Jay." She couldn't say no to her enthusiastic playmate, her partner in crime. Reining him in was Henry's job. "This question's yours. Go for it."

A quarter turn left Jay facing Henry with an open, earnest expression. "Does it have a bed as big as ours?"

She smashed her lips together, but the smile still pulled at her mouth. She covered her face. Jay's biggest concern, of course. Should've seen that coming.

"It's the most important question," Jay insisted. "I see you smiling, Henry. Alice is cheating with her hands, but she's smiling, too. 'Cause she knows I asked the best question."

She laughed until her cheeks ached.

"Well, Alice? Shall I answer Jay's question?"

She nodded vigorously.

Whoops. Henry couldn't see her while she was lying down.

"Yes, please," she choked out, lowering her hands. "It *is* important—but no offense, Jay, sweetheart, I think I'll keep the rest of the questions for myself."

"Yes, my dears, it has a bed as large as, or larger than, our own."

"S'okay, Alice." Jay stretched his arms out, raised them, and rested them behind his head, elbows out. "The important question's answered. You can have the rest."

She snorted and contemplated the car's roof. A sense of the timing would help her figure out Henry's motivation for rushing them into the car. "Have you been planning this for a while?"

"Define 'a while,' my dear."

Hmm. To get a cabin rental for Memorial Day weekend, weeks, maybe months, in advance. As far back as January? Or had it been a desire to give them space to process the last two weeks. The difficulty at the club. Meeting Emma and starting to understand everything her friendship meant to Henry. His history. "More than two weeks."

"No."

The latter, then. Henry worried about her and Jay. He wanted a safe space, but not the apartment, to help the three of them reconnect. He'd choose someplace familiar to him. But a place he hadn't taken Jay before?

Green leaves whipped past outside the car window.

"Have you run out of curiosity so soon, Alice?"

"Nope. Strategizing."

"Ah. A clue for you, then, my dear. We've reached the halfway point on our journey."

They'd been driving west for just over an hour. Unless a change of direction was in store, two and a half west—"We're going to the Berkshires?"

"Yes."

"You got a last-minute reservation for Memorial Day weekend?"

This little vacation had to be costing him a fortune. Four times the going rate and a kidney for the owner.

"Mmm. An interesting question, Alice. The answer, I suppose, is both yes and no, in that a reservation was not specifically required."

"Because your family owns the place?" That would simplify things.

"No."

"But you've been there before?" Not with Jay, though.

"Yes."

On the right track. Good. Keep going. "Are you paying a ridiculously high fee to make up for the lack of a reservation on a holiday weekend?" Fuck, this answer had better be no. He wasn't obligated to spend his money on her like that. She'd rather not take a vacation or vacation at home than have him shell out extra to give her and Jay a break from routine.

"No."

If the place wasn't his, and he wasn't paying extra—"You know the owner."

"Yes."

She sat up, seeking the smile evident in his voice. Their gazes met in the rearview mirror, a teasing hint of excitement widening his eyes. Close, then. If he meant to make her more comfortable, the place wouldn't be Emma's. But he obviously expected she knew or could determine the owner's identity from the facts at hand.

"Santa! You're taking us to Santa's cabin."

"Well done, Alice. And in a mere ten questions." Henry winked at her in the mirror. "Will graciously agreed to loan me the house for the weekend, as he won't be using it."

Jay whistled. "If his cabin's anything like his *house* house, I'm gonna be afraid to touch anything."

"Anything, my boy?" Henry chuckled. "That will make for interesting games."

"Maybe not anything." Jay's knees bounced. "I could touch some things."

So Henry had arranged this getaway for them at a potentially fantastic location, and the trip wasn't costing him a thing beyond food and gas. "Another thing I'll have to thank Santa for," she mused.

"Not to worry, sweet girl. We'll have dinner with Will next weekend, and you may thank him then if you like. For *this* weekend, however, I'd like you and Jay both to concentrate on yourselves." He squeezed Jay's knee and nodded at her in the mirror. "Simply relax and enjoy, my dears. Let your thoughts wander where they will."

They rode the rest of the way in silence, aside from Henry's occasional humming with the music. He turned off the highway west of Springfield, slowing through downtown Westfield before the view changed back to tree-covered hillsides and bare stone. A winding rural route, two lanes, barely any shoulder at all, with few crossroads and even fewer homes in sight. That gave way to another rural route, and finally to an unpaved road where the trees stood so close and the canopy so broad that the last flickers of twilight never reached the ground.

Henry turned into a driveway on the left and pulled up in front of a house where a porch light glowed with cheery yellow greetings.

Alice gasped.

Jay nodded. "Told you it'd be fancy."

The cabin was a cabin, all right, in that it mixed what looked like gray river stones with half-round logs in a classic motif. A sharp peak in the center with lower wings running to the left and right. Small windows on this side, round and half round, but then this was the north face. She'd bet the south side was a wall of glass.

Her attention kept straying to the light. "Is someone waiting for us, Henry?"

He turned off the engine and popped the locks. "No, we'll have the place entirely to ourselves. Will insisted on having a caretaker come through to freshen the linens and leave a welcome." He opened his door and got out. "Come along. Inside first. The bags may wait a moment."

Henry retrieved a key from above the door frame. Try that in Boston, and they might as well hang a sign out for thieves. Not that thieves could find this place. Hell, satellites couldn't find it under the tree cover. Henry wiped his shoes on the mat as the door swung open, and she and Jay followed suit.

Jay breathed deep. "I smell cookies."

Stepping inside, Alice leaned forward and sniffed. Yum. "Definitely cookies."

An overhead light flipped on, Henry's doing.

Jay made a beeline for the wide kitchen counter. A plate heaped with cookies waited. "Chocolate chip," he crowed, picking up some-thing else and waving it in the air. "And a note for Henry."

Her stomach growled.

Henry stroked her back and patted her ass. "Go on and have some cookies. I doubt you'll spoil your dinner, late as it is." He raised his voice. "Two cookies, my boy. Share with Alice, please."

Henry took the envelope from Jay's hand. He opened it with un-hurried precision, scanning the note he plucked out as she and Jay fed each other bite-size, broken-off cookie bits. Enormous, soft, chewy cookies, fresh-baked and not cold yet. A laugh had them both turning to Henry.

"Will assures me his caretaker was pleased to make a batch of cookies to split between us and her grandchildren, and he hopes my pets will find them enjoyable, as they could use some fattening up." He laid the note aside and shook his head, leaning in to lay gentle kisses on her cheek and Jay's. "But he's quite mistaken. You're both lovely as you are."

Henry snagged a piece of cookie for himself, chewing and nod-ding before swallowing. "Though the cookies are excellent. Jay, if you'll fetch the bags, the cooler and dry goods may stay in the kitchen, of course, and the others in the bedroom to the left."

Alice chomped another cookie bite, unsurprised when Jay shov-eled in the rest of his cookie and dashed outside. Henry's command plus nearly three hours trapped in the car equaled a Jay eager to stretch his legs.

She poked around the cabin, one large main room sectioned off into living and dining and kitchen areas by sumptuous furnishings. A hallway to her right with bedrooms and a shared bath. Stairs against the wall on that side led to a loft. Windows from floor to ceiling on the south side, split by a central stone chimney. A set of doors leading out to a deck.

Henry guided her to the lone door on the east wall.

"Master suite." He pushed open the door and turned on the light. "Where we'll be sleeping, among other things."

"Master suite for the master?" She teased him as she took in the space. Masculine, oversize furniture. A second door that probably led to a bathroom. A third out to the deck. "Sounds right to me."

"Master, Alice?" Tugging her against him, Henry slipped one

hand into the space between her back and her jeans—no, her underwear, even. He crushed her to him with a grip on her bare ass. "I'm not so demanding as all that, am I? That's a level of control far beyond what we need. Not when you're so beautifully obedient and responsive, hmm?"

Responsive, fuck, talk about understatement. Her nipples hardened beneath her shirt, pressed to his firm chest. She widened her stance to accommodate the warm pulse between her legs. "I like your demands, Henry."

"I know you do, my sweet. And I'm quite pleased when you tell me so." He sucked at her earlobe. "Do you know what else pleases me?"

Not a clue. The answer could be any of a million things.

"Making you *wait*." His deep voice resonated in her bones. A whimper escaped her as he stepped back. "Dinner first. We're two hours overdue."

Her own arousal captivated her for the next hour, as Jay brought in the bags and Henry put a quick dinner together and the three of them sat and ate around the table. But finally, as the antique clock in the dining area chimed ten, Henry spoke the words she'd been waiting to hear.

"Tell me your safeword, please, Jay."

"Tilt-A-Whirl." No hesitation.

"Alice?"

"Pistachio." A rush of adrenaline.

"Into the bedroom with you both, then. Leave your clothes as they are." Henry took a deep breath and exhaled with steady calm. "I'll remove them myself tonight."

She sauntered into the master bedroom with a bounce in her step, an extra sway in her hips. If Jay, following her, noticed, he held his tongue out of respect for Henry's mastery.

Standing side by side, she and Jay appeared cut from the same cloth. Henry's choice; he'd dressed them both. He trailed his fingers over the buttons down their shirtfronts.

"You both know you may use your safewords at any time," he prompted.

"Yes, Henry." They responded in unison. Maybe she'd gotten the hang of being a co-submissive.

"And you'll use them when?"

"If I'm—confused," she finished, as Jay ended with "scared."

Okay. They might be co-subs, but they were individuals, too. With individual needs. That Henry took care of. She wiggled her toes in her socks. Comfy.

Fingering the fabric between buttonholes, Henry nodded. "Or in pain of any sort, hmm?"

Emotional pain, most likely. She doubted they'd play games with physical pain until Jay—*be honest, Allie-girl*—until they both stopped thinking so much about the club. Henry encouraged them to show him their emotional needs. Like Jay had last week. As upsetting as his breakdown had been, as helpless as she'd felt to help him at first, he'd needed the emotional release.

Her answer followed on the heels of Jay's. "Yes, Henry."

"Lovely." He circled them, and she reminded herself not to turn.

Jay had no trouble staying still. Henry in charge gave him more comfort than not. The flirtatious charm Jay donned like a costume when he went out into the world seemed an outlet for nervous energy. He didn't lose his charm at home or in bed, but the contrast showed in his steadier, boyish expression of love. A reflection of the difference having Henry in his life made. Their love made a difference in her, too.

Henry's kiss took her by surprise, but following his lead came easy when his lips moved against hers.

He kissed Jay with the same thoroughness. Jay whimpered at the pleasure.

An answering cry built in her own throat. She breathed deep and quick.

Henry stepped back and studied them.

"I'm so very pleased with you both." Speaking in a conversational tone, he began unbuttoning her shirt.

She shivered at the brush of his knuckles against her breasts.

"Brave. Resilient." With each word, he loosed another button. "Beautiful. Brilliant. Eager." He pulled her shirt free of her jeans and pushed it from her shoulders, sliding his hands down her back and unclasping her bra as well.

Leaving her half-naked, he sidestepped in front of Jay and repeated the process. "Courageous. Obedient. Beautiful. Giving. Enthusiastic." Henry grasped Jay's jeans, sending his hips rocking and pulling him forward. Nimble fingers unfastened the top and lowered the zipper. Henry pressed his hand against the hard cock outlined by tented boxers. "*Very* enthusiastic."

She squeezed her thighs together. Jay hadn't cornered the market on enthusiasm. Her panties practically sloshed with anticipation.

Having stripped Jay bare, he returned. Her body hummed under his touch. He lowered her underwear, and the thick scent of her own arousal flooded her nose. His deep inhalation ...d satisfied sigh fluttered through her, tightening her stomach and provoking a downbeat of thumping anticipation. But he directed them to lie on the bed on their backs, a narrow space between, arms at their sides, legs comfortably spread.

Henry undressed himself with customary care, his gaze wandering over her body and Jay's. Each attractive to him in its own way, she supposed. To her, the body functioned as a system. A machine variable in the weight it could lift, the pressure it could sustain, the rhythm of its movement. God knew he'd built gorgeous machines when he made Henry and Jay.

But Henry had an artist's eye for anatomy. The private delights he saw in Jay's slender, boyish hips and long, lean muscles and in her own padded curves stayed locked in his head or flowed from the tip of a brush. She might never understand him with certainty or precision. But she was learning to accept that what he saw, he loved.

"Such beautiful creatures you both are." Nude, aroused, he knelt between them on the bed. "But far from delicate." He ran his hands down their arms, solid pressure crossing shoulder, bicep, forearm, palm. "So very strong. Inside and out."

Lowering his head, he raised their hands in his until he knelt, head bowed, with their palms on his cheeks.

Alice turned her head, a slow movement mirrored by Jay. An infinitesimal nod passed between them as Henry touched his lips to their palms. Humbled by their devotion, he meant to worship them tonight. A healing voice, a healing touch, for his wounded partners.

He ran his hands over her as he praised her. He moved with patient, sweeping strokes, leaving not an inch untouched before he rolled her onto her stomach and did the same to her back. Toes curled, she lay panting and trembling on the edge of orgasm when he finally pushed her onto her back once more. Christ, the intensity in the green depths of his eyes pierced her.

"Come for me, sweet girl." He ducked his head between her thighs. "Let me taste your pleasure."

Closing his mouth over her sex, he tugged her lips and clit inside and sucked with rapid repetition. His tongue pushed and rolled. Disobeying him would've been impossible even had she wanted to. Her climax had already begun, a flow of heat and pressure and release crashing outward, an earthquake with his tongue at the epicenter.

The wavering wail in her ears came from her own throat, her urgent plea for more answered with thrusting between her lips and a hard press against her clit. The cascade seemed never-ending, even when his tongue left her and he blew warm air across oversensitive flesh. Even when his fingers entered and his tongue bathed her clit. These quakes defied measurement on any scale. Unquantifiable. Limitless.

She lay dazed and sated. Her eyelids slid down. She forced them open. Amusement greeted her in Henry's soft gaze and pursed lips.

"Drift, dearest." He caressed her cheek. "You've earned a rest after providing such a delicious dessert. And I've a date for seconds."

He tapped her nose with his finger and turned away.

She struggled to keep her eyes open. Dessert. Seconds. Jay. Her body's sluggish wash of desire failed to dislodge the laxity in her muscles and the mellow contentment in her head. *Love you, Henry.*

"My patient boy. Such a kind, generous heart, with so little room for envy."

She lay quiet as he praised Jay, his hands moving over Jay's body as they had hers.

"Filled with love you want only to express. Your service accepted."

She'd burned with more jealousy watching Henry settle a coat on another woman's shoulders than she did as he stroked toward Jay's naked cock. Henry praising Jay, touching Jay, gifted her with redoubled pleasure, a joy to witness.

"Your beautiful submission appreciated and honored."

Every shift of the mattress rippled through her when Jay rolled over. Every buck of his hips into the sheets.

Henry kneaded tight, round ass cheeks under his hands.

She reveled in Jay's groaning punctuated by sharp breaths—interrupted by Henry's commands to wait a bit longer—and finally his pleading cries and thanks. She forced her eyes to stay open, grateful not to miss Henry dragging his mouth over Jay's cock. Twice in two weeks. Jay had to be in heaven.

Apology and affirmation both. Tender care, and Henry's promise to make them whole. Spreading Jay's thighs wide, he sank his lips to the base of Jay's cock. The muscles in his throat and jaw worked in flawless rhythm. Jay reached the finish line as quick as she had and with louder enjoyment. Bemusement crinkled in the corners of Henry's eyes.

Mumbling from Jay, and Henry nodded, bending forward and kissing Jay's chest. "Pillows."

Jay scrambled around the bed adjusting covers and pillows.

Henry turned his attention to her. "Still satisfied, my sweet girl?"

"Mm-hmm." She didn't feel . . . *shortchanged*, her brain chimed in, to silent laughter. Neither Henry's cock nor Jay's had filled her tonight, but she hadn't been left empty. Not like the nights when she'd wondered whether Henry desired her at all.

"Comfy," she added. "Humming." Staring into Henry's eyes made her own tear up. "In love."

"Exceptional," Henry murmured. "Come here, dearest."

Reclining into Jay's pillow-nest concoction, Henry tucked her into his side. He kissed her with slow deliberation, weaving one hand through her hair and cradling her with the other. Pulling back, he revealed Jay kneeling between his legs, head bowed, a perfect waiting pose.

Henry unthreaded his hand from her hair and stroked Jay's face, knuckles following his cheekbone. "All right, my beautiful boy. Show me."

Perfect. Front-row seat for gorgeous action. Resting her head on Henry's shoulder, she studied Jay's tongue technique and Henry's responses, his hand clutching her ass when Jay particularly pleased him. His fingers drifted, sliding between her cheeks. Unintentional. Hell, if Jay had his head between her thighs, she'd be distracted, too.

Legs tightening, Henry flexed his muscles. Jay splayed his hand at the base of Henry's cock. His fingers paled against the purple flush of excitement. His lips, wet and swollen, matched the color much better. He sighed as he sucked with greater speed, crooning his pleasure at being allowed to show his love and satisfy Henry's desire.

Henry's groans reverberated through his cheek and into her skull. Her hips surged against his side in echoing arousal, his approaching climax eliciting a sympathetic response.

"So close, my boy, you've such"—Henry took quick, panting

breaths—"delightful devotion to your task." Clenching Jay's shoulder in a white-knuckled grip, he squeezed her ass with the other hand.

Fuck yes. Henry'd trapped her between the pressure of his hand and her clit grinding against his hip.

With a harsh growl, Henry bucked his hips.

Jay rushed to swallow, gulping and gasping.

Tense and ready, she sent her fingers diving toward her pussy.

Henry got there first. He slid his fingers into her from behind, the heel of his hand bumping her ass as she rippled around him. Her climax arrived with sudden speed, her body shaking for one unending moment.

She lay in bliss, jolted into blinking finally when Henry's fingers left her. Accepting the offered fingers, Jay sucked them clean. Henry beckoned Jay forward, and they kissed with deep appreciation before kissing her in turn.

The three of them lay together, Jay sprawled on Henry's chest and Alice cradled at his side, until Henry patted their hips. "All right, my dears. Cleanup and sleep. It's time to put this day to bed, hmm?"

They agreed it was, stretching sated and sleepy bodies as they rolled to their feet and headed to the bathroom. Head drooping, she noticed little beyond the softness of the washcloths and the wide expanse of counter.

Less than ten minutes later, she lay under the covers, sleep claiming her almost before her men settled beside her. "Should go camping more," she mumbled. "S'nice."

CHAPTER 7

Alice pressed her head into the pillow and stretched. Her arms encountered no bodies. She popped her eyes open.

Jay lay on his side, cheeks stubbly and lips soft and full. "Hey, sleepy."

"Mmph." She yawned. The hour felt early yet. They'd fallen asleep so late. "Henry?"

Jay poked a hand out from under the covers and gestured behind her. "Outside."

Rolling to the edge of the bed, she spied him through the sliding glass door. Henry occupied a chaise near the edge of the deck, a closed sketch pad tucked beside him. "How long?"

"About an hour." Jay stroked her back. She rolled toward him until they lay face-to-face with their arms draped across each other's hips. Comfort, not desire, drew them together. Henry's moods rippled through the entire relationship.

"You haven't—"

"Tried to coax him back to bed?"

She nodded, and Jay shook his head.

When Henry was pleased with them, she and Jay magnified his joy. But when he was torn, his absence and distraction left Jay anxious and needy and her worried and maternal.

"I think it needs to be you this time." Jay drew tight circles on her skin. "If we're thinking the same thing."

She pressed her lips together. Jay might not be ready or even want to be. She'd pushed herself to model openness and share her uneasiness because Henry expected it and Jay needed her example, but his pain ran so much deeper. She carried a pebble in her shoe. Jay bent his back under a mountain.

"Alice?" He ducked his head. His breath tickled her throat. "I won't let you down again."

She clutched him tighter, flattening her breasts against his chest and pressing her mouth to his ear. "You've never disappointed me, Jay." Both of her lovers held themselves to impossible standards. "We agree he wouldn't still be thinking about it if the decision was an easy one, right?"

Jay bumped her shoulder with his nod.

"And the easy decision in Henry's mind is whatever is best for us, right?"

Another nod.

"Which means he wants to take the not-easy option and accept Emma's offer to teach. But he's punishing himself for even thinking about it."

"Exile. He's out there brooding."

"Because he wants something he thinks will be bad for us." Jay's hum of agreement vibrated against her throat, and she shivered. "But we agree it'll be good for us, right? To confront the situation? Make it something positive?"

"I'm . . . afraid, a little. But not like I was. I know what Cal did was wrong. And how he treated you. He'll do it again." Jay clutched her hip and breathed out, hard. "I dunno how many people got hurt 'cause I refused to speak up years ago. But I . . . I want to now."

She kissed him, a firm press on his cheekbone in front of his ear. Tried to buy herself time to work out how Henry would coax Jay to share more. "Why now, sweetheart?"

"You know I don't like being in control." Fidgety fingers tapped at her ribs. "But this is different. I should be able to give up control only when *I* want to. When it's safe. To Henry. To you."

The depth of his trust woke remnants of terror in her blood. He depended on her.

"When I saw Cal again, it was like I gave up control when I didn't want to. I couldn't stop it. I need—" He cleared his throat, and his voice strengthened. "I need that control back. Helping other subs is a good place to start. Isn't it?"

"You're the bravest man I know, Jay." Henry had fostered this bond between them for months. His careful crafting had created a place for her in this relationship, one allowing her to give and accept love, one allowing Jay to reveal more than the charming surface co-median. "And I think it's the perfect place to start."

His breath whooshed out. "Good. Then you'll go convince Henry to do what he wants, because we're both ready for it. I mean—shit. You are, too, right? If you're not, that's okay. You don't have to be just 'cause—"

"I am, Jay. You're not pressuring me. But what makes you think he'll listen to me and not you?"

A bitter chuckle broke from Jay's throat. "Because I'm a liar."

"Bullshit." She pulled back and stared him straight in the face. Cringing self-hatred twisted him in unnatural lines. "You're as honest as he is."

"You didn't hear me promising him I could handle it. I begged for weeks. He was gonna take you to the club alone, you know. I told him no, I was absolutely ready. That I'd gotten so far these months with your example. That staying home would be spinning my wheels."

Okay, he'd overestimated on his self-assessment, but he hadn't lied. Henry would understand the difference.

"I hounded him day and night. Told him *I'd* be good for *you*. Like a guide in case you got nervous. An example. And then I fucking lost it, and you had to save me. After I promised I'd be fine. He won't trust me now. He can't trust me now."

Fuck. This conversation wasn't one he needed to have with *her*. She rubbed his back. "You're gonna have to tell him that."

"What, I fucked up?" He laughed, and his gaze slid away from hers. "I think he knows."

"No, sweetheart." Cupping his cheek, she waited until he looked at her without immediately looking away. "That you're afraid he won't trust you. It's affecting your mood, eating away at you, and it'll attach itself to the rest of the pain if you let it. And that'll make Henry's job harder, won't it?"

Jay closed his eyes and mumbled.

"What, sweetheart?"

"I said you two really do think scary-alike sometimes."

"Good." She leaned in and kissed him, hard and controlling. "Twice as much love and attention for you."

He hummed. "Like catching nothing but green lights on a cross-town run."

She giggled. "Let's hope we get a green light from Henry."

She slipped out of bed, Jay whistling as she crossed the room naked. Bathroom first, a quick stop. She paused beside the bag Henry'd packed for her. They hadn't bothered unpacking last night. He might've included pajamas and a robe for lounging. But the house was isolated, the lot wooded. The lake access lay down a set of stairs in the hillside.

"Need a kiss for luck?" Jay scrambled onto his knees at the edge of the bed, as naked as she, and dropped into his waiting pose. A comfort. Somehow Henry had trained their fidget-prone boy to let go of anxiety and find peace in this stillness. He'd be here. Waiting.

"I always need a kiss." Stepping close, she pushed his hair back and proffered a gentle kiss. Sweet. "I don't have any idea how long this will take."

He smirked. "Good thing I know how to wait."

She breathed in Jay-scented courage and slipped out the sliding door. The air held the morning's chill despite the warm sunshine flooding her face. She shivered, her steps quick across boards beginning to retain heat. "Henry?"

"Is your delightful nudity an attempt to distract me from my thoughts?" He stretched out his arm, lifting the blanket across his lap with his opposite hand, and pulled her down. He hadn't bothered to dress, either. An excellent start. "A none-too-subtle hint that you're feeling neglected?"

He tossed the blanket over them both and cuddled her close, pressing his face to her neck and inhaling.

"Mmm. Not distract." God, his lap was comfortable. If anyone was doing the distracting here, it was him. "Clarify."

"Oh?" He danced his fingers down her spine and rested his hand at the top of her ass.

Fuck subtlety. Henry appreciated honesty, and Jay was waiting. "You're conflicted about Emma's proposal. Jay and I aren't."

"Because you rightly understand the two of you deserve my full attention?" He stroked her bare back with slow, steady sweeps.

"Because we rightly understand your desire to help newcomers at the club and stop a predator. Because we share it."

"You want me to do this." He defied interpretation, his face and his voice flat and neutral.

She threw herself into the breach. "We want you to do what you think is best. We just want you to have all of the information you need to decide that."

"Namely, that the two of you feel comfortable returning to the club despite the disastrous, traumatizing experience you had merely two weeks ago." Skepticism dangled from every word.

She didn't blame him. A week ago, Jay had been shaking and crying in their bed, and she'd been shying from contact. "I think we have to. Even if it's not comfortable. Especially then." She needed proof stronger than words. If she explained her certainty to Henry, he'd understand.

"When I was sixteen, I went to a haunted house with my girlfriends. A community-theater fund-raiser thing. Safe Halloween fun. But one of the guys playing a monster grabbed me. Copped a feel." The groping had seemed to go on forever, though it couldn't have been more than a few seconds before her horrified paralysis had given way to reaction.

"I was so angry. The night was supposed to be fun, not disgusting and scary. I rammed my elbow into his gut." The guy's pained groan and the way his hands had dropped from her chest to grab his stomach still made her cheer inside. "And then again in his face when he bent over. Monday at school, I saw a guy in my English class. We ran in different crowds, but I still knew him, you know? He had a black eye. His buddies were ragging on him, asking if he'd groped a guy by mistake."

The sick, angry feeling had swarmed like a cloud of bees, stinging her throat.

"I marched over and almost punched him again to see if I could make his eyes match, and I told him he ought to keep his hands to himself." Maybe he'd learned the lesson. Maybe not. "It was awkward, seeing him and knowing he saw nothing but a set of boobs to grab. But I think that's what we need now—me and Jay both—to reclaim that control. To act instead of feeling like victims."

Henry laid a hand on her hair and kissed her head. "Yes. You do. And you make a lovely argument for it, though I wonder why I'm only hearing of it *now*." His voice dropped to a low demand. "Why wasn't this experience included in your contract answers, Alice?"

"I—where?"

"Did you or did you not answer 'no' to the question of whether you'd experienced sexual violence?" His hold barely allowed her ribs space to expand.

"It wasn't—I haven't thought of it in years. I didn't let him control how I felt about it. I wasn't hurt, Henry. His touch wasn't anything more than a rough grope through my shirt."

"And Cal never touched you at all, but you wouldn't deny that his harassment and bullying is a form of sexual violence, would you? It's certainly one that has left a strong impression on your mind." He stroked her hair. "Touched or not, you were assaulted both times nonetheless, my sweet girl. You might have responded to our games in a way I could not have predicted. I might have harmed you for lack of information. You *cannot* withhold such details from me."

He whispered in her ear as he tucked strands of hair behind it. "Particularly not as we'll be spending a good deal of time at the club in the coming weeks. I must be able to predict your responses."

"We'll be—" Her mind took a moment to catch up. "You'd already decided." She pushed back, lifting her face from his neck and meeting his steady gaze. "Before I came out here this morning. You were waiting to see if we'd try to convince you."

"To see how committed you are to the idea, yes. To gauge the depth of your avoidance after the progress we made last week. Haven't I always encouraged you to confront fears and desires openly when you're ready?" He glanced toward the sliding glass door, which hadn't moved since she'd closed it. "I note Jay didn't accompany you on this little ambush. Did you draw the short straw?"

They'd had him all wrong. Rather than punishing himself or playing the overprotective dominant, Henry had been waiting on them to recognize their need and come to him on their own. To ask for it. "How long would you have waited?"

"As long as I needed to." He caressed her cheek with sliding knuckles. "Had you been unable to approach me with the idea, you also would have been unable to follow through and return to the club, where you'll certainly be forced to confront the emotions surrounding the event."

"You would've prodded us forward at home, though." Doing nothing wasn't his style. He constantly assessed the materials at hand, tested their weak points, and found ways to reinforce the overall structure. "Like you've been doing with Jay." He might call his work artistry, but the method was all engineering. "Using scenes that introduced me to new things and helped him confront his fears."

"I want you both healthy and happy." He pulled her closer, tucking her sideways in his lap and clasping his arms around her. "There's no timetable for that, Alice. No deadline you must meet." He brushed kisses over her face. "I won't grow tired of you. Nor of Jay. Whatever you need, I will provide."

"Jay's afraid." She blurted the words before overthinking could stop her. "That's why I'm the one out here convincing you of something you didn't need to be convinced about."

Henry stilled in midkiss. Neither a sigh nor a whimper, the soft hitching in his breath conveyed the same pain.

"He feels like he lied to you." Might as well get it all out. "But he didn't. I mean, I know he didn't mean to. Not any more than I meant to in the contract questions."

"He feels guilty." Henry relaxed.

She relaxed with him. She'd done right to mention Jay's problem, even if Henry'd already been aware.

"Something he desired so badly turned out so disastrously, and he's quite conditioned to blame himself in such cases."

"He thinks you won't trust him."

"Then we shall find more ways to show him what a wonderfully trustworthy boy he is. Starting now." He scooped her in his arms and stood, leaving the blanket to fall to the deck at their feet. "He's waited long enough to hear the outcome of your quest, don't you suppose?"

Henry circled the bed. Nude. Yummy. "A bit of fun to celebrate seems in order."

True to form, Jay'd been in his waiting pose when Henry carried her in and settled her beside him. Told him they'd return to the club in time. Skipped the lengthy explanation and said nothing of her confession or his intention to foster Jay's self-confidence.

"An activity I'm certain you'll appreciate, my boy."

Jay didn't need to hear those things, not like she did. For him, knowing Henry had made the decision was enough.

"Alice has a very talented mouth, wouldn't you say?"

If a full-body nod counted as a yes, Jay didn't need to speak.

"We wouldn't want her to lose her talent for a lack of practice, would we?"

"No, Henry." Jay's quick glance held a nervous edge.

Did he think she'd freak out? Hell, after the bastard's offer to fuck her face, she might, so maybe Jay had the right idea. No guy welcomed a crazy woman's teeth so close to his most treasured appendage.

"The two of you are going to play a game for me, my dears." Henry stacked the pillows and lay back against them, his sprawled legs an enticement demanding her attention.

"Jay will be the bold, fearless leader, and Alice will be his lovely little copycat." Henry's cock lay soft, relaxed, amid the short-trimmed pale brown hair between his thighs.

"Be sure to explain yourself as you go, my boy. Hands and mouths only." Henry crossed his arms behind his head. "You may have . . . we'll say thirty minutes, shall we? Thirty minutes to play with my cock as you like."

She exchanged a glance with Jay. He squared his shoulders, reached over, and took her hand in a confident squeeze. She forced her expression to seriousness despite her desire to giggle at his intensity.

"If I come more quickly than that, you'll have earned praise rather than penalties. A reward afterward. I trust you both understand the rules?"

Months ago, she'd imagined asking Jay for blowjob tips. And here was Henry, offering a teacher for her training, easing her concerns and giving Jay a task to shore up his faltering confidence.

"We understand, Henry." Jay answered for the both of them.

She'd watched Henry pleasure Jay twice in the last week. Commandingly so, both times. No way Jay would show her *that*—a dominant performance—and she trusted Henry to keep things relaxed.

"I'll leave you to it, then." He wanted this to go well. Of course he did. To banish any lingering panic in her. "Your time starts . . . now."

Lying on his side, Jay hugged Henry's leg like a full-body pillow and rested his head on Henry's hip. She hurried to mirror him, curling her leg over Henry's, pressing her palm to the inside of his thigh, her eyes aligned with Jay's.

His tongue came out, flicking his upper lip. She copied his movement.

He laughed. "Sorry. Thinking. I like to get the whole picture first. Like checking a map, knowing where everything is so you're not locked into a bad route when the GPS doesn't know a street's one way or closed for construction." He pinched his lips together. "Sorry, that maybe doesn't make sense."

"No, no, a survey. I get it." She slid her cheek along the smooth skin over Henry's hip bone. Fuck if she'd let Jay drown without throwing him a line. He'd rise to the challenge of being in charge. If he looked at things geographically, spatially, that wasn't so different from her own structural paradigm. "You're logging a status update and a menu of options."

Jay grinned. "You do understand." He moved in closer, nose trailing along the crease of Henry's thigh, inhalations loud and deep as he rubbed Henry's twitching cock with his nose and cheek. "Gotta get a feel for where we are . . . the scent . . . the muscle tension . . . the taste."

With his lips wrapped around Henry's cock, he gave a quick suck, down to the base and back in two seconds, no more. He waited, his eyes on her.

She belatedly remembered her role. Jay's mouth on Henry's cock was enough to throw anyone off their game. Kicking back and enjoying the show for the next thirty minutes appealed.

But she took a deep breath and followed Jay's example, nuzzling and caressing, tension melting away. Henry's cock was a treat, not a threat. His scent alone prompted a throbbing pulse between her legs. The man's smell seemed perfectly calibrated to attract every cell in her body. Jay's sweeter musk stirred a mix of arousal and the desire to cuddle him. But Henry's scent . . . she'd crawl over broken glass to fuck him. A soft bed, a mostly still soft cock fitting entirely in her mouth, yeah. Better. Much better.

Henry hummed a few bars. Something she didn't recognize, but he sounded happy. Good so far.

Jay teased his fingers along the inside of Henry's thigh and cradled his balls. Firm pressure, not a tentative touch. He knew the line between pleasurable and stop-right-fucking-now. She'd always erred on the side of caution and hesitance.

Hand cupped beneath Henry's balls, Jay massaged in a beckoning motion and encouraged her to copy him. He covered her hand, tightening up, and the grip felt . . . solid. The sort she'd use to squeeze her breasts while masturbating. A testable hypothesis, if she set up an experiment to measure grip strength and—

"Earth to Alice."

Oops. "Sorry, coach."

"See, you get too focused, you forget the bigger picture." Jay shot her his cockiest grin. "And the picture's getting bigger by the minute."

She choked on a laugh. Henry had hardened under their handling, his cock thick and expanding, lifting away from his body.

Jay released her hand, sliding his own up to grip the shaft at the base. He squeezed, once, without real motion, and Henry's humming developed a slight hitch.

"Once things are well in hand"—Jay waggled his eyebrows, and she groaned dramatically—"a little combo action sets the pace. Sometimes it's a leisurely ride on a two-lane road. Sometimes it's a wild drop down a mountain trail."

She smirked. "Got it. Sometimes you're melting tin, and sometimes you're cranking the furnace for carbon steel."

"If you say so. What I know about steel is it's a little heavy but it gives a great ride." He closed his mouth over the head of Henry's cock and sank down to the edge of his grip. He bobbed, his hand loosely following his mouth up and bringing lubrication back down. "A little straight up and down to start. No sense wasting your best moves. You gotta hold a little something back in case there's a long climb on the trail."

"Stoke the flames, keep that heat intensity right below melting." Copying Jay, she kept her hand loose and her mouth all lips and no tongue, adding her own lubrication. She held Henry's absolute attention, his eyes dark and fixed on their playground, throaty groans leaking from his closed mouth. "You were saying?"

"A little twist. Like you've hit a switchback. Zig, zag, pedaling hard." Jay moved his tongue like a wave, an upward roll, and covered Henry's cock. His hand gliding in a half-circle, he stroked toward the head, mouth popping off every time, tongue flicking out before coming down again.

Henry arched his hips as they switched control. She and Jay drew closer, straddling his legs, their weight holding him in place. The hair on his legs brushed her breasts and sex, a spur for her growing arousal. Blowing Henry in concert with Jay got a foreplay thumbs-up from her pussy.

She added the hand twist, the mouth pop, the tongue flick, every step as Jay had done.

Henry's cock swelled, the tip deep purple.

She shared a grin with Jay as he guided their hands back to Henry's balls, drawn tighter against his body and coaxing a low growl from him when squeezed.

"Race you—"

She nodded. Oh hells yes.

"—to the finish line?"

They set to work, tongues twining up the shaft, worrying at the head, backing off in turns to allow each other to engulf as much as they could. Less for her than Jay, but she'd ask for a lesson in that sometime, too.

Henry's rumbling growl proved her only warning as she pulled back, ready to cede ground to Jay's quick tongue. Heat splashed her cheeks, her chin, her neck with sudden swiftness. Surprise turned into giggles.

Jay cleaned off Henry's cock with a long pull and grinned at her. "You, uh, got a little something."

She pushed down her giggles. "Do I?"

"Don't worry. I got it." He waited for her nod, laid his tongue to her cheek, and bathed her in long strokes. Tipping her head back encouraged him to shift his attention to her neck.

"Delightful, the pair of you," Henry murmured. "And in under thirty minutes. You'll have to have a reward for such excellent work."

They wriggled up the bed and burrowed on either side of Henry as he brought his arms up and embraced them. Deep kisses for them both, entirely indifferent to, or enjoying, his salty musk on their tongues.

"Henry?"

"Yes, my dear girl?"

"Thank you for not, I mean, for trusting—just, thank you. And Jay, too." Lifting her head, she smirked at him across Henry's chest. "You're fun to play follow the leader with, stud."

Jay dusted his knuckles on Henry's chest and blew them off in a puff of air. "That's what all the ladies say."

"All the ladies?" She raised a what's-this-about eyebrow.

"Well, just the one. But she's the only lady I love."

She savored the warmth in her chest. Didn't blink back the tingle crawling along the edge of her eyes.

"So that makes her all of 'em, right, Henry?"

He hummed and ruffled Jay's hair. "Exactly right."

They loved her, and she loved them. No reason not to let herself feel the depth of their love, even when the feeling seemed bottomless.

Henry had let them play without interference or guidance. A no-pressure blowjob, because if she'd spooked, Jay could've finished. Her responsibility ended with herself. Which was nice, but . . .

She drew random shapes on Henry's chest and shoulder, fingers following no map. For all the control he exercised over them, he never treated them like toys to be teased and laughed over. A set of genitals to fuck. They'd been less considerate of his needs. Selfish.

"You aren't a toy to me, either, Henry," she blurted.

Jay's blank stare greeted her. "I missed something. What conversation is Alice having?"

Lifting her chin, Henry caught her gaze. "Your playful behavior was entirely in keeping with the exercise, sweet girl." He stroked her cheek and tucked a wayward strand of hair behind her ear. "My own pleasure was beside the point, though a beautiful bonus. Your comfort, and Jay's, are of far more interest to me."

"But don't you ever want anything for yourself?"

"For now, I'd like to watch the two of you play." Henry cupped Jay's chin in his other hand. "As a reward for your lovely leadership, my boy, you may pick a position."

"Alice on top." No thought required, from the speed of his answer.

Henry smiled. "Because you wish to lie back and let her do the work?" he teased.

Jay shook his head.

If Henry wanted playful, she'd do playful. "Because sex is like riding a bicycle, and you're the closest thing to a bike in this room?"

Jay burst out laughing. "I need to watch Alice ride a bike sometime. She's fantastic at sex, so it's gotta be cycling that confuses her."

She rolled up and over Henry and straddled Jay's thighs, hands on his chest, pushing him flat to the mattress as she started a rolling rhythm with her hips.

"I do a lot of pumping." She pitched her voice high and innocent. Pushed her hips down harder. "Am I doing it wrong?"

A slow shake, Jay's head moving though his gaze stayed fixed on her hips. Or, rather, what lay between them. He swallowed. His cock hardened in little jumps.

Power held the edge of addiction, the rush spinning in her blood.

His stomach twitched when the condom packet landed. A gift from Henry.

Four hands reached. Hers got there first. She sheathed Jay in latex with a steady stroke. He swept his hands up her legs from knees to hips and tugged.

"Not so fast, stud." Leaning forward, she rested her forearms on his chest. Lifted her ass and shimmied. "I gotta get to know my ride."

Jay pushed against her knees, his hips thrusting at the air between them.

A low rumble to her left swallowed his tiny whimper.

Henry had rolled up on his side. Stretching, he ran his hand down her back, shoulders to ass. She shuddered under his touch, sinful satisfaction begging him to stay a while.

"Our girl always manages to find the most inviting poses."

She'd meant to be playful. Like riding a bike. Legs pumping up and down. Ass swaying side to side. Bent low. She pressed closer to Jay, breasts firm against his chest. Pussy thumping in rhythm with her heartbeat and brushing over his gift-wrapped cock with each repetition.

Henry's fingers danced along the base of her spine. He traced the cleft between her cheeks with faint pressure.

The touch goosed her hips forward.

He hummed. "I doubt she yet realizes the depth of the temptation she presents."

Inviting. Temptation. With Henry lying at their sides, so close a single swift motion could bring him to his knees behind her. Where his fingers—

She dipped her head and sucked in a breath, body rippling against Jay's from where their foreheads touched to her toes curling alongside his thighs. Memory gave her the sensation of Henry covering her, his weight along her back, as easily as the present gave her the taut leanness of Jay's body beneath hers, his cock hard and waiting. She fumbled between them, aligning him in milliseconds and dropping her body onto his.

Jay's breath echoed hers. He squeezed his eyes shut. "I dunno, I think she gets it pretty well."

A fast slide, slick and open. Filled, now. But not as filled as she could be. Not as filled as her movements and her body tempted Henry to make her. Christ. The idea had taken root in her head, and she couldn't make it leave. Excitement or fear, either way adrenaline dumped into her system.

"She's a quick study, my boy. As are you."

He was?

"I am?" Jay panted out the question. Fingers splayed across her thighs, he fired his hips at her fast pace. Thumbs thudding like the bass line in a dance mix, he delivered a steady stroke to her clit, over and over. They moved to the beat together.

"Do you know why I so enjoy watching the two of you play?"

"Love." They'd answered together. She peppered Jay's face with kisses. Getting closer. The tightness pulled at her, every muscle responding to her unspoken demand, to the galloping rhythm eager to send them soaring.

Henry chuckled. "Yes, that, always. But more than that, my dear ones." Nuzzling close, he kissed Jay's neck where her hands had migrated, where she gripped the tense cords of muscle running up from his shoulders. "You've become so beautifully in tune. I've no worries when I place you in each other's hands."

His breath warmed her skin as he coaxed a whimper from Jay.

"I'm entrusting our precious girl to you, my brave boy, because you bring her so much pleasure." The faintest baritone rumbled as Henry murmured into Jay's ear. "You see the flush of her skin, hmm? Feel the trembling in her thighs?"

His words might've been for Jay, but fuck if they didn't make her moan.

"The pulse beneath your thumbs, faster now. Her nipples stiff and dragging over your chest."

Their dance neared its end. She hung on the edge, waiting for the final chord, the sustained note of triumph.

"Her legs tightening around yours. The sweet grip as she rides your cock. Wondrous, my boy. Every moment a wonder. Would I allow any man that gift, the beauty of her climax?"

"No." Jay mouthed the word, soundless. His hips snapped up hard.

Their bodies slammed together, his thumbs slick with proof of her pleasure as she ground herself against him.

"No," Henry echoed. "Only my diligent boy, who's learned his lessons so well. The only other I may trust to give our girl what she needs whenever she needs it. Like the good, hard fucking he's giving her right now."

She cried out as her climax hit. Maybe the note matched the music in her head. Maybe her body's shaking resembled a dance. Maybe the weight low on her back was Henry's hand pushing her tight against Jay, making sure she embraced each of his shallow, rapid thrusts as he joined her with a hitching whimper.

They collapsed in a heap, bodies trembling, Henry's quiet humming a soothing relief from the pounding rhythm they'd shared.

"Love you." Jay's whisper could've been for either of them. Probably both.

She captured his mouth with a slow, easy kiss. Nudged his face toward Henry's after and basked in joy as they shared the same. Shared a kiss with Henry herself, both of them trying not to laugh at Jay's appreciative whistle. Or what would've been his appreciative whistle, if his mouth hadn't been so dry.

She broke first, giggling. "What was that, the wind whistling in the canyon?"

He yawned. "Depends. Is the wind sleepy?"

"It most definitely is." She kissed his forehead and wiggled her hips.

He held the condom while she lifted off. Settling at his side, she snuggled him between herself and Henry.

"Is the canyon a narrow slot in a flash flood?" God, his sleepy smirk about killed her.

She snorted. "Flood's over. But it was a hell of a satisfying weather event."

They traded gentle teases as Henry left and returned. Lounged with legs open as he bathed them with the tender touch to which she'd grown so accustomed. Welcomed him back to bed with kisses. Nestled close for a nap, calm and relaxed, the morning's uncertainty washed away.

CHAPTER 8

"This is the kind of shower we should have," Jay called. "You could fit half-a-dozen people in here, no problem."

Heading toward the bathroom, Alice laughed. Sure, the shower was big, but not *that* big. Although it did boast a bench along the marble wall and multiple showerheads at different levels.

Henry touched her shoulder. They hadn't napped long. An hour at most. He'd sent Jay ahead to start the shower, presumably to have reason to praise him for completing the task later. "You haven't any water-related phobias in your past I ought to know about, do you, my dear?"

Teasing equaled good, because it meant he wasn't still angry about the omission on her contract answers. "No, Henry."

"How are your swimming skills?"

"You wanna see my butterfly? It's been a while, but—"

He breathed in sharply and spun her around, his hands firm atop her shoulders. Palms flattening against her back, he fingered the edge of her shoulder blades in a downward slide.

"Yes," he rumbled. "I very much want to see you undulating through the water in sleek, smooth motion. To watch the curve of your shoulders as your arms stroke forward."

Sliding his hands to her elbows, he lifted her arms above her head and rotated his hands to the inside of her arms. She was ready when the push came, sweeping her arms outward and down in the familiar movement.

"And the flex of your muscles as you force the water aside."

Her arms hung at her sides, Henry's hands circling her wrists. He growled, a quiet declaration, and nipped at her neck when he stepped in for a full-body press.

Her hips rocked. Her sex pulsed. Flaccid before he'd asked about swimming, Henry sure as hell wasn't soft now.

Despite the months of sex—almost a year, God, that long?—she'd collected few insights about his arousal triggers. He liked to watch. And he'd hung that painting of Jay's back where he'd pass it every night on his way to bed. He'd bent her over the table the first time he'd fucked her, she in a backless dress. He'd flogged her with tenderness, the suede caressing her like an extension of his hand.

"You're in love with my back," she whispered.

"I'm in love with all of you, my sweet girl. But your back is particularly lovely." He prodded her with his hips. "Into the shower with you. Quickly now. You've inspired me to play another game."

She hustled into the bathroom, equal parts curiosity and arousal.

"On the floor, Jay. Back to the wall." Henry called out commands as he pushed her into the shower ahead of him. Water rained down from two sides in a pulsing spray, fogging the glass. "Legs spread. I'm bringing you a treat."

She spread her legs, too, for balance, as Henry walked her right to the wall between Jay's legs and pressed a firm hand to her back. She shivered, nipples hardening. "Tile's cold."

"The water's hot. And so are your lovers." Full-body contact. Henry laid his mouth at her neck and his cock at her ass.

Jay's breath gusted between her legs. No penetration, not without Henry's command, but her muscles clenched with the sure knowledge they'd be tugging Jay's tongue or Henry's cock soon.

Extending her arms above her head, Henry grasped her wrists in a single hand. He squeezed.

Her fingers flexed, hands splayed, and she shuddered at the controlled power in his hold.

"Knees up, Jay. Keep Alice's legs together, please."

Crowding her with his muscled thighs and calves, Jay added strong palms and gripping fingers below her hips. She stood with her toes tucked beneath his ass, thighs together, pressure and need making her squirm.

"Oh, no, my sweet girl, that won't do at all." Henry dropped a dangerous whisper in her ear. "You must stand very still for me, Alice. You've been cut from the herd, marked by a predator. You've nowhere to run." He tightened his grip on her wrists. Water dripped from his face to her shoulder.

She opened her mouth, needing more air, deeper breaths, and wet heat coated her throat.

Henry's touch flowed over her, a long caress from forearm down—shoulder, side, hip, ass—turning narrow and flat to slip between her thighs. An easy slide over wet skin, fingers first and then the heel of his hand, thicker and pressing upward. He flicked her clit.

Her need surged with no outlet. Jay kept her from moving. Henry pulled his hand away. She loosed a frustrated whine.

He nipped at her ear. "One might think this prey wants to be taken. A desire my little minx can't contain, hmm?" He shifted his hips back with a quiet grunt. "A sense of joy in helplessness and danger?" He prodded between her thighs. "The hunt made easier with a partner."

Pulse at a gallop, she stood immobilized.

"Hold her tight for me, my boy, and you may use your tongue as you like."

The pressure on her legs increased. Jay captured her sensitized clit in a rolling wave.

Her low moan bounced on the tile.

"Lovely," Henry murmured. "I'm going to fuck your thighs now, my sweet girl, while Jay enjoys the taste of us both."

Kid stuff, the negotiation of a boy whose girlfriend wouldn't allow deeper access. But the illicit thrill tickled her, a sense of control despite the physical power he wielded with the weight of his body and his hold on her wrists.

He pushed forward, his cock a thick heat between her thighs. Bare. She clenched, ass and thighs and pussy pulling at her, a riot of need.

He unleashed a guttural groan.

She drowned in the satisfaction of his possession.

"I feel your desire, Alice. Your slickness, the heat and the wetness so different from the water beating at my back. Your skin, smooth and slippery, so tight and close."

He rubbed his cock along the cleft of her ass. Squeezing between her thighs, he grazed the fullness of her labia. Jay finessed her clit with his tongue each time Henry pulled away. An external massage of pressure and promise, enjoyable on its own, supercharging the corresponding internal pressure and promise low in her belly.

She tried to rock with the motion. Henry brought his weight down heavier on her back, plastering her to the shower wall. He slid his free hand up her neck and parted her hair. Gripping the back of her head, he turned her cheek to the tile.

Jay dug his fingers into the outer curve of her ass.

Trapped. Henry could do anything he liked to her, or order Jay to, and she'd have to take it. A shiver born of fear and excitement, too entangled to separate, raced through her.

"You're going to come for me, at once empty and fulfilled, Alice. Do you know why?" His thrusts grew shorter, faster, the ridge of his cock a mallet and her clit the drum pounding out their rhythm.

Suction sounds rose over the water spray. Jay's talented mouth pulling at Henry's cock. She struggled to form words, to answer the demand, but everything came out garbled.

Henry's chuckle was as soft as his thrusts were forceful. "I know what you need. I know how to give it to you. However I choose to fuck you, I do so because you're *mine*. And I love what's mine."

"Love. Fuck. Love." Her body finished before her brain, short-circuiting thought. She shook hard. Strong men held her, supported her.

Growling, Henry used his grip to angle her face toward him. He kissed her, fierce and demanding, thrusting until his hands tightened and his body stilled.

Muffled by her body, Jay moaned. Filling up on calories before lunch and loving every mouthful.

Henry sank to the shower floor, cradling her with him, nuzzling her neck and examining her wrists. She wiggled her fingers without prompting, to his quiet hum of approval. He wrapped his right hand around hers and guided them both to Jay's waiting cock.

"How quickly can you come for your lovers, my dear boy? Ten strokes? Nine? Faster?" Jay whimpered as Henry tightened their hold.

"With the taste of my cock on your tongue and the scent of Alice's heady musk in your nose?"

He hadn't moved their hands yet, but already Jay shifted and squirmed in their grasp, his ass sliding on the tile, his cock jumping under their fingers.

"No, no—faster than that. A boy who's done so well today, whose lips and tongue are so pleasing, surely he could come in eight strokes. Shall we say seven? I think you can come for me in seven strokes, Jay. No more, no less."

"I can." Dark, drenched hair gleamed as Jay nodded in unceasing, eager agreement. "I can, Henry. Seven."

"You will." Henry issued a clear demand, no give in his voice. He counted each stroke, moving her hand and his in unison, up and down Jay's cock. One. Two.

And fuck if Jay didn't come at the precise moment Henry's sibilant *seven* reached her ears.

Jay set plates, glasses, and napkins at three places and claimed the seat across from her.

Henry brushed aside their offers of more help with assurances that lunch preparations required no assistance.

Her stomach awaited the meal with eager anticipation. Her mind, helped along by the soft cotton of the robe Henry'd wrapped her in, drifted to their shower. She'd complimented Jay for being able to come so quickly on command, especially when he'd climaxed in bed with her an hour before. He'd chalked it up to Henry's skill with anticipation. But she hadn't asked Henry why.

Not why he'd kept Jay at their feet or brought him to orgasm in a controlled, commanding way. Submissive postures reassured Jay. Gave him the security he craved. After taking the lead in their blowjob game, Jay would've hungered for a strong reminder of Henry's leadership.

No, what she hadn't asked was why Henry hadn't fucked her. Mmph. Not the right word. He'd obviously considered it fucking, and she hadn't disliked the game. Hell, he'd gotten her off without penetration. Not a problem to complain about.

His forcefulness earned top marks. Mr. I'm-In-Charge Henry brought her to climax almost as quickly as he did Jay. He might've intended to reassure her, too, to gauge how threatened she felt by being overpowered. Building on her comfort from last Saturday when he'd taken her in the kitchen with little warning. Making preparations for taking them back to the club. Reinforcing their safety in his hands. Confirming their acceptance of his control.

Still, if that's what he'd been doing, why hadn't he just fucked her?

Henry stood assembling wraps at the counter from a row of open containers.

Fuck it. She'd ask.

"So why the non-sex sex?" Argh. Too blunt. Too loud, too. "Not that it wasn't fantastic for me, 'cause you know it was, but, I mean, didn't you want more?"

Jay surprised her, stretching across the table to clasp her hand. "It doesn't mean he doesn't want you or that you aren't worth more." He spoke with the sweetly reassuring and utterly confident tone of a man who'd heard those words a hundred times. "It's not about that. Henry loves us even without the sex. When we were—at the beginning, I mean, after I moved in with him, once he finally let things go past handjobs—it was the only way he'd take me, no matter how much I swore I wanted him to fuck me."

Henry hadn't said a word while Jay poured them out. Over the top of Jay's head, Henry's face showed tenderness. The curve of his lip, the crinkling at his eyes, and the gentle tilt to his head gave her a new perspective on the morning.

Aside from introducing a new kind of sex to her repertoire and building Jay's confidence, maybe *Henry* craved the reminder of tenderness and caring. A meaningful way to give them the love he needed to express while being the powerful dominant they wanted. Memories he treasured, the first tentative steps toward making Jay safe and whole.

Or she was overthinking, and the game had been an impulse brought about by their teasing play on the way to the shower. Henry had so many gears at work in his head she couldn't map them all. Not that she'd ever stop trying.

"Perhaps you'd care to tell Alice about that time in our lives, my boy. To share some of your experiences with her." Henry spoke casually, continuing to fix lunch, as if Jay's choice of conversational topics lacked significance. "Her own introduction to our life together, after all, has been entirely on display."

Fairness. With a prod like that, no way Jay'd keep quiet.

"He made me wait. Soooo long, Alice. Forever long."

"Forever, huh?" She teased, gently, awash in the uncertainty of those first months, when Henry hadn't taken her, either.

Jay snorted. "You thought you waited a long time. I waited two years."

Her mouth dropped open, but no words came out. Two years. They'd been living together. Sharing a bed?

"Yes, two years, my dear girl." Henry sliced finished wraps on the diagonal. "Patience and understanding were important for us both, weren't they, my boy?"

"I had nightmares." Jay dipped his head toward the table.

She rubbed her thumb across his palm.

"Sleeping in Henry's bed helped. But I felt like—" His gaze darted up and back. "Like I wasn't earning my keep, you know?"

She squeezed his fingers. Like her, he needed to contribute to feel valuable. For him, that meant pleasing someone, and he'd associated giving happiness with sexual games. A sex toy and a whipping boy for the people who'd touched him before Henry. Nothing more. "But Henry didn't look at it that way, right?"

Henry smiled at her as he carried a platter of spinach wraps to the table and set them down. She'd pleased him, somehow.

"He said I didn't have to earn his affection."

"You still needn't, my boy." Henry pressed Jay to his chest and kissed the top of his head. "My love exists regardless."

Jay turned, following their lover's progress to the refrigerator. "I still wanted to, though. Kept begging him to let me please him."

Ah. Increasing Jay's comfort with talking and sharing always pleased Henry. Jay needed to be proud of his place in the relationship, to be a senior sub sharing worthwhile knowledge with her. His sense of responsibility toward her made him stronger. Braver.

"He started slow. Let me feel him. He'd spoon up behind me and stroke me off." Jay flushed, the slightest hint of pink in his cheeks. "The first time, I came in two strokes. Just having him touching me was . . ."

"Thrilling," she murmured, and they shared an understanding smile.

Henry joined them at the table with a pitcher of lemonade and a bowl of chips. "Help yourselves. You'll need the calories for this afternoon's entertainment."

They both thanked him, though only she went on to ask about the entertainment.

"You'll find out later, my dear. Don't let me distract you from your discussion. I believe Jay was about to explain the sweet allure of his thighs."

"It's the muscles, right?" She faux-whispered as Jay beamed. "He's got great control."

Henry hummed, neither agreeing nor disagreeing.

Jay shrugged. "I kept telling Henry I wanted more, and he kept insisting on boundaries." Jay shook his head and rolled his eyes, the epitome of youthful impatience. "When he finally agreed I was ready for more, I figured for sure he'd fuck me. And he did—only my thighs, not my ass." He groaned. "I thought I'd die from wanting it, but he was right. It worked out better his way."

He reached for a wrap, paused, and grabbed a second, too. "So yeah. Two years before I even got the sex-sex instead of the non-sex sex." He smirked across the table at her, one eyebrow raised. "But I know he loved me a long time before he stuffed his cock in my ass."

Her chuckle grew into full-out, side-gripping guffaws. Only Jay would say it so bluntly and with such affection. She understood now. Why the non-sex sex.

More tactile intimacy than a blowjob, their bodies pressed together, cuddling with a larger sexual charge. But not threatening the way full-on sex would've been. Another way for Henry to accustom Jay to enjoying sexual activities that didn't demand more than was safe for him to give. To show Jay dominance could be comfort, because Jay wanted not pain but the freedom to be dependent.

For her, today, Henry had made it an illicit thrill, a safe way to feel helpless. Trapped against his body and knowing he could've done anything, taken anything, but that he *wouldn't*. That his dominance could be forceful without being invasive. Intimidating and exciting but safe.

For himself, too. He'd treated her gently as he had Jay, but with her preference for his commanding presence firmly in mind. The lesser severity of her emotional damage didn't mean Henry couldn't use the same technique to give them all what they needed. Even if maybe he needed it more than she did.

She'd been the one to give Henry something he needed. So what if she hadn't known that's what was going on? She'd still been the one to meet his emotional needs. The girl who would've rejected emotional involvement even a year ago. Now the deeper connection made her satisfied. Proud.

She sat straighter. Loaded her plate. Lunch tasted amazing, thanks to Henry's culinary skills and her own high spirits. This relationship puzzle got easier to examine every day. She'd label all of its pieces and functions eventually. And then what?

Henry sat quietly encouraging Jay's continued antics with his lunch. No need to worry. She'd never have a what-now moment, not with these two in her life. If Henry believed she'd gotten bored, he'd add a new mystery. She'd signed on for a lifelong investigation. The thought wasn't so frightening as it used to be. She tapped the new piece into place and set the puzzle aside.

Right now, her responsibility was to enjoy lunch. "Wait, you did what with the pickle spears?"

"Jay." Henry spoke without taking his gaze from her.

"Yes, Henry?" Jay paused in his work clearing the table, laying Alice's plate beside the sink.

"I'm putting you in charge of Alice for the afternoon. There are kayaks in the boathouse. Take her out on the lake and teach her to use one, please."

"Me?" Jay's surprised tone matched the *What?* in her head.

"Yes. Alice will follow your every direction with exacting precision. Isn't that so, Alice?" He raised an eyebrow.

She raced to figure out what he expected of her.

"Yes, Henry." Not enough. Something—ah. "If you want me to listen to Jay, I know he's the best teacher for the job."

His small smile told her she'd guessed right. He'd appointed Jay her guide in a specific task in line with Jay's expertise. Demonstrating trust. Rebuilding Jay's confidence. Inside the bedroom this morning and outside this afternoon.

"Alice has assured me she's an accomplished swimmer, and I'm certain you'll give her an excellent education in the art of kayaking."

"I will, Henry. I promise. She'll have a great time." Jay would kill himself to make sure of it.

"Come here, my boy." Henry tugged Jay into his lap. Their hard, bruising kiss flirted with gentleness, too, Henry's hands slipping over Jay's spine. "Finish clearing the dishes while I help Alice with her sunscreen and then come and wait your turn, please. I want you both well-protected while you're at leisure."

Henry led her to the bedroom, rummaged in their bags, and laid her outfit on the bed. He beckoned her with a crooked finger. She sashayed, as seemed fitting for one wearing a sash.

They shared a smile. Lifting one end of her sash, he tugged, her robe fell open, and he wandered inside.

"Now, where shall we rub that sunscreen? We wouldn't want to miss a spot." He stroked her stomach and breasts with a light, relaxing touch. "A sunburned girl is one who won't be allowed to play tonight." He pushed the robe from her shoulders.

She straightened. "Do you have credentials?"

"A license to undress you?" He reached past her. Swimsuit, a new two-piece in dark green. Henry's color. "I believe you signed the permission slip for that, my dear."

"Nope, not that." Stepping into the bikini bottom as he held it open, she smirked at him where he knelt in front of her. "Credentials for sunscreen application. What kind of liability insurance do you have? If I miss out on playtime because of improper application, I'll be terribly cross with you, sir."

"Mmm. 'Terribly cross,' you say? Such language." He kissed her belly above her trimmed curls before covering her flesh with the bikini. "I assure you, my skills are impeccable."

She hummed with satisfaction. Yeah, he was right about that.

Her shorts went on, followed by the bikini top, followed by a gauzy, long-sleeved shirt. Brisk competence in Henry's hands. Lying on the bed as he lifted her legs and coated them with sunscreen, she waved to Jay when he entered the bedroom.

He sat beside her at Henry's direction and waited his turn.

Henry finished rubbing sunscreen into her neck and face. He plopped a floppy fishing hat on her head. "There we are." With an entirely straight face, he added, "Lovely."

She wrinkled her nose. Looked up at the underside of the hat brim. Tipped her head back as if she might see it better that way. "Uh-huh. I'm not sure I believe you."

Henry smirked.

Jay laughed. "No, Henry's right. It's you. Wait, let me get my phone. I need a new profile pic of you."

She crossed her arms in front of her face. "No way, mister. There will be no photographic evidence of the hat."

Jay tickled her wrists. She nudged him back. They played until Henry had gathered Jay's clothes.

"On your feet, my boy. Let's get you properly dressed for this excursion."

She lounged on the bed, offering a teasing wolf whistle at Jay's naked behind. "I think my phone needs a new photo of you, too, stud."

He wiggled, and she giggled. "My ass is in high demand. It'll cost ya."

"Let me guess, the going rate is a bad hat picture?"

Henry pulled a pair of swim trunks over her view.

"Too late. My ass is safe from giggling gawkers."

"Sure. For now."

Jay got a short-sleeve shirt. No hat. She pointed out the inherent unfairness and found no traction.

"Your skin is much fairer than Jay's." Henry applied sunscreen with thoroughness over Jay's arms and legs and neck. "Our boy will tan. You will not. And I've already been informed I must be certain my sunscreen liability insurance is paid up."

Damn. Beaten by her own big mouth. She slipped on the water shoes Henry gave her while Jay did the same beside her.

Henry unfastened his watch and placed it around Jay's left wrist. "Five o'clock, please. You'll both wish to shower before supper. If you've been good, you might play as we did this morning, hmm?"

"Yes, Henry." Her voice and Jay's overlapped in their eagerness.

Henry kissed them both and handed Jay the key to the boathouse. "Go on, then."

CHAPTER 9

The boathouse proved to be at the base of the stairs leading down from the deck. Jay popped the padlock while she wandered to the end of the dock. The water sparkled under the sun hanging high and to her right, over the far end of the lake. Farther than she could see, at any rate. Not so big as Lake Mitchell, but big enough.

In her head, her little sister begged for a ride on the paddleboats. Dad scooped Olivia up and over his shoulders. He took them both out on the water. Her legs almost too short to reach, she sent the boat curving on an arc as the force of her pedaling fell behind Daddy's. Ollie had tried kneeling and pedaling with her hands. A happy day, full of laughter.

Making her way back to Jay, she ducked inside the boathouse. "Find some good stuff, stud?"

"Tons. You ever been in a kayak?"

"Not even once. Canoes, though."

Jay nodded. He'd folded back shutters, leaving streaks of light crossing the building. "Practice tipping?"

"At summer camp. Is this a prelude to a wet T-shirt contest? Because I demand an equal-opportunity competition, so you'd better get drenched, too."

"Nope." He pointed to a digital readout on the wall. "Water thermometer must be tied outside. Sends the data wirelessly. Pretty slick.

But it's too cold to practice tipping. Water hasn't flipped. We'll take a tandem instead of a rollover."

The thermocline. That's what he meant. The cold winter water in the lake hadn't warmed yet. So even though the sun was shining and the air was comfortably in the low seventies, the water temperature hovered below fifty. Way too chilly for a swim.

"You're the expert." She scanned the racks. A half-dozen kayaks, easy, plus other watercraft. Either Santa was obsessive about fishing, or he hosted parties here. Summer barbecues. Family getaways, or something else? She pushed the question aside. "Tell me all about how we'll work in tandem, stud."

Jay snorted and launched into a long explanation. Yes, it made sense that the more streamlined designs with a thin profile at the waterline would tip faster and right themselves more easily. The flatter, open variety—what Jay was calling a sit on top, she deciphered from the slurring *siddentawp* sound he seemed to think was a word—would provide a more stable platform for learning and be less likely to end with the two of them soaked and slogging up to the house in defeat. The kayak Jay drew out from storage appeared almost a single piece of molded plastic with plug holes to drain water away. He might not understand the physics or the materials the way she did, but he knew his boats.

"So we'll take this one, and you'll sit in front—see, it'll be easier for me to follow your paddling speed and sync up with you than the other way 'round." He handed her a double-ended paddle.

Light. Good balance. Not anything like the heavy wooden canoe paddles she'd used at day camp as a kid.

"Come sit on the dock with me, and we'll practice strokes and turns."

"Shouldn't we be in the boat for that?"

"Nope. In a tandem, we'll need to coordinate." He pulled her outside, lowered her to the boards, and knelt in front of her. "I'll call out commands for turns, and I'll stop paddling until you've switched up your stroke. You'll see." He stopped adjusting her legs and grip. "Actually, I guess you won't, since you'll be in front. You'll just have to . . ."

"Trust you'll be doing the right things behind me to keep me from dumping us both in the water," she finished, when he seemed unwilling to suggest it. She trusted him. Henry trusted him. They wanted him to trust himself. "That's easy enough."

"Is it?"

She pulled him into a hug, the paddle pressed awkwardly between them. "It is for me, sweetheart. I'm excited to spend the day kayaking with you. I couldn't be in better hands."

He squeezed her hard before pulling away.

"Right. Okay." Switch flipped, he dropped to the boards, sliding his legs alongside hers until their hips were snug. "Let's start with the paddling motion." He laid his hands over hers on the paddle. "Don't worry, ma'am, I'm a professional. I'm told I have great hands."

She giggled and let him play the charmer as they practiced strokes. He suited them up with life jackets afterward. Not too bulky, thankfully. It wasn't long before he held the kayak while she stepped in. He followed her, and they pushed off the dock.

Their first turning attempt resounded with a *smack* of paddles as she swung the wrong way, but they worked out the kinks quickly. Steering a kayak together differed from canoeing. The swaying, the speed, and the coordination didn't line up with her experience. But the lesson he'd given her on the dock helped with managing the double-ended paddle.

Now when he called out a direction change, she obeyed instantly. Left, to avoid the two anglers in the little motorboat with the open cooler. Right, to stay off the shoreline—did she see the mostly submerged tree trunk with the turtle sunning itself? Yes, she'd seen it.

He sprawled his feet in the foot braces near her hips. Tapping his toes, either from nerves or excitement, but eventually even her hyperactive boy settled down. The rhythm of the strokes became second nature, a kind of communion, with him following her pace as she listened for his directions. Give and take.

He checked in often, calling a pause and leaning forward to rub her shoulders. "Still good?"

She answered in the affirmative every time. She might end up sore, but their contentment together mattered more.

Fingers pressed against the back of her neck and pulled away. "No sunburn back here. Legs okay?"

"Fabulous." She made a face at her pale limbs. They never tanned. "As gorgeous as a line of vanilla frosting."

"I love vanilla frosting." Jay's voice turned sly. "If you tell Henry what a good boy I've been today, I bet he'd let me have dessert."

Hell, he didn't need to fill up on sugar. Her stud had the market cornered with natural sweetness. "One-track mind."

"It's a really good track. It takes me all kinds of amazing places. Places you haven't even seen." He paused. "Well, not without a mirror, anyway. Unless you sit around with a mirror between your legs and—"

She dipped her paddle and splashed water his way. They dueled, calling a truce when she leaned too far and Jay had to shift his weight to counterbalance her motion.

"No tipping, remember?"

"Nice save, sweetheart." She didn't have to see him to know how calm and confident he'd grown since this morning. Henry's campaign at work. "When was the last time you rolled a kayak?"

They pushed off in a slow turn, heading back toward the northern end of the lake. Jay keeping track of the time, no doubt.

"Oh, last summer. Pulled a stunt showing off for—" Silence from the back of the kayak. "Umm, the rest of the group. Speed. Flip and roll and bump upright."

Showing off for a woman, or he wouldn't have regrouped in mid-sentence. Last summer rang a bell. She paddled along in rhythm. Two strokes. Three. Four—ohhh. The woman he'd spent the Fourth with. Hadn't Henry said Jay met her kayaking?

She refused to be jealous of the women in Jay's past. He belonged to her now, and he hadn't then, and it wasn't like he had some continuing relationship going on. Lowering her voice to a smug flirt, she tossed words over her shoulder. "I bet you gave her a great ride."

His panicked squawk imitated a bird call. "Gave who what?"

"I mean, fuck, Jay, you give me orgasms like the bank hands out free lollipops." *C'mon, sweetheart, take the hint. I'm not upset, so don't you be guilty.* "Tell me the truth, she was singing your praises when the fireworks went off, right?"

"How'd you know I took her to the—Henry." He laughed. "Okay, no, not during the fireworks. But after, at her place, there was some definite praise."

"Knew it," she singsonged. "That's my stud."

"You don't mind? Really?"

"It was before I knew you could be mine. And you had Henry's permission, right?" He had to have. He wouldn't have done it otherwise.

"Of course. He's the one who suggested the fireworks date. Made the lunch and everything. 'Cause *somebody* needed a little rattling. An intimate dinner for two at home. Gave you a different perspective, didn't it?"

She craned her head over her shoulder. No way would Henry whore out Jay. "He sent you out to fuck another woman so he could see how I'd react to dinner alone with him?"

Jay flashed his sexiest I've-got-a-secret smirk. "The fucking was optional. I could've come home any time after midnight."

She could've been angry. Gotten mad about the manipulation. But it was damn funny. And Jay's date had obviously gone exactly the way he liked it. "Christ, did he tell you how many times I asked where you were?"

"Nope. He was in his studio when I dragged my ass home around sunrise. When he came out, he said the night had been 'promising.'" Jay shrugged, his fire-engine-red life jacket bobbing. "And I got a fantastic fucking, so whatever you did, it totally got his motor running. Plus I got dessert, 'cause he saved me a bowl. Best date ever, maybe."

She snorted. "You fucked and got fucked, and I had to cram my fingers in my panties. So not fair."

"Yeah, no offense to your fingers, but they aren't a match for Henry's cock."

They howled with laughter. When they finally got moving again, occasional giggles escaping, the day's exertion caught up with her. She paddled with less speed and precision.

"Alice, your arms are getting tired. Hold your paddle above the water and lean forward, okay?"

She obeyed. Sharp clicks sounded behind her.

"Okay. Scoot straight back and then rotate your paddle ninety degrees and lay it down between your legs."

She shifted a tentative inch but didn't run into her backrest. The seat folded flat, apparently. Extra gear allowance for a solo outing. She wiggled her way back, pushing off her foot braces, until she sat snug between Jay's thighs.

He sang to her as he lowered his arms, his paddle crossing in front of her stomach. "Put your floppy hat on my shoul-oul-der, whisper in my ear, baby."

"What a crooner." She tipped her face toward his and kissed his neck. "I love you, too, sweetheart."

He pressed his cheek to her head. "You're the first woman I've fallen for, you know. The only special one."

The muscles in his forearms flexed beneath a thin sheen of sweat as he paddled. Sweet, strong Jay. "Not even your first? Your sister's friend?"

He laughed. "No, that was a good summer, fun, but I didn't fall in love until I met Henry. And then it was slow." His words came as smooth as his strokes, easy and relaxed. "Not being submissive, I mean, that was immediate. I couldn't stop myself."

She leaned her weight on his chest. Sunlight flashed off Henry's watch on his wrist.

"But he did. He made me feel okay about myself. He didn't yell at me or tell me I was bad." Wonder filled his voice, light and floating. "Like everything I did pleased him. And when it didn't, he corrected me gently. Taught me a new way. I didn't feel stupid or punished. I was—"

"Happy. Special." She knew that feeling.

"Yeah." His hair rustled against her hat. "Happy. Special."

They glided back to the boathouse at a slow, steady pace. The turtle sunning itself on the broken tree trunk had gained friends. The anglers had moved on. The dip and lift of Jay's paddling seemed as much a part of the landscape as the birds calling to one another from the shoreline.

She sent Henry a silent thanks for giving her this time with their lover. He never hesitated to give them time together, sexual or not. Time to build bonds.

The trees on the hillside blocked her view of the deck as they approached. Kept her from knowing if Henry sat, sketch pad in hand, watching them, too. But she liked to think he was.

They raced up the stairs to the deck after securing the boathouse, Jay's longer legs an advantage as he peeled away from her. Being first to the top meant he had to stop to push the door open. She caught up, breathing hard. They muscled through the space together and collapsed in a heap on the floor.

"What an odd mess of limbs I seem to have left in the middle of the living room." Henry greeted them from a distance, volume growing as he neared. "How strange, that I would so carelessly leave such things lying about for anyone to stumble over."

Jay rolled and thrust an arm upright. Henry's watch glinted. "On time. Five, like you said."

"Quite right. Though perhaps next time the two of you will make a more graceful entrance. One with less potential for injury." Henry pulled Jay to his feet and kissed him soundly before extending his hand to her. "Up we go. Time to shower off your sunscreen." He kissed her with equal attentiveness and studied her face. "Which seems to have been effective. No need to invoke the sunburn clause."

She yanked the fishing hat from her head and sent it sailing across the living room. "No more floppy hats, either."

Jay pulled his shirt over his head, wadded it in a ball, and tossed it after her hat. "No more clothes!"

"No more clothes indeed," Henry murmured. "Go on. You may pick them up after your shower."

They left a trail all the way to the master bathroom, with her bikini top the last piece to come off. After they took quick bathroom breaks in private, Henry's authority resettled over them. A protective coating, like sunscreen. Alice giggled.

Jay trotted obediently into the shower and started the water.

"You're both in high spirits, my dears. Did you enjoy your afternoon?"

"Mm-hmm." She stepped under the spray while Jay gave Henry a thorough report of everything they'd seen on the lake. Face tilted up, she closed her eyes and let the water rush past her ears. She basked in the heat and twirled. Stepped forward to soak her hair. Opened her eyes.

"Beautiful." Henry leaned against the lip where the shower met the wall. Still clothed, not intent on joining them, but watching.

Jay, naked, stood with his back to the shower wall beside Henry. Also watching. His hands rested against the wall, too. Cock hardening, he made no move to touch himself.

"You'll want soap to wash away the sunscreen oils, Alice. Behind you."

She smiled to herself as she popped open the cap on the citrus-scented body wash. So Henry wanted to play a voyeurism game. A little control. She drizzled soap on the shower puff and replaced the bottle.

"From the top down, sweet girl. Slowly. We wouldn't want you to neglect even an inch."

Nope, wouldn't want that. Unless missing a spot would make Henry take charge of her shower himself. Her pulse thumped between her legs, and she squirmed. Her morning had been wonderfully sensual, but please God, let Henry give her his cock tonight.

Too greedy? She washed her neck and shoulders, leaving sharp-smelling lather with Henry's scent behind. Making a half turn, she teased her way down her arm. Water swirled past Jay's curling toes. He deserved Henry's exclusive attention, too. Watching them play would be more hell yes than hardship.

She skimmed the top of her breasts and hid her joy at Jay's soft whimper. Drowning out distraction, she attuned her awareness to the gentle chafing of the shower puff and the slippery suds on her skin. She rubbed tight circles across her stomach, sliding lower on each pass.

"Turn this way, my lovely girl." Henry stared with dark intensity.

She sucked in a breath through her teeth. The water beat down on her back, strong and thuddy like her suede.

"Spread your legs."

She widened her stance. Her hand crossed below her navel.

At the far side of the shower, Jay arched his hips forward. Even with his cock straining toward her, he obeyed Henry's order not to touch.

Henry sported a shapely bulge in his slacks.

Her eyes closed and body shuddered without consulting her brain. Clutching the soap-slick mesh, she slipped her hand between her legs, replacing reality with the slow slide of Jay's tongue and the thick heat of Henry's cock.

Her moan was doubled, echoing. The acoustics of shower tile accounted for a fraction, not the full echo. She tugged her lip into her mouth and bit down. Tug and release, over and over, mimicking the motion across her sex.

"Alice, stop."

Henry's command halted her in midstroke.

She clamped down on the whine in the back of her throat.

"You've neglected your legs. Do give them a thorough washing, please."

His sly tone and neutral face made imagining him a controlling bastard keeping her from her orgasm easy. But the flutter behind his fly proved he wasn't indifferent. Just teasing her, and Jay, and himself by making her wait. A patient man with a tempting cock. The definition of hell?

Thank God he made up for it by taking her to visit heaven so often.

Fuck if he had the patent on devilish. Raising her leg, she settled her foot on the shower bench. Let them look. Let them see her with her legs spread, lips swollen and flushed beneath a covering of white foam. An Alice-approved audience of two, all bright-eyed love and lust and—respect. Water ran in streams down her stomach and through her curls to rinse her clean.

"Our girl has a fine sense of performance art, doesn't she, my boy?" Henry took in Jay with a lingering glance and an approving hum. "You're doing well to wait so long."

She swept the shower puff down, rocking her hips with each stretch to her ankle. Lowering her leg, she added a shimmy and a flirty wink over her shoulder as she turned. "I hope you don't mind. It's so much easier to reach this way."

"By all means, Alice." Henry growled the words as she raised her other leg to the bench, her back to her boys.

Bending forward, she lathered soap from hip to ankle with her sex on full display. Her choice. Her power. Her invitation.

"I would hate for you to strain yourself." Henry's rumbling hum made her legs tremble. "Let's make it even easier, shall we?"

Jay's breathy, gratifying whine suggested the waiting game had reached an end.

"Jay, go and give our girl a hand. *Just* a hand, please."

She groaned. Christ. He meant to kill her.

"She'll need help with her back first. Why don't you wash it for her?"

They followed Henry's instructions, washing each other with rapt attention and simmering arousal, rinsing with roaming hands. When he ordered Jay to kiss her, their lips fused with unprecedented intensity.

"Step back to the wall, my boy, and take our sweet girl with you."

Henry's directions left them gazing at him through a curtain of falling water. Jay's back rested against the shower wall. Hers rested against his chest.

Jay worked his fingers between her legs. Deep, sucking kisses massaged her neck. His cock prodded her lower back.

But what she loved best, what made her knees wobble as Jay thrust his fingers inside and drew out her orgasm, was the water-blurred sight of Henry watching with one hand squeezing his cock through his pants.

Not even the fun of giving Jay a handjob once she'd recovered enough to stand compared. Though matching Henry's seven-stroke prowess for bringing Jay off in the shower satiated her competitive streak. Aww yeah. Nailed it.

She couldn't shake her smug smile as Henry toweled them dry and heaped praise and kisses upon them. Nor as he wrapped them in robes and ordered them to the kitchen to help prepare dinner. Breakfast for dinner. Jay's favorite. Another reward for being such a good boy today.

She cracked eggs for omelets while Henry diced meat and vegetables and Jay set the table. As comfortable a rhythm for three in the kitchen as kayaking had been for the two of them. They ate on the deck, lingering to watch the sun set over the western mountains. The slight chill in the air wasn't the cause of her shiver when Henry remarked they'd best clear the dishes quickly. He expected them naked and in bed in fifteen minutes.

They left the dishes to dry in the rack and made it to bed in thirteen.

"You're gonna get fucked so hard." Jay's eager whisper broke the silence. "God, it's gonna be beautiful."

They knelt naked on the bed, side by side, waiting for Henry's arrival. She tilted her head toward her playmate and whispered back. "How do you know it won't be you? Maybe I'll be the one watching the show."

"Nope." A slow smirk crossed his face. "It'll be you."

Okay, maybe. And yeah, she desperately wanted it. The suggestion and her own nudity, her awareness of the air passing between her thighs, provided a strong prompt for her body. Readying her to accept Henry's cock. Squeezing and welcoming the wet slide in response.

"It could be you." Her protest carried more form than belief.

"Nuh-uh. I got to play with you all day, and I got to come three times." His firm headshake scattered strands of black hair across his forehead. "Besides—"

Henry stepped into the room.

Jay bowed his head. Perfect stillness. She copied him, her heart hammering.

Henry paced around the foot of the bed without speaking. Undressing with slow precision, he hung his pants over a chair. Lowered his boxers, his cock hard and leaking already.

She squirmed, the tiniest shift of her hips, wishing for something to ease the ache building in her. The empty need. Something. Ha. As if she didn't know what she sought. The cock her covetous gaze tracked. Thick and hard and shadowed with color.

Henry gripped the base, and her muscles tightened. He angled his cock away from his body, positioned a condom on the tip, and rolled it down with exquisite patience.

It's me. Me-me-me.

"Such a shameless, wanton show our girl put on in the shower." Far from anger, his gruff tone streamed praise. "All for our viewing pleasure, my boy. Her initiative deserves a reward."

Henry rubbed his palm down the shaft of his cock and over his balls. His breath escaped in a hiss. He squeezed tight.

Her whimper matched Jay's.

"I was quite tempted to take you in the shower this evening, my dear girl. Waiting has made me more impatient to sample your depths."

He inhaled, slow and deep. "You're ready. Your eagerness scents the air. Your wet thighs shine for me. Show me. Spread your labia with your fingers and show me what's mine, Alice."

Fumbling and bumping as she rushed to obey, she splayed herself open, palms against her thighs and fingertips clutching slippery skin. Desire poured forth with the hope he'd see the greedy anticipation he caused. The near touch of her thumbs made her clit thump.

Rumbling approval, he ordered her to lie down. "Stretch out. Arms above your head. Quickly, now."

She lay back. Jay hadn't budged an inch.

"You as well, my boy. Lie on your side. Stay close to our girl."

Her boys moved together, but the similarities ended there. Jay lay still at her side, erect but seemingly content, his eyes gleaming. Henry grabbed her wrists and pulled them to her chest, wrapping his arm beneath her as he rolled her onto her side between the men. Raising her knee with his other hand, he breathed hot against her neck as he thrust.

She groaned her pleasure at the penetration she'd waited for all day.

Her body parted in a frictionless slide, absorbing the force of his thrust and displacing it, sending ripples rolling through her.

He bucked his hips without pulling back and growled in her ear. "Is this what you needed? What you missed this morning?"

She nodded against his shoulder behind her. Fuck yes. She needed this every morning and noon and night.

"With words, Alice." He pulled his hips back, his cock so close to leaving her.

She whined an urgent plea.

"Say what you need."

"Need your cock. Need it." She sucked in a breath, her lungs tight, his hand pressing her wrists between her breasts and making her work for air. "Please, Henry. Need you, all of you."

He thrust hard. His tight grip on her thigh kept her from sprawling into Jay.

God, that low, guttural moan couldn't be hers. Had to be. Inches away, Jay hadn't made that sound.

"You have it, my sweet Alice." Henry's rapid thrusts left her shaking. "Everything I have to give you. All of it yours."

Her vision blurred. She grew numb where their bodies didn't touch and burned where they did. The heart of the fire, the source of all heat, centered her awareness. Her body clenched him with a rhythmic pulse as he advanced and retreated, advanced and retreated, a battle promising victory for all. She babbled a string of incoherent pleas.

"Yes," Henry growled, his melodic baritone grown hoarse. "You make me burn."

She wailed. Stiffened as fire consumed her and her hips battered him with speed beyond her control. Offering no water to douse the flames, he rolled them onto her stomach and kept going. Yes. More. She flexed her ass and pushed up.

Her arms lay curled and trapped beneath her as her face met the pillow, his body a red-hot brand at her back. He drove her deep into the mattress. Soft sheets clutched at her stomach, her breasts, her thighs. Tried to drown her in their cool waves. No. No, not yet. "No waves," she mumbled. "Don't stop. Want the fire. All fire."

A huff of breathless laughter tickled her ear.

A pause, his. A whine, hers.

"Hush your worries, my sweet girl." Hoisting her back and up, he settled her on her arms and knees. Thrust deep and drove a moan from her. "I've fire enough left for you."

The ocean of silk fell out of focus beneath her. Musky maleness, clean sweat and pure desire, surrounded her. She gripped the sheets in numb fingers and reveled in the hard slap of Henry's hips. Shuddered as his hands spanned her back, thumbs pressing on her spine and fingers curling around her sides below her ribs.

Heat-friction formulae. Fluid dynamics equations. Variables dancing in the flames as Henry fucked her hard and deep, until he'd fucked the last thought from her head. Until they became beings of motion and emotion.

Faster and faster, hips driving, linear growth in speed bringing exponential growth in feeling. She burned with love, with lust, with Henry. Her eyes closed tight. Stuttering groans slipped from her throat.

"That's it, dearest. Burn it all away. All but this."

He thrust, and her scream rivaled the crackle of the flames in her mind as they came together. Impurities burned away. Shining, heated perfection left behind. Solid. Strong. Lasting.

Henry tumbled them to the bed, his body curled around hers. He pressed a kiss to her hair, nuzzling the curve of her ear. An attempt to distract her, maybe, from his hand slipping between them and holding the condom secure as his cock withdrew and didn't return.

She sighed, a quiet protest.

Humming to her, he offered another kiss.

Henry stretched past her shoulder, a shadow behind her eyelids. She blinked the world into focus.

He cupped Jay's cheek, fingers threading through his hair with tenderness. "Did you enjoy the show?"

"Yes, Henry. Thank you." With a full Jay-smile, all bright eyes and not a trace of jealousy or disappointment, he winked at her. "Told you it'd be fucking beautiful. Or beautiful fucking."

She giggled. He was incorrigible. Adorable. Theirs. "C'mere for a kiss, you silly boy."

He looked to Henry first, naturally.

"As she says, my dear boy. Kisses first, washcloth after."

If the kisses numbered more than two, and the washcloth-fetching delayed several minutes—well, that, too, was only natural.

She lazed between the sheets, waiting on her boys to emerge from the bathroom. Ladies first seemed a staple of Henry's lexicon, both in bed and out, so she'd already finished her presleep routine. Henry had bathed her first, his hands sure and tender on her sex, his eyes soft.

She yawned and stretched, pointing her toes and splaying her fingers. Seldom-used muscles reminded her of their vigorous workout today, on the lake and off it. She closed her eyes and sighed. Henry's idea of a weekend getaway might kill her. But Christ, she'd die happy.

"Uh-oh. Alice has orgasm smile. We weren't in the bathroom that long, were we?" The mattress rocked as Jay flopped beside her. "I gotta brush my teeth faster if I'm missing spontaneous orgasms."

"Shortchange your brushing and you'll lose your beautiful smile," she murmured without bothering to open her eyes. "And then I'd be missing that."

He leaned in and pecked her cheek, his breath minty fresh. "If you think it's beautiful, I guess I'd better keep it."

A *click* brought deeper darkness behind her eyelids. Henry, turning off the light on his way to bed. The sheets lifted to her right, cooler air slipping beneath and Henry with it. She hadn't expected to end up in the middle tonight, not when Jay needed cuddling more than she did.

An offer to switch flitted through her mind, dismissed as Henry laid his hand on her stomach. If he intended to play musical sleeping spots, he'd manage it subtly without saying a word.

Jay tangled his feet with hers, teasing and pushing, and she indulged him. A squirmy, playful boy not ready for sleep. Not seeking sex, though they all slept nude in what had seemed a decadent thrill to her at first.

Wearing pajamas had been a habit ingrained after sharing a bedroom for years. With Ollie, at home. With roommates through college and afterward. She hadn't stayed the night with lovers after sex or let one stay with her. Even getting her own place hadn't broken the habit. Only Henry had done that. He and Jay slept naked, so she did, too, on nights she spent with them.

Now she spent every night and never wore pajamas. She wore nothing unless she was bleeding, and only underwear then. Not even as a silent "no, honey, not tonight." The panties acted as her nonverbal clue. If Henry planned to play penetrative games, she'd need a minute. Not help he required, because he probably paid closer attention to her cycle than she did, but the panties added to her comfort. And he hadn't objected.

But tonight she lay bare beneath the sheets and pressed between two warm, naked bodies. What would Henry say if she came to bed covered from neck to ankles? Order her to take them off. Turn up the thermostat. Cut strategic holes?

She giggled, bobbling his hand on her stomach. No, the scissor-wielder would be Jay. He'd give her an adorably innocent smile and insist he was just helping.

Henry hummed. "What's made you so amused?"

Opening her eyes, she rolled her head to face him. He lay shadowed in the darkness but beautiful to her eyes nonetheless, and at her side. Always. "Trying to remember when it became normal to sleep naked."

"You didn't before?" Jay paused his footsie campaign. "Why not?"

"Did you? Before you moved in with Henry?"

"Well, yeah. Once I had my own place. Slept naked, watched TV naked, ate dinner naked." Tossing out a smile, he ran tickle-fingers up her arm. "Who needs clothes?"

Mmm, naked Jay sprawled on the sofa. Across the dinner table. "Obviously not you, stud."

"Whatever Alice's reasons, perhaps we ought to be grateful for how quickly she has grown accustomed to our preference for skin-to-skin contact, hmm?" Henry stroked her stomach with his thumb, his fingers spread and resting above her curls. "A lovely way to enhance our bond with her."

Jay eagerly agreed, bouncing the mattress as he assured them he'd be more than happy to demonstrate his gratitude whenever they desired.

Henry pulled him in and worked magic above her, relaxing Jay with a single kiss as if he drew out every drop of excess, playful energy and stored it away to return at a more appropriate time. They broke apart and snuggled down on either side of her.

"Nudity encourages pair bonding and enhances calm, soothing feelings." Henry picked up the conversation as if he hadn't interrupted it to care for Jay. Of course not. Their needs were never an interruption for him. His tone turned sly. "When it isn't enhancing other needs."

If denying her pajamas had been a calculated part of his strategy, she'd better get a bigger chessboard to play with Henry. "Is that why you started extending our time? Letting me spend the night?"

"Aside from the two of us simply desiring your company?" He squeezed her waist in a half hug. "Certainly. The more I was able to increase your attachment to us without speaking of it, the more your comfort level grew."

"Lowering my defenses." He'd waged a sneaky little war under her nose. No—under her clothes. She snickered.

"Parents of newborns are encouraged to spend time holding their offspring skin to skin."

She pushed at his shoulder, a teasing shove. "I know you're not calling me an infant."

Henry chuckled. "No, dearest, certainly not. But you are a new member of our family. The more Jay and I snuggle against your bare skin, the more the chemicals in our bodies attune to each other." He inhaled at her neck. "Recognize our bond with you and wish to spend even more time deepening it."

"So I was right all along." An unexpected victory. "Love is just addictive substances changing my brain structure, and you're my dealer."

"If it helps you to think of it in such a way." He kissed her neck. "Though I would never say love is 'just' anything."

"For me it's home." Jay wriggled until she made room for him to lie with his head cradled at her neck. "Wherever I am, I know where home is. And that's you and Henry."

Christ, he'd make her cry. She closed her eyes tight. Jay made the most intimate complexities easy to explain in two words. It's home. Simple, and somehow everything.

"Exactly right, my boy. So it is."

Jay's happy little sigh tickled her skin. He slung his arm over her alongside Henry's. Sleep came courtesy of all-natural, chemically induced contentment. Who needed pajamas when they had love?

CHAPTER 10

"Allllllice. My sweet girl." Henry's breath warmed her ear.

She grunted into the pillow. It felt early. Opening her eyes to check the time would take too much effort, but it felt early.

"I thought we might enjoy the sunrise."

Was he joking? That would make it, what, five o'clock? On a Sunday morning. Was this really something she needed to be awake for?

"Sleeping," she mumbled. "Take Jay."

A hard cock pressed into the small of her back. "I'm taking *you*, my dear."

She squirmed, her hips pressing back of their own accord. A sexy wake-up call appealed, so long as she didn't have to move too much. Or open her eyes.

A chuckle rolled from across the room.

"Not this time, Alice." Jay sounded awake. Like, awake-awake, not just-rolled-out-of-bed awake. "I'm on my own this morning."

She cracked open an eyelid. One of the lamps brightened the room. Somewhere behind her, thankfully, not the one in front of her face.

Jay had donned biking gear, tight little shorts and one of his sweat-wicking T-shirts. Damn. Sorry she'd slept through him dressing.

He stepped closer to the bed and tapped the nightstand twice with his palm. "But I left you all the gear you'll need."

She tipped her head back. Her brain took a moment to interpret the dark outline beside his hand. Binoculars. She snorted. Figured he hadn't been kidding. "Bird-watching?"

"Bird-watching," Jay confirmed. "Have fun with that. I'll be flying down hills."

"And crawling back up them," she grumbled at him. Teasing him was too enjoyable to pass up. "So have fun with that."

"I will." Bending down, he kissed her cheek and Henry's. "See you both later."

"Don't forget to grab your bag from the kitchen. I've packed high-energy snacks for you." Henry leaned over her shoulder to kiss Jay more thoroughly. "Be safe. Call if you run into trouble."

Jay promised to bike safely, be back around lunchtime, and call if he'd be late. And then he was gone, wide-awake and eager and out the door. At five in the morning. He'd grown up rural, even more than she had. He might miss biking less-traveled roads, even with all the hours he spent roaming city streets.

Henry descended on her shoulder, nipping and biting with gentle tugs. Parts of her were definitely waking up.

"Are we really going bird-watching?"

"Mmm." He sucked at the cord of muscle running up toward her neck. "We're really going outside, Alice. What you watch while we're there is entirely your choice." He rolled away, and his feet thudded against the floor. "Best bring the binoculars in case you want them, though."

A drawer opened, and a zipper, and the sliding doors to the deck. Footsteps faded and returned. The lamp switched off, leaving the room bathed in pale predawn light.

The binoculars landed beside her chest. "Hold these, my dear."

She'd hardly gotten her fingers around the strap when she was scooped up, blanket and all. He carried her out, pausing to let her tug the screen door closed behind them. A few minutes' work had them settled in a deck chair, the binoculars on the table beside them along with Henry's cellphone and a sketch pad and pencils.

Yesterday they'd gone inside and played in bed with Jay. Henry obviously had something else in mind today. Being naked and in his lap boded well. Except Henry had thrown on a robe. Soft and warm as it was, it wasn't *him*. She'd much rather touch skin to skin, especially if she was going to be woken up and dragged outside so early on a non-workday.

Yawning, she rested her face near his neck. He tucked the blanket around her shoulders with care before slipping his arms beneath.

"It's all right to sleep, Alice, though I do hope you'll enjoy this." He clasped her waist in a gentle squeeze. "Perhaps such an early arousal on vacation is a bit much to ask of my sleeping beauty after a late night." His voice vibrated in her ear. "Do you see the light beginning its journey?"

The deck faced south-southeast, out over the lake. The edge of the sun invisible yet, but its effects made its presence known—the lightening sky, the orange-and-purple tint, the calls of birds in the morning mist.

"It's beautiful."

"Predictable," Henry murmured.

A boring word, yet he'd said it with approval. The way she might when a materials test returned the result she'd expected—the proper tolerance for heat or weight or other stresses the design demanded—and a project could move forward.

"Predictable?"

"Mm-hmm. Predictable. Sunrise. Predictable in its timing. In its path." His stroke across her stomach lengthened, his palm running up and over her breast, and she shivered. "We know where and when it will occur every day. It keeps no secrets. It spills its light across the earth with a steady hand."

He swept down again, not stopping at her stomach but rolling over the top of her thigh. She parted her legs in answer to his unspoken demand.

"Fingers first, Alice." He stroked the inside of her thigh.

She clutched fistfuls of his robe.

"The smallest rays of light, tentative tendrils creeping across the landscape, outlining what they find there."

His touch matched his words, slow and light, tracing the outline of her sex, the outer lips as they swelled, the inner concealing the slickness building within. Jesus. She'd never look at sunrise the same way.

"And all the while, the sun is rising. Its reach is growing. Steady and patient." He nuzzled her neck with soft kisses. "It knows time is on its side."

Henry, her sun, imposing his will on the land below. Mmm. The sweet compulsion and confidence she loved. "Because the sun knows it always wins. Every day the landscape submits."

He tapped her clitoris, and her hips jumped. "This isn't about winning, my dear girl. Not like that."

Returning to soothing strokes, he teased the seam of her lips and parted her with slow attention. "The sun offers light and warmth, and the earth responds with a welcoming embrace. The flowers turn to greet the day, their petals opening."

He added more pressure, opening her, eagerness seizing her as he circled her entrance with a single finger. "Their nectar sweetly flowing."

He thrust. One hand held her hips down as the other moved. He pumped steadily, quick to add a second finger. "Watch the lake, sweet girl. When the sun crests the horizon, the water ripples and shines like colored glass."

She turned obedient eyes toward the lake, though her mind fell prey to Henry's fingers within her and his hard cock pressing from the other side, his robe between them.

He abandoned her hips for her stomach, sliding over the curl-covered curve that led to fiery bliss. He rubbed her clitoris with lazy strokes while his fingers inside her increased their speed. She whimpered at the contrast.

The sun reached its tipping point, a broad curve almost too much to watch, at the southeastern end of the lake. The light spread across the water, burning away the morning mist, leaving shining reflections to sparkle and dance.

"Oh! It's beautiful, Henry." Her words emerged in a breathy rasp, her mouth too dry and her breath too short for anything else.

"Beautiful. Predictable. The sun spills itself out across land and water every morning. Always the same. And never the same." He spoke directly into her ear, a hushed, urgent rumble, as he drew her closer to climax. "A unique beauty each and every time. A fresh palette of colors. The earth stretches, and wakes, and breathes—"

Tension tightened her limbs. Her breath stopped in the split second between need and fulfillment. His fingers pushed her forward, made her body wake for him. Her cries rivaled the birds. Her hips rocked with more speed than the waves lapping at the lakeshore. Unfettered exuberance rippled as if she were what Henry named her, a landscape of natural, wild beauty.

She trembled with aftershocks.

Resting his hands on her thighs, he pressed his lips above her ear. "And begins every day with a glorious climax stirring everything touched by the sun's heat." His quiet chuckle tickled. "Good morning, Alice."

"Henry?" Jumbled thoughts coalesced. The sunrise this morning. The way he made every moment special, memorable.

"Yes, my sweet girl?"

His words and his touch stirred something deeper than lust. Nothing before had come close to the intensity of her life with Henry and Jay. *I was sleeping. And now I'm not.*

"Thank you for waking me up." She managed a shaky, intimate whisper.

His hum told her she'd pleased him, though long moments passed before he spoke. "I find great joy in it, Alice. Thank you for trusting me enough to allow it."

She twisted sideways and pressed kisses to his neck.

He patted her thigh and encouraged her to turn fully, helping her shuffle and wiggle and slide until she'd settled herself straddling his hips. The heat of his erection radiated between her legs. Her movements had dislodged his robe. The knotted belt served no purpose, not with the fabric gaping. She nudged her hips forward, her weight on his cock drawing a sharp breath from Henry.

"Can I have this, too?" She teased with her smile, folding her arms across his chest.

"There are condoms in the pockets of my robe, Alice." He tucked her hair behind her ear. "I certainly wasn't saving them for anyone else."

Score. She quested for a condom. If it necessitated shifting her weight while she dug for the pockets, and if that meant she rocked against his erection, well that was hardly her fault, was it?

She smirked.

The blanket slipped down her back as she sat up.

He smirked.

But she found a condom all too quickly, and he allowed her to unroll it over him herself, his hand holding his cock steady at the base. They'd been skin to skin a moment ago. And when he'd slid between her thighs yesterday in the shower. Henry. Not latex.

Even the thrill of being on top, of watching her body accept him as she sank onto his cock, didn't silence the voice in her head. This power belonged to her. She sat flush against him, tightening and releasing muscles to enjoy his thickness buried inside her. Feeling him bare would be negotiable, wouldn't it? Surely he wanted to forgo condoms, too.

He watched her with narrowed eyes, though that might be the sun. Her body blocked a slice of the light. She might have a halo, her outline backlit by the rising sun. Maybe he allowed her to ride him for the aesthetic high.

His reason for granting her power remained irrelevant to her pursuit. The important things numbered two. One, she had him pinned under her. Two, she intended to give up condoms for good.

Steadying her weight with her hands on his shoulders, she rose and sank. Henry cupped her ass. She repeated the motion and touched her tongue to her lips.

"Henry, you know I'm consistent about taking my birth control pills." Ease into it, nice and slow. Like a lazy morning fuck in a deck chair. "And we've been monogamous for months. Most of a year."

"Polyamorous."

"What?" His quick response hadn't been in her script.

"The word you want is polyamorous. A closed, faithful poly relationship. A triad, if you like." Gripping her ass tight, he interrupted her rhythm with a sharp upward thrust.

Fuck, he was fantastic and thick and—no. Focus. Get to the point before he fucked her brains out.

"Okay. Polyamorous. Whatever we're calling it, I have the pregnancy issue covered and there's no threat of disease. So, I want—" God that felt good. She rocked harder, grinding her pelvis down and relishing the pressure against her clit. "I want us to stop using condoms."

He spread his hands wide, lifting her ass and letting her slide down his cock from her own weight. Unhurried, he slipped fingers beneath her and stroked her sex from behind. "You've given the practical reasons why condoms are unnecessary, but I have yet to hear why you wish to eliminate them."

"Don't you?" She'd assumed he'd jump at the chance. Every other guy had pressured her to give them up, and she'd refused every time. But Henry had never been like every other guy.

"Ah—that isn't the issue, Alice. Tell me why you desire this change." He brushed her with a fluttering touch where their bodies joined. Rubbing, back and forth, spreading her slick lubrication.

"Because I—because—" Fuck. Her train of thought derailed between Henry's cock and his fingers. "Wouldn't it be better?"

"For myself and Jay, or for you, dearest?"

"Both. Right?"

He wore his patiently-waiting face. His fingers stilled. His cock stood hard but at rest within her. She might be on top, but he owned the pace. He'd make her wait until he had his answers.

"Because I've never, umm . . ." Sighing, she struggled to put her certainty into words. "I guess because I trust you. I love you, and I want to feel your skin sliding against me, and I want to feel you climaxing inside me. I never let anyone—I didn't trust them enough or feel comfortable enough." A wash of heat covered her shoulders and swept down her back, excitement and embarrassment too intertwined to separate. "And you might let Jay's tongue play washcloth sometimes if we didn't have a latex-and-spermicide aftertaste."

Henry surprised her with a fierce kiss, lifting his legs and rocking her forward. Raising a hand to her head, he drew her closer for a harsh clash of lips and pushed his tongue into her mouth the instant she opened to him.

Growling, he let her go.

She panted to catch her breath.

"Those are fine reasons, Alice. You have the loveliest thoughts." He stroked her back, encouraging her to sit up, settling her weight across his lap once more. "I'll think on your suggestion. Will you think on one for me, as well?"

"Of course I will." Whatever the proposal, he wouldn't force her to accept his view. He'd only ask she consider it.

"Without impugning your responsible nature, if I may point out, pills are a daily method prone to error and sensitive to timing." Slowly, he traced the slope of her pelvis and cradled her lower abdomen. He blew out a breath and glided his hands to her breasts, gentle and firm at once, thumbs rubbing. "Unless you've a wish for a child soon—in which case we've other things to discuss—you might consider a more long-term management method."

"What, you mean a patch? Or shots?" She let the mention of

motherhood slip by. No fucking way she'd entertain a discussion of that now. In a decade. Or never. No matter how much she liked the tender way he held her.

"More long-term than that, dearest. An implant or an IUD, perhaps. Something proven reliable and requiring no action on your part to maintain."

She'd nixed them before because of the upfront investment and the rarity of partnered sex in her nights. But now she got laid more every month than she had in some years. Work insurance would cover the cost. She wouldn't have to worry about slipups.

"I'll make an appointment. To talk over the options." A small concession. If finding a method that worked as well as her pill with less effort convinced Henry of her safety enough to go condom-free . . . so worth the switch.

"Lovely." Holding her steady, he leaned in and kissed her, his mouth slow and sure.

She rocked in his lap, moaning each time he flexed his hips. The sun warmed her back, and the blanket covered nothing but Henry's legs behind her.

"Hold on to me, dearest."

She gripped his shoulders, balancing her weight.

He spread his hands and clasped her ass. Lifted her. Let her fall. The angle put pressure on her clit, created friction as her flesh dragged along his, made her hips jump and her thighs clench and her body respond with a ready rush of new lubrication.

"That's it, Alice, my sweet girl." He slipped his hold lower with every thrust, until she alone controlled their movement. "You know the rhythm you want."

She pushed herself, chasing the building need, the excitement of his reactions adding to her own. The way he stared into her eyes. The way his lips parted and his chest expanded as his breathing grew rapid.

He jerked his hips beneath her in counterpoint, as if he couldn't hold still any longer when her body gripped him so. He stroked with firm pressure, his left hand holding her open to him while his right moved, fingers slick, rubbing and circling and Jesus was he going to—

Eyes closing, back arching, she shuddered. Her orgasm came hard and fast and violent, astonishment and pleasure rolling through her in equal measure. Henry groaned, clutching her painfully, holding their bodies together as he gave three hard thrusts.

She collapsed onto his chest. Moving would be impossible, which suited her fine. His every breath resonated in her bones. As did his finger inside her. Alongside his cock. Not where she'd thought he'd go, but fireworks-worthy nonetheless. Fullness and pressure. She'd been so sure this time, and her certainty had brought on her climax.

She burrowed her face against his neck. Her body shivered in reaction. She wanted him in her ass. Fingers. Toys. Whatever he preferred to start with. However he'd played with Jay that ended with a blissful look of love and trust and incredible pleasure.

He shifted, coaxing her hips up. She feared he'd insist they go inside and clean up when she yearned for cuddling, but he stripped off the condom and pulled his robe across his lap before pressing her back down. He wrapped the condom in a tissue and laid it on the side table.

"Henry?"

"Hmm?" He reached past her, grasping the edge of the blanket and tugging it over her back.

"You've been—all weekend—you've—your fingers—" For fuck's sake, was she a scared virgin? About anal, yeah, okay. Even if she wanted it. "You've been awfully handsy with my ass."

"Handsy, my dear? Is that a euphemism for fondling? Caressing? Rubbing?" He trailed his fingers down her back.

She squirmed.

The movement stopped. "Does it make you uncomfortable, Alice?"

"I—no. Not uncomfortable, exactly." Not at all, exactly.

"What, exactly, sweet girl?"

"You haven't, I mean, you've teased, but you haven't . . . penetrated."

"Ah." His slow turn brought his mouth in line with her ear. "Did you want me to?"

He'd dropped into the deep rumble that made her shiver from the inside out.

"I think yes." The thrill of saying it, of admitting it, quaked in her gut.

"Good." He kissed her forehead. Sliding one hand up her spine, he cradled her ass more tightly against him with the other. "We'll play new games soon."

"You always do that."

"Do what, dearest?"

"Wait. Wait for us to ask. To say what we want." From the very first night. He would've walked away if she hadn't asked for what she wanted. Even if he wanted it too.

"It means more to me to know you want the things I offer you, Alice."

He pushed her, sometimes. Prodded. Tested her reactions.

"That you accept them not only willingly but eagerly."

He never moved forward unless he was certain she felt ready. Confidence, caution, and care. Her Henry. She squeezed him tight.

"I don't think we're gonna eat outside today."

The rain came down in fits and starts, stray drops pinging off the windows and beading up on the deck. The sustained patter grew into a steady drumming. Wind whipped the trees. Anyone hosting a Memorial Day picnic on Sunday afternoon was destined for disappointment.

"No, it seems not, my dear."

She wandered back to the kitchen. If Henry's presence wasn't lure enough, the eggplant parmesan bubbling in the oven smelled intoxicating. The garlic butter he slathered on a split baguette loaf added to the enticement.

They'd spent most of the morning cuddling on the deck, but that didn't stop her from pressing herself to his back now. No such thing as too much touching. She wrapped her arms around his waist and rested her chin on his shoulder. "Big lunch."

Chuckling, he kissed her cheek. "Half of it will disappear into Jay's stomach once he finishes his shower. And a large, late lunch eliminates the need for supper. A light snack later will suffice to keep your energy up."

Mmm. They'd expended lots of energy at sunrise. He might have more games in store for them tonight. "I like things that keep you up, too."

His soft snort rippled his stomach under her arms. "You and Jay do that quite well on your own."

"What do I do well?" Jay called to them from the bedroom doorway. "Aside from everything, I mean."

She burst into laughter. Not at his words. She wouldn't have expected less from confident comedian Jay, and he was in fine form. But she'd mistakenly assumed he might, at the very least, dress himself.

He strode out to the kitchen naked. "What?"

She shook her head, wheezing as she attempted to catch her breath.

"Henry said I should clean up." Jay shot them a sly smile. "He'll wanna inspect the job I did."

"In a moment, my boy." Henry finished anointing the garlic bread.

She released him and stepped back, her laughter coming under control.

He tented the bread with foil and swapped it for the eggplant, adjusting the oven temperature. "Very well. We have fifteen minutes until lunch."

Jay grinned. Henry stepped out from behind the kitchen counter. She rested her elbows on top and leaned forward, waiting for the show.

"Stand straight. Arms out." Henry delivered precise commands in a deep voice. "Feet spread."

Jay jumped to comply, standing like a living da Vinci drawing. His chest rose and fell as Henry circled him. God, he was the most beautiful boy. Long, lean muscles. Squeaky clean from his shower. She licked her lips, a bid to make him blush, and Henry winked at her over Jay's shoulder.

"Let's see how you've done." He ran his finger down the curve of Jay's ear. Flicked the earlobe. "Did you wash behind your ears, my boy?"

"Yes, Henry."

Henry leaned in and traced the same line with his tongue.

Jay's breath stuttered.

"Mmm. So you did. Well done." He ran his hands along the tops of Jay's arms. Over the gently rounded biceps. The sloping forearms. The farther Henry stretched his arms, the closer he stepped to Jay's back. He slipped his hands under Jay's and curled the fingers upward. "Beneath your fingernails?"

"Yes, Henry." Jay etched anticipation in every syllable.

Henry hummed. "I'll require a closer look to be certain." He bent Jay's arms inward, bringing his hands above his shoulders. "No obvious dirt particles. A taste test will tell us the full tale."

One digit at a time, from pinky to thumb, disappeared between Henry's lips and emerged sucked clean. Whining like an anxious puppy, Jay scrunched his eyes shut.

He scraped his teeth across his lower lip and swallowed hard. His pose pushed his chest forward. Sparse black hair formed a soft, swirling T down his abdomen, past the rib cage heaving with his breath. The ridges of muscle alongside his narrow, boyish waist led straight to his erect cock jumping with excitement.

Arousing. Sweet. Jay in two words.

Lucky bastard. Also Jay in two words. Affection, not jealousy, smoldered in her chest as Henry pressed himself to Jay's back and murmured in his ear. She bathed in the exquisite empathy of one who'd stood in the same position filled with desperate desire, the urgent need to please.

Jay raised his arms straight up, and Henry inspected his sides. Checking for cleanliness required slow strokes from the curve of Jay's underarms along his ribs to his waist. Henry held him in a tight grip, his fingers pushing into sleek skin. Jay's cock bobbed against his stomach.

She breathed out easy and left her arousal to simmer. She'd had Henry to herself all morning. Jay hadn't gotten laid today. If he wanted attention, time with Henry's hands and mouth on his body, he deserved Henry's indulgence.

Pushing forward, she hugged the counter. The edge dug into her stomach the way Henry's table had in August. She'd stretched across a vast expanse and waited to see what he'd do. What she'd given him permission to do to her.

Henry spanned those sweet ridges of muscle arrowing toward Jay's cock. Told him what a good, clean boy he was while Jay emitted near-silent whimpers.

She vibrated with readiness to carry out any task he might ask of her. The words she ached to hear went something like *fetch the lube from the bedroom, my dear, and we'll see if our boy looks as happy as you do when bent over the table and fucked.*

Henry raised his mouth from Jay's neck.

She bounced on her toes. Ready for anything. Commands, demands, requests, suggestions. Whatever he wanted, the instant he wanted it.

Henry opened his mouth.

A shrill ring sent her bolting upright.

Jay groaned.

"That's time, my dears." Henry nodded toward her. "Alice, turn off the timer and rescue the garlic bread from the oven, please. It seems we're ready to eat."

Holy fuck. No more showtime? But—but the table. It was right there. And Jay was right there. And she wanted to see—

The timer rang again.

"Alice, the bread, please."

"Right. Right. Sorry, I'm on it." Her back protested the bending to retrieve the goods. Ugh. Too much exercise yesterday. Overexertion had settled in her muscles. She turned off the oven and set the pan on the stove.

Cock wilting, Jay heaved an exaggerated sigh. "I love garlic bread. Who knew it could be such a buzz kill."

"Vampires," Henry deadpanned.

Jay snorted. She followed suit. Their eyes caught. Grins widened. Heads shook.

"Go and throw on some clothes, please, my boy. I declare you clean enough for lunch." Henry patted Jay's ass and sent him on his way. Jay made it four steps before Henry called after him, "Do try to stay clean. I'll finish my inspection this evening, and I would hate for you to fail the taste test below the waist."

Jay whooped and slapped the top of the bedroom door frame as he passed through.

She woke blinking and yawning and stiff.

"Don't move, please, Alice," Henry whispered.

The quiet, steady rhythm of breathing in her dark-haired mattress proved Jay still asleep. She left her head on her crossed arms atop his shoulder blades and opened her eyes.

The stacks of board games and the jigsaw puzzle they'd found to entertain themselves after lunch waited to be returned to their cabinet. Jay rested beneath her on the rug in front of the half-finished puzzle.

Henry overlooked them from the nearest chair, a sketch pad balanced against the curve of his left arm. The scratch of his pencil accompanied the near silence in the room. Even the rain had stopped its drumming outside.

Henry's right arm danced, his hand hidden behind the pad he held. "Did you have a nice nap, dearest?"

"Comfy pillow." She matched his quiet tones. Jay had been up as early as she, and he'd spent six hours biking up and down mountains afterward. "That why you didn't . . . you know . . . earlier?"

Pausing his hand, he met her gaze over the edge of the sketch pad. "He'd have fallen asleep in his lunch."

She twitched her lips but stifled the laugh. "He needed the calories more than the cock?"

Henry granted her a gracious nod and a closed-mouth smile before the rustling scratch of the pencil returned. He seemed intent on his work, but unbothered by her distractions. Content, as if he'd succeeded in his purpose for the weekend. Tomorrow they'd go home.

"Thank you for bringing us here. I can't remember the last time I had a long, lazy weekend." She yawned into her elbow. "How long have we been sleeping?"

"About ninety minutes." His gaze flicked between her and the paper before him.

Fuck. She struggled not to jump to her feet. Or her knees.

"It's after seven?" Henry's time. A nice waiting pose and a heartfelt apology might make up for their lapse.

"It is." He surveyed her in full, his slow sweep chasing away anxiety. "Not to worry. You're following my directions by lying still." He flashed a smile. "Astonishingly enough, you followed that direction in your sleep, as well. I'd no idea you were so agreeably submissive."

She clamped her lips together to avoid waking Jay with laughter, but air chuffed through her nose and her stomach muscles rippled.

Jay snuffled and shifted beneath her.

"Close your eyes a while longer, please, sweet girl. I haven't quite finished here."

A deep breath calmed her. Closing her eyes, she crooned to Jay and drifted, buoyed by the scratch of Henry's pencil and the surety of his love.

CHAPTER 11

"Pistachio. Pistachio."

She gasped the word after the pain hit but before the mortification flushed her face.

Two male voices, one deep and even, the other thin and cracking, called her name.

Back blazing, she crumpled to the bed, unable to move from a near-fetal hunch. God-fucking-dammit. One wrong twist, and her lower back throbbed. She'd ruined Henry's plans for Sunday night. Jay's inspection. Their relaxing weekend away.

Guilt tightened her muscles, and she sucked in a breath through gritted teeth. Hands touched her back but didn't attempt to uncurl her from her naked ball.

"Where does it hurt, sweet girl?" Henry delivered firm, kneading pushes with the heels of his hands. "Muscle spasm, hmm?" He issued orders to Jay, sending him dashing to the kitchen.

"M'sorry, Henry." She yelped as he found the center of the pain.

"Ahh, there's the trouble spot." His hand lay flat, a slight, soothing pressure. "No need for apologies, dearest."

"But I ruined tonight." The pain grated like a spike in her back, and she wanted to beg Henry to lift his hand and pull it out.

She kept her eyes closed, refusing to witness his disappointment in her failure. Christ, she'd cried like a baby over a tiny spanking at the club, and now she'd stopped the game for a fucking pulled muscle. Because she couldn't manage to roll from her back to her knees without injuring herself. Fucking idiotic move. Thank God they'd been in foreplay-land. Any later, and she'd give Jay a complex.

"Nonsense. You haven't ruined a thing, my dear girl." Henry's matter-of-fact tone carried no sting of disappointment. "You used your safeword, as you should, when something went wrong."

Safewording stank of failure, even if he'd handled run-of-the-mill problems like pulled muscles dozens of times. The pain hadn't ebbed. Their last night here, and she'd knocked herself out of the game.

"Is she okay?" Jay barreled through the doorway. "I got everything you wanted."

"Sad and pouting a bit." Henry laid his lips to her forehead. "But reasonably fine, I expect." He lowered his voice, a tender prod. "Shall I add embarrassed and guilty to the list, my dear? I'm sorry you are hurting, but I'm proud of you for taking the correct action rather than attempting to pretend you were fine."

"I stopped the game," she whispered. The last night she'd done so had been a clusterfuck of epic proportions.

"Temporarily, and with good reason." He murmured thanks to Jay and warned her of the cold.

She hissed at the chill of the towel-covered ice pack he draped on her back.

"I never want you to suffer in silence, Alice." He deepened his voice and leaned in, his face inches from hers. Brows lowered, mouth a thin line, he hadn't looked so serious all day. "You're to speak up. Always. Am I understood?"

She must've twanged his memories of the lesson Jay'd learned the hard way. As if submission only and always involved suffering. Wrongheaded thinking. A hypothesis he'd hate to see her test.

"I understand, Henry." The ice muted the throbbing in her back. She managed a wry smile. "I can't promise not to be mortified, but I won't let embarrassment stop me from telling you the truth."

"Good girl. We'll leave the ice on for another ten minutes." He kissed her cheek. "Jay, the ibuprofen, please. Alice, if you'll lift your head."

With Jay's careful assistance, she managed to get the pills down without spilling water all over the sheets. He sat beside her afterward and rested a hand on her calf.

"Sorry you're benched for the night." He scrunched his face in a caricature of unhappiness. "It sucks, I know. Not even in the fun way."

She'd have hugged him if not for the pinch in her muscles. "I'm the sorry one, sweetheart. Once I'm all popsicle-back, can you help me up?"

"And why would you want Jay to do that, Alice?"

"I'll get out of your way—go sleep on the couch or in one of the other bedrooms." She met Henry's gaze, resolute in her intention to ignore the beautiful expanse of bare flesh below. "It's our last night here."

His chest, broad and firm.

"I already messed up your plans."

His abdomen, sloping toward a delicious center.

"You guys don't need me third-wheeling it while you're trying to restart the mood."

Henry sighed. "Utterly ridiculous."

Jay nodded. "Where does she get these ideas?"

"What?" She tentatively uncurled her legs. The pain was tolerable, in that she didn't stop breathing. Walking to the living room would be no big deal. "What's wrong with my ideas?" The sooner she moved, the sooner Henry could get Jay's head back in the game. "I'm holding up the fun."

Henry looped her hair around his finger. "Did I demand Jay leave the bed in January when he was so bruised and in pain?"

When Jay had tangled with a delivery truck, been flying on painkillers, enjoyed a slick blowjob, and watched Henry fuck her tenderly for what had seemed uncountable hours of bliss. Oh. Yeah, that. "No, Henry."

"No." He trailed his hand down her cheek to her neck. "Do you suppose your presence here is more of a distraction for him than our beautiful boy's presence then was for you?"

"He wasn't a distraction," she whispered. Henry had shredded her argument in two questions. She'd been thinking of herself as an inconvenience. But when her night had been interrupted, she'd wanted nothing more than to make sure no one felt left out. "I wanted to share."

"As do we, sweet girl." Henry's teasing smile softened her pain. "If you wish to adjourn to the living room, Jay and I will simply have to follow you. Light the fireplace, perhaps."

Jay whistled. "Sex in front of a roaring fire? I haven't done that. Is there a bearskin rug around here?"

She let a single giggle escape. Her back twinged, but not terribly. "Me neither."

"Ah." Henry traced her mouth with his thumb. "No fireplace tonight, my dears. We'll save it for a lovely winter's evening when I may take you both on the floor before the hearth. Your skin glowing and warm. Shadows dancing. The spice of wood smoke mingling with your sweet scents."

Jay clutched her leg and whimpered, his eyes dark and eager. If not for the lingering ache in her back, she'd be right there with him.

Henry lifted the ice away. The surface chill, the numbness over the deeper pain, helped some.

"Return this to the freezer, my boy. We've an hour before we ought to ice Alice's back again. I believe we might make good use of our time."

Jay snatched the ice pack from Henry and grinned at her. "I'll try to put on a good show, so don't fall asleep, okay?" He dashed away without waiting for her answer.

"Your pulse is slower." Henry took his fingers from her neck. "Tell me your pain level, dearest."

"Not great, but bearable. I'll live."

Something flickered in his eyes before he reached for the pillows and swiftly rearranged them. When they'd gotten her settled, she had a firm pillow under her back for support and two under her head to elevate her view.

Jay hustled back into the room.

Henry crooked his finger and called to him.

They knelt on the bed, Henry's knees surrounding Jay's. He leaned forward, gripped Jay's chin in one hand, and kissed him. Hard. Enough to push Jay's head back, tilting his face upward and arching his back until his chest met Henry's.

There. There came the happy whimper she loved.

Henry switched his grip to Jay's hair, the thick, baby-soft strands at the back of his neck.

"I haven't finished inspecting you." He ran his tongue up Jay's neck from the notch in his collarbone to the underside of his chin. "Did you wash every inch?"

Jay moaned a wide-mouthed affirmation.

Henry nipped at the sloping muscles above Jay's shoulders.

A tug on his hair and a push at his chest sent Jay to the bed. He sprawled on his back, his breath fast, his cock hard and straining.

"Yes, you wouldn't have neglected anything that belongs to me, would you, my boy?"

Jay shook his head.

"No." Henry teased a finger up Jay's thigh. "And every inch of you belongs to me, doesn't it?"

"Yes, Henry." Eyes gleaming, Jay watched Henry with an unwavering gaze.

Straddling Jay's hips, Henry rose on his knees and stroked his own cock. Once. Twice.

Jay licked his lips, and she echoed the movement. Almost like still being in the game, sharing his enjoyment.

"Mine to protect." Henry dropped his hand to Jay's cock. Curving over the shaft and pressing down, he squeezed Jay against his stomach. "Mine to encourage to grow."

Whining, Jay rocked his hips.

Henry held him pinned between his legs. He rubbed the tip of Jay's cock with a single finger in a slow, swirling motion. Lifted the shining fingertip to his mouth and sucked. "Mine to sample whenever I wish."

She opened her mouth. Had to. Couldn't breathe otherwise, as panting and excited as Jay to see what Henry would do. A magician. Keep a close enough eye, and she'd learn his secrets. But no matter how close her scrutiny, Henry never lost his magic. He retained his ability to surprise and delight and command her attention.

"However I wish." Henry lowered his hips toward Jay. His cock hung stiff and dark an inch above Jay's. He pushed forward, a slow thrust, and his balls swayed, brushing along Jay's shaft.

Jay shuddered. He dug his hands into the sheets at his sides, one within her reach. She resisted the urge to touch. Fuck if she'd interrupt the spell Henry had woven around him.

"I know you want my touch. The climax I denied you this afternoon."

Jay nodded, a frantic need, his hips surging as Henry raised enough to create a gap between them.

"Ask for it, Jay."

"Please. Please, Henry," he begged, with adorable intensity. "Please take me."

She chanted along in her mind, a chorus of pleas. She knew the urgent desire when climax wasn't enough, when the physical release fell behind the emotional need to be owned. To have Henry claim her.

"However you want." Shadows danced across Jay's abdomen as he twisted and squirmed. "Make me yours."

She'd run from such terrifying needs for months. Now she silently urged him on. *Yes. Take Jay. Love him.*

Henry bent forward and rested one hand on the bed. He stared into Jay's face.

Jay stared back, open and needy. He gasped and groaned as Henry whispered, "Mine."

She'd missed the moment—Henry's other hand. Holding Jay's cock. Kind of. The darkness between their bodies justified the extra time she spent staring. Nope, nothing to do with how fucking hot Henry's cock looked sliding against Jay's. Or how Henry kept Jay's cock pressed tight to his own with his palm. Or the way he rubbed his fingers over the tips and slicked pre-come down the shafts.

Jay's stuttering whimpers signaled his approaching climax. Henry didn't stop, didn't clamp Jay's cock hard or demand he wait.

"That's it, my boy." Their cocks rubbed faster as he cupped Jay's balls and squeezed. "Show me the orgasm I've given you."

A jerk of his hips and Jay came with a desperate whine, a sigh of relief as ejaculate splashed his stomach and chest. Her clit throbbed in empathy, the warmth and desire pushing her pain to the back of her mind. Watching her boys fuck was the best medicine in the world next to getting fucked herself.

Henry kissed Jay with bruising intensity, hard and growling and nipping at his lips. "A beautiful Act One, my dear boy. No intermission tonight. The show must go on schedule, hmm? Act Two is already starting."

Act Two? *Please God, make him work himself to climax over Jay.*

Henry gripped his cock at the base, angled it down, and dragged the tip across Jay's body through splashes of come. An artist signing his work. Fuck, she'd let him sign anything he wanted on her stomach any day.

He worked his way up Jay's body until he knelt over Jay's face, cock in hand.

Jay parted his lips.

Henry swiped his cock across them.

Jay lifted his head, chasing the brief touch.

"Tongue out, my boy. I want to see you licking."

Jay extended his tongue with perfect obedience. Splayed it wide and lapped at the head of Henry's cock. Eager and moaning, he begged to take more without saying a word. The sheen of his lips and the deep magenta of his tongue paled alongside an even deeper shade.

Henry pressed forward. Not much. Enough to pop the very tip of his cock into Jay's mouth, but no more.

"Suck. You taste yourself on my cock, don't you?" He pushed in and out as Jay swayed and tugged, muscles tightening in his neck. "The taste of us together. A strong flavor. An excellent blend."

They developed a suction-pop rhythm, the head of Henry's cock disappearing to the edge of that sweet ridge begging for attention. Jay's lips clung to that curve for a long moment every time Henry pulled back.

"You can take more, can't you? I've seen you take more than this. Such a delightful mouth and an expert tongue." Henry rubbed his cock over Jay's waiting lips. "I'm going to give you more this time. Clap your hands for me first. Twice, please."

Jay scrambled to raise his hands across his chest. He clapped twice, the snap hard and sharp over their breathing.

"Good boy. Twice to stop."

Jay nodded.

"Repeat the words so I know you understand."

"Clap twice to stop." He flicked Henry's cock with his tongue and ended with a cheeky grin. "Do I win a prize?"

"You do," Henry murmured. "Now open your mouth and take it."

Her mouth dropped open with his, but only Jay's received the prize. A slow, steady thrust, his lips stretched around Henry's cock.

Henry kept his hand tight around the base. Gave Jay half, up to the edge of his knuckles. Pulled back and thrust again.

Eager whimpers accompanied every wet plunge. The bed rocked, Jay thrusting at the air as his cock hardened. Sucking Henry off might be his favorite activity.

Henry thrust faster, but still controlled. Still limiting his depth with his hand.

Jay sucked, his lips formed a tight seal, but their game wasn't a run-of-the-mill blowjob.

Her heart stumbled, skipping a beat before racing.

Henry was fucking Jay's mouth. And Jay wanted it. Couldn't get enough of it. Had a way to stop if he needed to, a temporary replacement for his safeword. Had Henry's unwavering attention, ready to pull out in an instant if Jay needed a break.

Christ, they were beautiful. Jay's cheeks hollowed out as he sucked during the pause between each thrust. Henry slipped his hand back. Three fingers, then two, then no more than a circle of thumb and index at the base of his cock. Guiding his thrusts more than limiting their depth.

Jay's throat worked, his Adam's apple bobbing as he swallowed and whimpered and begged to claim his prize.

Henry thrust and didn't pull back. Thrust twice more, his hips jerking, his cock deep in Jay's mouth. Growling, he lifted free, spilling ejaculate, coating Jay's lips and questing tongue.

She could've come herself if he'd ordered her to. One finger on the button and it would've been over. Fuck the muscle strain. She'd happily end up in traction.

A single rock of her hips put an end to her grand notion. Clenching her teeth, she waited for the pain to subside. The chill in her back had faded without her notice.

Henry shuffled back and kissed Jay. "Thank you, my boy." He kissed his forehead, the bridge of his nose, even his come-smeared lips. Gently, now, no longer possessive and demanding. "Such attentive service pleases me. My loving, obedient boy."

Jay beamed. "I love you, Henry."

"As I love you, Jay." He pressed one more kiss to Jay's lips. "I've a task for you now. Can you guess what it is?"

"Ice pack and washcloth." He listed her need before his own without hesitating.

"My brilliant boy." Henry rolled to the side and let Jay escape. "On your way."

Jay edged off the bed with care, an utter mess from face to thighs. He raised his arm with a salesman's flourish and lowered his hand. "This model comes—"

"I can see that," she interrupted with a giggle. "I think I'll talk to the owner about buying the demonstration model. They put on quite a show."

Jay sauntered around the bed. "Told you it'd be worth staying awake for."

"I can't wait to see the encore performance." She winked at him and ogled his half-hard cock. "It seems like there's always one in the works."

His gasp dared her to laugh. "Is there an encore, Henry? If Alice wants an encore, I can be ready."

"Tasks first, my boy."

"I'll be right back." He raced toward the door. "Don't start the encore without me."

"It's a two-man show," Henry called after him. "I'd hardly attempt it alone."

He laid a hand on her cheek. "How are you feeling, truly?"

"Good. Really, really good." She tipped her face into his hand and nuzzled closer. "And looking forward to that ice."

"I'm pleased to see you in such high spirits, sweet girl."

"You mean after you just fucked Jay's mouth?"

"Such a quick study," he murmured. "And so willing to speak the truth with blunt precision." He kissed her, tender and soft. "Yes. I mean after I fucked Jay's mouth. Tell me how you felt watching."

"You made sure you wouldn't hurt him. I saw your hand. And he couldn't get enough of it."

"*Your* feelings, dearest. Did those things reassure you?"

"I had a split second of panic, when I figured out what you were doing. But then it was okay. Better than okay, because I knew Jay was safe and you were giving him what he wanted. It's not the acts. It's the people. The intentions."

More kisses, sprinkled across her forehead and cheeks. "Good girl."

Positive reinforcement. That and repetition. He'd work to make sure his lessons sank in the way he must've done with Jay to build his confidence. Teach them both to accept their sexual desires and their emotional needs and find greater fulfillment. She wrapped her arms around his shoulders. "I love you, too, Henry."

"You had better." He mock growled at her. "You've signed me up for a second show tonight."

She giggled. "Am I going to get one?"

He lay beside her and took her hand in his. Pressed it to his cock, soft now but still slick. "If you play nicely while we ice your back." He nodded past her. "Hand that here, please, my boy."

She spent twenty minutes with the ice numbing her back and her fingers dancing along Henry's cock. Jay's fingers joined hers once he'd settled himself beside Henry. By the time he trotted off to toss the ice pack back in the freezer, he and Henry were ready for their encore.

A tussle this time, mock wrestling at slow speed before Henry pinned Jay to the bed. He held Jay's thighs down with his hands and Jay's arms with his legs. Mouths closed over cocks in the same moment.

Henry, solid and commanding, carried the weight of his authority, taking hard pulls.

Jay, supple and slim, writhed like smoke in search of a chimney. Drawn upward, a helpless slave to his own nature.

Fuck, she'd watch this show every night. Listen to the whimpers and groans and the harsh breaths. Inhale the heady musk of two men eager for release. The maleness hung so thick in the air she tasted it in her throat.

They shouted as one, Henry working his magic. Holding off Jay's climax with his hand and driving himself toward his own so they could share the moment together.

Cleanup was quick, while they iced her back and readied for sleep, cocks at rest. Henry settled beside her, on his back as she was. Jay curled along Henry's far side with an arm and leg flung over Henry, his hand brushing her arm. She slept.

Low laughter rippled in her ears. A slight chill hardened her nipples. She fumbled for the covers.

"You'll wake our canvas, my boy."

"But she'd be sorry to miss this. I know she would."

An answering chuckle from Henry. "Yes, she might wish to open her eyes before the fun ends."

She struggled to raise her eyelids, blinking rapidly. What was she missing? Ah, fuck, a matinee. "So this is what middle-school boys do every morning before breakfast. Mystery solved."

Henry laughed. "I usually managed to wait until I'd gotten in the shower."

Of course. Clean, discreet, thoughtful. The three corners of the Henry triangle. Except when she and Jay made up two of the corners. That was a good triangle, too.

Jay shrugged, one shoulder higher than the other, not interrupting his rhythm. "I fucked my pillow and hid the pillowcase in the laundry."

She giggled, imagining him tiptoeing through the halls and stuffing the hamper to overflowing with wadded-up pillowcases. His poor mother. "But today you decided to share? Lucky me."

Waking up to the two of them kneeling side by side, Jay's left knee pressed to Henry's right, their hands moving over a pair of gorgeous erections, was a sight she could get used to.

Henry knelt closer, his cock angled toward her breasts. Jay seemed to be targeting her stomach, though his wandering gaze roamed beyond her body. He checked in with Henry every few seconds, an adorable tilt of his head as he watched Henry move and adjusted his own grip.

God, she'd wondered for months, and here was the answer. Jay followed Henry's lead, even in this. She loosed an appreciative sigh, half a moan, and laced her hands behind her head.

"One for the road," Henry murmured. He winked at her.

Jay came first, popping like a champagne cork under pressure and whimpering with relief. Warmth dotted her stomach. Henry came more slowly, with tighter control, in long arcs across her breasts.

Kisses followed. "Good morning, sweet girl. How are you feeling?"

Her back ached when she tried to move. Hardly unexpected. She sat up, with help, and joined them for a shower.

Henry held her against him, supporting her back with his chest. The water rinsed the evidence of their passion from her body while he brought her to a gentle climax with his fingers.

"Mmm. All praise to Henry, bringer of the endorphin rush."

Jay laughed, and Henry chuckled and kissed her cheek. "We'll add ice and more ibuprofen while Jay and I square away the cabin, my dear."

She took it easy, walking to stretch her muscles before the long car ride ahead, while Jay followed directions with good cheer. Towels and sheets into the washer, running as Henry made breakfast and Jay returned yesterday's games and puzzle to their cabinet. The dryer declared the linens done as the last breakfast dish was washed and set on the drain board.

Henry demonstrated exceptional familiarity with the cabin. The location of extra towels and sheets. The laundry room and detergent. He'd been here often. He and Santa might've brought other players here.

Jay loaded the car, making trips back and forth as he filled the trunk with the bags Henry had packed and zipped.

Henry pulled the ice pack from the freezer. "I believe a final application is in order."

"You know this place really well, huh."

Raising an eyebrow, he beckoned her into the kitchen and cuddled her to his chest. "Many years past." The ice chilled her lower back. "Before Jay came into my life."

"Were they special?" The girls, she meant. Or boys. The ones he'd brought here.

"Will's picks, for the most part. Victor's, ages ago, when he and Em had submissives in training."

"You didn't come alone? I mean, not alone, but—"

"For a weekend away with my dear ones? No, Alice. Never." He stroked her hair with his free hand. "They were all of them special in the moment, and in the moment only. You and Jay are special to me in every moment, whether your lips are around my cock or across town speaking to a coworker."

"Car's packed." Jay's shoes squeaked on the floor. "We ready to go?"

"Are we ready, Alice?"

Time to go back to the real world, carrying a deeper appreciation for both of her men and their needs. "Ready."

The ice pack went back into the freezer. Last-minute bathroom breaks for all. Henry took a final look through the rooms and declared Jay's cleanup successful.

She held back a sigh as Henry locked the door and left the key atop the frame. "It's been a wonderful weekend, Henry." Santa's cabin had been good to them. Good *for* them. "Thank you for bringing us."

"Fantastic weekend," Jay added. "And I didn't watch a single bird."

Henry snorted. "As if you ever did before. You're a much more able cock-watcher than birdwatcher."

Jay preened. "I play to my strengths."

Henry chivvied them to the car, lowering her into the front seat with care and directing Jay to take the back.

"Perhaps we'll make a winter visit if you'd like to ski, Alice." Henry started the engine. "And warm up by the fire afterward, hmm?"

Her happy moan echoed Jay's. "Yes, please."

CHAPTER 12

"Alice!" Jay swooped down and kissed her before dropping into the seat across from her. Twelve forty-three. Less than fifteen minutes late, but still unusual for him. "Sorry, I got pulled into an extra hand. Order yet?"

"Pulled pork sandwiches and a shared plate of fries. Should be up in a minute." They lunched at the same diner every Tuesday, five blocks from her office. In ten months they'd worked their way through the entire menu twice. The sandwiches were a favorite treat. "You have a good morning?"

They traded stories and jokes until the food arrived, whereupon he wolfed his down and she took a slower approach. By the time she laid her napkin on her empty plate, Jay had reached the middle of a story about his regular Tuesday morning delivery customer whose sons lived out of state. They'd paid for weekly grocery delivery and pre-scription service since their mother's hip surgery last summer.

Sweet, can't-say-no Jay usually spent extra time chatting with Mrs. Eickhoff when he made his weekly drop-off. But this week Alice only half listened to his recounting of the widow's latest news. Her mind strayed back to Sunday morning. To Henry's voice. *We'll play new games soon, Alice.* She shifted in her seat.

"Does it hurt?"

Jay stopped in midsentence, his lowered brows and parted lips the definition of confused. "Umm, putting the groceries away or playing gin rummy? 'Cause the answer to both is 'no,' only I don't know why you'd think either would."

"No, I mean—" Clearing her throat, she checked out the neighboring tables. "With Henry. When you're *with* him."

"Ohhh." He swapped attitudes in an instant, his eyes softening as he leaned in. "Nervous, huh?"

He might think her braver than him, but he had it backward. Henry hurt her when she asked for it. Like the flogging. Anal sex might hurt the same way. Pain-with-pleasure during. An ache later. She lacked context. "Maybe a little."

He dodged soda glasses and condiments and clasped her hands. "It won't hurt. Promise." Muscled forearms flexing, he squeezed her fingers. "The first time, it's kinda uncomfortable, 'cause it's odd, you know? Like your body's not sure what's going on. And then it feels amazing. Full. If it hurts at all, even the first time, you gotta tell Henry right away. He won't be mad if you need to stop."

"I know." She did. She just needed to hear it from Jay. Her expert.

"I think—" Concentration added tiny lines to Jay's forehead and the corners of his eyes as he squinted. "It helps to breathe nice and slow. And relax your muscles. And listen to Henry's voice. If you feel like you're starting to panic, listen to Henry. He loves you. He knows what you're ready for. He won't try to give you more than you can handle."

He let go of one hand and pointed a stern finger at her. "If you're getting your information online, stop right there, young lady. You'll make yourself crazy worrying."

She stared at her empty plate with its smear of barbecue sauce. Caught. Jay sported a sweet and playful surface, and he liked things simple and decided for him, but he wasn't stupid.

"People do weird and unnecessary stuff. They spread stories when things go wrong." He held understanding in his eyes, as wise as Henry about her need to research and analyze from every angle. "Things go right, they're too busy enjoying brainless-orgasm-land to babble about it online."

When she needed him to play senior submissive, he stepped up and got the job done without thinking less of her. Her fears slipped away, floating free. "Thanks, Jay."

"If you need more convincing, I can go first. Sacrifice myself as a demonstration model for your needs." He flashed his charming flirt smile and waggled his eyebrows. "I'm willing to take one for the team."

She laughed until she was out of breath. "Eager, you mean."

"Always. And so are you."

Well, that was true enough.

Jay stood, dropping bills on the table to cover the tab. "C'mon, I'll give you a lift back to work on my pegs."

She let him pull her up from the chair. "You just want my arms around your neck and my breasts bouncing against your back every time you brake."

"Of course I do." He tugged her toward the door. "You're gonna say yes anyway, right?"

She ducked her head, grinning as she followed him outside. He was such a horndog. And a sweetheart. And hers. She answered in a soft voice. "Of course I am."

On Wednesday night, Alice didn't remove her shoes at the door.

She was ready by far to shed her work clothes. The day had been a long one, filled with complications caused not by the nature of the work but by the client. New demands requiring revision to a project already well under way. Time constraints forcing the team into a brainstorming session of epic proportions. Wrung out, she needed more comfort than flopping on the couch until dinner could provide.

Jay's sweet smile proved an intoxicating lure, a reminder of the domestic tranquility she enjoyed these days. And the spicy aroma emanating from the kitchen promised another delicious dinner delivered by Henry's capable hands.

Her lovers greeted her with cheerful voices and gentle kisses.

The last of the table settings found its place courtesy of Jay, which necessitated thanks and praise from Henry. Hands-free, as his were coated in some unnamable sauce. A homemade marinade. Certainly the origin of the spicy scent.

Jay gave off his own scent, fresh and woodsy, from his post work shower. His hair hadn't fully dried. The ends curled under.

She ran her hand up the back of his head, threading her fingers through his hair and shaking it out. Her frisky puppy wriggled in place.

"It smells great in here, Henry. How long until dinner?" A casual question unlikely to draw Jay's notice. But Henry's brief glance at her would give him a wealth of information.

"Oh, I think we might have an hour, my dear. Perhaps more. You might wish to relax a bit beforehand." Yeah, he knew. The lightness of his answer, the slight twitch at the corner of his mouth, and the tilt of his head added up to pure Henry amusement.

"I will, I think. I can't wait to get out of these clothes."

Jay twisted to face her, widening his eyes with exaggerated innocence. "I could help with that. Chief unfastener, at your service."

She tapped the counter. "I think helping me with my clothes is a task reserved for very good boys with very clean rooms."

Odd, how a Jay so still could be so alive with energy. The potential for action crawling under his skin, waiting for the explosive rush into kinetic energy, practically made him vibrate.

"I'll be going to my room to undress in four minutes." Fair warning, enough time for him to clean up any lingering trouble spots. "If I like what I see, the person who's done such a wonderful job taking care of my room can take care of me until dinner."

Jay whipped his body around. "Henry, may I be excused? The table's all set."

Henry's gentle nod came with a straight face and no hint of a tease at her game. "Of course. You're free to amuse yourself until I call you for dinner."

"Thank you, Henry." He trotted away at a more-than-fast walk. Wanted to run, probably, but Henry had a no-running policy to prevent Jay from slipping and cracking his skull open. A necessary measure, no question.

Leaning in, she nuzzled Henry's neck and inhaled below his ear. Sharp citrus. Musky leather. She left a kiss behind, as soft as her voice. "Yes, thank you, Henry."

He turned to catch her lips and gave her a more thorough kiss than a simple welcome home. Pulling away, he left her close-eyed and shuddering, drawing energy from his attention.

"You're settling in well, my sweet girl. The eager anticipation on Jay's face tells me your rewards have been thoughtfully chosen. Tell me, are you comfortable with your role?"

She leaned against the counter beside him. His long-fingered hands conducted casserole like a symphony as he layered thin strips of meat in a dish. Modified beef stroganoff, from the mushrooms and onions and sour cream on the counter.

"He makes it easy." No, that wasn't right, exactly. "And hard." She shook her head. Giving Henry the wrong impression might make him stop the game. "I mean, it's complex, but not." She crossed her arms. "I'm not explaining well at all."

Henry chuckled. "If I may?"

She gestured with one hand, serving up the conversation on a silver platter. "Be my guest, o eloquent one."

"You find Jay responds well however you praise him, so long as you do so verbally and provide a task he enjoys. This is an easy matter to accomplish, as he enjoys any task that makes you happy. And, paradoxically, a difficult matter to accomplish, as you cannot tell if the reward truly makes him happy by itself or if it is merely the action of pleasing you that rewards him."

Henry magic, taking a jumble of complexity and turning it linear with such quickness.

Practice. Experience. Tonight would be her third attempt at enforcing the spot checks on their shared bedroom. Henry had years of experience, not only with the submissive mindset in general, but with Jay specifically.

"Not to worry." Henry kissed her cheek. "You've done nothing thus far to upset him, and I don't expect you will. Have you considered that you may simply ask him if he's enjoying himself? In your room, he's duty-bound to answer you honestly."

She nearly smacked herself in the face. "Checking in. I should check in with him even when I'm rewarding him. I don't know what I'm doing otherwise."

"Asking questions is not a sign of failure, sweet girl. Your ability to intuit his needs will grow with time."

He'd told her something similar the night of their anniversary dinner, when he'd held her in his lap. Then he'd been talking about himself. "Like you did with me at first."

"And still do. A question is not a weakness but a strength. Information gathering. A tool to sharpen your mind just as you do at work. Now—are you comfortable in your role?" He winked as he asked. Gathering information about her, still, and in no way relinquishing the dominance in the conversation.

Damn, he was good. She'd have to work on questioning Jay the way Henry questioned her. She didn't have to anticipate Jay's answers the way Henry did hers. That skill would grow. The appearance of confidence and the deep desire to know would get her through in the beginning.

"More than I was three minutes ago." She breathed deep and exhaled slowly. "If you'll excuse me, I have an appointment to keep."

"Have fun," he murmured. "I'm certain Jay will."

Her shoes clicked on the hardwood in the hall. She crossed onto the bedroom rug in silence. Jay stood at the foot of the bed with his feet spread and his hands clasped behind him. At ease. Not raised or hunched, his shoulders signaled eagerness, no tension.

He didn't look up, and she didn't speak. Not yet. Earning his reward had to mean something to Jay. She'd taken her cue from Henry here. Stillness. Waiting. Jay struggled with those things. So she started her spot checks the same way every time, requiring him to be still and quiet while she pulled a dominant cloak over her mind.

She went to the vanity, the one Henry had loaned her the first day they'd met. Other than the lone double bed, she had her furniture and Jay had his, which left the bedroom cozy rather than crowded. A good fit, like Henry's bed and their bodies. She bent at the waist, giving Jay the chance to ogle her ass. Waiting would be easier if he had something fun to think about.

She slid open the thin center drawer, the one intended as a jewelry tray, and lifted out her pen and notebook. A basic Moleskine, but it served her purpose. She'd splurge on a leather cover when her budget had more wiggle room. She wrote the time and date at the top right on a fresh page.

"Jay." Her quiet call brought his head up immediately, his eyes focused on hers. "Show me what you've done this week, sweetheart."

She took notes as he led her around the room. Everything in its place. Laundry in the basket. Items lined up across the top of his dresser. Clean clothes folded in the drawers rather than tossed in. The bed made. The closet tidy. The rug vacuumed. She noted each task he'd completed and praised his thoroughness, his dedication, and his courtesy in keeping their shared space immaculate.

"You've been very good, Jay. Do you know how proud it makes me to come home and see this?"

He shook his head, his face sweet and open to her. No, he probably didn't. Organization was something Henry had trained in him, not an inborn trait. A well-ordered space didn't calm his mind the way it did hers.

"No?" She laid the notebook aside and took his hands. "When I walk in the door, sweetheart, I only want two things—to see my beautiful boys and to relax. And here's my Jay, keeping everything in order, so there's no work to be done here. Nothing I need to worry about." She raised his hands and kissed his palms. "You've earned a reward for such generosity. Would you like to help me relax even more, Jay?"

"Yes, please, Alice." He squirmed, a subtle ripple.

She didn't have to look down to know he'd be hard.

"On your knees, then." She squeezed his hands once and let go. "Help me undress. Shoes first, please."

He sank to the floor in a single fluid move. She rested a hand on his shoulder as he lifted her right foot. Ran the other through the hair on his bowed head.

He caressed her feet as he slipped off her shoes, his fingers warm and firm through her thin socks.

She moaned soft encouragement. "Your hands are so much more comfortable than shoes, sweetheart. Socks next, please."

His slipped his hands inside her pants leg and rolled her dress sock down to her toes, first one side and then the other.

She flexed her foot.

He squeezed.

"Tell me what you're thinking right now, Jay. Are you enjoying your reward?"

"Yes, Alice. I'm thinking about how small your feet are. How they fit in my hands. How soft your skin is. How it tastes when you let me kiss you." His words tumbled out unfiltered, without pause.

"Would you like to kiss me now, sweetheart?"

He answered with a sharp nod and a whispered *please*.

"You've been such a good boy this week that I'm going to allow it. You may kiss any skin you've uncovered, Jay."

He curved over her bare feet like a territorial puppy guarding a toy, his elbows out to ward off nonexistent challengers. Kissing the tops of her feet first, he sucked at her skin with strength. Placed the gentlest of kisses on her ankles. Rubbed his cheek against her.

"Thank you, sweetheart. I'm feeling nice and relaxed thanks to you. Do you know what else will help me relax?"

He sat back on his heels, eyes bright, smile sly. Henry's little co-median. Her playmate. "No pants?"

She laughed, nodding. "No pants. Can you help me with that, Jay?"

His fingers were at her belt before she'd even said his name. "Yes, Alice."

Oh, yes. God knew Henry had him undress her often enough. Jay could probably do it blindfolded. Something to consider for the future, but one she'd have to ask Henry about. Blindfolds had to count as toys, and toys required permission.

Opening her belt and unzipping her slacks, Jay inhaled on an almost-silent whimper. He curved his hands around her ass over her panties. She hummed in happy agreement with his solid grip.

The pants slid to the floor.

He leaned into her, resting his forehead against her panties. His breath gusted across the silk. A new pair. Dark green. A welcome-to-our-home gift from Henry.

Jay traced the edges with his fingers.

"Do you like my panties, Jay?"

His nod brushed dark hair along the hem of her shirt.

"Do you want me to leave them on for now?"

Stillness, but not a no. A yes he didn't want to voice? She ran her hands through his hair. "Do you want to know why *I* want to leave them on for now?"

Fingertips stroking silk, he nodded in rapt fascination.

"They give me courage. And love. All wrapped up in Henry's touch. And this pair is my new favorite. Do you know why?"

"His eyes," Jay murmured. He nuzzled at her, his nose bumping her clitoris.

Her desire ticked up a notch, and she forced herself to set it aside. She hadn't been so blatantly sexual with his last two rewards, and she wouldn't make this more than comfort and foreplay. Bonding.

"The color matches. Like he's watching over us. S'why I like my shorts with the green stripe best."

"Exactly right," she whispered. "Come up here and unbutton my shirt, sweetheart. The bra matches, and what's underneath is for you."

"Kisses?" Popping his head up, he set to work on the bottom button of her shirt.

"For any skin you reveal."

188 • *M.Q. Barber*

Her shirt followed her pants to the floor, and she ordered Jay onto the bed. Not out of his clothes. She'd work up to those rewards eventually. He curled against her in his T-shirt and tented shorts. She laid his fingers on the front clasp of her bra. "Do you want to give me kisses here, Jay? Would you like that?"

He wriggled at her side, cock pressed to her hip, and whimpered. "Yes, please."

She squeezed his hand and let go. "Go ahead, sweetheart. As many kisses as you like, until Henry calls us to dinner."

He opened the clasp and brushed aside the silk with his hand.

She breathed deep, her chest lifting into his touch, the instinctive first breath of freedom after the day's confinement. Henry had chosen surprisingly comfortable undergarments for her. She wasn't denying that. But a bra was still a bra, and her breasts were not so large as to demand constant support, and off was always more comfortable than on.

Jay smothered her breasts in kisses. Light kisses first, lips dragging, cold as he inhaled and warm as he exhaled. His tiny, contented sounds, between a grunt and a hum, made her smile.

They lay side by side, bodies tilted toward each other. Her eyelids drooped as she stroked his back and his hair, murmuring to him of what a good boy he was. How much he deserved this time with her. How she appreciated his love.

She'd gotten it right. She felt the difference, the confidence filling her as Jay tugged at her nipples and his hands curled and flexed against her stomach. This time she'd balanced the comfort and relaxation she wanted and needed with the security and praise Jay wanted and needed. She wouldn't wonder later how she'd done or wish she could ask Henry to grade her performance.

Things might be more playful on other nights. They might be more power-oriented. But in this moment, she'd listened to Jay's needs and given him the right reward. She sighed, happy, relaxed. Her eyes drifted open, fastening on Henry, a silent witness in the doorway.

She raised an eyebrow, her hands pausing on Jay's back, but Henry shook his head.

He raised a finger to his lips, curved in a gentle smile. *When you're ready*, he mouthed. *Not before.*

She gave the slightest nod, a movement Jay might interpret as her resettling her head, assuming he noticed. His fascination seemed trancelike.

Supper was served half an hour late Wednesday, with no complaints.

Alice adjusted numbers on her computer screen. Silently swore. Adjusted them back. Listened to Jay's laughter from the living room, where Henry provided contemptuous commentary for the reality show Jay had stopped the TV on. Hard to resist a train wreck. And that's what she had here, too.

June would start in two days. Tomorrow was Friday—Henry's time. Saturday they'd be dining with Santa, a nerve-racking prospect even though she'd suggested it. Her June budget had to get ironed out tonight. With a lease demanding thirty days' notice before vacating, she'd still be paying June rent on her empty apartment.

By itself, not a problem. Except now she lived *here*, and she ought to pay her share of the June rent, and she didn't even know what that was. Sitting at the dining room table staring at the numbers for over an hour brought nothing beyond embarrassment and frustration.

Whatever one-third of Henry's rent came to, she couldn't pay it. Not while paying her old rent. Her student loan payments. Her little sister's rent and a stipend for her expenses, because she refused to have Olivia dividing her attention between medical school and a job. Ollie deserved the best opportunities. The path with the fewest obstacles.

"Alice, come join us." Henry's voice rose above the varying modulations emanating from the television. "You've sequestered yourself quite long enough for the night."

"Uh-huh." If she didn't contribute to the food budget and didn't eat lunch all month, she could offer a partial payment on her share of the rent. "In a minute." She could go without lunch. The breakfasts and dinners he made for her and Jay would—

"*Now*, please, Alice."

Huh? What—shit. She'd blown him off in her distraction. And it wasn't as if she were making progress, because there was none to be made. Time to suck up her courage.

She powered down the computer and joined the men on the couch.

Henry sat sideways, his legs stretched along the cushions. Jay lay on his side, his head pillowed on Henry's thigh.

Jay sat up enough for Henry to pull her into his lap before settling down again. His weight sprawled across both of them, head near her hip, shoulder a gentle pressure between her legs. He shifted as he made himself comfortable.

She fought not to squirm.

Henry clasped her shoulders and touched his mouth to her ear. "I'll gladly allow some leeway in your conduct, Alice, but I do expect to be treated with more respect than an irritating insect swatted away without thought."

"I know. You're right, Henry. I was distracted. I'm sorry." Not because he was her dominant, but because he was her lover and her friend, and he deserved better than her inattention.

He pressed his thumbs deep into the back of her neck, digging tiny circles in her muscles. "More than distracted, I'd say."

"Rude, then." Her eyes drifted half-closed. "I'm still sorry."

Uttering a noncommittal sound, Henry sank his thumbs lower and dug deeper, pushing out toward her shoulders. "I was speaking of your tension, my sweet girl." He kissed the top of her ear. "What has you so distressed tonight?"

The perfect opening. "Could I—would it be all right if I waited to start paying my share of the rent until July?"

Henry's hands stopped moving. Shit.

Jay rolled to his back, tipping his head into her stomach. "What share of the rent?"

"Mine. My third?"

Jay moved his head from side to side with slow, regular motions. "You aren't paying rent?"

"Paying the rent isn't his responsibility, Alice." Henry resumed the massage. "Nor is it yours."

Rebellion bolted through her. "I'm living here. I'll pay my fair share." When you lived with someone, you split the costs down the middle and paid for your own food. "I always have before."

"You're been living with roommates before. Such is not the case here." Henry crossed his arms in front of her and held her tightly to him. "Providing a home for you and Jay is my privilege."

"But that's—" Fuck. She didn't mean to sound ungrateful, but she didn't like feeling beholden, either. She needed to pay her share. She just couldn't until July. "I don't know if I can do that."

Jay looked up at her with wide eyes.

Henry rested his head against hers. "Tell me why not. What is it about the idea that makes you uncomfortable?"

"I guess—" Dad had handled the financial stuff until his accident. When Mom had taken over, homework had come with a chorus of angry voices in the background every night.

Not paying rent meant handing Henry another kind of control over her. Wiggle room to push for authority over her bank accounts. Not happening. Had she inadvertently picked a man who felt worthless if he didn't control the cash flow? She should've asked before she fell in love.

"I want to be an equal partner, Henry." Christ, she sounded like an idiot. An equal partner in a relationship built on inequality. Power exchanges she'd agreed to. "Financially, I mean."

"When you lived with roommates, Alice, an equal share of the rent earned you an equal voice in decisions, did it not?"

"It was supposed to, yeah." Her last roommates hadn't given a shit about keeping common areas clean.

"Payment served as a kind of protection. A guarantee." Henry's even tone offered no clues to his thoughts.

"Right." God, navigating this minefield would be easier if she knew whether she'd offended him.

"Because your roommates had no particular concern for your welfare beyond your ability to pay, did they?"

"We weren't friends, if that's what you mean."

"I do mean." Henry dropped his hand to Jay's chest.

Jay's heavy exhalation sank chest and hand both. He tracked her with his eyes. Tension clung to his lips and jaw.

"Am I someone you need protection from, Alice? A roommate you fear might throw you out if you can't deliver? Perhaps you feel paying rent is a safety clause. A backup in the event you somehow fail to satisfy me as a submissive or as a sexual partner? A way of showing you are worth more than your actions in our bed?" Henry's harsh whispers slashed at her heart.

"That's not—I wouldn't—" But she trembled. He wasn't wrong.

She wanted proof, something she could point to and say she'd contributed, some security that this relationship wouldn't dissolve into nothing. Or worse. Paying an equal share from the start, she'd avoid angry bickering over money.

"It's all right, sweet girl." Henry pressed his lips against the side of her head. "You're unaccustomed to thinking of your lovers as family. Unaccustomed to living with them. To considering a future with them." He coaxed her with a gentle, low tone. "You've adjusted to a great number of changes in the last year, Alice. If this is one for which you feel unready, that's fine."

Henry's deep breath lifted her as his chest moved, and he tightened his arm around her. "We'll call June a trial month of nonpayment, hmm? If, come July, you remain uncomfortable with the notion, we'll settle on something appropriate then."

He hadn't said no or dismissed her concerns. He'd give her time to work through them. Of course he would. He was Henry. "I can live with that."

"Good." He traced the edge of her collarbone. "As you're considering, perhaps you'll think on how you might handle such a situation in my position?"

"In your position?" She'd never be in Henry's position. Hell, if she hadn't met him, she wouldn't even be in her position.

"As the established leader in a relationship. Imagine—ah. Yes. You're close with your sister, are you not? Despite the geographic distance between you?"

"I try to be, yeah. She's in California, but we do our best." Not so much contact as she'd like, but Ollie had been so busy with internship rotations this year that their schedules had rarely matched.

"If you had a comfortable home, well within your means, and she were to come live with you, would you insist she pay rent?"

"Of course not. I'd be paying the same for my place whether she lived there or not. I'd want her to save her money for more important things." What a ridiculous question. "She's my little sister. I love her."

Silence from Henry. A smirk from Jay.

"Oh." Closing her eyes, she swallowed through the tight warmth in her chest she hadn't understood how to quantify before. Something she welcomed now rather than fighting against.

"Yes, 'oh.'" Henry turned her head and delivered a kiss over her shoulder. A long, slow kiss, his tongue stroking hers, his fingers caressing her neck. "You are my lover, Alice. My sweet girl. I want no less for you than you want for the ones you love, hmm?"

Henry patted Jay's chest, and Jay threaded their fingers together. He tugged her right hand with his until they, too, lay on his chest.

She ruffled his hair with her left hand. Instead of the grin she expected, Jay studied her with unaccustomed seriousness.

"Henry's never asked me to pay rent. And he's never threatened to toss me out. Not even—" Jay squeezed their hands. "Not even when I had nightmares. And I hated going to work and facing the guys I used to hang out with. Even if they didn't know, I felt like they did. Like they saw everything that was wrong with me."

Henry rubbed Jay's chest in slow strokes, their hands moving together. "There's nothing wrong with you, my boy," he murmured.

Jay nodded against her stomach. "I couldn't keep working there. But I didn't have the money for my own place if I wasn't working. And I was too . . . ashamed . . . to go home and have to explain." He shrugged. "When I moved in with Henry, I didn't have a job and we weren't having sex. He let me sleep in his bed, and he didn't ask me for anything. He only asked what I wanted. What my perfect day would look like."

There was the grin she'd expected.

"That's when I put together the business plan and found the right target. Henry gave me the capital to buy out the messenger service. I built up the expanded services myself. And now I get to spend every day on my bike helping people and every night in Henry's bed pleasing him and myself. And now you."

Jay crushed her fingers in his. Understanding gleamed in his eyes.

"Alice, I still have my own bank accounts. I could pay the rent on this place. If I'd made a mistake and this was something abusive, I could get out. Not 'cause I thought of it, but 'cause Henry did. He insisted I keep my money separate. Made sure I understood I could . . . escape . . . at any time." Jay shook his head. He'd never want to leave this relationship.

Neither did she. Even if it meant rethinking the meaning of equal partner.

"I let Henry pay the rent himself because providing a home is part of how he shows he loves me. Like the way he makes sure I have a good breakfast and dinner every day." Jay squeezed her as if he could imbue her with his own certainty by the press of a hand.

Her subconscious agreed. Jay had the greater experience here. He was a fine guide in this.

"It's okay to be nervous. Just don't think it's something it's not, okay? Henry's not trying to trap you or make you some second-class person."

"You do so enjoy spilling my secrets to Alice, my boy." Henry spoke over her shoulder in a fond, teasing murmur. "But I believe we've trapped her between us rather well here, don't you?"

Pressed to Henry's chest and pinned by Jay's weight, she giggled. With Henry's ruthless logic and Jay's earnest confession rattling in her brain, financial independence wasn't a concern. Henry wouldn't shove her into some historical housewife role. She knew that, when she wasn't swimming in a sea of panicked mortification. Now she swam in a sea of warm bodies and rising arousal. Much better.

"It's no secret that you love us, Henry." Grin growing, Jay shrugged against her thighs. "Not anymore. And if Alice doesn't know by now how much you show it—" He wriggled and squirmed, dislodging their hands as he twisted onto his stomach and pushed himself up, taking the opportunity to rub his face between her breasts like a cat ready for a petting before he was high enough to look her in the eyes. "Then it's my job as senior sub to enlighten her."

Henry's nod rustled her hair.

Jay kissed her. Tender and sweet, but with definite intent, rocking his hips against her. Her head fell back on Henry's shoulder. He nudged her, sucking at the side of her throat. Jay echoed her moan. Her hands met Henry's across the muscled span of Jay's back as they clutched him.

Jay pulled his lips from hers, his smirk firmly in place. Not the only firm part of him. "We don't want Alice unclear about the benefits of being in love with you, right, Henry?"

"Mmm. At the moment, those benefits include an early bedtime." He flexed beneath her, erection hard against the curve of her ass, pushing her toward Jay. "Exercise is an excellent way to ensure a good night's sleep, wouldn't you say, my boy?"

"It always does for me." Jay waggled his eyebrows.

She loved him confident, secure, and playful, and she didn't doubt

Henry felt the same. Sharing with her, using his past as a lesson for her, made Jay feel useful. Needed. Loved.

"We ought to see what it does for Alice, then." Henry growled against her throat and made a teasing lunge to nip at Jay.

They shivered, bodies rocking with his movement.

"Off to bed, my dears."

CHAPTER 13

When Henry emerged from the closet Saturday evening, Alice felt certain the scrap of black fabric in his hand was for her. He'd already laid his own clothes on the bed, though he hadn't changed into them yet.

She and Jay stood waiting, naked, fresh from the shower, toweled off and tranquil. In theory.

Henry had permitted the two of them hands-only play in the shower, which she suspected had been an attempt to settle their nerves. Jay had pressed her to the wall, water making her skin slick as skillful fingers pulled an orgasm from her. And then she'd plastered herself to his back, off center, her head resting against his shoulder, and stroked him to a beautiful climax. A better job than she'd done at the cabin, if she did say so herself.

The strategy had worked for Jay. He stood with a quiet focus, watching Henry move, his cock at rest. He'd slipped into the proper mindset for tonight, the subservient watch-and-wait they'd practiced last night.

But last night had been for fun. A dress rehearsal, with Henry teasing them with ridiculous commands and laughter sprinkled throughout their education. Tonight was the real deal. William was a true guest, another dominant and a friend of Henry's.

She wanted Henry's skills acknowledged. Her own performance flawless, a credit to his training. *Do not fuck this up, Allie-girl.* The pressure wasn't the weight of Henry's expectations but her own need for perfection.

"Jay. Sit, my boy."

Jay sat on the edge of the bed, his body loose and his smile mellow. His cock didn't even stir when Henry raised the black fabric up to his thighs.

"And stand, please."

Jay stood. Perfectly calm. Perfectly obedient. While Henry dressed him in boy shorts that hugged his ass and outlined his cock. The amount of skin on display drew attention directly to the small black band around Jay's hips.

Henry grasped Jay's chin in one hand and delivered a bruising kiss to his mouth. "My beautiful boy. You need no adornment, hmm?" Their second kiss proved softer. "Fetch the trays from the refrigerator, please. We'll want them to warm to room temperature. And listen for the door. You'll be in charge of buzzing our guest in when he arrives."

Jay nodded. When Henry let him go, he left the room with no more than a small, encouraging smile for her. Focused. Like she ought to be.

She wasn't worried, exactly. Henry had laid out guidelines for her thank-you. She wasn't trading favors with her body, wasn't property to be passed to a friend. He'd assured her Santa would enjoy the night, even if he left with nothing more than a few kisses and a hard cock.

Henry approached her and touched her face, knuckles brushing her cheek.

She quivered with excess energy, spilling weakness the way an incandescent bulb shed heat.

With a soothing hum, he disappeared into the closet. He returned with something white and flowing. Gauzy. He urged her to feel the fabric draped across his hands.

She pinched the cloth between two fingers, rubbing back and forth. Soft, with lace edging. Thin. Sheer. Definitely see-through. Her fingers wouldn't stop moving. Her nipples tightened.

"All right, Alice?" He tossed the gown on the bed atop his own dinner clothes. Holding her head between his hands, he tipped her back until she had to meet his gaze. "If you're not ready, sweet girl, there's no shame in stopping things before they begin. You've nothing to prove to me, or to Jay, or to Will. Do you wish to use your safe-word?"

Henry standing so near, smelling so good, and putting his hands on her skin worsened the problem. Combined with her nudity, it didn't matter that Jay had made her come twenty minutes ago or that she'd played with them both this morning. Wet and needy, she'd embarrass herself if she couldn't find the post orgasmic tranquility Jay had. Back out, or be honest?

"Henry, I—I need *you*."

He inhaled, a sudden, sharp breath. His eyes flashed wider. He rubbed circles on her cheek. "We've little time, dearest."

She knew. She'd manage without the peacefulness somehow.

"So you'll have to be quick for me, Alice."

Legs trembling, she moaned her relief.

He dropped his hands to her shoulders. "How quick can you be, my sweet girl? Are you ready to come for me now?"

"I am. I am. Please, Henry."

He spun her, his hand firm on her back, and pushed her facedown into the mattress.

She stretched her arms over her head, hands clasped, imagining the embrace of restraints on her skin.

"Spread your legs for me. Show me how ready you are."

She widened her stance and tipped her pelvis. Her clit brushed the duvet. Her body clenched in anticipation of Henry's entrance. A rustle of fabric, the hiss of a belt.

His casual khakis thudded on the floor at the same time foil ripped. He'd carried condoms in his pocket all day. For her. Not much longer, though. She'd already made the appointment.

Henry nudged her entrance and stroked her hip. "So beautifully wet for me. Let's see if we can't fulfill your need *now*."

He pushed in hard, deep, without stopping.

She gripped his cock as if she could pull him in faster by force of will.

His hands stayed on her hips. He wasn't using his fingers to rush her, but she didn't need the help. Once he'd hit his depth, he set a hard pace, rapid thrusts forcing her against the bed and grinding pressure on her clit as she jerked beneath him.

Her breaths became whines.

Henry's vocal encouragement turned to grunts with every thrust.

He delivered the hard fuck she needed. Pinned beneath his body, she provided the lubrication while he provided the piston.

She shouted a silent count. Three thrusts before her body grew rigid, tension locking up every motion, every hope of motion. Two more released it, her pleasure shrieked into the sheets as Henry kept going, driving her harder and higher to reach a second peak. Only then did he let himself go, his hips slamming hers, his growl rattling above the buzzing of her blood rushing past her ears.

She sagged against the bed.

Bending over her back, he extended his arms alongside hers. "My lovely temptation." He kissed her shoulder blade. "We haven't time for another shower. You'll have to spend the evening with my scent on your skin."

"Mmm." She stretched beneath his weight. "It's my favorite."

He chuckled. "We'll at least get you cleaned up and dressed." He kissed her other shoulder. "You have what you need now, hmm? Feeling more relaxed?"

"Relaxed and ready to serve." The importance of her earlier anxieties fell away. She'd asked Henry to fulfill her needs, and he'd provided for her. He hadn't questioned her need. He wouldn't question her performance tonight. He understood she'd do her best.

"Good girl." Henry squeezed her hands before rising from her back. "Now, Jay, was there something you needed?"

Jay, washcloth draped across his arm like a waiter at a fancy restaurant, stood at the bedroom door. Hoo boy. Those shorts didn't hide a thing.

"I heard a noise." Jay's lips twitched. "It seemed like you might want some fetching done. Sir."

Henry snorted. "Such a thoughtful, brilliant boy. The reasons to love you, my little charmer, are too numerous to count. Bring that here, please." Henry slipped free of her body, planted a kiss on Jay's cheek, and cleaned her before himself.

Finally upright, she eyed Jay's shorts and gave him a sheepish grin. "Sorry, sweetheart."

Jay shook his head, tranquil despite the stiffness straining the fabric. "Don't be. You've helped me hit three orgasms since midnight. I doubt I could come again if I tried. This"—he waved at his crotch—"is me appreciating one of my favorite sights. If Henry told me to sit still and watch him fuck you like that all day, I'd do it with a smile."

He smirked. "Die of blue balls by the end of the day, probably, but I'd die a happy man."

She kissed his cheek, the one Henry had left untouched. For balance. "Love you, stud."

"I love you, too, Alice. You know that, right?"

"I know." She patted his chest.

Henry, having swapped the rest of his day clothes for sleek black slacks, buttoned on a dress shirt that matched his eyes.

"But I bet Henry's about ready to dress me."

"An excellent wager, my dear. You win the prize." Henry pointed at the white gown on the bed. "It consists of two parts." He picked up a scrap of fabric even smaller than Jay's. "First, some lovely panties."

She stepped forward and raised one leg at a time at Henry's direction. The panties seemed hardly less sheer than the gown, and the back was a thong. Because her boys were ass men and wanted something to look at, or because Henry was playing more games to get her thinking about things rubbing against her ass all night?

Both, of course, sweet girl. Her mind provided the answer in his voice, her mental mimicry a match for reality.

She raised her arms, and he dropped the gown over her head. Sheer was an understatement. The darker tips of her breasts stood out easily. The gown channeled more lingerie than dress. A nightgown in virginal white, if the virgin didn't intend to hide a thing.

The vee cut, front and back, came to a high empire waist with a bow Henry tied below her breasts. Tied, she wasn't in real danger of spilling out of the fabric. Untied, she'd have offered easy access for hands or mouths. The gown fell above the knee, an embroidered floral motif running around the bottom edge.

The intercom chimed as Henry kissed her forehead. "Ah. Will always has had an excellent sense of timing. Jay, the door, please."

"Yes, Henry." Jay trotted off ahead of them. His voice drifted back as he asked who he might say was calling and were they expected this evening?

"Please inform the master of the house it's Santa Claus calling." The speaker distorted William's voice. "My naughty-and-nice list indicates both are true for the well-behaved little ones at this address, and I'd like to speak to him about clearing up this discrepancy."

Jay snorted. Alice giggled.

"We may as well let him in, my boy." Henry shook his head, but his voice was fond.

Jay pressed the button to talk. "Certainly, Mr. Claus. The door will admit you momentarily. If you'll please head straight back to the stairs, you'll find those well-behaved and *extremely* deserving youngsters on the third floor behind the door to the left at the end of the hall." Holding the button to unlock the building's main door, he grinned at her with infectious enthusiasm, eyes dancing, body relaxed.

"Well done." Henry squeezed Jay's shoulder. "You'll both do quite well, I'm certain. If you've any confusion, you know how to gain my attention or Will's."

A hand on the shoulder or knee and patient stillness, like the club. Otherwise, follow directions, answer when asked, and enjoy themselves. Not significantly different from any other night at home. Except, of course, for who'd be giving the directions.

She took a slow breath. In. Out. Nothing to worry about. *I got this.*

Footsteps in the hall preceded a knock at the door. Henry nodded to Jay.

Alice waited to Henry's left while Jay opened the door with a smooth flourish. Standing behind it, he stepped back as it swung open to admit their guest.

William, dressed not unlike Henry, filled the frame. Gray slacks, dark purple dress shirt open at the collar, gray suit jacket with the buttons undone. In the crook of one arm he carried a bottle with an unfamiliar label. A small gift bag dangled from his fingers.

"Charming, Will. Quite the fashion statement."

Henry's laugh made her glance up.

That was all right. Watch-and-wait didn't have the same rules as the club's eyes-down policy. She needed to read her dominant's cues to attend him for the evening. Tonight, a red Santa hat with white trim perched atop William's white-blond hair.

"Christmas in June?" Henry clicked his tongue. "A bit early, isn't it?"

"Ah, but Christmas in July is such a cliché, and I hate to be boring." William winked at her and projected innocence at Henry. Stepping forward, he let Jay close the door. "If your girl's going to call me Santa, I can't arrive without looking the part and bearing gifts. Imagine the disappointment on her sweet face."

"Gifts are entirely unnecessary, Will, but I won't turn them away." Henry leaned to his right. "Is that a Graham's port?"

"Mm-hmm. A thirty-year tawny for us." William raised his arm, displaying the bottle, and waggled his fingers, making the dangling bag dance. "And something sweet for the young ones."

The bag was suddenly the most important object in the room, if the speed at which Jay's head turned was any indication. She stopped herself from snickering at his wide-eyed interest.

"Yes, because what they need most is more indulgence." Henry's dry tone made William laugh. "Jay, please take Will's gifts to the kitchen. The port should be fine on the counter. The bag—" He looked to William.

"Needn't be refrigerated, either. The chocolates ought to keep as they are."

Jay loosed the barest hint of a moan as he accepted the bottle and the bag. Loot in hand, he headed toward the kitchen.

Henry chased him with his voice. "No sampling yet, my boy."

"Yes, Henry." Jay disappeared around the corner. He'd find an excuse to busy himself for a few minutes.

Alice folded her hands behind her back. Her turn. She'd agreed to this game. Santa wasn't likely to turn her down, but the nervous thrill of waiting to be picked for dodgeball, of standing in the hall as a professor posted grades, soaked her in a burst of adrenaline.

Henry drew her forward. "The most special woman in my life feels she owes you a debt, Will."

Aside from an eyebrow raise, William gave zero feedback. Damn Neutral Mask 101, the intro class for all dominance majors.

"I see." He tucked his Santa hat in his coat pocket while he studied her face.

He scanned her body once, a casual glance, and with less of her on display than he'd seen at the club. No cause for embarrassment, not in front of a man who'd seen Henry and Jay make her climax in less than a minute.

"I'm owed no debt, but I'm happy to accept her gratitude in whatever way she feels the need to offer it."

"I thought you'd see it that way, Will. As it happens, she has chosen to offer you a novice submissive for the evening." Henry clasped her shoulders, his fingers firm on her collarbone, thumbs rubbing her back. "May I introduce you to Alice?"

"Mine, Henry? For the evening?" William's thick blond eyebrows soared. "I can't imagine you allowing *that* even if I'd found the bastard a shallow grave to lie in."

"No, not even then, Will." Henry's voice was quiet but unyielding. "Domestic play. Victor's rules, you remember?"

William nodded, his face and voice uncharacteristically serious. "With the utmost respect and restraint, Henry. On my honor."

"Then I've no doubts all will be well." Henry squeezed her shoulders and released her. "Go ahead, sweet girl."

She stepped forward, breathed deep, and spoke her first words to her temporary dominant. "May I take your coat, sir?"

"Are you certain you can reach, little one?" William lifted her hands.

He dwarfed her. She wasn't tiny, but she was used to Henry and Jay, and he had as much height on them as they had on her. The top of her head met his chin.

"You won't need a footstool?" He smiled, ducking his head. "Henry must have a pedestal here with your name on it."

Laughter threatened. He was as bad as Jay. "No, sir. I can reach."

"All right then, little one. You may take my jacket, with my thanks." He released her hands.

She moved behind him and curved her fingers under the jacket collar with only minor tremors. William's broad back hid Henry from her, though he'd watch her closely, at least at first, ready to smooth over any confusion or nerves.

William held his arms out and down. "But we'll stop this *sir* nonsense immediately, pet. We're not so formal as all that, are we? I thought we were friends."

She stripped the suit coat down his arms and clutched it. A misstep so soon. She'd promised herself perfection.

William turned and lifted her chin. "You'll call me Santa, little one, else I'll wonder if you're doing so in your head where I can't hear you. We can't have that, can we?"

"No, sir—no, Santa." Embarrassment swamping her, she curled her arms around his jacket. She'd never live their introduction down. Twenty years from now—yeah. Yeah.

Confident contentment rallied. Twenty years from now, she'd still be calling Henry's best friend Santa. She'd still be Henry's sweet girl. She had no doubt the grin on her face rivaled Jay at his goofiest.

"Ahh, what delightful color in your cheeks." William paused. If he'd recalled the color in her other cheeks on the night they'd met, he had the sense not to mention it. "Go and put my coat away, little one, and then come back to me."

"Yes, Santa."

He touched her arm as she turned. "First, though, you'll tell me your safeword."

"It's 'pistachio,' Santa."

He repeated it, and she nodded.

"All right. On your way, pet."

She eavesdropped on Henry and William's conversation as they moved to the living room. Henry sounded happy to reconnect with an old friend. He'd devoted so much of his time to her in the last year, and she'd only recently understood how much. He'd probably practiced with Jay, held run-throughs before every one of her contract nights with them the way the three of them had done last night to prepare for William's visit.

She was as important—no, more important to him than William was, even if William had been his friend since who knew when. Henry would've made certain he and Jay were properly prepared and in sync. Like they'd been for her birthday.

Shifting her weight forward, she grabbed a padded hanger from the rod in the armoire. Her thong stretched and rubbed with her. Mmm. Henry always thought ahead. Now he had her anticipating. She hung William's jacket and closed the doors before crossing the room with quick steps.

Jay had done impressive work this afternoon. While she'd played kitchen helper, he'd rearranged the living room to Henry's specifications. The coffee table had been draped in bright tablecloths, layers of overlapping colors matching the large floor pillows surrounding the table and the slipcovers thrown over the chairs and couch, which had been pushed back to create a floor-level dining space. Moroccan, Henry had said, though the menu was more traditionally Spanish.

She paused to let Jay pass her, tray in hand, before making her way to William's side. Her drop from standing to waiting pose wasn't as graceful as Jay's. Jesus, how did he do that so naturally while he balanced dinner on one hand?

But William smiled and stroked her hair, so she couldn't have done too badly. She laid her hand on his knee and waited.

"A question already, little one?" He lifted her chin.

"For your comfort, Santa."

"A topic I take great interest in." He tickled her jawline.

Unusual, but not uncomfortable. Odd to have a man who wasn't Henry or Jay touching her so familiarly, even one who wouldn't expect anything when the night was over.

"Ask, then, pet."

"May I take your shoes and bring you a drink?" Her head felt stuffed with knowledge of the menu. "We've a fine dry sherry, a Manzanilla."

She'd practiced her pronunciation, at first as a way of teasing Henry, who'd laughed long and hard when Jay had pulled the bottle from the refrigerator and asked what "man vanilla" was and whether it was good for licking off breasts. Jay's wink and sly grin told her he'd known exactly how far off his pronunciation was. He took his post as Henry's little comedian very seriously. Was that irony?

"Both delightful suggestions, little one. I see we'll get along famously. You may, in fact, do both." William lowered his hand from her face.

She slipped off his loafers and carried them to the door.

The kitchen next, where Jay poured two glasses of sherry.

"I pulled the cork while you were getting your temporary transfer," he teased in a quiet undertone. "So it's been resting a few minutes already. If you come back for a refill, don't forget to return the bottle to the bucket. It's gotta stay under room temperature for the best flavor."

She bumped his hip. "I know, goof. I listened to Henry this afternoon, too." Across the room, their lover relaxed into his cushions and laughed at a quip of William's. Beautiful. "But thanks for the reminder, sweetheart."

Jay bent toward her ear. "That's senior sweetheart to you." He grinned before dancing off with another tray and Henry's glass.

She followed with the glass for William.

"No, no main meal this evening, Will." Henry accepted his glass from Jay and lifted it to his nose. He took a breath and a sip. "I thought we'd dine tapas style tonight."

Alice knelt, offering the sherry with her hands cupped beneath the glass, thumbs atop the base for stability. Jay had spread the trays on the coffee table, displaying all of the bite-size treats she'd helped Henry make, the combinations of cheeses and olives and figs and ham and sausages and mushrooms. The list seemed endless, though they'd limited the menu to a restrained half-dozen recipes. All made to serve well at room temperature, so no one needed to tend the stove away from the conversation, Henry had said. Little appetizers. Finger foods.

"An excellent choice, Henry. I've often found eating with one's fingers to be a delicious experience." William took the sherry, raised her hand to his lips, and kissed the tips of her fingers. "Especially when one's fingers are so lovely."

He resettled himself on the pillows, one propped against a chair as a backrest. "Tell me, little one, did you have a hand in preparing this feast?"

"As an under-chef, Santa."

William's eyes sparkled.

She had five seconds to realize why before he pounced.

"Ah, so you spent the day under the chef? And left Henry's poor boy to finish by himself?"

He tsked twice while her cheeks heated. If he only knew what she'd been doing five minutes before he arrived. Or did he? The man had been friends with Henry through an uncountable number of sex-capades. He recognized freshly fucked on a girl.

She schooled her face to blandness and mustered her driest tone. "A girl can learn a lot working under the chef, Santa. I can't imagine anywhere I'd rather spend the afternoon."

William barked out a laugh so loud it startled her. "Henry, you've found another comedian. I swear you're building a clown troupe to entertain yourself. Do they juggle and tame animals, too?"

Henry stroked Jay's bare chest, coaxing him to nestle deeper into the pillows. "Not as yet, no, Will. But they're both wonderful acro-bats. Quite . . . flexible."

Jay preened under the attention.

Her shoulders twitched as she stifled a laugh.

Will gave an exaggerated groan. "I cry peace. At least until I've tried this delicious-looking assemblage." He surveyed the table.

She waited for her cue.

"The bacon wrap first, little one."

She retrieved a bacon wrap and offered it to William, one hand on the toothpick and the other cupped beneath the appetizer.

For such a bear of a man, he took it delicately between his teeth and chewed slowly, savoring the flavor, before declaring it a success. "Was this a piece you made, little one?"

"No, Santa." The almond-and-cheese-stuffed dates with bacon around them had been the last menu item to be prepared. Henry had sent her and Jay off to shower and finished them himself.

"No?" William patted her shoulder. "Then you pick me out your favorite. You must have had a taste or two in advance."

She relaxed into her role as a charming-but-submissive dinner companion, catching snatches of Jay's interactions with Henry on the other side of the low table but focusing on William. Their guest's wishes were hers tonight. Playing with him was fun and low pressure. Her anxiety drifted away long before she realized it. William was witty, kind, and gentle. No wonder his friendship with Henry had lasted so long. Not that she knew how long, exactly.

She accepted a cherry tomato stuffed with an olive puree—her work—from William, nibbling and teasing his fingers as she considered the question. Finishing the treat, she raised her gaze to wait for another command.

He shook his head in three slow movements. "Alice, little one, you've something on your mind."

Christ. Had he and Henry learned attentiveness together?

William laid a hand on her head. "Tell me your thoughts, pet."

"Just silly thoughts, Santa." It wasn't her place to ask him about Henry. If she wanted to ask those questions, the decision of whether she ought to have the answers lay in Henry's hands.

"Wonderful. I adore silly thoughts. I entertain them myself all the time. Tell me yours, and I'll be doubly entertained." His voice teased, but he held her gaze with serious intent.

Withholding her answer might disrupt the entire night.

"I was wondering how long you and Henry have been friends. How you'd met." She shook her head. "But I don't need to know. It was idle curiosity, Santa."

William looked past her. "Henry, I'm heartbroken. You haven't shared the tale of our meeting? The adventures of our youth? However could you be filling your time together if not with that? Surely you won't mind if I rectify the situation."

"Be my guest, Will." Even when she couldn't see Henry, his familiar baritone quelled her doubts. "Do try and stick to the truth, if you can manage it. Your flair for the dramatic is legendary."

"Embellish a tale? Me? Nonsense. I'll tell it as simply as possible." William paused, pursing his lips. "To start, I'll need crucial information from you, Alice."

"From me?" She couldn't possibly hold key details for a story about how William and Henry met.

"Indeed. Quite crucial. When were you born?"

She blinked before rattling off the date on automatic pilot.

"Excellent. I believe I recall Jay's birthdate, so we're ready." William sipped his sherry and cleared his throat. "As our story begins, young Jay has mastered the art of toddling a few steps before falling on his ass. A fine ass, undoubtedly, but many years away from the delectable vision it is now."

Henry hummed in quiet agreement, and Alice and Jay giggled.

William raised his voice, amusement threaded through every word. "Dear little Alice has only just learned to stand on two feet by the expedient method of gripping everything in sight. Furniture, pant legs, the dog if she has one—no?—very well, no dog in this tale. Pity. Every children's story needs a dog."

"Were you telling a story, Will, or merely rambling to yourself? I'm certain I could tell the story in the same amount of time you've spent on the prologue."

William waved a dismissive hand. "You're always in such a rush, Henry."

She guffawed at the blatant untruth and clapped both hands over her mouth to stop more from escaping.

William patted her thigh at the knee, his expression triumphant. He must love teasing Henry as much as Jay did.

"In the wilds of New England, we find Henry, a strapping lad of eleven, already taller than all of his classmates—ah, wait, no, that's me. Let's see. We find Henry, a sensitive, focused *artiste* of eleven years, beginning the sixth grade. It's the youngest grade offered at this academy, and both boys are new to the school. As luck would have it, the class is scant on W's and lacking V's entirely. Thus 'Upton, William' and 'Webb, Henry' are forced into cohabitation."

Jay'd been right about Henry and William meeting at school. She'd imagined them older. Teenagers. Boarding school at eleven sounded lonely. Luck indeed.

"It is, of course, much harder on William, as he's such an angel to room with. Perfect in all ways. This goes without saying, I'm sure."

"If one were capable of not saying something, certainly. But we'll make an exception for you, Will."

"I'm exceptional in all ways, Henry."

A snort in reply.

"But I'll forgo sharing tales of my amazing athletic prowess and general brilliance, as I suspect the crowd at this story time is far more interested in hearing about young master Webb." Eyebrow cocked, William gazed over her head. "Who, it must be said, was as devoted to the people he loves and as unconcerned about the opinions of others at eleven as he is at thirty-nine."

"Mind you don't make me a candidate for sainthood. My dear ones will develop unreachable expectations."

Impossible. He'd always exceeded hers so far.

"Says the man who called his mother after dinner every day for the first semester to make certain she was coping well without him."

"Will—"

"And—*and*—mind you, as this was before children ran around with cellphones in hand, made those calls from the public phone in the floor lounge with the taunts of 'baby' in his ears, to which he replied—" William cast a pointed glance across the low table. "Come now, Henry, you recall better than I."

A story from Henry's childhood was too good to pass up.

Henry sighed, and sipped his sherry, and stroked Jay's cheek with one finger. The king of his castle with his jester lazing at his feet. "It was *one* day, Will."

"And they never said a word about it after that day you spoke back to them, did they?"

Chuckling, Henry outlined Jay's mouth and tugged at his lip. "No, they never did. Which was partly your doing."

"You can't leave your pets with half the story, old friend." William leaned forward and touched Alice's chin.

She jerked toward him, flushing with the awareness that she'd neglected him to stare at Henry.

"They obviously want to know you. And you want that, too." His gentle push turned her until Henry filled her vision once more. "Now, the idiot boys were running their mouths about babies who needed to be tucked in and must be afraid of the dark, and our young hero said . . ."

Henry cleared his throat. "Why? Are you afraid to call your mother? Do you worry bigger boys will call you a baby? I'm sure she'd want to hear from you. I know mine does." His tone stayed calm and even.

Oh hell. She knew what had happened next. No bully would hear that and not feel patronized.

Jay rocked side to side. "And then?"

William stroked her hair. "Oh, and then they thrashed us both, of course."

"Only because you wouldn't stand clear, Will." Henry hugged Jay to him, kissing the top of his head.

"What, and let my roommate take a beating alone? Absurd. And then Henry calmly pulled out his handkerchief, wiped his bloody nose, and called his mother to tell her about his day." William laughed. "Everything but the thrashing. It ruined their sport entirely."

"I suspect your punches might have had something to do with that, Will."

"Can I help it if my father put me in boxing lessons from the time I was eight? Certainly not."

Henry made a sound of dismissal, if not disagreement, and gave Jay another hug before patting his ass. "Clear the table, my boy, and we'll have games before dessert."

Jay gathered dishes, rose to his feet, and headed to the kitchen without complaint.

Instead of sending her to help Jay clear, William crooked his finger. "Come closer, little Alice."

She knelt on the pillow, her knees touching William's hip. He clasped the side of her neck. His thumb brushed her ear. Leaning close, he whispered, "Was that the sort of story you wanted to hear, pet? Do you see things more clearly now?"

She tried to picture the two of them as boys, Henry calm and composed, William throwing punches, but her mind kept returning to the night at the club. Henry. Calm and composed. William. Throwing punches.

"You've been friends for a long time." Understanding clicked. William didn't feel she owed him anything because he'd been doing what he'd always done. "You'll always have Henry's back."

He pressed a light kiss to her forehead. "And yours and Jay's, little one, so long as you're his." Pulling away, he gave her a slight push. "Now, go and help young Jay clear. I'm eager to see what entertainment Henry has planned for the rest of the evening."

She scrambled to gather plates. William's satisfied sigh and Henry's quiet hum informed her she'd flashed her ass at the former and given the latter a view straight down the front vee of her nightgown. She savored the heady sense of her own power, even now, when she'd technically handed that power to another. The extra sway in her hips as she walked to the kitchen wasn't an accident.

The games would be fun, though Henry hadn't agreed to her original suggestion. For the best, anyway. Her mouth had been running on pure bravado when he'd sat her down at the table and asked what sort of thank-you she'd wanted to give Santa.

"You could give me a spanking. The good kind. So I can get it right this time." Right almost certainly did not involve sobbing like a child.

"Get what right, sweet girl?" Neutral-Henry acted as if he didn't know what a poor reflection of his training she'd demonstrated.

"Show your friend that I'm not such a baby, that you *did* train me and I *can* take it."

Henry looked at her for a long moment. "No, Alice."

She leaned in, reaching for him. "But—"

He laid a finger to her lips. "Your response wasn't babyish. Nothing was shameful in any of your actions that night, Alice. You've nothing to prove." He cupped her cheek. "Neither you nor Jay is ready for that, even in play. Something more entertaining is in order, I expect. We want Will to laugh with us."

Between Jay's story about Santa's wife throwing a hissy fit and Emma calling the woman a harpy, Henry's reasoning needed no further explanation. "To see our happy home."

"Precisely. We'll give Will an evening in a happy home, with a charming companion."

She shook off the memory as she set her dishes on the counter alongside Jay's. He was already on his way to get the rest. Santa had been right about one thing, for sure. Jay had one fine ass. And she got to play with it.

She picked up the bowl waiting on the counter. No food in this one. She and Jay had spent part of last night filling it with slips of paper. Henry had set down a few rules but otherwise allowed them to write whatever they chose, refusing to vet the slips on the grounds that it would give him an unfair advantage.

Passing Jay in transit, she carried the bowl to the coffee table. She knelt and waited. Jay returned with a tray of two glasses of port, two dessert plates with thin slices of Henry's chocolate torte, and a plate of truffles that had to be William's gift to them.

"Lovely, thank you, my boy." Henry waved toward the open space beyond the coffee table. "Will, if we may borrow Alice for a bit, she and Jay will do some acting for us in a game of charades." A curving smile overtook his face and lightened his eyes. "There are, of course, valuable prizes to be had."

"Going head-to-head, are we?" William sank back against his pillow. "All right, then. Bring it on. I'm feeling brilliant tonight."

"Mmm. I'm feeling motivated to win, myself."

They haggled over the rules, settling on alternating guesses, with her and Jay allowed to act out their words singly or together, at their option. The first correct guess earned a kiss from the primary actor, with placement at the winner's discretion. As William was the guest, "his" submissive would be up first.

She drew a slip from the bowl and unfolded it. Jay's handwriting, not hers. She suppressed a grin. *Why am I not surprised?*

She beckoned him up beside her, turned their backs to the men, and showed him the slip. After waiting for his goofy grin to subside, she whispered, "Stand still and look happy." The second part would be easy. The first part would give him fits.

Turning him sideways, she held up a finger toward William and Henry in the universal charades sign for "one word."

She slid to her knees, trailing her hands over Jay's bare chest, warm and firm, kissing the skin below his navel. She lacked permission to remove Jay's shorts, but William wouldn't have trouble guessing once she brought her mouth in position.

Kneading Jay's ass, she dragged her cheek up and down alongside his cock and listened to his choked-off moans. Tsk-tsk. No sounds during charades. No climaxes, either. Bet he wished he hadn't written "blowjob" now.

"Let's see." William stretched out his words in a syrup-thick drawl. "I've two minutes to figure this out before you'll have a chance to steal, is that right, Henry?"

She hadn't factored in William's sense of fun. Logically, the object of charades was to guess as quickly and as often as possible until coming up with the right word. That's how she'd have played. Obviously why she'd never played sex charades before. She'd have ruined the fun too fast.

"Two minutes, mm-hmm."

"I must say, this is a difficult game. I think 'ways to make a man moan' would be a good guess."

"It does run into that pesky one-word problem."

"Oh, true, one word. Well. That makes things harder."

She muffled her laughter against Jay's shorts. No way he could get any harder in this fabric.

"Would you like to pass, Will? I'm happy to make a guess if the game is too difficult for you."

"No, no, I'll take my full two minutes. Is 'ass massage' one word, Henry? Do you have a dictionary for these tricky problems?"

"I could find one, I suppose. But the search might take a while, and you've only ten seconds left to guess, Will."

"Oh dear. I'll have to go out on a limb and say 'blowjob.' Do I win?"

"I believe Jay wins," Henry murmured, laughter in his tone. "Though perhaps it's more of a torture."

She stopped her torment and raised the slip to display the word.

Broad smile in place, William clapped his hands. "Excellent. A kiss for me, then. Come here, please, little one."

She trotted over for instructions.

He pulled her into his lap.

Straddling his thighs, not quite brushing the bulge in his pants, she waited for him to claim his kiss or direct her. Mouth? Neck? Some earlobe nibbling?

He raised his left arm, rolled his sleeve up, bent his arm back, and patted his elbow. "A peck here, pet. My elbow has felt terribly neglected all night. No fault of yours, of course. How were you to know it was crying out for attention?"

Giggling, she bestowed the kiss, the kind a child might give, or a parent kissing a boo-boo.

"Ah, such miraculous healing power in your lips, little one. My elbow feels much appreciated." He patted her shoulder. "But I suspect your playmate is in need of your assistance now."

Jay, holding a new slip from the bowl, had directed his watch-and-wait intensity at her with William.

"Run along, pet."

She hurried to Jay's side. He pulled her in front of him, dropping his arms around her, and showed her the slip. Her handwriting.

"I've seen how this works." He tickled her ear with soft, full lips. "You seem to like it."

His eager nudges and sultry tone promised he'd pay her back for the faux-job. He took his hand off her long enough to hold up two fingers to Henry, and then he gripped her hips tight and pulled her hard against his groin.

She went to her knees.

He followed, a solid wall behind her ass and thighs.

She about died of cuteness the way Jay imitated Henry, hips rocking against hers and hands skimming up her back. The side effect pushed up her nightgown, which left her bare ass rubbing Jay's shorts.

Should she? Aw hell, why not?

Henry made a smart remark about whether "rug burn" counted as one word or two. She missed William's reply as she crossed her arms on the floor and laid her head on them. Back arching, she shoved her ass into Jay's crotch.

He sang out a groan as quick and automatic as his cock thumping against her. But the way he dropped over her back, his hands coming down alongside her arms, and the kiss he pressed to her spine demonstrated pure intent.

Pure intent to mimic Henry.

She closed her eyes, reminding herself this was just a game of charades.

Heated air coasted across her ear. A breath. Two. And then a growl.

Hips jerking, she shivered and moaned. "Unfair."

"No talking, remember?" Jay was quick to tease.

"Ah, yes, I recall the term now. 'Doggy style.'" Henry spoke warm, liquid syllables. "It's the growl that sells it."

Henry-style was more like it. Jay kissed her hair and helped her to her feet.

"Vocalization, though, hmm." William tapped his fingers against his thigh. "That might be a violation of the rules, don't you think?"

"What would you suggest, Will?"

"This little play did have two actors."

"It did."

"We might split the prize. A kiss each?"

"That seems a more than fair compromise."

Henry and William wore matching grins.

They played several rounds, and she bounced between hovering on the edge of orgasm or collapsing into giggles. Both made for a hell of a good time. Henry and William finally agreed to call the game a draw.

William treated her to a sip of his port—fruity, with an aftertaste like thick caramel on her tongue—and one of the dark chocolate truffles he'd brought, which had a maple syrup center. She kissed his fingertips as he fed her.

He tipped her chin up and kissed her cheek. "Will you come snuggle with me, little one? It's traditional to sit on Santa's lap."

Warmth flooded her face. *Traditional* conjured memories of the birthday traditions Henry and Jay had celebrated with her.

Though William held his arms open, he didn't tug, prod, or pressure.

She settled into his lap, comforted to find him flaccid beneath her despite the arousal he'd obviously felt off and on throughout the night. He wrapped her loosely in his arms. Trying to guess his cues, she leaned into his touch and tucked her head against his shoulder when he stroked her arm or hugged her to him. Seemingly content, he made no demands.

From across the coffee table, Henry let out a soft hum. Jay massaged his feet, intent on his task.

She felt relaxed. A little sleepy, even. Santa warmed her back with steady strokes. Nestling closer, eyelids drooping, she glimpsed Henry's smile.

"Your girl has given me quite a gift, Henry." William spoke in a low tone, as if he feared to disturb her. "She's shown lovely poise. And such comfort." The light touch of his fingers tickled her arm.

"My Alice has taken a liking to you, Will." Henry shook his head and loosed an exaggerated sigh, his voice teasing and soft. "Heaven knows why. As if you aren't entirely too jocular, always jumping in without looking, always finding trouble—"

"Oh-ho, I'm the one who finds trouble, am I? I seem to recall—"

"Now, Will, let's not be hasty. Little pitchers have big ears, and they've had their story time today."

William snorted, waving aside Henry's words. "If you found my boyhood antics so troublesome, you'd hardly have gone and chosen a joyful pup for your own household. You're too serious, Henry. You need lighthearted souls around you."

"They are a wonderful comfort, that's true." Henry ruffled Jay's hair and tugged him to lie half atop him in their nest of pillows. "My home is never short on laughter."

"Would that mine were the same." William sagged into the pillow, his chest deflating beneath her.

She tilted her head back in question.

He frowned, his eyes distant, before he laughed and chucked her under the chin. "But you say your girl's taken with me, hmm? I admit, I'm hard to resist. Is that true, little one? Have you been comfortable in my hands for the evening? Speak freely."

She twisted to meet his gaze. "I trust Henry's judgment. He chose you as a friend. His best friend, I think." The evidence suggested it was true. "So when he tells me I'll be safe with you, I know it's the truth. He wouldn't lie. And he didn't. I'm not uncomfortable, Santa."

William stared at her. He blinked, twice, sharply. "My God, Henry." He pulled her in tight and kissed the top of her head. "What I wouldn't give to have half—a quarter, even—of that trust and devotion."

His chest expanded beneath her shoulder as he breathed. "The faces that come and go over the years are fun for play, but they're so focused on short-term needs. All wanting me to be someone or something else for them. I can hardly offer them more, can I?" William laughed. "Emotional connections. I'm not sure I recall how to make them. My wife acts as though my slightest touch will contaminate her with unspeakable desires."

Henry hummed a soothing melody. "It's all right, Will. Alice is an excellent cuddler—the consummate lap warmer."

He knew how much she enjoyed touch, how she'd come to depend on his in so many ways.

"I guarantee you she won't tire of it, and she already has affectionate emotional ties to you."

To soothe the stresses of the day, to comfort her, arouse her, and to make her feel she belonged.

"Her needs are being met."

She'd isolated herself, afraid to mix love with sex because she refused to risk emotional involvement. William had been isolated by circumstances, wanting love but unable to have it. Along came Henry, determined to fix everything for everyone. She was glad he was so good at it. Be nice to know why, though.

William rested his face against the top of her head, his breath warm. He didn't see her as a potential sex partner. Or not simply a desirable woman who might be available to him if she weren't with Henry and Jay. He could find sex with willing partners at the club. Despite his apparently sexless marriage, what he lacked wasn't sex but affection.

That explained why Henry had been comfortable allowing her to offer her thank-you to William as a temporary submissive. The subs Santa played with wanted something from him, and they negotiated to get it. She'd only wanted to give him something.

The conversation moved on, Henry asking William about his son. He'd be a senior in high school in the fall. The near dozen years between her age and Henry's had never seemed such a vast distance. But she had the same number of years on Santa's kid. If life had worked out different, Henry could've had a kid that age by now. Jesus.

"One more year, then." Henry's quiet, knowing tone suggested he meant more than the kid and his graduation.

William bumped her head as he nodded. "The marriage has been hell, but I did get an amazing son out of the deal. Her hatred and deceit was worth living with to have a son who knows I love him instead of one who's been told nothing but lies." Pain and determination mingled in his voice. He shook it off, patting her knee. "But who knows, Henry? Maybe you'll have a son of your own soon, now that you've finally found perfection."

A mother? Her? Soon?

"*Alice?*" Jay echoed her own surprise before he clamped his mouth shut.

"A premature notion, Will." Henry's voice was firm. "I'm content with the joyous blessings already in my home. My Alice is young yet."

"Ah. I've overstepped. Forgive me, little one. It wasn't my intent to startle you." William kissed her forehead. "I've heard nothing of any plans in that direction, Alice, and any such decisions would undoubtedly rest in your hands."

"As they should," Henry murmured.

Laughing, William ran his hand down her arm. "Tell the truth, Henry. It's those sleek muscles you love so much. You want more time to capture them on canvas before trying your hand at beautifully swollen curves."

Henry shook his head, smiling as he stroked Jay's cheek. "Alice has delightfully swollen curves with the proper encouragement, doesn't she, my boy?"

"Yes, Henry." Jay licked his lips and met her gaze. "Delicious curves."

Her nipples hardened. The sheer, gauzy fabric of her nightgown did nothing to hide them as she shivered. William followed her spine down and rested his hand above her bottom. Larger than Henry's, with wider fingers, his hand didn't make her heart thump the way Henry's touch did. The way Jay's eyes were doing now.

William twitched under her thigh. "My God, Henry. Living with these two, how are you not walking around with a permanent hard-on?"

"Meditation. Willpower." He tousled Jay's hair. "An unending succession of exquisite blowjobs."

Will groaned. "Have a heart. I've a cold bed waiting for me. A man can only take so much torment." But he rubbed her back with a light hand and kissed her head. "You've been a charming companion, little one. It's no wonder Henry's so ass-over-teakettle in love with the both of you. Go and join your playmate, and I'll leave you to your games. Whatever debt you felt you owed is more than paid."

She grazed his lips with hers and wrapped her arms around his neck in a quick hug. "Thank you, Santa," she murmured. "I'm glad you're such a good friend to Henry and to us."

Henry welcomed her return with a tight hug and a whisper in her ear. "My dear, sweet girl. Such a beautiful gift." He settled her on the pillows beside Jay, who clutched her in a fierce grip. "You're both at leisure while I see Will out, my dears."

They lay in silence, Jay curved as tight around her as Henry's slacks hugging his ass when he walked to the door. Yum.

"I had a wonderful evening, Henry." William slipped his shoes on. "It's been a long time."

"Too long." Henry handed him his coat from the armoire. "We'll plan something again soon."

William smiled at her and Jay in their nest, and she smiled back. "They're a credit to themselves and to you, Henry." He must have said something else as he turned away, because he and Henry chuckled together.

"I wish you luck, Will. Give our best to Em if you see her."

Ah. Santa was off to the club, to find a playmate of his own before he went home to that cold bed. The rest of her night would probably be much more fun, even if it involved cleaning the kitchen and falling asleep. At least her bed would be warm and full of love.

CHAPTER 14

The door opened seconds after Henry buzzed. Unmarked, unobtrusive, no different from the half-dozen doors he'd driven past as he threaded the car down the alley and parked. Tuesday evening. The shadows hung deep in the alley between buildings though the sun hadn't set.

Jay brushed Alice's fingers.

She clasped his hand.

Emma ushered them inside and down a narrow hall. An oddity, coming out to the main reception area from the back. Past small offices and a coat room, all dark.

No one stood behind the curving counter to greet them. Emma didn't request their electronic devices or log their visit. Her heels echoed on the granite with each step. She flipped a switch, and the sconces along the wall highlighted their path up the stairs.

"No one will be here tonight but me, Henry. It seems we're undergoing a 'pest extermination.'" Emma appeared immaculately coiffed as always. Dress, hose, heels. Pearl choker.

Did she sleep that way, or did she don a persona every morning?

"Even those with private rooms have been informed they won't be accessible this evening."

Ugh. Distracting herself by worrying about irrelevancies like Emma's perfection wouldn't cut it tonight. Henry had brought them here to confront their lingering unease. To excise that fucking bastard Cal from whatever corner of Jay's mind and hers he occupied.

"Take whatever time you need." Emma's mouth softened as she glanced at Jay and Alice. "I'll lock up behind you when you're ready."

"Thank you, Em. Your attention to detail is most appreciated." Henry kissed Emma's cheek.

A brief kiss. A friend kiss. An entirely nonromantic kiss that still left Alice grateful for the squeeze of Jay's hand in hers.

"Come along, my dears." Henry held out his hand. "We'll begin with a tour of the second floor. Alice hasn't seen it at all yet."

They'd taken the elevator straight to the third floor the night she'd been here. Dressed to attract attention. To see and be seen.

Tonight they'd dressed for comfort, covered from head to toe. Her coziest flannel, her softest jeans, her well-worn sneakers. Jay sported equally scuffed sneaks topped by loose sweats and a thin, long-sleeved T-shirt.

"Second floor." She stepped onto the stairs, Jay half a beat behind, their hands entwined. "Can't wait. What's up there?"

Henry settled his hand against her back and played tour guide as they climbed the grand staircase. The rise and fall of his voice soothed. At the top of the stairs, he led them left, past a separate reception area and expanded cloakroom.

"Not everyone arrives dressed to play. For those with more elaborate tastes, such would be unthinkable." Henry pushed open a door and turned on a light. "Changing rooms on this floor. A non-play area. The rules of respect, the code of conduct, still apply, of course, but contact must remain nonsexual. Locker rooms, as well, for post-play showers."

"But the bathrooms upstairs have showers." She and Jay had climbed to the fourth floor because the showers in the third-floor bathrooms had been in use.

"Those are not for bathing so much as playing, my dear." Henry flipped off the light and closed the door. "As we did at Will's vacation home."

Shower sex. She laughed, an edge of nerves beneath. "I can't believe I didn't think of that."

"Really, Alice." Jay tsked at her, mock-sorrow on his face. "After all the showers we've taken together. How could sex not be the first thing you think of when you see a shower? It's the first thing I think of."

"Sex is the first thing you think of as soon as your eyes open in the morning." She smiled to take the sting out of the tease. "I'm pretty sure it's what you think about when you're asleep, too."

Jay splayed his hands in the universal sign for *eh, what're ya gonna do?*

Henry made a soft sound between a hum and a grunt. "The salon and the attached kitchen command the largest space on this floor." He led them back past the stairs, threw open a pair of oversize doors, and lit up an enormous room.

"Whoa." She pivoted to take in the dozen or so seating arrangements. Cozy, intimate spaces for two. Larger groupings of short sofas. The room clamored for men in formal dress discussing weather and war while women in Victorian gowns played the piano or embroidered. A movie set from some period piece where the electricity would get edited out. "Fancy."

Jay's sigh seemed almost relaxed. Her estimation had been way off. He hadn't shown a hint of upset, no fidgeting, no clinging to Henry. Maybe he'd find confronting this easy.

"Tell Alice about the salon, my boy." Henry's fond smile matched Jay's. "What does this room remind you of?"

Jay wandered right, weaving from seating area to seating area. Stopping at a pale blue chair, he frowned. "Where's the other one?"

"I'm not certain." Henry led her toward the grouping Jay had picked out. "Emma is likely to know. We may ask her if you wish."

Jay gripped the chair back in both hands and shook his head. "I thought it would look the same. Silly. But I . . . I counted the steps, you know. I was watching your feet so I'd know when to stop." He dragged his shoe against the rug. "Twenty-three steps from the salon door to the chairs, and you told me to sit and I sat on the floor."

Their first real meeting. That's what this room meant to Jay. The week after Cal's assault, he'd said.

"I remember," Henry murmured. He gestured her to the short couch beside the chair. "I asked you to sit in the chair instead, and you apologized for displeasing me."

Bruised from the week before, an emotional wreck in search of a new dominant, Jay had gone back to the club.

She sat. "Your first date."

Henry raised his eyebrow, but Jay beamed. "Henry didn't look at anyone else all night. He didn't go back upstairs. He stayed here with me the whole time, and I didn't have to do anything bad to earn it."

"That must've been exciting." Smiling back took effort. She had a limited idea of what Jay considered bad ways to earn attention, and none made for pretty pictures in her head. "A good night."

"The best. He asked so many questions. I thought he must be planning a huge scene and he'd take me upstairs when he had all the answers, but we just talked."

"It ought to have been a familiar experience, my boy." Henry stood straight, his shoulders unbowed, his tone even, but his eyes— tightness lurked at the corners as he tracked Jay's every motion. "I hadn't intended our talk to be quite so novel."

"It was—" Jay ran his hand across the back of the blue chair. "The first time I went home hopeful instead of empty. Like I didn't have to leave everything at the door."

She studied her shoes. The place Jay feared was the place he loved, too. The place where he'd met Henry.

"I had a red ribbon and a homework assignment. Henry wanted to see me again. I mattered."

He'd found his first spark of self-worth in submission here with Henry. Of course he'd felt empty. He'd been a toy to the people before Henry. His pleasure had lasted as long as he was pleasing and being praised. When the game stopped, the feelings stopped, too.

"That's what this room reminds me of." Face sweet and open, he gazed at Henry with naked adoration. "You told me, 'You're a good boy, Jay'"—he'd dropped his voice, the lower register a credible mimic of Henry's dom tone—"'and your red ribbon tells everyone here that you're *my* good boy. I want you to take good care of my property this week. Treat it well. If you do that, you will have pleased me very much.'"

Henry had given him something to look forward to. A way to respect himself.

"You still please me, my boy." Henry pulled Jay into a hug, cradling him tight to his chest. "Very much."

As nervous as the club made Jay, this room, this space, stood outside that feeling. It had its own memories, happy associations. A tree with their initials carved in the trunk. Their relationship had started here.

"Alice, you're missing the hugging." Jay's voice was muffled against Henry's neck. He flung one arm wide in a blind search for her body. "You don't wanna miss out."

"Nope." She rose and nestled herself at their side. "Wouldn't miss it for the world."

The little kitchen off the salon had finished their tour of the second floor. Nowhere to go but up. No going back, not if they intended to confront the thoughts drying her throat and making her pulse race.

The third floor's silence seemed eerie. She irrationally expected a soundtrack. The plaintive whispers of violins below a chorus of chatter and moaning and the slap of skin against skin in the hall.

She came to a dead stop.

"Alice?" Henry paused beside her. "Tell me."

They'd been here. Right here, between that bench and this viewing window. Hemmed in. Herded like cattle, and Cal with a mind for slaughter.

"I thought someone would help us." She meant to speak up, to provide a good example for Jay and make Henry proud. Her words emerged in a whisper. "I couldn't figure out why no one was stopping him. But no one thought it was strange. Just the way to talk to submissives. Perfectly okay."

Humming to her, Henry kissed her temple and rested his forehead against hers. "They would have expected such things had been negotiated, sweet girl. That if he were speaking to you, red-ribboned as you were, he'd already obtained your consent and his behavior was consistent with your preferences."

The idea of giving that man her consent made her skin crawl like a cockroach colony. She shook off the creeping disgust. "I got that, eventually. That's why I talked to him. Defied him. Another man—I don't even know his name—he started asking questions. Gave us the opening we needed to get away." Not soon enough, though. Not for her paralyzed playmate. "Jay?"

"Huh?" His head jerked. Jittery, foot tapping, he'd been staring at the wall. "I'm listening. Bad night. So many people, and he—I mean, what?"

She stepped toward him and gripped his trembling hand. "I'm sorry I let him say those things to you, Jay."

He shook his head, his mouth a stubborn line. "I'm sorry you had to protect me. If I hadn't stopped moving, you wouldn't have had to talk to him. It was my fault."

"It was not." Her voice and Henry's sounded as one.

"His behavior was an egregious breach of protocol and common courtesy. You are not at fault for his actions, my boy, and your response to his presence was neither unexpected nor unwarranted." Henry touched her face, gently turning her toward him. "Nor are you at fault for Cal's words. His speech is his own. The responsibility to conduct himself like a gentleman is his own, even if he chooses not to exercise restraint in word or deed."

Silence drifted in. She lacked the stomach to head down the hallway and into the room where she'd been publicly disciplined. Unjustly so, since Cal had instigated the entire event. But she'd agreed to accept punishment. The way Jay'd agreed to sign the papers and pretend he could forget Cal's assault. To avoid making trouble.

Henry tucked her arm into his own, and her feet moved automatically to keep up. The hall opened with unexpected quickness.

The distance had seemed insurmountable that night. An endless search to find her way back to Henry. She'd dreamed, in the week afterward, she hadn't found him at all. That Jay's hand had slipped from hers and she'd been alone among strangers wearing Cal's face.

Thank God waking up had brought her face-to-face with Henry. He hadn't disappeared, and Jay hadn't disappeared, and she wasn't lost.

Tears blurred her vision.

Henry squeezed her hand. "Tell me how you feel now, standing here, Alice?"

She rotated in a slow turn. Breathed in and out. Rocked with the shame and confusion. The fear. Cal's laughter. But underneath, too, rolled her initial excitement. Will's courtesy. Jay's loving attention. Henry cradling her in his arms . . . and Henry lowering her panties and turning her over his knee.

"Too much," she murmured. "I feel too much."

"Jay?"

"I don't know." He shook his head. "Not—I don't know." He stood on jittery legs, one knee twisting in and out. "Fine. This is for Alice. She got hurt. I'm fine."

Henry frowned. He didn't challenge Jay's answer. A bullshit answer, for sure. Maybe Jay didn't know exactly how he felt, but he wasn't fucking fine.

"Angry," she blurted. "I'm really fucking *angry*, and I don't want that jackass to make anyone feel as helpless and small as he made me feel ever again. And I'm angry at myself for not doing something different, and I'm angry at Henry for not finding another way, and I'm angry at Jay for not fucking saying how he feels."

They stared, Henry approving and Jay with wide eyes.

Her lungs heaved. Streaming tears itched her cheeks.

"And better." She sucked in air. "I feel better, because I'm not afraid to be here. He doesn't win. He doesn't get to defeat me. He's nothing, and I'm still me. I still have both of you. He hasn't taken a damn thing from me. I win. I win."

She laughed, and cried, and let Henry soothe her with sheltering hands and whispered encouragement. But Jay watched with an uncomfortable fear, his anxious expression reforming into a smiling mask every time they looked at him.

Henry's quiet sigh warmed her neck. He stepped back. "Jay? Perhaps you'd like to share your feelings now, as Alice has done."

"I'm good. This was good. I'm glad Alice feels better." He delivered a toothy grin, as if Henry would agree they'd exorcised their demons and take them home.

"Upstairs, then, my dears." His words sucked the joy from the room.

Jay halted at the top of the stairs, on the edge of the fourth floor, and she stopped with him.

"Straight ahead, Jay." Quiet but firm, Henry allowed no argument. "Keep moving, please."

Jay stepped forward. "One foot in front of the other, right? No problem." Swinging his legs and dragging his toes, Jay babbled fast but walked slow. "I can dance if you want. Fancy footwork."

Henry took her hand when she would have moved with him. No way in hell could he expect Jay to do this alone.

He shook his head at her. "Patience," he murmured. A grimace crossed his face.

Memory flashed, Henry's pleading expression as he urged her into bed after the night had gone so badly. He needed her to follow his lead. His forcefulness had gotten Jay moving until he could break down in safety. Tonight, Jay had to confront the source of his pain.

Jay acted as if being here didn't affect him, but he crept along like a child in a house of horrors. Even with the rooms empty and silent. Even with the hall brightly lit. Even with her and Henry walking behind him. He looked to both sides as he walked, shaking his head. He slowed as he passed each door.

He . . . didn't know.

Horrified understanding shivered through her blood.

The entire floor was an open wound in his mind, a terror beyond imagining, built up from year upon year of pretending he'd put it behind him. He couldn't identify the place where his nightmares lived.

Henry laid a hand on Jay's shoulder. "Stop here, my boy."

They stood between two doors, one on either side of the hall.

Jay swung his head between them.

"The left," Henry prompted.

Jay's memories might be indistinct, blurred by pain and fear, but Henry's had to be absolute. Frozen and sliced and dyed in shades of blame on slides for him to examine under a microscope. How often did he wish he'd noticed the scene sooner and saved Jay some pain?

Guilt and regret crippled as effectively as fear. Dozens of times she'd heard Henry say he wanted them healthy and happy. When he'd met Jay, Jay had been neither. Henry would've been a boy who'd driven his parents to distraction caring for wounded creatures.

Jay took a cautious step and pushed the door wide. He stood in the door frame.

Henry reached past their shoulders for the light switch. Spotlights illuminated the room's centerpiece, an X-shaped piece of equipment fastened to the far wall.

Stepping into the room, Jay flinched. And then he laughed.

"Nothing to be scared of here. It's only wood and metal and padding." His forced chuckles grated at her nerves. "Silly to get all worked up over it. I'm glad, I'm glad we, uh, visited"—he tugged at his sleeves, hiding his wrists—"to get that cleared up. We can go home now. Whenever you're ready."

Hell no. No fucking way Henry bought his bravado either. Pushing away the pain because it hurt to feel it.

"Jay. My brave boy." Henry's shoes tapped against the wood floor. He stopped beside Jay, the two of them facing the illuminated frame.

Metal rings stood out at the corners and various points along the X. Attachment points. "No one but Alice and me will ever know what happens here."

The first night Henry had tied her down, he'd chosen soft cuffs and shown her how to escape. Anyone tied to this frame would be splayed like da Vinci's Vitruvian man, vulnerable and exposed. Doubtful Cal cared whether restraints chafed. He probably preferred they did.

"Do you still wish to hide from this? To feel it controlling you when you want to let go?" Henry lowered his voice. "Will you give this moment that power and deny it to me, dear one?"

"No!" Jay's fierce headshake scattered his hair and twisted his torso. "I want to be yours, Henry. Just yours."

"Then you must reconcile with the past, Jay. Feel the truth of it. Accept your own blamelessness." Henry tipped his chin, a brief glance at the floor. Would he ever accept *his* blamelessness? "You called out your safeword and were ignored."

Jay moved forward. His shoulders shifted with every breath, his exhalations audible in the silence. He stopped less than a foot from the frame. His leg twitched. His hand clenched.

He stood, back rigid, unmoving, for long minutes.

Henry turned toward her. Expecting he'd shoo her away to give Jay privacy, she took a half step back.

He thrust out his palm in a curt *stop* gesture.

She froze, waiting.

He beckoned her to him. The soft soles of her sneakers barely made a sound.

Jay never twitched.

Henry's gaze shifted between the two of them. He pressed his mouth to her ear.

"He needs a push." He whispered so low she strained to hear him even at this distance. "A painful one."

Understanding ached. He'd seen her react badly before, misread his intentions, try to defend Jay against harshness when Henry had a purpose for it. Her challenges had made Jay's wait for comfort longer.

"I trust you." She breathed out the words.

Henry kissed her temple and rubbed her back. Stepping forward, leaving her behind, he took a slow, deep breath.

"Step away." Henry had a new tone. Anger. Disgust.

Jay's head came up.

Henry clenched his jaw. "It's an interesting technique you have, but I think you've outstripped your skills." Now his words came light as an observation on the weather. "And it seems your sub has had enough for the night."

Jay trembled, a full-body motion. Henry wasn't speaking to *him*.

She curled her hands into a single tight fist, fingernails pressing deep into her skin. Henry had walked a fine line that night, if she'd understood properly. Said he'd nearly had to apologize to Cal for interrupting the scene. Even if he'd sized up the trouble in an instant and burned to free Jay.

"Perhaps you ought to release him. Pause to check his status? These things are so easily overlooked in the heat of the moment, aren't they?" Henry's friendly, cajoling tone didn't match the snarl twisting his lips. Eyes hard and glaring, he wrinkled his nose as if the air offended him.

An expression he'd likely had to hide from Cal at the time. His pauses might represent Cal's side of the conversation, if he heard the voice in his head.

Head cocked, Jay stood almost still. All but the shudders that rolled down his shoulders and twitched in his fingers and wobbled in his legs.

"Boy!" Henry's voice gained volume and command. "What are you called here?"

Ten seconds. Long enough for Cal to have answered for Jay, she knew not what.

Jay's howl rattled her bones. He attacked the padded frame with fists and feet.

"Not yours. Not your slave. Not your slut. Not your *bitch*." His voice cracked. He fell to his knees in an ungainly heap of limbs, a rare lack of grace, and pounded the frame with animal ferocity. "You're not my master, you fucking horrible piece of shit. You never were. You lied to me. You told me I was safe. You wouldn't stop. You wouldn't stop. You wouldn't—"

Her entire body strained to go to him.

Gaze fixed on Jay, Henry waved toward her. *Wait.*

They stood in silence as Jay exhausted himself, until he stopped beating at the frame, until his voice grew hoarse and his anger turned to sobs. Only then did Henry speak.

"Jay. My sweet, playful boy. You've a soul bright like sunshine, dear one. Clear and shining in your every smile. You give so much of yourself. Do you understand now, my brave boy? Will you tell me what you deserve?"

"I don't—" His voice shook. He coughed, and tears fell unchecked down his face. "I don't deserve what C-Cal did to me. I didn't deserve it then, and I, I don't deserve it now."

"Beautiful, my boy. An excellent answer, entirely true. Do you know what you do deserve?"

Head hanging down, Jay swayed slowly. No.

Henry sank to his knees in front of Jay and smoothed back his hair. "Love, my boy. My love. Alice's love. Unending, no matter what demons must be confronted."

Jay sobbed, his slender body heaving.

"Will you let me hold you, my dear boy? You aren't alone in this. You're never alone."

Jay tumbled forward, babbling, curling his body half-fetal in Henry's lap.

Relief raced through her. With Henry's leadership and her support, Jay would move past this. He'd know he was safe and loved and that he deserved to be.

Henry beckoned her forward even as he answered Jay's incoherent speech. "No, my brave boy, it hasn't tainted you. There's nothing dark and dangerous in you, my love. You're still my Jay."

She settled beside them in silence, trusting Henry to lead.

He kept up the steady, slow petting down Jay's head and back. "Nothing you could tell me would change that, Jay."

Hunched and hidden, tucked in tight against Henry, Jay sniffled. His shuddering set off little waves in his thin shirt, currents Henry smoothed with each pass of his hand.

The desire to scoop up their boy and take him out of here, to end the pain in his face and the full-body sobs, pulled at her with unbearable urgency.

Henry fumbled for her hand and squeezed. Seeing Jay this way hurt him, too, even if he wouldn't show it. Couldn't show it and remain the strong, powerful man Jay needed him to be in this place.

But this moment belonged to Jay, not them, and he hadn't purged everything he associated with this room. With *that man*. The same need she encountered when Henry unlocked emotional doors for her.

Once the path opened, the landslide came through in an uncontrollable rush.

Squeezing Henry's hand to draw his attention, she lifted her other hand toward Jay and waited. She wouldn't normally need permission, but right now, on delicate, unfamiliar ground, checking couldn't hurt.

Henry's small nod and return squeeze fueled nerves and hope.

She touched Jay's shoulder. Light. Cautious.

"It's scary." She swallowed. Every word needed to be perfect. No room for error, not with her sweet, sensitive lover. "It's hard to know, isn't it? When you feel like, like something's wrong with *you*."

Jay's breathing slowed.

"Like if you say it, it'll be true."

The trembling subsided, but Jay didn't emerge from hiding. His tiny, jerking nod stopped almost before it started.

She paused to gauge Henry's reaction. Pushing might help, but it might harm.

He rubbed his thumb across her knuckles and mouthed, *"Keep going."*

As much as Jay needed Henry's comfort right now, Henry couldn't leave. But if Jay felt he couldn't say whatever it was in front of Henry, Henry would make himself invisible.

He'd use every tool at his disposal to help Jay. Right now, his best tool was her. Like the night Jay had first told her about Cal, about how pathetic and worthless he'd felt. He'd needed Henry's comfort to be able to tell the tale, but he'd needed *her* reassurance. On some level he'd wanted confirmation from an equal, and he would always see Henry as a superior.

Terrifying, to be the one guiding. Surely Henry didn't feel this fear. Maybe greater comfort with it defined a dominant. But she found confidence, too, knowing he believed her up to the challenge.

"Do you know what makes me feel better when I'm scared, Jay?" Like when she'd been terrified Henry would find out she harbored feelings for him. Or tell her he wasn't in love with her. Or that there'd never be a place for her in this relationship.

Shaking his head against Henry's chest, Jay turned in Henry's lap. She slid down until their heads were level.

"Telling Henry." She whispered the words, snuggling in close.

Henry released her hand and embraced her, his strong arms encircling them both.

"The longer I waited, the more scared I was. The harder it was to tell him. But then I felt so much better. It's okay to be afraid, Jay."

His hand crept forward.

She tucked it inside her own. "But you know what Henry will say, right?"

"Be honest," Jay mumbled. "I can't help if you won't let me."

Yes. He'd met her halfway. Giddy warmth pumped through her. "You're Henry's brave boy. You can do this, sweetheart."

"But I"—brown eyes shied away—"I want to hurt him."

Cal? Hell, she'd like to fuck him up, too. Henry probably wouldn't throw a punch no matter the provocation. He'd find another way.

"Like he, like he hurt me." Pressing his head to hers, Jay whispered as if he imagined he could be so quiet that Henry wouldn't hear him. "Like a bully. Henry hates bullies, Alice. I don't want to be a bully."

Henry tightened his arm around her.

"You think maybe Cal made you like he is." She squeezed Jay's fingers. "That he taught you to want to hurt people."

Slow and tentative, shoulders flinching and soulful eyes trimmed in red, Jay nodded.

Christ, what could she say to that? Instinct told her Jay was incapable of bullying. The anger and pain he'd poured into the whipping stand, the way he'd beaten the frame until he almost couldn't lift his fists, raised fear *for* Jay, not *of* him.

Jay's anger bore nothing in common with Cal's sadism. But her argument wouldn't convince him. His fear wasn't a rational one.

"Do you want to hurt Alice, my boy? Right now, at this moment?"

Pale and gagging, Jay spat, "No!"

"To hurt me?"

"No." Blinking fast, Jay blew out a hard breath. "No, Henry. I love you."

Henry had shocked Jay out of his shame-filled stupor. With . . . an irrational argument?

"Cal is a bully because he abuses others from a position of power, my dear boy. To be angry with him for what he's done is justified. You have never sought power of any sort. Never struggled with obedience. Wanting Cal to receive the treatment he doles out isn't anything like the indiscriminate bullying he practices. He doesn't love. What you feel for me, for Alice, your instinctive distaste for unwanted violence toward us, Cal has never felt for his partners, nor do I expect he ever will. You are nothing like him, Jay."

"You aren't disappointed in me?"

Henry cupped Jay's chin, tipping his face up until their eyes met. "On the contrary. I'm proud of you, my brave boy. Think of everything you've confronted here tonight. You will be happier and healthier for it in the long run, able to give yourself to me more freely. And as for Cal—" Eyes narrowing, Henry frowned. His disapproval seemed a structural weight, lowering the ceiling and shrinking the room around them. "We *will* hurt him, but where it matters most to him. His pride. His reputation. The aura of power he hides within."

"Pulling back the curtain," Alice murmured. "Not so great and powerful now."

Henry hummed.

Jay actually snickered.

Her heart lifted. Jay's emotions had traveled all over the map tonight, but a true laugh, even a small one, was a huge improvement over his earlier avoidance and terror.

"I don't have to wear the ruby slippers, do I?" Jay sniffled, his voice raw.

She wished for tissues.

"I'm more a sneaker kind of guy."

"Silver." Henry dug in his pocket and came up with a handkerchief. Of course. "The shoes are silver in the original. Something to add to our reading list, I expect. Blow your nose, my boy."

While Jay made use of the handkerchief, Henry tilted his head and raised an eyebrow at her. "Alice, you recall how to find the serving room off the salon?"

She nodded and rose, seeing the gambit. "Just a drink, or a snack, too?"

"A drink only, thank you, my dear. Something soothing for Jay's throat, please."

"Will do."

She left Jay to Henry's tender care, following the trail of lights they'd left on behind them, down the stairs to the second floor. She'd take her time. Let them find the closure they needed together. Jay had been the one who'd broken down, but she wasn't naïve enough to believe being in that room with him again hadn't affected Henry, too. He'd keep that to himself, though.

234 · *M.Q. Barber*

The sharp tang of fresh-brewed coffee wafted from the salon. The aroma grew as she crossed to the kitchen and reached for the light switch.

"There's more in the pot if you'd like a cup."

She bumped her shoulder on the door frame, missing the switch on the first pass. "No, thank you."

The lights came up. Emma stood beside a prep counter at the far end of the room.

An intruder, Alice's hackles said. It might be her club, but she didn't belong in their cozy little world of three, not tonight, with Jay so vulnerable.

"Henry asked me to get some juice." She kept an eye on Emma as she carried out her task, finding a small bottle of apple juice in the fridge.

"Is young Jay all right?" Emma waved a dismissal. "No, no, that's a silly question. Of course he's not. But—" She cradled her coffee mug as if seeking warmth. "Is he handling it well?"

Henry had promised Jay no one would know. Whatever happened tonight stayed in the room.

"He's with Henry." A simple truth, and not breaking Henry's promise. For almost anything involving Jay, Henry was the answer.

Emma nodded as if she understood that truth, too. "I never felt better than when I was at Victor's side, no matter the difficulties in our path. I'm certain Henry is equally attentive to Jay's needs." Lines appeared around her mouth and eyes as her face tightened. "Would that we'd been able to make things right years ago."

The rigid sense of threat in Alice's spine softened. "I think—"

Far from trying to insert herself in their relationship, Emma felt some sense of responsibility. Guilt.

God knew Alice understood that weight. "It was incredibly important for Jay to come here and do this."

Emma had voted to banish Cal from the club. She'd seen Jay, then, in the aftermath of Cal's attack.

"Helpful."

And Henry was one of this woman's closest friends.

"So thank you."

Natural for her to show concern for his subs.

"For helping."

"Important for you, as well." Emma's gaze was shrewd. She

sipped her coffee. "You're not one to run and hide, are you, Alice? A poor introduction to this scene can leave lasting scars on a submissive player. I've seen it happen too many times. You have a better handle on yourself, I think."

Her skin itched. Tiny, dancing tingles beneath the surface like this near stranger had tugged a zipper and peeked inside the polite-company-Alice suit. They weren't confidantes. They shared a truce shaped by Henry's love. If he expected them to cede territory to each other, she'd need a map of the boundaries. "I have Henry."

Emma nodded. "You do."

The juice bottle chilled her hand. Henry and Jay were waiting. She raised the bottle and moved toward the door. She'd been less nervous her first day in the high school cafeteria, for chrissake. Her tongue nearly betrayed her and asked Emma for a hall pass.

Fuck. She was Henry's envoy here. He had to have known she might run into Emma.

The training. Cal. She paused in the door frame. "I'm sure he'll be in touch with you soon about moving forward on the classes. Tonight's—" *Just for family,* she almost said, grateful for the twitch of compassion that stopped her. "Busy."

Emma had set aside her plans—or hadn't had any to change—to be here and open the club for them. A woman Henry protected like a favorite aunt or a younger sister.

"No, of course. He's focused. I wouldn't expect any less."

A woman without a family who stood in the dark drinking coffee and feeling guilty for events beyond her control and five years gone.

"But thank you, Alice, for your kindness."

"Sure. I mean, same to you." She shot through the halls and stairs. Something about that woman made her feel small.

Shoving the discomfort to the back of her mind, she delivered the juice to a somewhat calmer Jay.

He drained the bottle at Henry's insistence and flexed the empty plastic like a makeshift stress ball, crush and release.

They made their way down the stairs, Alice turning lights off behind them as they went, Jay holding tight to Henry's hand with the one not creating a steady stream of pop-and-crunch noises.

Henry settled Jay in the car, letting him keep the increasingly crumpled plastic.

Emma exited the club's back door a moment later and set the

alarm. Scanning her surroundings, she paused and nodded to Henry and Alice before going to her car.

She didn't approach, didn't intrude, and Alice wasn't certain whether that made her feel better or worse. She almost wanted the woman to give her a reason for her dislike. Some imperfection. Something Emma wasn't the number one, all-time best at.

They drove home with the light strains of classical music and the occasional, fading crunch of plastic for accompaniment. Weary. That's how she felt, and Jay no doubt felt the same a hundredfold, and Henry, too, after navigating such a rocky shore.

They readied themselves for bed with none of the innuendo and teasing the activity normally engendered, only an abundance of small gestures. Touching of hands, steadying comforts declaring *I'm here* and demanding nothing in return.

When they slipped under the covers, she and Henry cradled Jay between them like new parents, lying on their sides, hands resting together on his chest, feeling his every breath in the darkness.

"Henry?"

"Yes, my boy?"

"Tonight was—" Jay gulped in a raw breath. "Thank you for making it less scary. And Alice, too. When I, in my nightmares it's always, I'm always alone. And it's worse. I made it worse in my head. But you made it better."

"The hard work was yours, Jay. You must take credit for it, hmm? For being the brave boy I know you are. That strength, that willingness to bare your fears and confront them, is yours to claim." He laid a gentle kiss on Jay's brow. "You make me so very proud to call you mine, Jay."

"Make you proud," Jay repeated, and the wiggle in his body communicated his joy better than words ever could. Nothing in the world—not a bike ride, not chocolate, not orgasms—made him happier than pleasing Henry. He yawned, lifting their hands.

Henry hummed a slow melody. Jay's eyelids fluttered.

She lay silent, studying his smooth face, feeling the lingering tension drop from his frame as he let go. The sandman owed him sweet dreams.

She ought to roll over and find sleep herself, she supposed, when she'd watched Jay for longer minutes than she could count. But

Henry shifted his hand, covering hers. He wouldn't be sleeping for a while yet, either.

"Thank you for tonight, Alice," he whispered. "He follows your example, you know. Mine is too distant for him at times, I think. Unattainable, as he sees it."

His soft sigh pained her. Henry prided himself on providing for them. His ache must run deep when the gulf between dominant and submissive prevented him from giving Jay what he believed he needed.

"He sees in you the balance he needs to find in himself. Your willingness to continually confront new things gave him the strength to pierce the veneer, the well-adjusted gloss hiding the pain he couldn't address. I'm more hopeful for his sense of self now than I've been in all the time I've known him. Before I loved him, even."

She sucked in a breath. Henry rarely shared such thoughts with her. And that . . . that was what made her hackles rise around Emma. Henry's heart and body belonged to her and Jay, but she worried about his mind. His soul, if she wanted to be poetic.

It wasn't something she would've fought for with previous lovers, wasn't something she'd cared about or known existed. Fucking was fucking, and talking was optional and likely to lead to troublesome attachments. She'd dumped guys for less emotional intimacy than this.

"This is, these are the sorts of things you talk about with Emma." With Henry, she wanted everything. Wanted to *be* everything.

"Hopes and fears." His intimate tone carried no surprise. Her chess master would've guessed seeing Emma tonight would make her wonder about her own role in his life. "For Jay. For you. Never specifics. He needs confident leadership from me. You, at the outset, needed a sense of freedom and control. The ability to walk away, as you'd done before."

"While you made it so appealing that I wouldn't want to." She hadn't considered how difficult that would have been for him, the balance he'd struck as she'd struggled with her feelings, wavering between pushing them away and wanting them closer.

"I'm not much of a fisherman, Alice." He cupped her cheek, his hand warm, his grin wry. "And you would have fought the line doubly hard if you'd seen the hook for what it was. I did try to tell you."

He had? "When?"

"The morning of our anniversary dinner. I blatantly offered to declare my love."

"You—but that was a joke." He'd brought her breakfast and teased her about . . . getting down on one knee.

"Only to you, sweet girl. You weren't ready to hear it." He slipped his hand behind her head and cuddled her close as he could with Jay asleep between them, his grip firm, as if he feared she might yet leave him. "For me, it was very real."

"And I told you love wasn't my style." God, she was an idiot.

"Mmm. Your response solidified my belief that something more . . . structured. Solidly built? With a sound contractual foundation, perhaps? Might prove a more effective lure than an outright declaration of my intentions." He let go, smoothing her hair and sliding his hand down her arm to interlace their fingers. "But I always meant to lead you here."

Here. Terrifying at first, but growing more comfortable with every day that passed. More secure. More confident. More right for her. Because she was . . . maturing? Standing in one place long enough to pour concrete footers reinforced with rebar. Certain she could give Henry the submission he wanted and keep the flexibility, the independence, to be an equal partner. Far from competing, their needs dovetailed. Even closer, now, when he shared his thoughts with her.

"You said Jay needs confident leadership. And when you've felt . . . less than confident . . . maybe you've gone to Emma for advice." The idea might sting less as time went on, as Henry came to see he could lean on her, that she was capable of seeing weakness from him without it diminishing his strength in her eyes. "But I'm not Jay. Sometimes I need to see your vulnerability and help you with it the way you've helped me find and accept mine."

"Maybe so, my sweet Alice." He raised her hand, turned the palm up and laid a gentle kiss within. "Sweet, and strong, and smart. Our balance is perfected with you here." He kissed her again and returned their linked hands to Jay's chest. "But for now I want you to obey me and follow Jay's example. Sleep. If you aren't well-rested in the morning, you'll be using a sick day from work. No arguments."

She snorted, quietly, as she twisted and wiggled to make herself more comfortable. No arguments, right. If she had pressing work to do and Henry felt she needed to stay home, she'd use her safeword, explain the situation, and carry on as she needed to. His power was her gift, and sometimes the rest of the world would interfere. But when it didn't . . .

"No argument," she agreed, eyes closing. "Love you."

"And I you, my dear girl." He sighed, soft and low. "You and Jay saturate my soul with indescribable beauty."

His declaration echoed in her mind until sleep came.

Turn the page for a special excerpt of M.Q. Barber's

BECOMING HIS MASTER

From rescue to romance . . .

Teach a wounded submissive the value of his service. The task ought
to be an easy one for an experienced dominant like Henry Webb.

But novice Jay Kress challenges his teacher like no other. Still
bearing the bruises of an encounter outside the bounds of safe
consensual play, Jay is desperate to submit to the man who saved
him—and shamed by his desires.

Henry recognizes the dangers of a relationship built on hero
worship. He'll teach Jay how to stay safe, that's all. He won't take
advantage of the younger man's trust. He won't share his fantasies
about his dark-haired, athletic student. He'll never claim this
submissive for his own . . .

A Lyrical e-book on sale March 2015!

CHAPTER 1

As a boisterous crowd climbed the winding grand staircase to the adult playrooms above, Henry Webb took a quieter stroll down the narrow hall behind the front desk.

After last week's utter debacle, he'd intended to spend the evening relaxing upstairs. A request from Victor, however, carried the weight of a summons.

A few of his own pieces graced the walls thick with three decades of club history. Victor's office awaited him behind an intricately carved door of well-polished black walnut. His knock skimmed the falling whorls of Persephone's hair.

"Enter."

He stepped inside.

Victor dropped his pen into its holder. "The boy is back."

Clicking the door shut behind him, Henry traced the cool, sinuous antiqued brass handle. If Victor intended to shock him with the announcement, he'd failed. Henry had expected the boy's return. Anyone who'd spent more than five minutes in the novice submissive's company would have predicted it.

"Is that why Emma sent me straight back to your office like an errant schoolboy?" Unbuttoning his suit coat, he claimed a wing chair across the desk from Victor. Firm with a hint of cushioning, the chair, as with every piece in the room, conveyed a power and authority commensurate with Victor's role as president of their little social club.

"My wife hasn't thought of you as an errant schoolboy in a decade." Wolfish amusement lurked in Victor's smile. "Did you tell her how exquisite she looks this evening?"

"Of course." To do otherwise would have offended a beautiful woman and been a lie to boot. The corset shaped Em's body into a feast for the eyes, a centerpiece at a front desk staffed by a handful of beauties of both sexes. "Is the blue a new piece?"

"Mm-hmm." Victor delivered the distant nod of a man chasing fantasies and returned bearing a frown. "She wanted it laced tighter, but it's her first night in it."

Henry favored the cautious approach. Breaking in a new corset demanded time and patience, much like a marathon runner shaping a new set of sneakers.

Pale brown eyes gleaming, creases gathering at the corners, Victor confessed, "She begged so prettily I had to turn her over my knee and deny her satisfaction."

Henry settled back in the cozy leather with a chuckle. Given Emma's masochistic needs, she'd undoubtedly reveled in the attention. "Thus the glowing smile she's wearing while greeting the players tonight."

Victor grunted. "She loves the denial almost more than the completion." He stretched his jaw, sharp and shadowed by his short-trimmed beard. "I have plans to take her this evening, but I've yet to decide whether she'd enjoy it more if I leave her unsatisfied. A bit of time basking in her arousal out front might convince her to climax sweetly for me when the time comes." Flaring his nostrils, he savored a slow breath. "She makes the loveliest sounds."

A truth Henry had witnessed often enough, and one requiring no response. He'd learned from Victor in much the same way, as the older man verbalized his thought process for a scene before directing it. The tutelage had granted Henry deeper insights into the how and why of the choices made—and, perhaps more importantly, the opportunity to see them change on the fly when a sub's needs dictated something different from the anticipated performance.

Victor waved, a dismissal of the subject though likely not of his attention to Emma's upcoming satisfaction. "But that's not why I wanted to speak with you upon your arrival."

The bloodied back. The wrenching cries. The *snap* of the bolt cutters bringing freedom. Henry forced the wash of images aside. "The boy."

Jay Kress, the latest victim of Calvin Gardner's sadistic pleasures.

"He signed the papers. Consensual, inadvertent error." Victor's flat tone struck with all the joy of an untuned piano.

Another missed opportunity to eject a bully from their ranks. A dues-paying dominant couldn't be tossed on his backside without cause, and Cal was clever enough to choose fresh-faced submissives unlikely to make a formal complaint.

Submissives like Jay Kress. "And now he's seeking a new dominant."

"Or the same one."

"Cal is a problem." They'd never be rid of him so long as the subs held their tongues and Cal's father sat on the governing board.

Victor splayed his hands, palms up. "One that time and training might fix."

"He preys on the new faces." He struggled to keep the anger from his tone and didn't quite manage. "He delights in their pain, humiliation, and degradation."

"Some of them want that, Henry." Victor waved off the objection already forming on his lips. "A small percentage, yes, but some do. Most of them young men like our Mr. Kress. Would you tell them their desires are in error?"

"I'd tell them if they're among the vast majority of submissives who want to feel cherished and secure, they'd do well to stay away from Cal." His grip on the chair arms left impressions in the leather. He smoothed them with strict attention for each dark ripple in the surface. "A man or woman who violates a safeword has no honor and deserves no trust."

Preaching to the choir, but Victor hadn't seen the novice after. Hadn't wiped the blood from his back or bundled him into a robe.

"Yes, as Emma told the other board members, to no avail." Victor tapped the desk, his fingers reflecting in the glass atop the mahogany wood. A match for the shade of Emma's hair. "She spoke to the boy in private after his testimony and gently suggested he consider not playing again until he'd listed boundaries for himself and his future partners."

"He couldn't articulate a single one, could he?" An all-too-common problem among new players. Seeking acceptance, they neglected safety. Those with specific fantasies found negotiating easier. Confused submissives lacking self-awareness, however, required careful handling.

"After Cal stalked out in a fit—he left the boy tied, Victor, with no guarantee I'd clean up his scene for him, for God's sake—and I unbound the boy, he was a sobbing, bloodied wreck."

"An outcome that can be the result of a good scene as much as a bad one." Victor wore his lecture face, one eyebrow raised above a chilly gaze. "Would you have me outlaw whipping? My Em loves the sting on her back. Blood and tears can be a component of satisfaction."

"Not for this boy." The cries had pierced him. Not a shred of pleasure in them, and no reason for the young man to have endured the pain. "You didn't hear him calling pitifully for Cal to return. Apologizing for using his safeword, saying he knew he wasn't to do it and it wouldn't happen again."

The blatant betrayal of consensual play strung him tight with rage. "You know as well as I do a dominant can create a vivid mental picture to satisfy a sub's need for pain and swap out the dangerous threat with a safe toy that fulfills the purpose without causing harm."

If Jay Kress wanted to be tortured and violated, the fantasy could have been accomplished without the potential danger of perforating his colon with a whip handle. "The boy didn't want any part of it, Victor. He only wanted to please his master."

"I agree."

Victor's soft tone and expectant stare thrummed awareness of the gap between his spine and the chair. Henry eased back and resettled his shoulders. He ought not allow emotion so much control. Less so in the club and least of all in a situation whose principal players had ceded none to him.

Ever the teacher, Victor nodded. "Which is why my darling Emma is even now putting a bug in the ear of every dominant who enters. She'll encourage them to stay away from the beautiful dark-haired boy in the tight leather shorts with the vivid welts across his back. Unless they want to find themselves in my office explaining their actions."

"He'll beg until he finds someone." Back a week after such an intense, devastating session? The lack of self-control blared alarms.

"He's a danger to himself." Denying him access would be a wiser course.

"He is, that's true." Victor frowned, pulling his features into craggy canyons. "If I ban him from the club, he'll find a more dangerous playground."

"The boy needs a teacher." Solution found, he crossed his leg over his knee. Victor would recommend a good one, and all would resolve itself. His own conflicted emotions would subside in time. "A caring dominant to help him find his boundaries and learn to assert himself in negotiation."

"Such was my thought as well." Victor's accompanying stare clarified with nary a waver.

"Me?" No and no again. "He'll associate me with his torture." Better to leave him to someone else. Healthier for all concerned. "Possibly even resent me for stopping the scene and costing him Cal's dubious affection."

"Emma says the boy called you his savior." The return of the wolfish smile didn't bode well. Victor only let the look out to play when he meant to win. "Asked incessant questions. Had she met you, how well did she know you, did you play with boys or girls, didn't you have just the dreamiest green eyes. . . ."

The chair's embrace suffocated. Henry launched himself free. "Hero worship, then." Condensation slipped down the carafe of ice water on the sideboard and joined its fellows in a spreading patch on the robin's egg blue linen beneath. "It'll fade."

"Until it does, why not take advantage of it?"

He tucked his face toward the bookcase. Disgust and fear suffused him. Victor knew where to twist the knife.

"*Positive* advantage, Henry. The boy needs a guide, and you'd be an excellent one. You've a light touch with wounded souls, and he deserves it, doesn't he? If nothing else, the psychological challenge ought to appeal to you."

Shoulders tight, Henry tipped his head back as if he might shake off the suggestion and the problem with it. He whispered his confession to the silent row of unaccusing spines, the pages within full of their own secrets. "I'm attracted to him, Victor."

He'd stood and watched because of the boy's beauty. The lines of his back in sharp relief as Cal had wielded the whip. And then the blood. The shouting. The urgent need to stop Cal without provoking more harm. "He deserves delicate handling, not yet another dominant who might confuse their own desires for his."

"At least talk to him. You enjoy denial almost as well as my darling wife does."

The impropriety of lengthy silence forced him to turn and attend to Victor's words. Their shared gaze acknowledged truth. But the words wouldn't come.

Folding his hands on the desk, Victor leaned forward. "Wouldn't you enjoy the opportunity to sit across from the boy knowing you could have him with a word and forcing yourself to strict control instead?"

Breath flooded his lungs. "You know me too well."

"Age and experience, Henry." Victor relaxed into his seat and straightened his tie. "Talk to the boy. My runners say he's been wandering the third floor as a green-ribbon in search of a partner. Why not give him one?"

Wearing a green ribbon. Attention-seeking behavior. Meat for the lions, tender flesh and a heart more tender still. Henry paced. He'd already lost this battle. The conclusion foregone.

"A talk, then. Tonight only." He'd help Mr. Kress see the need for balance and turn him loose. Perhaps the damage had been superficial, easily remedied with a stern reminder to take care for his own safety.

"Cal's been banned for two months." Victor's blandness only ever disguised spear points beneath. "The boy could explore his desires more freely with your assistance."

"Non-sexual, Victor." Henry bent his back and gripped the top of the wing chair. Smooth, supple leather. The submissive's skin would be even softer. More supple. Twenty-four, twenty-five at the most, youth clinging to smooth cheeks. A crime not to paint him.

"I won't touch him when his need is so raw and untrained." He'd cross any number of ethical lines by becoming involved with the younger man, even if the lines were of his own making and meant nothing to others at the club. No, Victor would understand. William would understand.

"A hands-off approach, certainly, if you like." Victor ran a finger along the edge of his desk. "So long as you don't mind Emma and myself wagering on the outcome."

Henry forced his hands from the chair. "Two months of instruc-

tion, and I'll turn him over to an ethical dominant who suits his desires."

Two months ought to be enough. It would have to be, if he meant
to keep this innocent from playing with Cal once more. Even an abusive dominant could prove more alluring than loneliness for a submissive desperate for a place to belong.

Victor's casual grunt betrayed his disbelief. "My lovely wife
thinks you'll like this boy, and she has a sixth sense about these
things. I wouldn't bet against her."

"And her wager is?"

"That you'll put a leash on him and take him home. Not tonight,
of course. But eventually."

"I don't collect strays, Victor."

He left his play partners better off than he'd found them and took
pride in doing so, but their games stayed at the club. The married
straight boys who wanted more punishment than their wives delivered. The sweet-faced girls seeking validation for desires that shamed
them.

Short-term or long-term, impact play or sexual possession, it
made no difference. None of them had enticed his senses or inspired
his passion enough to bring them home. When he found his muse, he
would know. He was in his early thirties yet, and the post-college set
still found him attractive enough. He had time.

Victor shrugged, an elegant gesture rippling the fabric of his dress
shirt. "Then there's no harm in spending the evening with the boy and
offering him some friendly advice."

"No harm at all." Henry straightened and buttoned his suit. "If
you'll excuse me, I need to track down young Mr. Kress and inform
him he may stop searching for a new dominant. For tonight, at least,
he has found one."